FALLING TIDE

Kirsty A. Wilmott

BEAR PRESS

ISBN
Hardback: 978-1-999-710255
Softcover: 978-1-999- 710262
eBook: 978-1-999-710279

A CIP record for this book is available
from the British Library

For Bear Press
Development: Jutta Mackwell
Editor: Bridget Scrannage
Art Director: Sarah Joy

Set in 11/15pt PT Serif

1v00

For Mike,
I write because he stands beside me.

Chapter 1

There was a gentle tap on the door. Anna jumped. She hated this, when the reality, the audacity of what they were trying to do overwhelmed her. She was sitting in her favourite chair, which had moulded itself to her shape, had held her through some very difficult moments. She placed her fingers over the handprints she'd made on the arm and gripped tightly.

What did she have to offer four disparate souls seeking an encounter? It didn't matter that Simeon said it had nothing to do with her; she knew there were expectations. She could feel them draped around the vicarage, hiding in the corners like large, sticky cobwebs. Then there were the draughty, shared rooms with the mismatched bedding, the noisy cistern and the central heating that – despite the horrendously expensive new boiler – would start singing and hissing with exuberance whenever anything deep and meaningful was about to happen.

"Are you ready?" Harriet asked, peering around the door. Anna shook her head.

"Oh Anna, you'll be fine."

"But what if it's not what they expect? What if I'm not what they expect?" Anna tucked her hair behind her ear. It was fair, no definitive colour, wispy and flat, hanging just below her jawline. Harriet had made her get it cut. It was easier to look after, but she missed being able to drag it out of her eyes and pull it up into a ponytail. By contrast, Harriet's long, dark, curly hair was twisted into a large, untidy bun, loose tendrils hanging about her face. No effort required. The thoughtlessness of it shouting to the world how attractive she was, how she didn't have to bother.

Anna thought she might let her hair grow out a little, at least until Harriet noticed – and she would notice, which made Anna realise how much her friend had taken her in hand. Harriet had made her introduce a bit of fruit and the odd plate of vegetables to her diet, for which Anna was grateful, she really was, but she knew that none of it was of any use unless these little changes filtered down into the bits that mattered. The bits inside her that still felt wobbly and out of control.

"We have made it quite plain that the accommodation is not en-suite and that the vicarage leans towards draughty," Harriet said gently, her eyes narrowing. Anna knew that she was annoyed. They'd had this conversation a million times before and the small line between Harriet's eyes was getting deeper by the second. "You have to remember that the price reflects what we have to offer. We're hardly charging the earth."

Anna took a deep breath. She knew Harriet was right. Harriet was always right and Anna couldn't have managed any of this without her. It had been Harriet who had arranged the rooms after the fire, who'd spent hours listening to Anna and Archie deciding what they should provide for the first couple of weekend try-outs. It had been Harriet who'd overseen the redecoration; bright white to cover up the grubby, flame-shaped marks that had bloomed up the walls, smeared their clothes and made everything stink. Harriet had taken those tired, breathless rooms and created spaces that were pleasant and welcoming, filled with a jumble of second-hand furniture that somehow managed to make the vicarage feel arranged, perhaps even a little loved. It was also Harriet who cooked the meals and sorted the housekeeping. She and Archie had worked tirelessly so that everything was in hand and manageable. At the thought of Archie, Anna sighed. Now there was a man who had your back. A man who truly believed in what they were trying to do. On top of which he bubbled a gentle love and enthusiasm for all things God and church that made Anna feel rooted and safe within the parish.

He was training to be a Reader, though Anna thought he was on the course purely because he and the bishop were good friends, a relationship that had started back in their Navy days. She thought it was optimistic to be starting a Reader course when he was just shy of seventy – she hoped Archie was up to the three years of intensive study.

Harriet cleared her throat and folded her arms.

"But we've never had four before," Anna wailed before she could stop herself.

Last time there had been two retreat guests. A battered Skoda Fabia and a Mercedes, shiny black with tinted windows. Anna had nearly had a heart attack when that had purred down the drive. Thank goodness Harriet had been on meet-and-greet duty and had not been fazed by Angela's obvious wealth. Actually, Angela had been nice, relatively easy and had left a large donation in her room. Mrs Skoda on the other hand had been a nightmare. Had wanted extra blankets, a wake-up call of all things and hadn't bothered to let them know beforehand that she was a vegetarian and gluten-free because 'most people are nowadays, aren't they?'

"It's better, safety in numbers. Breakfast will be less awkward than last time," Harriet said firmly.

Anna just wasn't sure she could do this. She'd even been flooded with guilt when, on the strength of their marvellous plans, they'd got the diocese to shell out for an extra loo upstairs. Bloody Archie and his brilliant ideas – turning the vicarage into a small retreat centre for those who needed time out from their busy lives. He'd even got Simeon to sort out a website. *Oh God, we have a website*, Anna thought and had to do some slow breathing to calm down again.

"I wish you'd take your own advice," Harriet's voice had hardened, her annoyance beginning to spill over. "You can do this. You're good at this." Then, because she knew Anna well, she smiled. "And if you don't come through to the lounge this minute, I'll get Simeon to have a word."

***

In the lounge the fire was blazing, the pale rose-pink curtains drawn against the draughts. A bargain, where the woman selling them had been staggered to find that there was another house with windows large enough to hang them. Archie had driven over to Truro to pick them up, using it as an excuse to pop in to see the bishop for coffee. Anna had imagined the two of them sitting together, the bishop desperately trying not to salute his old colleague and Archie trying to remember to call 'Pearly' Longbottom, 'Your Grace' or Frank if they were alone. 'Pearly' apparently because his front teeth were overly large and white. They didn't look anything out of the ordinary to Anna, but you had to have a nickname in the Navy. Anna wondered what Archie's had been.

She was taking a deep breath when Harriet pushed her further into the lounge. There were two young women seated together on the sofa, one with bright orange hair, the other with plaits and a fringe, a little long. Anna thought they must know each other well, for their arms touched at the elbow. They both looked up and smiled together, as if they had practised. Wide mouths, open hearts, sweatshirts and jeans. On the other sofa, but with a seat between them, sat a young man and an older woman. Anna guessed the woman was in her late fifties, possibly early sixties. The man looked about twelve, but he'd arrived in a van so was obviously a little older than that. He looked tired, dressed in a dark blue suit that was well-worn and a little shiny. The woman was narrow, from front and side, and was sitting upright, her hands loosely clasped over her stomach. She reminded Anna of someone, though she couldn't quite think of whom. Probably a distant relative of her mother. Anna dragged herself back to the moment. It was time to begin.

"Hello everyone. I'm the Reverend Maybury. Please call me Anna." She'd practised this bit many times, though to her it still sounded a little desperate. "For the next couple of days please treat the vicarage as your home. Harriet, who you've met, and Archie and I will be about the place most of the time so if you need anything ..." Anna forgot what she was supposed to say next. Was it the bit about eating together or not being worried if the heating system made the odd noise? She cleared her throat. "It's all very informal. There is a timetable of meals, Morning and Evening Prayer, which we will say down at the church, just along the lane. You can't miss it. It will be open for the length of your stay during daylight hours." That was Simeon's part. They had spent nearly twenty minutes trying to work out what was meant by daylight hours. Was it the quality of the light or a set time after sunrise? In the end Archie had given Simeon some times based on sunset and the time Anna wanted to say Morning Prayer. She smiled, though she hadn't felt like smiling at the time.

She continued, "It's a good place to muse on life and—" She was about to say 'stuff', but remembered that Harriet didn't like the word. She said it was too vague and harsh. "And I will be available to listen and to pray with you at certain times. Harriet will organise that, so you won't have to hang about trying to find me." Anna looked at each of them. "I hate name badges, so if we could just go around and introduce ourselves, that'd be tremendous."

Anna had no idea where that had come from. Tremendous was a ridiculous word to use. Useful, good or even nice would've been more appropriate.

"Harriet, let's start with you." At that moment Anna's phone began to chime. Simeon had found her a ringtone that he thought she'd be able to hear wherever her phone had been left under or down the back of. It filled the room with its tuneless clamouring. She managed to switch it off and was dismayed to see as the light dimmed that it had been Tom. *Bugger*, she thought and wondered what he wanted.

"My name's Harriet. I live in the village and I work here at the retreat centre." Retreat centre! Anna shivered. It was just the vicarage, her home! "And I also work the odd shift at the pub. I love walking and there are some absolutely beautiful paths around the peninsula. But I would always take a waterproof. When the weather comes in, it comes in hard and fast."

Harriet turned and stared pointedly at the first of the young ladies sitting to her left.

"I'm Georgie. I work in Exeter, for a church, St Andrew's," she said a little fiercely. "I deal with youth." She had the short orange hair and pink cheeks. Her eyes were large and startlingly dark. Anna couldn't decide if she was devastatingly attractive or scary. Georgie had obviously decided that that was all for now as she nudged the young woman next to her. She peered at Anna from under her dark fringe, her thin face dull with makeup.

"I'm Dani. I'm currently living with Georgie. I've had some problems ... with my family and Georgie suggested I come to catch a break."

Anna nodded and quickly turned to the young man. Dani was about to spill her troubles to the room and that wouldn't be helpful at such an early stage. This first night was difficult enough without some stranger making you feel as if your life wasn't as bad as you thought.

"Hello, I'm Laurence. I'm not quite sure why I'm here." He sat back. He yawned. It seemed to surprise him as much as everyone else. "Sorry," he muttered.

"Perhaps you're here to get some rest," Anna suggested, smiling encouragingly. He nodded and looked relieved that nothing else seemed to be required of him. "And what about you?" Anna added, turning to the lady on the end.

"Hello, I'm Catherine Edwards. I'm from Wiltshire, and my son recommended the Lizard. He said it was a good place to come and find yourself."

Anna glanced across at Harriet, who raised an eyebrow. Harriet knew exactly what she was thinking. Tom's mother?

Here? Anna blinked rapidly as she tried to slow her breathing. He must have known that she was coming. Couldn't he have rung to warn her? Or was that what the missed call had been about? If so, he'd left it bloody late. She took a deep breath, trying to calm down.

"We eat at 7.30. That should give you time to unpack, to have a little rest. The dining room is across the hall." She smiled around the room, a general, all-purpose, my-job-is-done smile, and then almost sprinted to the door. Harriet followed her out and laid a hand upon her arm.

"Anna, take a breath. It's probably just a coincidence."

"She's from Wiltshire. For goodness' sake. 'My son said …'"

"We can't be sure."

Bloody, bloody hell! That was all she needed. Tom's mother on retreat!

Chapter 2

Simeon sat in the church. It was almost dark, but last time one of the lady guests had come down to church after dinner even though it was the first night. She'd jumped when she'd noticed him sitting in his pew, but had still said hello. He'd nodded. She'd worn flat, pale grey lace-up shoes and dark blue trousers. She'd walked around reading the memorials and leaflets and had called goodbye when she'd left. She'd added a thank you, as if she'd known that it was his job to lock up. Not long after Archie had appeared, just to make sure Simeon was alright.

Today, while Simeon waited, just in case the church was required, he read one of Archie's books, *Reconciliation, where do we start?* Archie had been very worried that he wouldn't know as much as the others on the Reader course, as it had been years since he'd done any studying. Simeon thought he'd be alright, but had decided that, if he read the books too, then Archie would've someone to discuss them with. Simeon paused and lifted his head to look round. The church was as familiar to him as his own home. The undressed stone walls, the simple, open-backed pews and the square altar pushed to the back of the tiny sanctuary. The book on his lap was heavy and he was finding it difficult to concentrate on it. Belle stood up and stretched, her claws clicking on the slabs. She looked up at him and he nodded. She was right, it was getting late. He still didn't like wandering about after dark, particularly when he knew there were strangers around.

He walked slowly down the aisle to make sure that everything was as it ought to be, touching the old tenor bell sitting behind his pew just the once. The metal was reassuringly cold. It was the only thing he allowed himself to brush with his fingers, otherwise he had a tendency to get stuck. Once past the bell and heading towards the door he stuffed his hands into his pockets, just in case he was tempted. Belle waited patiently. She knew the routine. After he'd locked the door, pulling it past the squealy stones, she waited for him to clip her lead onto her new collar, fluorescent pink. A gift from Derek and Harriet because he'd mentioned one day in the pub that, often, he couldn't see Belle in the dark, even though she was a light honey colour.

He kept his eyes on the ground as he made his way up to his lane, just across from the end of the vicarage drive. Through the hedge he could see some of the vicarage windows rimmed with light. The guests would be settling in, Harriet organising tea and Anna worrying about whether she'd be good enough. Anna was Simeon's second favourite person to be with. Archie was always going to be number one, because Archie had very quickly understood what Simeon needed. The next person on the list after Anna was Derek. He asked questions, talked about interesting things and hardly ever mentioned the weather, which was where most other people started. Derek and his dog Dolly joined Simeon and Belle for a walk nearly every morning. Dolly and Belle were both old dogs and were used to each other, and Simeon was used to Derek. It was a good arrangement.

Archie had made Simeon fit a sensor light, which came on as he passed the farm, blanching the lane white, turning the puddles into mirrors. They'd had a lot of rain recently and some of the muddy gashes were deep. Belle didn't like mud either and managed to pick her way round them.

"We match, you and I," Simeon said to the top of her head. At the sound of his voice Belle lifted her snout to sniff the air, which pleased him because Dolly was almost stone-deaf.

***

Archie looked around. The two young women had been whispering, but stopped when he cleared his throat. The girl with the plaits – was it Dani? – looked bored. Catherine was scribbling something in her retreat book. Archie had thought it'd be a good idea to provide a pen and notepad for each of

14

their guests. He wasn't expecting them to use them, particularly if they'd brought their own, but having time with God was worthy of a blank page. The boy, Laurence, was sitting staring at his knees, his complimentary pen and notebook nowhere to be seen.

"Hello," Archie said, sitting a little further back in the chair. He'd turned it slightly so as to be able to see them all. "I'm Archie, the churchwarden. I'm going to run this next part of the evening. You can totally ignore what I'm going to say or you can use it as a place to jump from over the next few days. Tuesday through to Thursday are all yours to do with as you will. All we ask is that if you're going to be late for a meal, please let us know." He smiled again. "Otherwise, we'll worry."

That was a legacy of the Terry year – that, if someone wasn't where they were supposed to be, the first thought was that something awful had happened. They'd all become quietly adept at telling one another where they were. 'I'm on my way, I might be a few minutes late.' None of them had actually discussed it, but it had become a way to manage the anxiety, to move past the time when looking over your shoulder was instinctive. Even Simeon had been known to send a text, particularly if the weather was bad. He knew that when the clouds drooled over the Lizard, Archie liked to be sure that he and Belle were safely tucked up inside their cottage, front door locked, hatches battened down.

Archie took a deep breath. He had to read the meditation slowly and with a gentle emphasis. He'd tried it out on Anna, then Simeon and eventually Phil at the pub. There had been some tweaking, but the general gist of it was to get comfortable. To give to God all the things that were bothering you so that God could have a clear run. Of course Archie knew that laying down your troubles took some doing and wasn't always appropriate, as sometimes they were precisely what God wanted to deal with. Anna had taken ... well, she'd taken

15

forever to sort out some of her baggage, was still a work in progress, as she liked to say. But then they all were a work in progress. He was far from perfect himself and so felt this was a great privilege. He liked to think that he was simply leading a small group of strugglers like himself to find a moment of peace. The rest was up to God. Pearly, Bishop Longbottom, had said that people tried too hard, tried to do too much, that God was big enough to fight his own battles. But a battle wasn't what these folk needed in what Archie hoped was their own open-hearted expectation. For a moment he was disarmed by his own part on their journey. The words blurred just a little.

"So, get comfy, and here we go," he squeaked.

Half an hour later on cue, Harriet brought in flasks of coffee and hot chocolate. Archie was fairly sure the boy, Laurence, had fallen asleep. He looked wide-eyed and a little disorientated.

Anna yawned. Just before nine thirty she would say Evening Prayer, usually down at the church, but on the first evening they would stay here in the lounge. She'd argued that trailing out into the darkness before you'd had a chance to get your bearings wasn't a great idea. Archie was glad they'd agreed to it as he could hear the rain splattering the windows and, if truth be told, seeing the church for the first time at night could be a bit spooky. Catherine stood up, stretched discreetly and came over to get a drink.

"Thank you, Archie. That was very helpful," she said, picking up a hot chocolate. "What a treat. I never bother at home. I just have a cup of tea."

"You're welcome." Archie always had a cup of hot chocolate before bed. Full-fat milk and fairly traded chocolate powder. He was discovering that, once you unleashed the sweet tooth, it was quite difficult to get it back on the lead.

Behind Catherine, Laurence slipped out of the room. When Archie had first arrived he'd been wearing a suit. When next

Archie saw him, he'd replaced his jacket with a thick jumper, baggy and a bit pulled in places. Archie wondered if he'd come formally dressed because he'd thought that was what was required. Or maybe he'd simply come straight from work. He'd take another look at the boy's form, remind himself what he did for a living. The girls watched him leave too, their eyes swivelling after him. Archie thought they might be of a similar age. He was glad. He'd assumed they'd get mostly older people, retired folk with time on their hands, because the retreat was held over the working week. Of course they might have got this batch of young people simply because this was at the cheaper end, or rather the cheapest, end of the market. Perhaps it was all they could afford. He'd not thought of that.

"So, do you live in the village?" Catherine asked.

"Yes, have done for quite a while now. What sort of place do you live in?"

She frowned. He supposed it was a little ambiguous.

"I mean village or town?"

"Village, but my church is in the local town." She stirred her chocolate. Archie eased forward to stand up. He really didn't want to spend another minute sitting down, his back was singing, the muscles tight, and craning to look up at her was making his neck ache.

"So, what are you hoping for over the next couple of days?" Catherine tipped her head to one side and blinked.

"I'm not sure. I suppose that's the nature of God – he doesn't really do what we expect."

Too soon, thought Archie. You weren't supposed to lead the guests, you were only supposed to listen and follow where they wanted to go. Bugger. He had a lot to learn.

"Quite right." Now he sounded like a school master. Harriet came across.

"Just checking, Catherine, that you have everything you need?"

Archie flashed Harriet a grateful smile and stepped back, out of the way. Harriet was really competent at putting people at ease and never seemed to get tangled up. Not like the rest of them. He wondered whether Laurence would come back for Evening Prayer.

Dani stood up.

Rather loudly she said, "Harriet, I wonder if I might make an appointment to see Anna?" Everyone fell silent for a moment while Harriet pulled the timetable from her pocket.

"Well, you're first up so any time tomorrow afternoon." Harriet spoke quietly, normally, allowing the room to set itself right again.

"Oh, I'd hoped for something a bit sooner than that."

Archie wondered if she'd ask for an alarm call next or suddenly decide she was vegan. He sidled over to Anna, who was looking brightly around the room.

"Archie, you did well tonight," she said, nodding. He nodded back. As it was only his second go at taking the meditation he was really pleased. She'd said that she'd take special note of anything he could improve on, so he was hoping for a list of useful tips. Anna's phone jangled and her cheeks flushed pink.

"Archie, do you mind if I answer this?"

"Of course not." A vicar was never really off duty. She disappeared into the hall.

"Tom?"

"Anna?" At least he hadn't called her Reverend Maybury!

"So is it your mum?" There was a silence, longer than was reasonable. Anna kicked herself for being so sharp at the outset.

"You know, that's what I like about you. There's absolutely no beating about the bush. No 'How are you Tom? How's the job?'"

Anna was disheartened that the phone call had so quickly tumbled into misunderstanding.

"Sorry, Anna. Long day."

"So how are you? And I'm not just asking now because you told me to."

"I know you're not." He paused and then began suddenly, "I'm not great, and it is my mum. I'm so sorry. I didn't know she was coming down. She wanted to surprise me."

It sounded reasonable, yet Anna couldn't help the thought that she'd probably been at the bottom of a very long to-do list.

"Someone at a friend's church saw your email about the retreats and sent it to her. I'd told mum about Terry and the Lizard and that ... I knew some people there."

Anna's mouth stretched into a smile. She was glad she was perched on the bottom step of the stairs and couldn't see herself in the mirror that Harriet had hung by the front door. 'Somewhere to check you don't look like a scarecrow before you open up to the world,' she'd said. Anna hadn't been one bit offended. Looking like a scarecrow was the least of her worries. It was just that she wasn't used to the mirror, and now and again she caught sight of herself unexpectedly and didn't always like what she saw.

"I'm quite glad you didn't tell me," she said. "With advance warning I think I might have hit the stratosphere. I get worried enough as it is."

"You shouldn't, you know. You're really good at this stuff."

"I wish people would stop telling me that," she said, grumpily. "And what is this stuff anyway?"

"Now you're just fishing for compliments." She hadn't been. He paused. "And I think I mean simply walking alongside people. Helping them do life."

Anna laughed. She could hardly manage her own life, let alone anyone else's. She had to go; she was already late for Evening Prayer.

"Tom, I'm going to have to hang up. Um, thanks for letting me know."

"Too late. Sorry again."

Since the incident out on Beacon Point, she'd bumped into him at the pub, just the once. He'd bought her a drink and they'd chatted, mostly about the village. He'd also phoned her a couple of times to give her the heads up on some break-ins, parishioners who needed more than the usual reassurances from the police. The calls had drifted into more personal matters and had lasted longer than necessary. He'd even mentioned how much he'd like to walk down to the point, the Lizard. She'd waited to be asked. Only then there'd been a long, drawn-out murder enquiry in Falmouth, followed by a couple of police courses, and she'd had Easter and Pentecost, and as autumn had approached it was like he'd given up trying. She didn't blame him.

Anna was still sitting on the stairs staring at the wall when Harriet appeared patting her watch.

"Come on Anna, you need to get on with Evening Prayer."

"Must I?"

"You know you must. Is it his mum?"

"Yes. Let's talk later." Anna said, following Harriet dutifully into the lounge.

**

Laurence looked around the room. It was tiny, though there was a certain comfort in being able to see all four walls. His bed faced the door. That was good. The curtains twitched and burped cold air through a large sash window that took up nearly half the facing wall, so it wasn't particularly warm. But he'd slept in much worse places, particularly over the last three nights. He would've liked to have been able to see what he was overlooking, but didn't want to peer into the darkness in case someone saw him. The bed looked like any other single bed though there was a small cushion and a pile of towels as if he were in a proper hotel. It was nice that someone had gone to some trouble. No en-suite of course, just a bathroom and loo along the landing. He shrugged. It was infinitely better than his van, which had been freezing. He didn't bother washing, simply climbed between the sheets and lay back.

He slept deeply, before he'd even switched off the bedside light. When he woke a couple of hours later, he was out of bed, feet on the rug before he could stop himself, heart racing, sweat beading on his forehead. Once he'd calmed down, worked out where he was, it didn't take him long to decide that he probably wouldn't ever work out why he was here. Deciding to come away to the Lizard was nuts!

He was on retreat. He was hiding. He was trying to work out what to do and Georgie was here! Sitting large as life in the lounge with her friend. All shiny bright, all smiley and sweet with orange hair. He hadn't been expecting that.

He hadn't seen her properly for five or six years, though a while back he'd bumped into her at the shopping centre. They'd had a coffee and an awkward chat. It had been a rainy day, dull and miserable. He'd had nothing better to do than wander about, to be where other people were.

When Georgie had seen him, there'd been a moment when she'd beamed, a broad, wide smile that had stopped him in his tracks. But as soon as she'd taken a few more breaths, the smile had faded, and she'd looked sad, perhaps disappointed. From then on, she'd been deliberately off-hand. They'd swapped news about life, other kids they'd known. Had said they ought to exchange numbers, but hadn't quite got round to doing so.

Once they'd parted there had been a moment when he might have turned back to get hers, but what if she'd been hurrying away? Glad that their chance encounter was over? So he'd walked on.

He wasn't surprised at how she'd been at the café, just a little hurt. He knew that most of the kids from the home didn't want to remember, didn't want to hold on to that time, but wanted to talk about what was going on now. He'd been really pleased to find that she'd gone on to do a degree in youth work. Georgie had always been a good kid, and he'd always thought, even back when he'd first seen her, that she had a bit more about her than some of the others.

He didn't like to admit it, but meeting her for that coffee on that rather unremarkable afternoon had been the catalyst, the kick up the bum he'd needed. At the time he'd been working for a supermarket and had been wondering for ages if he ought to try something else. Something with a few more prospects. If she could climb out, then why not him? God, that had been a good moment! When anything had been possible. A moment when he could still walk with a straight back, unbowed and undamaged. Oh hell! He lay back, switched out the light. He closed his eyes and rolled over. He opened his eyes and rolled back to stare at the ceiling. A thin line of light was coming from under the door. He guessed they kept it on in case one of the guests needed the loo in the night.

He knew better than to check his watch. It would only pile on the pressure to sleep again. He tried hard not to think of meeting Georgie. Drinking bitter coffee, on plastic chairs behind a window hazy with condensation. He squeezed his eyes shut to stop them leaking his regrets.

Chapter 3

Anna knew she wasn't supposed to, but after breakfast she decided to speak to Laurence. He'd come to Morning Prayer in the church, but had looked as if he should have stayed in bed. He was pasty, almost grey around his eyes and didn't look as if he had slept at all. At breakfast she'd watched him pick at his food. She'd tried offering toast, eulogising Archie's wonderful porridge, but it hadn't made any difference. The jeans and the large baggy jumper he was wearing made him look skinny and underfed. He did seem to be in a bit of a state. She wondered if he'd lost his job or perhaps his girlfriend. She moved down the table and slipped into the chair next to him.

"Look, can I help in any way?"

He scraped his chair back. There wasn't anywhere else for him to go, so Anna sat back too. She hadn't meant to sound so keen or to corner him. He looked just like an animal, big eyes scanning the room for a way of escape. He shook his head.

"I thought I'd go for a walk. Left or right at the bottom of the lane?" His voice was distant, as if he were already out there.

"Go right. It will bring you to the point itself, and there's a lovely café."

She turned away, disappointed, got up to go. Catherine rose too and came around the table to speak to her.

"Did you sleep alright?" Anna asked. One of her stock questions at breakfast.

"Yes, I did. The bed is quite comfortable."

Good old Harriet and her bargains, thought Anna.

"He looks like he could do with a long sleep and a good hot meal," Catherine said, as they watched Laurence slip from the room.

"Yes, he does." Anna realised she'd just gone and broken

the other cardinal rule of retreats that you should never discuss one guest with another. She was really terrible at this.

"So, I wondered ..." For an awful moment Anna thought Catherine was going to ask to speak to her, one-to-one. That would be impossible. Would she want to talk about Tom? Anna wondered what she might say. What this woman thought of her police officer son? Anna supposed that she should at least say that she knew him. Or shouldn't she? Was that breaking any of the rules? Round and round she went, musing this way and that on what she ought to declare should the moment arise. God, it was exactly like being back at school. "Sorry, God," she said quickly to herself. Catherine was looking at her quizzically, a frown that made her pale eyes appear almost rectangular, just like Tom's whenever Anna felt he was getting annoyed with her.

"What did you wonder? Sorry, mind elsewhere." Now Anna was sure she sounded as if she didn't care.

"Well, my son is coming over for lunch, and I hoped he could join us, or would you rather I took him to the pub?"

"Here is absolutely fine," Anna said, brightly. *No, it wasn't! Here was a terrible idea.*

And how come Tom could find time to have lunch with his mother? Wasn't he in the middle of a murder investigation? Perhaps he'd solved it already or perhaps he was just making time for Catherine? Anna hoped that Harriet would come down early to sort out lunch; she really needed someone to unravel to, again.

"Well, I'm off for a walk. Which way at the bottom, left or right?"

"Left is nice." Only they'd had a lot of rain recently and that part of the path got a bit squelchy. She knew she'd only said left because Laurence had already laid claim to the right. He patently wanted to be alone, but Anna felt as if she was playing favourites. "Actually, both routes are nice. It's just that turning left is less busy!"

"Thank you, Anna."

Anna smiled at the woman's back and wondered if starting the day with a large brandy wasn't such a bad idea.

***

Derek was still chuckling. It made his cheeks wobble, and his eyes almost disappear into the creases under his eyelashes. Harriet had told him about Anna and Tom, and the surprise appearance of Tom's mother. She supposed it was quite funny if you weren't Anna or Tom. Derek could hardly believe that Tom's mum had actually come on one of their trial retreats!

Harriet looked around the kitchen. It still seemed too full of things. They only had a couple of weeks left in the bungalow. After that, they were moving into a small rented house at the top of Archie's road, conveniently close to the pub, Derek had said, smiling. A six-month lease until their new home was fit for habitation. For a second, she felt a little overwhelmed, something that Derek never seemed to be. Harriet knew he was excited about the renovations, even though it would be more building site than cosy cottage for quite a while. He didn't seem to see that there was still a lot to do. She sighed. She'd always travelled light, had only had a few suitcases and boxes to deal with. He had a whole bungalow with a lifetime of memories and she knew he was finding it difficult sorting through it all.

"Honestly, Derek, you should have seen her face."

"Anna's or Catherine's?"

"Anna's of course. I'm not sure Catherine knows what's going on. Not yet anyway."

"That Anna and Tom know each other?" he asked.

"I think there's more to it than that, but snails would get it on faster than those two."

"I'm not sure snails are the best example."

Harriet shook her head.

"Derek, it's the spirit of the conversation, not the words. Snails are associated with slowness." She leant back against the sink and folded her arms.

"Well, then it's a good analogy." He twisted round in his chair and looked up at her. "What did I ever do to deserve you?" He was staring, his eyes wide, his forehead puckered like a small boy seeing a steam train for the first time. Harriet had persuaded him to grow his hair a little longer so she could see the curls, but he was rapidly fading from fair to grey. His becoming cragginess was settling into chubbiness now that he was eating properly again. The year after Fiona's death had been a little hit-and-miss with respect to food.

"Everyone's allowed a second chance," she said, "me too, don't forget." He looked gratified.

"Granted, but not with a beautiful young woman who takes my breath away."

Harriet smiled and turned back to the sink, wondering for the hundredth time whether Fiona would've been happier if Derek had spoken to her like this. It felt so mean to be living her new life on the back of her old friend's misery.

Dolly nosed at the door. Harriet dried her hands to let her out.

"Will you have another go at sorting out your office? It's the only room we've not got into boxes." *And the main bedroom, and the spare room and the kitchen*, she thought.

"And it's the only one you can't really help with. I know, I know. I'll make a real start on it today after I've taken Dolly out. I didn't manage to go with Simeon this morning. I hope he didn't hang around too long." Derek poured himself some more coffee. "What time will you be home?"

"Late tonight. Sorry, luv. I promised Phil that once I'd finished at the vicarage, I'd go and give him a hand behind the bar. You know what Tuesday evenings can be like." She turned back to the sink; how could there be so much crockery from just two people? He'd promised her a dishwasher in the new place and she couldn't wait.

Dolly whined. Derek had taken his coffee into the lounge

26

so Harriet let her in. She was such an old dog. Would she manage in a new house, settle down alright? Harriet hoped it wouldn't be too much for her. She left the breakfast things to drain and went through to find Derek. Though it was a little early, she decided to head down to the vicarage. It was only a three-minute walk, but it would get rid of some of the cobwebs.

***

Any wind out on the sea funnelled up the lane from the cove and today Harriet could smell seaweed and rotting leaves. It was an aroma that fitted the day, the place and her mood.

The back door was still locked, so she had to walk back round to the front. Anna let her in before she could fish her key out of her pocket.

"How's it going?" Harriet asked, shrugging out of her coat.

"Oh Harriet, I don't know what to do!" Anna took a deep breath. "Tom's coming to lunch. He's taking some time off to see his mum, and I said it was fine for them to meet here."

Harriet laughed.

"It's probably best to get it over with and at least you'll see him again."

Anna pursed her lips. She refused to countenance, at least out loud, what Harriet thought was obvious: that she liked Tom and, more to the point, that Tom was drawn to her. Anna led the way down the hall to the kitchen, where she'd piled a few things from breakfast. Harriet began to reload the tray with all the items that actually lived in the dining room. Sometimes Anna made more work for her, which was a bit of a pain.

"The thing is, Harriet, even if he did like me, he would be too busy to do anything about it," Anna said, pulling open the dishwasher. She straightened up. "You and Derek seemed to realise straight away that you were meant for one another. It certainly didn't take you very long to move in together."

Harriet had always wondered whether Anna had been a

little shocked.

"Actually, we wondered about it for quite a long time. Nearly six months after Terry. Neither of us wanted to hurry anything." She turned away from Anna's questioning look. There were still lots of things unsaid, things she and Derek hadn't talked about, things that Harriet was having difficulty articulating. They worked on so many levels, but there was always Fiona standing between them and lately he'd looked old, or rather she'd felt too young. Harriet hoped this slightly odd, dislocated sense was the feeling of looking forward because a fresh start was what they both needed.

"Sorry, Harriet, I haven't done as much clearing as I ought to have done."

Harriet shrugged. It was what she was paid to do, part of the job description, and she had a good system except when Anna messed it up.

"How was breakfast?" she asked.

"Good, but I'm worried about Laurence. There's definitely something wrong."

"Well, I'm pretty sure God will do his thing and the Lizard will do the rest. He probably just needs someone to talk to."

"He won't talk to me. I wonder if I ought to get Archie to offer."

Harriet swung round, her tray loaded with crockery. It was heavy, so she rested it on the edge of the table.

"What did we agree?" she said, sharply. Anna looked confused. Harriet sounded like her mother, not her friend. "You promised not to interfere. You have to wait for them to be ready, and if they are never ready, that's not something you carry. Ok?"

Anna bit her lip and gave a little shake of her head.

"I've done it again, haven't I?"

"Look Anna, no harm done. Just be there for him, but don't fill the space with your worries and thoughts. Allow God to fill the space with his things instead."

For a second, she thought that Anna was going to cry, but though her bottom lip trembled, she held it together.

"Thanks, Harriet. I don't know what I'd do without you." Anna rinsed her fingers at the sink and reached for the towel. "Now what about lunch? Do you think I ought to find something else to do? Shall you and I go to the pub?"

Harriet shook her head, laughing. Anna was only joking. Anyway, if she went to the pub, she'd only end up helping Phil behind the bar. With a quiet sigh she headed to the dining room to sort the rest of the breakfast chaos.

Harriet had tried to simplify the menus as she couldn't be around to supervise all the meals. The accounts clearly showed they wouldn't be able to afford her being full-time for quite a while, and even Anna shouldn't be able to mess up porridge and toast, though she'd burned the bottom of the saucepan on their first ever try-out. After that Harriet did pop in to help at breakfast whenever she could.

Back in the kitchen she began to unload the fridge onto the table to check that Anna hadn't had the night-time munchies. Harriet had hidden the chocolate cake behind the biscuit tins, just in case.

Anna came through with another tray of things from the breakfast table. Half of them would have to go back. It was obvious she didn't have her mind on the job.

***

Georgie was cleaning her teeth. She found herself staring in the mirror, her toothbrush dripping into the sink, and ran her other hand through her hair. The dye was beginning to grow out, dark roots showing through the orange. It was still very bright and made her jump whenever she caught sight of herself.

Alf, her boss, the vicar of St Andrew's, had done a double-take the first time he'd seen it, but had quickly decided it made her look cool. Having a youth worker with orange hair was alright, she'd overheard him saying to his secretary. She spat into the sink. She really didn't want to think about Alf and work.

She'd heard Laurence say he was going to head right along the path so she would go that way too. She couldn't stand another minute with Dani. It had been Alf's suggestion to invite her on the retreat, even though Dani had already been staying with Georgie for nearly a month by then.

Georgie shared a small house with a couple of other young people from church, but they both worked away in the week, and Georgie was so busy on the weekend she hardly saw them. It worked and yet it didn't. She always felt that she was the odd one out, that she was the one that didn't fit even though she'd been there the longest.

And now Dani was installed, spilling out of the tiny box room at the back. Making her presence felt in ways that Georgie could only marvel at.

Dani seemed to talk all the time, worming inside your brain so there wasn't any space left for your own thoughts. Georgie needed space. That's what she'd told Alf, the man with all the ideas and no time to do anything except muck up his diary and blame the rest of them for not being close enough to God.

She was supposed to have a day off, just one day a week, but in the last eighteen months, apart from when she'd actually gone away, he'd managed to find something for her to do on every single one of those days. It was so difficult to say no. Everything was always so urgent, so important, God's work! She was exhausted, and now he expected her to look after Dani too. She would talk to Anna at some point because it would be nice to have someone to listen to her for a change. She wanted to do her best, was doing her best, but apart from setting her alarm earlier and earlier it seemed there was never enough time to get anything straight, particularly the thoughts in her head and the admin scattered across the bedroom floor.

She crept down the stairs, her walking boots in hand, her coat stuffed into her rucksack. Dani was talking to Anna in the dining room and when she leaned forward to reach for the sugar, Georgie scooted past the open door. She didn't breathe properly until she got to the bottom of the lane. She felt guilty, of course she did, but if she didn't get some time to herself, she'd explode. Anyway, she wanted to catch up with Laurence. It had been a while since she'd seen him, and after their quick coffee at the shopping centre she'd felt unsettled. She thought she'd probably come across as offhand rather than grown-up, which had been what she'd been going for. She wondered when it had become so important to show him that she was alright, that she was getting on well. That she'd shaken the dust off her feet and managed to walk away from their less than easy start. She checked her watch; she was only a few minutes behind and she could walk quite fast when she wanted to.

***

The cove at the bottom of the hill was tiny, the tide high. Georgie didn't have a clue as to whether the water was coming in or out, but it looked as if there was no more space for it, lapping against the concrete of the ramp, nearly at the front door of one of the cottages. There were three stone buildings that must have done something useful at some point. Now they were holiday homes opening onto the waves. They must be awesome places to stay, but way above her pay grade. It was lovely, the sea bright blue, wrinkled with white foam and speckled with sea birds. Georgie breathed in deeply for the first time in a long while and then, hearing voices behind her, hurried up what she assumed was the coast path. It was narrow and climbed steeply, but she quickly turned the corner and was soon out of sight of the road. She relaxed her shoulders, thanked God for the sea and the beauty of his world and began to walk. Once she'd got past the lifeboat station, sitting at the bottom of some horribly steep steps, and out onto the next promontory she could see Laurence not that far ahead of her. He was walking slowly, his head down. It wouldn't take her any time at all to catch him up.

Chapter 4

Dani was cross. She'd wanted to get some fresh air, but was worried about getting lost. She'd assumed Georgie would wait for her. Dani had only had a very short chat with Anna and one more cup of coffee. When she finally got upstairs and worked out which was the right door to their room, Georgie was nowhere to be seen.

Dani was disappointed in Georgie. She wasn't great company and though she'd been alright on the journey down, the previous night she hadn't wanted to talk at all. Dani had told her a couple of things, difficult things, and all Georgie had done was mumble, turn over and begin to snore. *Rude,* Dani thought. *Very rude.*

In the hall pinned to the wall was a large map of the walks around the area. She'd go and have a look at that. She really didn't want to get lost and she didn't believe Anna who'd said how difficult it was to do that, walking around the point. All paths led into the village apparently. Dani sighed. Why had she agreed to come in the first place? This wasn't her thing at all. She supposed she'd only said yes because the Reverend had suggested it and the church would pay for most of it. Of course then her mum had got really angry, had screeched things like 'Why on earth do you need a retreat? What are you retreating from? You never do anything to help ...' Her mum never seemed to understand how hard it all was, so after that particular episode, Dani hadn't thought she'd had much choice. She had to come away.

The place felt empty when she came down the stairs. So much for there being someone around at all times. She wondered where Laurence had got to. He still looked quite sweet, a little pale, older and definitely not drunk like he'd been when she'd last seen him. She hooked her bag over her shoulder and zipped up her coat. She wasn't interested in Laurence; he wasn't her type. Georgie had been a bit weird;

she'd pretended not to know him. Dani supposed Georgie didn't remember that she, Dani, had been one of the girls with Georgie at the club all those years ago, that she'd seen them together, had heard at least a little of their story. At some point she would have the pleasure of reminding her.

***

Simeon hadn't needed to unlock the church that morning. Anna had said that she would do it. Instead, he'd waited patiently for Derek to walk by with Dolly, but had finally received a text to say they weren't coming because Derek needed to sort out a couple of things with Harriet. From then on, Simeon's day had refused to slot into place. Everything was behind time. Disconcerted, he tried to breathe away the scratchiness inside. It worked to some extent, but it wouldn't go completely. In the end, he decided to walk to Archie's. That settled, he began to wonder about the retreat and how it was going.

The day before, Archie had said, "We are like a well-oiled machine, and this is only our second attempt." He'd seemed very happy.

Simeon's job was to keep an eye on the church, Harriet cooked and Anna dealt with anything spiritual. Simeon decided to tell Archie that he agreed that they worked well together; it would please Archie. Archie liked things to go smoothly. Simeon thought about that for a moment. Obviously most people wanted things to go smoothly, it was just that Archie showed his joy. His back would straighten and he would bounce from foot to foot. Sometimes he would put one of his hands in his pocket, a sure sign that he'd forgotten himself. He even seemed to enjoy the endless meetings about what needed to be done. He kept saying it was a good way to use the vicarage, to make the most of where they lived. And that to do something positive after the awful months dodging Terry and her madness was an excellent remedy for what they had all been through. Though you couldn't say madness in front of Anna, that made her cross. Terry was sad, not mad, used by her husband until her longing to be loved had consumed her. Simeon didn't care what Anna said. Terry had been clever, and sly. Sadness didn't make you want to kill someone and she'd murdered Derek's wife, Fiona. Simeon was absolutely certain of that. It had left Derek adrift and lost for months.

Simeon didn't want to think about that. Such thoughts made him want to shut out the light, crawl under his blanket and listen to the sound of his house at rest. Of course now that wasn't so easy, as Belle would often potter about and when he was having a difficult time, she'd come and push her nose under the covers, breathe her doggy breath into his face until he wrapped his arms around her neck and pulled her close. Not allowing her on the bed was the one dog rule he didn't abide by.

He took the lead down from the hook. At the clink of the catch, Belle climbed out of her bed a little stiffly and came and sat at his feet. She was nearly eleven years old, but the vet said that she was an excellent weight and still moving well, with only the tiniest bit of arthritis in her joints. Simeon decided on walking boots because the first part of the track, down past the old radar station, was muddy from the cows. In deepest winter he often had to go the other way, out onto the lane that ran past the church and down to the coast via the lifeboat station or Church Cove itself.

Every day, unless the weather was stormy, he and Belle walked the path round the Lizard. If it was a Monday or a Thursday, he turned in at Archie's gate, and they would spend a couple of hours together talking about Archie's latest book. Simeon read a great deal now, and the walking enabled him to ponder what he'd read. It was important to give yourself processing time; it was what Anna was especially bad at. She said she loved reading too, but mostly what she called 'unsuitable' novels because you didn't need to think about them too much to work out what was going on.

The air was fresh. It had been a gentle October, but with lots of rain, so the paths were particularly muddy. Still, he liked this time of year when the colours were settled and muted. Grey through to green with the odd splash of rich-red bracken when the sun shone and the lichen, orange and yellow, softened the rocks, with their crinkly flowering. There was a front coming in. He could see it bubbling out across the sea, but he reckoned he'd got plenty of time before it made landfall. Gulls were wheeling about as usual; he also saw a stonechat and a jackdaw but not much else.

When he reached the cliff edge, he looked back to Beacon Point. The promontory rose up, a wedge of solid rock clothed in short grass that petered out towards the edge. Just below the point was the place he used to stand, a place where the cliff was tall and sheer down into the sea. Where he'd thought very seriously about jumping because he wanted to see what happened next. It had been a difficult time, and he didn't like to think about it. He'd come a long way since then.

He looked east and then west to make sure that the path was empty and began to stride towards the Lizard. Belle lolloped along beside him. He slowed down a little so that she had time to mooch about. At the next headland, looking across to where the hotel sat back against the sky, he could see two figures walking. They were a few metres apart, the first a young man, plodding along, head down, a black beanie pulled over his ears, behind him a woman, her hair bright orange. He watched them disappear into a crevice where a stream dropped down onto the beach and from where another path ran straight up into the village. He waited for them to appear on the other side. They climbed slowly as the path was steep just there, twisting and turning with the cliffs, which were grainy and dark, rearing above a line of rocks. That would've been a good place to jump, except the path was too close by, and people would've wanted to call out 'Good morning,' 'Are you alright?' 'It's a bit of a drop, do be careful.' His favourite spot back by Beacon Point was much further from the path, which had, on the whole, discouraged people from interfering.

Simeon followed the couple, but walked more slowly. He didn't want to catch them up, acknowledging the resentment he felt at them impinging on his walk. There were often people about, but not usually too many in October. He wondered if they were from the retreat. Then before he could help himself, he glanced over his shoulder, just to make sure there was no-one behind him. To begin with, every fifty steps, then every forty. He began to sweat and his heart rate rose. Belle whined and licked his hand.

Dogs were clever; they knew when there was something wrong. Simeon began to speed up. After another fifteen minutes he walked around the last point, from where he could see the roofs of the three buildings squatting precariously at the end of the Lizard. A café, the wildlife lookout station and a serpentine workshop. They were the last structures before the land dropped into the sea, apart from the old lifeboat station tucked down below, where shore became ocean.

His first problem was to get past the end of the National Trust car park. If he was going to bump into anyone, it would be there. Then he had to walk across the small turning space where the café people parked their cars and where visitors who had overshot the main car park turned around. The sunken lane was too narrow for a vehicle and a pedestrian, so they had built a wide flat path that cut through the fields either side of the road. Simeon hardly ever went that way because it was too often filled with strangers, people who'd paid for the car park and then didn't want to waste their money; leaving the car while they had a cup of tea looking out over the old lifeboat station, watching the wildness of the sea, perhaps even spotting a seal or two before wandering up into the village. There was a pub, a couple of shops and a few more serpentine workshops, turning out lighthouses and ashtrays, even though hardly anyone smoked anymore these days.

Simeon could see all along the path now. The woman wasn't visible, so either she'd gone into the café or up to the loo in the car park. The young man was standing in the turning area. A large black car appeared, obscuring him for a few seconds, then slowly turned around and headed back up the road. Simeon thought it odd that, having come down so far, they hadn't stopped to look at the view. Perhaps they had just missed the entrance to the car park and were saving it for later. As far as Simeon could see there was no-one else around. When the young man disappeared onto the lower shore, Simeon broke into a jog until he was almost across the turning area. He would've made it completely if he hadn't looked up to see where the man was. As it was he stumbled on a tussock and sprawled forward, his hand taking most of the fall. He sat for a minute, nursing his wrist, checking his watch hadn't been scratched.

"It's ten past ten," he practised, out loud. Actually, it was twelve minutes past ten, but Archie said that people sometimes got annoyed when he was precise. Another two minutes, no more, and he'd be round the other side, the wild side, where the westerlies whipped the waves into mountains that smashed against the coast, filling the air with foam. He got up. Belle was beginning to tire, so he would have to take it slower again. He looked around him. The young man was far below, walking down the narrow path to the old lifeboat station, now no more than a couple of sheds at the top of a slipway, a line of pillars sticking out of the swell like old teeth. The ramp ended abruptly, as if someone had taken a saw to it. Even down in the shelter of the buildings, it was a desolate place. Padlocks and warning signs, iron rings sunk into the rocks, rusting and sharp-edged. Simeon had been down there once or twice, but had been overwhelmed by the cliffs rearing up behind him, the ramp and lifeboat station blotting out the view of the sea in front. It had made him feel very small and disconcerted. He shivered at the thought of it. He spotted the woman. It looked like she'd nipped up into the car park to use the loo, but instead of coming across towards him, she turned down after the man, disappearing behind the café. Another figure appeared briefly at the bottom of the lane. Simeon turned away and quickly walked onto the next spit of coast. From there he could see Archie's house nestling into the land, squat and hunkered down, ready for anything the weather could throw at it. Simeon's pace began to slow. Archie's house was safe. Archie would know how to calm him. Archie would put everything into perspective.

He made his way into a small gully. At the bottom was the path that ran back up into the village. It was very narrow with tall hedges either side, but he rarely met anyone coming along it. Glancing back, all he could see was the sea, a grey swell to the horizon. The Lizard was invisible from there. Simeon jumped when a man appeared, coming down towards him from Archie's lane. He was small, his hands hidden in his pockets, with a set of binoculars hanging over his right shoulder. He wasn't wearing a hat, so Simeon could see that he had short, grey hair. Simeon dropped his eyes to the path, had to gulp a couple of quick breaths. It had been the suddenness of the man's appearance that had made him start, just when he'd thought all danger of bumping into anyone was over. He noted a dull-green coat and mud-spattered, blue trousers. Scuffed leather shoes and, peeping between, yellow socks. The man didn't speak as he passed. Simeon waited until he was clear of him and then began to run, Belle wheezing as she struggled to keep up, to stay close.

Chapter 5

"So, what shall I do with these?"

Phil looked up. Kyle was standing in the doorway with a bundle of used sheets. Except some of them looked suspiciously clean and freshly ironed.

"You did get them from rooms two and four?" Kyle looked confused. Phil sucked his top lip and counted to ten. "I've shown you twice now. The book tells you which rooms are occupied. If it's one night, you change the sheets. If they are staying for longer, but have used them for two nights, you change the sheets. If the room hasn't been used, you don't change the sheets."

"I thought you said one and four."

Phil wondered for a moment if he could have got it wrong. It was possible. He walked over to the book lying open on the top of the fridge.

"We only have one couple in and a single gentleman. The single gentleman was a bit vague about when he would be checking out, so that's why I've put a question mark over the room for the next few days. For now, we simply tidy it up, make sure he's got soap and doesn't need clean towels." Kyle's expression didn't change. He blinked, and Phil, who was already feeling a little irritated, was reminded of a koala. He wondered if anything made Kyle move at speed.

It was just one more thing on his list of grumbles that morning. The guest hadn't come down for his full English, but his holdall was still stuffed under a chair in the corner of his room, so he hadn't done a runner. He'd probably gone out for an early morning walk and got carried away, but even so, it would've been courteous to have let Phil know he wasn't going to be around for breakfast. "The couple left this morning. So only the one room to change. Kyle, check the book. It's not hard."

"I'll sort it out," the boy said, sullenly. "I can easily put the clean ones back on."

Phil looked at the tangle of sheets.

"No, get fresh ones for all of them. And do it nicely," he called after him, "like Harriet showed you." *Not a bloody hope*, he thought. But Harriet was coming in later, so he would ask her to check that Kyle had done it well enough. The bell tinkled on the door. He put on a smile and turned to serve a young woman. She was small and neat and looked as if she'd washed behind her ears. He wondered if she'd like a job.

"What can I get you?"

"A coffee, please. I've just walked up from the Lizard."

"Stunning, isn't it?" She looked along the bar vaguely, as though she didn't quite understand. "Are you staying round here?" he tried instead.

"The vicarage."

So one of the lost souls. He was glad she'd asked for coffee because at ten-thirty, if she asked for anything else, he might have had to ID her. She had dark hair, plaited from just behind her fringe, which hung a little long and made her look as if she were peering up at you all the time. A thin face, powdered to cover freckles running across her nose.

"So, how's it going?"

She was leaning on the bar, and he readjusted her age a little. She looked quite comfortable standing there.

"How's what going?" She narrowed her eyes.

"The retreat? If you're up from the vicarage, you must be on the retreat."

"Oh, that. Yes, it's alright, though it's not very warm. I had to put on a jumper to go to bed."

"Those windows can be a little draughty." Phil turned away to smile. Anna would be worried about that.

"And rattly. I didn't get a wink of sleep. I came because I'm having a difficult time at home, and I need a break."

Phil poured himself a coffee and settled in. This young woman clearly needed to tell someone why she was here, and he didn't have anything better to do. There was a crash from the kitchen. Kyle must have started on the breakfast plates. Phil got up to shut the door.

***

"So, you see, I wasn't ready to have a baby, but I couldn't just get rid of it." Dani sighed.

"Even though you weren't sure who the dad was?" Phil asked. He slipped off his stool to fetch the coffee pot. She shook her head when he held it over her cup.

"Well, I was extremely vulnerable and anyway, it wasn't little Selena's fault."

That word, vulnerable. As a lad he'd hardly known what it meant. Nowadays the kids used it as a matter of course.

"Selena. Is that a family name?"

"No, I just liked it and Mum didn't."

Phil frowned.

"So who's looking after little Selena now?"

"She's not so little, almost three, and Mum has her." She took a sip of coffee. It was probably a little cold by now. "We don't always get on that well. There's nothing in the rules to say we have to," she said, a little defensively.

Phil wasn't sure where to go with this and was relieved when the door opened and Archie appeared, bringing a draught of leafy air with a slightly fishy tang.

"Archie, how are you?"

"I'm well, thank you."

He marched over to the bar, down at the far end, away from the young woman. Phil smiled apologetically at her and moved across to serve him.

"Archie, am I glad to see you."

"Isn't that one of the young ladies from the vicarage?"

"Yes. She's been in here for ages."

"I won't disturb her." She had indeed completely ignored Archie's nodded smile. "When I spoke to Anna earlier on the phone, she said they'd all gone out for a walk."

Phil smiled. The retreat was certainly a joint venture.

"Well, technically this one walked up from the vicarage and then down to the point, but she wasn't very impressed. She fancied a coffee and, as it happens, a chat. Now I know all about her." He rolled his eyes.

"She looks so young. How can she have that much to talk about?"

"Now you know that age is no barrier to life."

Archie nodded. He looked thoughtful.

"What's up, Archie?"

"I'm not sure, Phil. Everything seems to be working as we planned. Simeon seems settled, though he was a bit rattled this morning, Anna is ... well, Anna, and yet ..." He broke off.

"And yet ...?"

"I don't know what's wrong, but something's bugging me." He looked across at Phil and shrugged. "I can't go and talk to Anna as I'm not exactly sure what to say."

Phil looked carefully at his friend. His overcoat was still buttoned up to the neck as if he weren't staying. He had his beanie on (a present from Anna), pulled down nearly to his eyebrows. His face was clean-shaven as always, but his cheeks were a little pale and he looked worn, his eyes dull under heavy eyelids. He wasn't a young man, though he always walked with purpose, very upright. That was the Navy for you, it glued your backbone straight with salt, Archie always said.

"You're allowed to be normal, like the rest of us." Phil poured Archie a coffee. "Everyone relies on you to some extent. Aren't you about to embark on a bit of an adventure?" He meant the Reader course. Archie nodded, but Phil could tell he wasn't really concentrating. "You're also allowed to be worried. How about taking some time out for yourself for a change?" Phil pointed to the rum.

Archie smiled, but shook his head. Phil had known that it was far too early in the day for Archie, but he liked to offer anyway. He knew Archie thought that worrying about yourself only made things worse, that introspection was self-indulgent. So Phil was surprised when Archie asked, "Have you got time for a quick chat?"

Phil looked back to his only other customer. Dani was now chatting to Kyle, who had slipped through from the kitchen, unobtrusively. They both had fresh cups of coffee. Phil was pretty sure the breakfast hadn't been cleared away properly, but he was fed up with taking Kyle to task and he was more than a little pleased that Archie had sought him out. Lots of people talked to Phil, mostly because he was there, like a good hairdresser. Archie never did that, never made him feel as if he were just part of the furniture, even when he was nagging him about church.

"Where are they all from, your guests?" Phil asked, topping up their cups. He was pleased to see Archie taking off his coat.

"Exeter, except for one woman, Catherine, who's from Wiltshire. She saw the advert because a friend of hers from Exeter thought she'd be interested. We're only advertising in a small number of dioceses to begin with. Still honing the way we do things. Making sure we can manage before opening up to the wider world." He smiled.

"Well, I think it's marvellous. I was worried they'd close the church down altogether after what happened."

"No, the bishop was determined to keep us going and he really believes in Anna."

And in you, Phil thought.

"It's a shame she has such trouble believing in herself," Phil replied.

"Oh, none of us are much good at that."

"You have a point, Archie, but wouldn't life be simpler if we cut ourselves some slack now and again?"

Archie nodded.

"I suppose it would help a little."

"So, what would you like to talk about?"

45

Archie took another sip of his coffee, frowning in concentration.

"Well, I'm not sure, but I think I'd like to talk about Anna."

Chapter 6

"And just before we go through for lunch, perhaps you'd like to say grace," Harriet said firmly. It wasn't a question. "Anna!"

Anna jumped. She wasn't listening. Tom hadn't arrived yet. Catherine, Dani and Archie were sitting uncomfortably around the lounge. Archie had arrived only a few seconds before and was still out of breath, a little pink. Said he'd been chatting to Phil and had forgotten the time. Georgie was upstairs, running late. Anna had no idea where Laurence was. Dani kept looking at the door and then at her watch, as if she were waiting for something to happen. She had a way of raising her eyebrows and biting her lip that made Anna think of a religious painting she'd studied at college. A mother and child by Bellini, mother exceedingly peeved and child grumpy. It wasn't how she saw Jesus. In fact, she had real problems seeing him as a baby at all. Babies were scary, cried and weed at inappropriate moments, and she simply couldn't imagine praying to someone who was bawling at his mother because he needed his nappy changing. Harriet cleared her throat. Anna shook her head.

"Thank you, Lord, for this morning. Bless this food to us and the hands that made it. Amen."

Well, this will seal it for Catherine, Anna thought. Now she would know Anna obviously didn't have an original bone in her body. She wished she'd thought to prepare a grace that was a little more deep and meaningful.

"I don't suppose you mind, do you, God, as long as we're grateful," Anna muttered quietly to herself. Anna was always grateful for Harriet's lunches. Fluffy quiches and nutty salads, fruit and yogurt. As if she were on a proper diet, only it tasted really nice.

She wondered where Tom had got to and, for that matter, Laurence. The phone in the hall rang, and Harriet disappeared to answer it. Anna's mobile was somewhere about the place but on silent.

"This way, ladies. Lunch is across the hall," Archie said, jumping up as if he were the butler, which made Anna smile. She followed behind them, like a good sheep dog. At the top of the stairs Georgie appeared. She looked dreadfully pale and yet flushed at the same time, almost as if she had a fever. Anna sighed. That wasn't how you were supposed to look after a wonderful walk around their beloved peninsula. What she hadn't realised when planning any of this was how responsible she would feel for everyone. She tried not to, but they had all come here looking for something, and Anna felt it was her job to help them find it – and so far, it wasn't going well.

Harriet was standing with her back to them, the phone clamped to her ear. When Anna sidled into the dining room, she could see Catherine surreptitiously checking her phone, too.

Oh Tom, Anna thought, *it's not just me you are letting down.*

Harriet appeared and motioned for Anna to follow her back into the hall, where she pointedly shut the door.

"That was Tom," Harriet said.

"Of course it was. What's the excuse this time?"

"A body down on the point. He's left you a message, but knows you have your phone on silent when you're with the guests and it was Laurence who found the body, so he won't be back for a while either." Anna looked at her watch. It was just one fifteen. Her hand was trembling. Harriet had her arms folded tightly across her thin frame and her face looked almost green. Anna sat down heavily on the bottom stair.

"Oh Harriet, I don't think we can do this again."

"It won't be like last time," Harriet said, quickly, but her voice shook and faded. Anna needed to breathe, needed to think, but instead she hauled herself up and wrapped her arms around Harriet. Just for a second, they held onto each other, remembering Terry.

"Oh, bloody hell. What am I supposed to tell his mother?" Anna whispered. Harriet pulled away and checked her reflection in the mirror.

"Tom says to have lunch and then, if you wouldn't mind taking her down to the café. He'll try and snatch a few moments."

As if it were all about a missed lunch!

"I can't. I've got that one-to-one with Dani."

"Oh, bother. I'd forgotten," Harriet said, leaning forward and tucking a strand of Anna's hair off her face. "Well, don't worry, I'll go."

Anna began to move, until the obvious question stopped her in her tracks. She quickly turned back.

"Do we know who? The body, that is?" she asked, in a small voice.

Harriet pressed her lips together.

"Tom said you might do that. They don't know yet. Laurence is in a bit of a state, but try not to worry."

"Then I must go to him."

"Tom thought you'd say that too. He said he'll bring him back when they've finished with him. That he'll be gentle." Harriet was having real difficulty suppressing a smile, which annoyed Anna. She became aware of the anxiety in her stomach. Acid bubbling unpleasantly. She breathed deeply, and Harriet touched her arm.

"Are you ok?"

"Just feeling a bit overwhelmed."

"Get in there and do your stuff."

"I hate small talk," Anna said, wearily.

"Then skip that bit and go straight into the deep and meaningful. The girls look just about ripe for some TLC. I wonder if they've fallen out?" Which was all they needed.

Archie was tucking into a large plate of food. For a man who was stick-thin, he couldn't half-eat. Anna supposed it was all the energy he spent standing ramrod-straight and doing the right thing. She felt bad immediately for being so catty, particularly as Archie was one of those people she leaned on rather heavily.

"Archie, may I interrupt you?" He and Catherine were talking about being churchwardens. "Sorry Catherine." Archie frowned as Anna leaned towards him.

She whispered, "When you've finished, could you take some food down to the Lizard? Poor Laurence is being questioned by the police. He'll have had nothing since breakfast."

The room fell silent. Everyone looked up. Georgie dropped a spoon and coleslaw splattered across the table. It was hard being discreet in such a confined space.

"Of course," Archie said, already rising from his unfinished plate.

"No, finish your food. A few minutes won't make any difference. Catherine, I don't suppose you've got a signal on your phone?"

"No, I haven't had more than half a bar all morning. That call was Tom, wasn't it?"

Anna nodded.

"A police incident down on the point. He'd like you to go and meet him there later. There's quite a nice little café. He's hoping to get five minutes once the body has been moved."

Bugger, Anna thought. She hadn't meant to say that.

Catherine nodded. Her hair, thick and well cut, bobbed around her face as if it had just been brushed. Her eyes were pale where Tom's were dark, but they still reminded Anna of him, particularly the way they widened just a little when there was something unusual going on. Like Tom's, the rest of Catherine's face remained passive, unreadable, until she smiled, and then she instantly looked ten years younger. Anna decided that that was how she wanted to age. Gracefully and with quiet dignity.

"You've met my son, or so I hear. There was a nasty case

last year," Catherine spoke quietly, but the room went silent again.

"Yes," Anna said, wondering if she should elaborate or whether Catherine already knew about Terry. Dani and Georgie of course would now want to know what constituted a nasty case.

"One of our parishioners got a bit lost because she'd been hurt really badly by her ex."

That was an understatement. Derek's wife, Fiona, had been bludgeoned to death in the churchyard. There had never been any hard proof that Terry had done it. It had been a horribly stressful year. Derek and Harriet had spent the first six months disliking one another intensely, caught up in the maelstrom of Fiona's sudden death. Anna had been stuck in the middle. It had been difficult for all of them. Then out of the blue, during a brief cessation of hostilities, a miracle in itself, a remarkable relationship had blossomed. Two lost souls etc. Maybe that was a bit cheesy, but they did seem really happy. Of course Anna knew that Harriet would be relieved to move out of the house that Derek had shared with Fiona, even for such a short time, into something that was theirs.

"Didn't she try and push you over a cliff or something?" Catherine asked, looking intently at Anna, and Anna began to explain why she and Terry had ended up on Beacon Point with Dolly the dog and Tom.

**

Harriet rang Derek when she got to the centre of the village. She'd virtually passed the bungalow on the way up, but that would've meant introducing Catherine and he would've asked too many questions.

"I hope it's nothing sinister," Catherine said quietly, turning her back to the wind. It was blowing steadily from the west and rain clouds were beginning to blot out the horizon.

"You mean, simply a body washed up from a passing ship?"

51

Harriet replied. *No-one I know*, she was praying silently, over and over again. She'd immediately thought of Simeon. Only if he'd gone missing, Archie would've realised straight-away. Harriet normally saw Simeon at church, but last Sunday Phil had been short-staffed at the pub, so she'd served pints instead. One of these days she would have to ask Anna what going to church was all about. God, she got on some levels, but church, not so much. Simeon always went and he never did anything unless he could see a purpose to it. Plus, he didn't find the services easy. He said it was because he didn't like breathing air used by so many others, that it made him prickly and uncomfortable. So he sat in the tower with the door ajar. His own private space. Sharing a pew sometimes made Harriet feel a bit uncomfortable too.

Harriet and Catherine turned south, leaving the houses behind, and the wind began to skip past them, whisking across the headland like a great big child who had no idea of its own strength. The path ran alongside the road at field height, so that the Lizard spread out either side of them. The lighthouse and cottages were perched along the eastern edge, the sky a dark grey backdrop. It made the buildings glow, like seagulls turning in a ray of sunlight, and Harriet felt as if she were wearing 3D glasses. The large car park at the end of the point, with the useful loos wouldn't be very full at this time of year. Already she could see the lights from the police vehicles, a blue disturbance in the air. It made her stop. They had filled up the village with their glaring presence when Fiona had been killed and then when Dolly had disappeared.

"Are you alright, dear?" Catherine asked.

"Sorry, it's the lights. They always remind me."

"That must have been a difficult time for all of you."

Harriet wondered how much Tom had told his mother. She'd heard the first part of Anna's conversation over lunch, but then Dani had wanted to tell her about her morning and she'd had to turn away and concentrate.

"What really got to us was the not-knowing, particularly in the last few months. We all began to look over our shoulders. Wondering what had really happened to poor Fiona." She turned back towards the point and shrugged. "Tom tried to help, I know he did, but in the end, it was Anna who worked it all out."

"She sounds pretty amazing."

"She is and she's not," Harriet said, laughing. "I'm not being mean. She'd tell you herself that she is ordinary and flawed. I think it's just that she's less good at pretending than the rest of us, which makes her ... real, I suppose." Catherine gave a tiny shake of her head. Harriet wasn't surprised. It was an odd thing to say about someone. That what she loved about Anna was that she was ordinary and not very good at putting on a front.

"Oh, my," Catherine said, stopping abruptly. "This is a wild prospect. It takes your breath away. Though I guess you get used to it."

"Not really and once we drop down onto the point itself the scenery is even more incredible. The end of everything until you hit America. Normally I would be hurrying you down there to see it. It's just that ..."

"Why don't you go back? I'm positive I can't get lost in the next hundred yards or so."

"No, I'll be fine." Harriet swallowed the rising anxiety and strode forward. Anyway, she still wanted to check it wasn't anyone she knew.

***

Simeon looked up the path. Two women were walking down from the car park. He was surprised the police had let them through. They'd blocked off the lane just above the main entrance and there were constables standing on each of the coastal paths, east and west, turning people back. He didn't envy them that job. It was a cold day, the waves marbled dark green, were edged with white foam, and any second now it

53

would start to rain. Archie, who was standing next to him, began to wave.

"It's Harriet and Catherine."

"Who is Catherine?" Simeon asked, staring at the tall woman, walking just behind Harriet.

"Tom's mother."

"Oh," Simeon said quietly. He wondered what Anna thought about that. She and Tom had become friends. Not like him and Archie or even him and Anna, but Simeon knew that Tom had been over to visit. Simeon had seen them at the pub, sitting at one of the little tables around the corner. Where people sat if they didn't want to be disturbed. Simeon knew that Anna was quite good at helping people, even if she didn't always sound as though she really believed or understood what she was trying to say. Tom perhaps had needed someone to talk to who wasn't in the force.

Simeon quickly smiled at Harriet. He then carefully nodded at the other woman, but kept his eyes fixed on her knees. She was wearing light blue trousers and stout walking shoes that he thought had been well cared for. He didn't risk glancing up to see what she looked like. He was teetering on the edge of anxiety as it was and there simply wasn't any slack in the system.

He'd left Archie's at eleven forty, had been on his way home when he'd seen the young man down on the old ramp, trying to reach what looked horribly like a body. He'd been trying to clamber round the fencing along the edge of the lifeboat building, fencing that should have kept him out. The young man ought to have phoned the coast guard. It had been foolish to try to do anything without the proper equipment or someone to help him. The water, sucking up and down the stanchions, was unpredictable, and sometimes a wave would rise up and break over the entire structure. There were signs everywhere warning people of the danger. The dead man wore a dark-green coat and blue trousers, though it was hard to be completely sure of the colour because they were wet. His body had been hanging across the angled struts that used to hold up the ramp. High tide had left him draped there, folded over like a sheet on a washing line.

For a moment, Simeon had stood there, trying to decide what to do. It had been eleven forty-seven. For once he felt he could be precise without annoying anybody, and Tom was sure to want to know timings as exactly as possible. He'd also known he couldn't touch a body or even get close, not after Fiona. So, instead of running down to help, he'd jogged to the café, and they had phoned the coast guard from there.

Tom was now standing beside an ambulance. They'd had to call it because the young man had fallen into the sea.

Simeon knew that he had to tell the police what he knew, but Belle was getting cold and a little restless. He'd kept quiet about things before, but Anna said it wasn't necessarily the best thing to do. Which meant she thought it was wrong. Sometimes he had to trust her and not his own instincts, which at the moment were to go home and hide under his blanket. He was trying very hard not to do that. He'd been getting almost beyond his limit when Archie had been let through with some sandwiches for the young man. Tom had then allowed him to stay with Simeon until he was able to take a statement. Simeon still didn't feel right, but having Archie close was better than nothing and his breathing was getting a little slower.

"Where's Anna?" Simeon asked Harriet.

"She had an appointment with one of the guests," she replied.

"I think you should tell Tom that is why she's not here."

Archie smiled one of his little smiles, the ones he used when he was trying hard not to smile at all. A small flattening of his lips and a fluttering of his eyelids.

"Have I said something funny?"

"Oh no, Simeon. It's just that that is very thoughtful of

you. Tom might indeed be wondering where she is."

"And she'll hate missing out on what's going on," Simeon said. Archie turned away. Simeon thought he was definitely laughing. But he was sure that Anna would hate missing out on what was going on. Sometimes he really didn't understand why people reacted like they did, and now and again even Archie could be a bit of a mystery.

Chapter 7

Tom saw his mother picking her way down from the car park, and he was surprised and a little disappointed that she was accompanied by Harriet. The constable at the bottom of the steps pointed to him, as if his mother might not recognise him. Though they were still a little far off Tom waved. This was going to be awkward. He really didn't want to interrupt what he was doing to make small talk with his mum. He wondered if she'd understand.

Laurence was still in a bit of a state, kept mumbling things that needed to be checked out. The body, which even he could see hadn't been long in the water, looked pretty bashed about. The right hand was folded into a claw, bruised and livid, an eye half closed and swollen. Tom hoped Anna wasn't staying away because she was cross with him. He'd meant to come over a couple of times recently, ask her to go for a walk or something, only now, out of the blue she'd met his mother. It was all getting a bit complicated. The problem was he was used to giving orders, not having to give explanations. He scooted on past that excuse. It didn't sit well and he knew she'd argue the toss, quite rightly, he supposed. Damn, he needed to concentrate.

He stepped away from the ambulance. His mum and Harriet were now standing with Archie and Simeon. Simeon was a priority before too many people asked him what had happened. He had been the one to call in the incident and Tom knew there would be all sorts of details floating around in Simeon's head, which Tom would like to get hold of.

He strode over, knowing that the constables around him were watching carefully. He supposed having the boss's mother on site was a big deal. For him it was annoying, something he'd try to ignore. What should he have done? Left her waiting at the vicarage? Actually, come to think of it, that wouldn't have been such a bad idea.

"Hi Mum," he said as casually as he could. She smiled and nodded.

"Hello darling. I can see you've got your hands full. Why don't you get on with what you have to do? I'm happy to wait for you at the vicarage." He filled in for himself, 'away from all these prying eyes'. She wasn't stupid.

"Thanks," he said, marvelling that she sounded as though they saw each other all the time. "I'm sorry." He leaned forward and kissed her on the cheek.

"Not to worry," she replied brightly. But he knew she was disappointed. When she smiled properly, her eyes were a mass of crinkles. Not something she liked to be reminded of. This time there was barely a line, as if she were smoothed flat by the wind.

"Thanks for walking her down, Harriet."

"Anna couldn't come. She has an appointment with one of the other guests," Simeon said, unable to hold it in any longer.

"Oh, thank you, Simeon," Tom said, quietly. Harriet and Archie both looked away. It was bad enough being a standing joke with the constables, now he had to contend with Anna's friends too. For goodness' sake, he was forty-four, not fourteen. Petulantly, his teenage self was thinking that he didn't have to tell them everything. Actually, looking at his mother, the word that sprang to mind was 'anything'. She didn't know anything. Why would she? There was nothing to tell. A little more sharply than was warranted, Tom turned back to Simeon and said, "Come over to the café, and we'll take your statement." He began to walk away. Simeon didn't follow. Tom knew why. Grudgingly, he turned back and said, "And yes, Archie can come too."

They followed him across the tiny car park. Laurence, from the back of the ambulance, saw Simeon and nodded. Tom stored that away. Simeon of course had his eyes on the ground and didn't see the acknowledgement. He was surrounded by strangers and blue lights. It wouldn't matter how close he stood to Archie or how much Belle leaned into him, he wouldn't be comfortable enough to look up at a relative stranger.

Holding the door open, Tom said, "They'll bring us coffee and Sandra can take notes. You remember Sandra?" She was following them in and smiled at Archie. She wasn't threatening in any way, which was useful for putting people at their ease. Archie straightened up a little as he smiled back and Tom wondered if it was simply the presence of a woman. Archie was a man who always remembered his manners, a man that Tom wasn't at ease with and, though Archie was shorter than Simeon, just now he seemed taller, protective of his friend. He was standing just behind Simeon, close but not touching, so that he was not invading his personal space. Archie would worry about things like that, would know how close was close enough. Simeon, tall and lanky, was engulfed in his old parka, the hood pulled down so that his eyes were invisible. Simeon rarely looked up at someone unless he knew them really well or they were a long way off. Tom supposed it was a small miracle that Simeon hadn't already had a complete meltdown. He knew he'd have to tread carefully.

His radio crackled. He ignored it.

The café looked out over the point, one of the most spectacular views in the country. In the summer months, you couldn't get a table for love nor money. Sadly, at the time of the incident there'd only been a couple of walkers sitting inside. They'd drunk coffee, eaten cake and read their newspapers. They hadn't even been able to agree on how many seals they'd seen coming round the headland, and in their statements there certainly wasn't anything useful, like whether there'd been a body in the water or even when they'd first arrived. They'd both noticed Laurence leave the café, but neither had been able to give a half-decent description of him or had been sure of the time. They'd simply had a quick look round for wildlife, choughs mainly, and then had settled back. Tom had gotten contact details and let them go.

The girl working at the café had been a little more useful. She'd been wiping tables over by the window when Laurence had come in, she thought at about ten twenty. She'd gone over to talk to him at the counter for a couple of minutes while he'd placed an order. He'd then sat down, in fact at the table Tom was now heading for.

The café was on two levels, the lower one overlooking the western coastal path and, below that, the old lifeboat station. They'd moved the new lifeboat to just beyond Church Cove back in the sixties so they could launch it more often in bad weather. Some visitors did walk down the steep, narrow path to stand at wave level, but the views were from above, where you didn't feel quite so vulnerable, quite so small. Even on a quiet day the old station was a reminder that the sea was treacherous, the horizon distant and that, between, there were sharp granite rocks able to peel open a hull like a tin opener as cross-currents drove a vessel this way and that. It was a view you didn't take lightly.

Tom could see his men putting tape around a patch of cliff that looked as if it might have been where the man went over. There'd been a few scuff marks and some of the ice plants looked as if they'd been pulled up by their roots. Archie and Simeon shuffled in opposite him. Simeon, sitting next to the window, peered down, perhaps to check the body had definitely gone. Sandra sat at the next table and pulled out her notepad. She was shaping up nicely and Tom hoped she'd have a go at her Sergeants' Exams in the next few months. He needed to push her a little harder, ironically so she could move on to another posting. For him that would mean starting again with someone new, which was not a great prospect.

"Ok, Simeon, tell me what you saw."

Belle was under the table, her head on Simeon's lap. His

60

hands were clasped in front of him.

"I was coming back from Archie's ..."

"Could you start a bit earlier?"

"Alright. On my way over to Archie's I saw two people, a man and a woman. They were ahead of me. I thought they might be guests from the vicarage." Which of course they were. "They were a long way ahead. It was ten o'clock when they passed the hotel." Tom knew it would be worth speaking to Simeon. Those timings would be spot on and would help with an accurate timeline. "They may not have been together because when I first noticed them, there was approximately twenty feet between. When I came round the corner about twelve minutes later, I could only see him. When he got to the small car park, just here, a large black SUV appeared. I don't know if the man spoke to anyone in the car. He could have done before it turned around and went back up towards the village or back up to the National Trust car park. The man then continued to the point and disappeared as if he were heading down to the old buildings at the bottom. By the time I crossed onto the other path, the young woman had re-appeared behind me and also headed to the old lifeboat station. I saw them both because after I had walked about a hundred metres, I turned around and looked down." Tom thought he'd probably been checking there was no-one following him. Simeon's anxiety was often set off by the appearance of a stranger. Archie bit his lip. "As I was turning away, at ten fourteen, I saw someone else. They must have come down the lane. If they'd used the coastal path, I'd have seen them earlier. I spotted them just beyond the old café, but they very quickly disappeared. I'm not sure which way they went or what they looked like. A man, I thought, but I only saw them for a second. I thought it was dangerous for them to have walked down that part of the road. It's extremely narrow and the sides are tall and steep. If a car comes down or goes up, there is nowhere for a pedestrian to go. Though it's further, the safest route is along the footpath through the big car park." Tom nodded. It suggested that the person wasn't local, though it was only the last few metres that were truly dodgy. He revised his thoughts; a local would know that if you kept your wits about you, you could scurry along that narrow bit without too much difficulty. The way through the car park was definitely the long way round.

Simeon described what the man and the woman had been wearing. The man was definitely Laurence Weller, sitting in the ambulance. Tom was fairly sure the young woman was Georgie Harbrook. Archie confirmed their names, as long as it was a young woman with orange hair. Simeon said that it was. He then added, "As I continued on to Archie's, a man came down the path that runs past Archie's house. I didn't note the time, I'm sorry." Tom shook his head. Poor Simeon would've been thoroughly put out by all these strangers.

"It's alright, we can work it out from your other timings."

"I'd say it was only two minutes at the most from when I saw the other person at the bottom of the lane. The man I passed had short, grey hair and pale blue trousers, pale yellow socks and scuffed, brown leather shoes. Lace-ups. But I cannot be any more precise than that. Oh, and he had a set of binoculars." That was interesting. Tom would have to get the constables to search the path and the beach below. "I'm afraid I don't know what sort. I was already anxious; there were too many people about." Archie pursed his lips and clenched his fists resting on the table in front of him. Simeon grimaced as if trying to remember something else. "I jogged the rest of the way, as fast as Belle was able to go. I got to Archie's at ten nineteen. I left at eleven forty to walk home, back the way I'd come because Archie had to be at the vicarage for lunch. It wasn't my usual day, and he wanted to talk to Phil on the way."

"Why didn't you go home through the village?" Tom asked.

Simeon looked up for the tiniest moment. Tom knew he'd sounded a little aggressive, but it was odd, considering the levels of anxiety that Simeon had been struggling with.

"I'd got very agitated walking to Archie's. Archie suggested I retrace my steps to prove to myself that I could do it. He didn't want me to get into a destructive loop."

Tom looked at Archie, who was staring out of the window, supposedly admiring the view, but Tom reckoned he was praying. Praying for Simeon, for the poor guy who was dead, for the young man in the ambulance and for Tom, too, he had no doubt. Archie turned back, his mouth a tight line.

"I didn't know that, on his way home, he was going to find a body," he said, quietly.

Simeon glanced up at Tom, probably no higher than his chin.

"I didn't find it and I never got close to it. It was only as I came around the point that I saw the young man trying to get over the barrier to get near enough to pull the man off the beams. I knew it was the same young man I'd seen earlier because he was wearing the same clothes. I thought about going down to tell him to come away, but decided he probably wouldn't listen. He might not have realised that the man was dead and that it wasn't worth risking his own life."

"And I'm sure not everyone realises how dangerous this bit of the coast can be, Simeon," Archie said gently. Simeon nodded.

"I ran to the café and asked them to call you. My phone doesn't have a good signal round here. They rang the coast guard and the police. Then I went down the track to the shoreline. As I came around the bend, the man cried out and slipped into the water. I couldn't help him, but I shouted that he should try and hold onto one of the pillars. The tide was on its way out, so I hoped he'd be able to manage that until someone arrived to help."

He'd held on and fortunately the coast guard had called

the lifeboat station, who'd sent a contingent in the Land Rover to assess what was needed. The vehicle was still parked opposite, the four-man crew standing around drinking coffee, their yellow boots giving the place a bit of a festive air. Tom was thinking Father Christmas, though he knew it didn't make sense, but it made him realise he'd have to leave some money on the counter. The café had lost some custom that afternoon and had been supplying everyone with hot drinks, almost continually.

"Thanks Simeon. Is there anything else you think I should know?"

Simeon shook his head, then stopped.

"What is it, Simeon? You often notice things others don't," Tom said. Simeon simply nodded.

"When the orange-haired young woman headed down the old ramp, she walked as if she was happy. I'm not always sure about people's faces, and she was too far away for me to see it properly, but she sort of bounced. I was up there." He pointed to the path above where the police tape fluttered, where it ran level for a few yards. Beyond that it quickly dipped into the gully from where you could walk up to Archie's house. You had to climb down some granite steps to a small area of grass with large cracks in the turf that made it feel as if everything was falling into the sea. Tom had walked along it himself to see the lie of the land. From the bottom of the gully you couldn't see anything but the sea, not the café or the boat house. He'd peered up the path into the village, where Simeon had inadvertently walked past the drowned man. Tom was sure they were one and the same from the man's clothing.

If you carried on along the coast path, followed it far enough, you got to Kynance Cove – a lovely spot that was jam-packed with tourists in the summer, with its overhanging rocks, a stony beach that gave way to sand at low tide and another very nice little café. That would be a good place to walk with Anna. Spectacular at all times of the year.

"Thank you, Simeon," Tom said, then ran through the timings again so that Sandra could double-check them. The only thing he needed to ask was what time the waitress thought Laurence had left. Sandra checked back through her notes. She'd said about eleven forty, but he wanted to be sure.

Simeon began to open and close his hands.

"May we go now?" Archie asked, ever alert to Simeon's needs.

"Yes. We'll type up your account and get you to sign and date it later."

Sandra stood up too, waiting for them to slide out from behind the table. Belle stretched and yawned. She'd fallen asleep on Simeon's feet and was a little stiff.

"I'd like to go home via the village. It'll be quicker," Simeon said. Archie nodded. Was Simeon checking that it was alright with him? That his friend didn't still think it necessary for Simeon to walk home by the coast path to prove that he could? Even Tom could see that Simeon needed to get home and under his blanket as quickly as possible.

"Good," said Archie, doing up his coat, "I want to pop into the vicarage and let Anna know what's going on."

"I'll be down later myself," Tom said.

"Anna will probably be pleased," Simeon said, quietly.

Tom noted the word probably and agreed. He could never be quite sure with Anna. He patted Simeon on the arm, which made Simeon jump. He shouldn't have done that, but hoped Simeon realised he was only trying to reassure him. He liked the guy, had misunderstood him to begin with, but had learnt that the main thing with Simeon was to ask the right question.

Chapter 8

"So, Dani, is there anything else you'd like to talk about?"

Anna hoped not. They'd been closeted away for well over an hour. She'd been advised to have a clock clearly visible. Sadly, the one she'd brought through from the kitchen had stopped. She kept thinking she must change the batteries because looking surreptitiously at her watch wasn't easy or professional.

Dani probably could have done with a bit longer. She was in such a muddle. She'd been living at home with her mum because (and Anna wasn't absolutely sure about this) she'd had a baby a few years before and her mum was helping her take care of it. Only they didn't seem to get on. In fact, they'd had a massive falling-out and now Dani was living with Georgie. No wonder the girls were a bit annoyed about having to share a room. Anna thought that Dani was being a little hard on her mother, who seemed to be working full-time as well as doing all the childcare. Dani said she just wanted some freedom, a bit of fun. But could you have that when you'd had a baby, when you were a parent, even one who couldn't have been more than seventeen at the time of the birth?

"Georgie is being a real bitch. Sharing a room with her is not easy."

Anna and Harriet had expected some niggles, but this was a step beyond. Anna hunted about for the right response.

"Why? What has she done?" She immediately regretted asking that. It felt as though she'd already taken sides.

"Well, last night we were chatting until, without warning, she rolled over and then completely ignored me."

"I expect she was tired. Hadn't she driven down?"

"Yes, but she drives everywhere and she told me she loves driving, so it can't have been that."

"Well, I suppose she's here for a reason too. Perhaps she

needs a little understanding, a little space." Anna tried to sound gentle and reasonable, but Dani seemed to have an answer for everything. If truth be told, she seemed a little self-centred, a little spoilt. Anna frowned, then tried to look kind and understanding again. Dani hadn't noticed. She was off again. She clearly wasn't going to let it go.

"Georgie's doing fine," she said, crossly. "She works for our church. It's a cushy number if ever there was one. I've had some awful jobs. The chip shop was the worst. The owner was very handsy, and I always stank to high heaven."

"Working for the church can have its tensions and anxieties." Anna laughed. "That I do know."

"Well, whatever your problems are, you don't have to be rude and selfish, do you?"

Anna shook her head and rose to her feet.

"Let's go and find some tea. There might even be some of Harriet's chocolate cake somewhere. It's gluten-free, but you'd never know it." Dani reluctantly got up to follow her. Anna led them into the dining room. She checked her phone as casually as she could. There were no new messages. She wondered what was going on down at the Lizard. Should she have cancelled her chat with Dani, who was now peering at her own mobile, looking grumpy and frustrated? It certainly didn't look as though the last hour had made any difference. Golly, people led complicated lives.

Harriet had left a tray for her in the kitchen. Anna added more cups, just to feel useful, though they probably didn't need them. Talking to Dani had made her feel as though she was skating over the top of everything, that she was probably missing something important. The poor girl did have it tough on one level, but on another, she seemed to be getting quite a lot of support. Of course, all the help in the world sometimes wasn't enough.

There had been one elephant in the room, which Anna had carefully avoided: Who was the dad? She hoped it wasn't the horrible chip shop man, that Dani hadn't been confiding some form of abuse. Anna went cold at the thought of that and knew she'd now have to speak to Dani again. She picked up the tray and carefully manoeuvred out into the hall. Harriet and Catherine were there, taking off their coats, and Anna felt a wave of relief.

"Oh, fantastic. I've made tea, and I have your cake, Harriet." She didn't want Catherine thinking she'd made it herself.

Catherine nodded and smiled, but it was tight and forced.

"I'll just pop up and get a thicker jumper," she said.

She was definitely getting the hang of the vicarage.

Anna hardly waited until Catherine was half-way up the stairs before she hissed, "So, what happened? Was Tom there? And what about poor Laurence?"

Harriet hung her head; her hair fell forward as if she were shielding herself from Anna.

"I didn't like the lights. They sort of stained the air. It reminded me of last time."

"Oh Harriet. I should have taken Catherine down. I'm so sorry."

"I'm alright. Honestly." Harriet peered up from under her mane. She looked brave and frail. "Tom is hoping to pop in on his way back so you'll be able to get some of your answers then. The body was a man staying at the pub. He probably went in some time this morning. It looks as if Laurence was trying to rescue him. Just off the old slipway."

"That ramp is a death trap. How long was he in the water?"

"I don't know. You'll have to ask Simeon. He saw it all."

Anna blinked. That wasn't good.

"I'd better go round. It'll bring back some awful memories for him."

Simeon had found Fiona in the graveyard, just after she'd died. Much earlier on in his life he'd been chucked into a harbour at low tide. He still couldn't even paddle on a boiling hot summer's day. Dead bodies and freezing water were not a good combination for him.

"He's alright. Archie's with him, and Tom allowed Archie to stay while he questioned him."

That was kind of Tom. Or clever.

"Still, it would've upset him."

Anna was fairly sure that anything out of the ordinary would knock Simeon sideways, so watching someone trying to pull a body to safety would've made him feel all turned inside out. He'd told her that was how he felt when things didn't go as expected, when things were scary or out of the ordinary. She thought it described exactly how a lot of people reacted, though many just got sad or angry to cover it up.

"I'd be more worried about Laurence," Harriet said. "Now he was in a state."

Anna swallowed. Simeon and Laurence to take care of. Where should she begin? She picked up the tray, which she'd rested on the side table, as Catherine came down the stairs. Anna whispered to no-one in particular, "Just to warn you, Dani is in the dining room, and she's a bit grumpy."

"Where's Georgie?" Harriet asked.

"I'm not sure, but she and Dani are definitely not getting on," Anna was still whispering. She really didn't want Dani to hear them talking about her.

"Tom wants a quick word with her too," Harriet said.

"Georgie? Oh, I wonder why?"

Catherine pointedly looked away. Was she uncomfortable talking about Tom, or perhaps she didn't think the body was a suitable subject for the bottom of the stairs? They filed into the dining room. Dani was wandering around, looking at the pictures on the walls.

"I wondered where you'd all got to. Thought I was being left on my own again."

Anna wanted to ask if she'd seen Georgie, but in the end didn't dare. Harriet took charge of the tray and began to cut

70

cake and pour tea.

Dani suddenly jumped up, marched to the door and, as she walked into the hall, said, "I'm going to find a signal." They heard the front door open.

"Don't you want any cake?" Anna called after her, but there was no reply.

Anna breathed out loudly and straightened up. She wondered if Dani had heard them talking after all. She'd left the front door open, letting in a sliver of colour that made Anna want to walk out too. The vicarage suddenly seemed too small and very draughty.

She turned to Catherine.

"So, did you enjoy your walk this morning?" she asked.

"Yes, I did. I got as far as Cadgwith. It's a lovely path, just a bit sticky in places." She sighed. "I should have asked Tom to meet me at the pub there, then perhaps he wouldn't have got waylaid."

"Oh, that wouldn't have made any difference. Work always comes top of his list."

Anna stopped. That sounded peevish at best.

"I suppose if you're a police officer the things that keep you busy are quite important," Catherine replied, taking the smallest piece of cake. "You sound as though you know him quite well."

"Not that well. Really, I hardly know him at all." Anna chewed her lip. What if Catherine told Tom what she'd just said? Would he be surprised by her hurried denial? "Do we know when Laurence is coming back?" she asked, trying to pull the conversation back onto safer ground.

Catherine shook her head. Anna didn't dare look at Harriet, but wished that Catherine wasn't so tall, so competent. She took a step back, trying to move out of her shadow.

Anna decided to find Georgie and see how she was doing. She began to edge away. She knew she ought not to disturb a guest in their room, but it hadn't been an ordinary morning. Anyway, she wanted to be seen to be doing something of worth.

"Just going up to check on Georgie." She smiled at Catherine and Harriet without really looking at them and made a run for it.

She tapped gently on the girls' door, which swung open part-way.

"I'm sorry to disturb you," Anna said, stepping into the room.

Georgie was sitting by the window, staring out. From there you could only see the trees ringing the garden and a bit of the drive as it swept across the front of the house on its way round to the back. She could hear the rooks along the lane, a noise she rather loved, but she could understand that for some of the guests it could be a little desolate. Mrs Fabia, their first-ever guest, had complained that they kept her awake. Georgie turned to Anna, her face wet with tears and scrambled to her feet. Anna didn't know what to do. She'd trespassed and that was against the rules. After all it could be a God moment, one that Anna absolutely should not interfere with.

"I'm really sorry. I should leave you alone."

Georgie remained standing, blinking, her bright orange hair garishly topping her rather pink face. Anna backed out of the door and then, just as she'd pulled it closed, pushed it open again.

"I came to tell you that there's tea and cake downstairs. You look as though you could do with it."

"I'll be down in a minute," the girl mumbled.

"You know I'm around if you need to talk. You don't have to make an appointment if you don't want to."

The idea of cake suddenly seemed very appealing. Anna was hopelessly out of her depth. She wondered if she could invite Irene, her spiritual director, round for an afternoon's proper listening with the guests. Now there was a woman who really knew her onions.

On the way down Dani passed her, her hands thrust into the pockets of her jeans. She looked at the wall. Anna hesitated, wondered if she ought to follow her back up, try and talk to her. But it was too hard. She hoped Dani would be kind to Georgie, who looked as if she needed some space and a lot of love.

When she returned to the lounge, Tom was there with his mother, laughing. He had a cup of tea, and Harriet had cut him a huge piece of her lovely cake.

"Where's Laurence?" Anna blurted out.

'Hello Tom' would've been a better place to start. He looked chilled to the bone, and his hair was recently cut. It always made him look like a convict. Ok, that was over the top, but it did make his eyes seem too big, and he definitely looked as though he could do with a couple of early nights.

"Laurence will be here shortly. The paramedics decided to bring him as they had to get him out of his wet things, and he's basically sitting in one of their red blankets."

"I hope he has a change of clothes apart from his suit. We'll have to put the damp ones down by the boiler."

"Perhaps he'd be more comfortable if Archie went out to greet him," Tom added, gently.

"Archie's not here. I'll have to do." Anna began to panic. A horrid rush of adrenalin that made her feel hot and slightly nauseous.

Tom filled his mouth with cake and nodded to Harriet. Anna felt a spike of what was probably jealousy. He'd realised that a cake of that quality had to be made by her. Anna was still only one level above toast and scrambled eggs.

"I'll go and make a new pot," Anna said, suddenly wanting to be anywhere but there.

"I'll give you a hand," Tom said.

"No, stay and talk to your mum. I'm sure you've got lots to

catch up on."

In the end, Harriet trailed after her to the kitchen. Anna didn't need to see her expression to know what it was like. She emptied the pot into the sink and said, "I know. I should have let him come and help me." Harriet didn't say anything. Anna chanced a quick glance. Harriet was leaning against the back door with her arms crossed. She was wearing a rather lovely rose pink jumper with little threads of silver running through the weave. She was staring resolutely over Anna's left shoulder. "But what would his mum have thought? I mean he hasn't seen her for ages and ..."

"Oh Anna. One of these days I'm going to lock you two in a room and let you get on with it."

"Get on with what?" Anna said.

Harriet elbowed her out the way and filled the kettle.

"He obviously likes you. It's just that you never give him any encouragement."

"I thought he was supposed to woo me."

Harriet began to laugh. Anna couldn't remember the last time she'd done that.

"You are ..."

"A numpty, an idiot, a banana."

"None of those," Harriet said, waving the kettle around.

They both turned to the window when they heard something coming down the drive.

"The ambulance. You'd better go and get Laurence sorted," Harriet said. "I'll give Archie a call and get him to pop over just in case we have to tuck him in or something."

Chapter 9

Anna didn't come back into the dining room, and Tom and his mum were running out of things to say. Eventually Harriet appeared to tell them that Anna was making sure that Laurence was alright. Tom thought she'd run away. He couldn't quite look his mum in the eye, and he thought he knew how Anna might be feeling. His mum wasn't stupid, but she wouldn't dream of saying anything without an invitation. Just occasionally Tom wished she would, wished she'd have a go at him for being such a crappy son with a terrible taste in women. Not Anna of course. He'd always hoped she and his mum would get on because they both had such an all-consuming faith. All-consuming … sadly that fitted the bill, for it did seem that sometimes it was all Anna could see, her calling, her bloody parishioners, being needed twenty-four seven. Perhaps his only hope was to come and live in the parish, to become one of them. It would mean a long commute to work, a nuisance, but not a deal breaker.

Tom needed to have a first go at the statements, needed to speak to the young woman who had followed Laurence down the ramp, Georgie Harbrook, the girl with the orange hair. They wouldn't get anything from forensics for at least two or three days, and Anna wasn't going to like the fact that he wanted to come back and talk to Laurence again. He'd also drunk enough tea to float a battleship and eaten enough cake to see him through to next week, but still his mum seemed keen to keep him there.

"I'm just popping to the loo. I'll be back in a minute," he said. She nodded, but his need of the facilities clearly didn't fool her.

The kitchen was in darkness, so he knocked on Anna's private door. There was no reply, but he heard the creak of the stairs as someone began to descend. He went back along the hall and waited at the bottom.

"Tom!"

"Anna. I'm sorry."

"What for?"

Classic Anna, making him work hard.

"I don't seem to have seen you much lately."

"You're busy, and now your mum's here. I wouldn't expect you to make time for me."

He had to take that one on the chin. At least she came down another couple of steps so that they were just about at the same level.

"But I'd like to try. I'm entitled to a life."

She looked uncomfortable.

"Yes, you are. And I do understand." She was whispering so that he could barely hear her. That would be so no-one else could eavesdrop.

"No, I don't think you do," he said.

And then she smiled, as if he'd won her over.

"Come into the kitchen, just for a minute. You mustn't leave your mum too long."

He followed her down the hall.

"Tea?" she asked, automatically, he supposed.

"No, I'm awash."

"Harriet told me off. Said I never encourage you."

"Do you want to encourage me?" he asked, hopefully.

Harriet came in carrying a large casserole and some part-baked potatoes.

"Oh, sorry, you two."

"How do you do it?" Anna asked her in wonder. "You genuinely seem to magic the most awesome meals out of the air."

Harriet bowed. She was a lovely girl, beautiful, but Tom had always felt that she held back, stayed aloof. He was never completely comfortable around her. Perhaps it was the copper in him. Open and honest he liked. He supposed that was why Anna was so appealing.

"Derek just dropped it off. There's plenty, Tom, if you'd like to stay," Harriet said.

"I don't think the local constabulary hanging about will do your ambience any good at all, and I must get going."

Anna was clearly desperately trying to think of something to say. Her lips were squashed together, and he wanted to rub away the lines wrinkling her forehead. He wondered if this was how Simeon felt when overwhelmed by one of his compulsions to touch something and to go on touching it.

"I'd best go and say goodbye to mum. I'll be back tomorrow."

Anna's eyes narrowed.

"Why? Surely it was just a stranger who slipped off the cliff."

"I don't know. I think your Laurence knows more than he's telling, and I need to speak to the girl who was following him along the path. Georgie Harbrook, Laurence said." Tom shouldn't really have said that. He might allow himself to say a little too much in front of Anna, but not Harriet as well. She was emptying a carrier bag onto the countertop and hesitated, stiffening just a little at his words.

"Oh Tom, he's just a lad with a weight on his shoulders, and she's ... so young," Anna pleaded. "Please don't tell me you think they had something to do with the death." She stepped back and shuddered. Muscle memory, a deep rift within her that might never go away. *Bloody Terry*, he thought, *hanging over them like a sodding vulture.*

"Dani walked up to the pub this morning," Harriet added helpfully.

That made him decide which of the young women to tackle first, but Anna's face was crumpled and hurt.

"It's probably nothing. I'll ring and let you know what time I'll be back."

He was just doing his job. He wished she'd try and see that. He pulled the door shut behind him, unnecessarily hard, and the crash echoed down the hall like a judgement.

***

When Harriet phoned, Archie was still with Simeon. He'd stayed to make sure that Simeon settled, that the anxiety didn't overwhelm him. Archie was glad because now it was only a three-minute walk to the vicarage, though another part of him wished it was further. He didn't seem to have had any time to do the things he felt he ought to have done that day, and now he'd have to nursemaid the boy, Laurence, too. That sounded harsh, even inside his own head.

"Sorry, God, that's not very kind."

He could hear Simeon's voice immediately, saying, 'God doesn't mind, and sometimes it's better to speak out the thought that's bugging you. Get it into the open where God can deal with it properly.' Archie smiled. Simeon taught him a lot, though sometimes it could be a bit tiring. The front door of the vicarage was open so he rang the bell and stepped inside.

"Anna, you said you needed me." He undid his coat as she came down the hall to greet him.

"I'm so sorry, Archie. I expect you could really have done with some time by yourself."

She looked stiff, as if she were really cold.

"Are you alright?" he asked.

"Tom," she said, without explanation.

"He's just doing his job."

She slumped, her mouth an actual upside-down 'u' shape.

"Oh Archie, it's not that."

Archie felt as if he was standing on the edge of a large puddle, that if he made one false move, he'd put his foot right in it.

"Is it that you don't ever seem to get any time together?"

Her face crumpled.

"I don't think it's that either." She breathed one little, shallow breath. "How can I be drawn to a man who barely

78

recognises God? I'm a vicar! Doesn't that count for anything?"

Anna seemed to be getting angry. He took a tiny step back.

"Sorry, Anna. I didn't mean to upset you."

"Of course you didn't. I know that." As she turned away, she patted his arm, which felt better. He didn't like being at odds with her. "It's just that Tom isn't sure the body in the water is as straightforward as he'd like." Archie was confused. Anna had jumped from Tom's faith to the body in the water. He wondered what was going on inside her head. "He's going to come over again tomorrow and question Laurence, who's in a real state as it is."

"He did seem to be a bit incoherent. To begin with, the paramedics thought it was just shock. After all, he did fall in the sea, so he was very cold, but even after he warmed up, he didn't seem to make any sense."

"What did he say?"

"I only heard the odd phrase. We weren't supposed to be listening. But he did say, 'Why would he do that?'"

"I wonder if he saw him jump? That would've been awful."

"I don't think so because he was draped over the ramp. Only the tide could have left him there, and it was about an hour after high water when Laurence was trying to rescue him."

Anna sighed.

"Look, stop and have dinner with us, and then you and I can take a tray up to him. I'm not expecting him to come down after his ordeal. We can see then if he needs someone to talk to."

Chapter 10

It wasn't quite the full house at dinner, and Archie could see there would be far too much food. Harriet had gone up to the pub, even though she must have been exhausted, and of course Laurence was upstairs. Georgie looked very pale, as if she were coming down with something. Dani made a fuss about where she'd like to sit, so in the end everyone got up and moved around. Catherine looked calm, perhaps a little sad. It hadn't been the day she'd planned. She was bound to be feeling disappointed. Of course he wasn't that good at reading people, so he knew he might be getting the wrong end of the stick. Still, even he could see there was a lot going on. He slipped onto the chair beside her.

Anna asked him to say grace. He kept it simple, and afterwards she looked over and whispered 'thanks'. He thought she might sit on the other side of Catherine, but she went and sat by Dani, who looked pleased.

"So not the most restful and God-centred day," he said to Catherine, who was unfolding her napkin.

"Oh, it's not been so bad. Except for poor Laurence of course. I actually managed the most glorious walk to Cadgwith this morning."

"That's one of my favourites. Did you look in at the pub?" She smiled and nodded. "They do a fabulous cream tea," he added. Catherine looked like a scones-and-jam lady. The last time he'd gone there, he'd ordered one of their beef burgers. It had given him indigestion for hours after, but had been worth every mouthful.

"So, a good walk and ..." Archie didn't know how to go on, but she didn't seem to mind.

"A good talk with him. Tom is right, this place helps you look at things from a different point of view. It's not even about getting it in perspective," she said thoughtfully. "And I hadn't realised you were all such good friends. It's a really special community."

"Is it? Are we?" Archie regretted that slipping out of his mouth. As he quickly realised, she was including Tom. Archie had never quite got the hang of the DI from Falmouth, had resented his intrusion into their lives. He always brought trouble, or rather he always troubled Anna, and she could definitely do without it. Now that was interesting – he'd never managed to articulate it quite so clearly before.

"I think he looked comfortable around you. He was less the policeman and more my son. Apart from Anna, of course." She tipped her head to one side. Archie didn't want to be rude, but saying anything on that subject wasn't his place. "Sorry, Archie. I should have pretended I hadn't noticed."

He sighed.

"It is pretty obvious," he almost whispered, for fear anyone else might hear them. "I'd like her to find someone, I really would. But Tom's faith is ..."

"It's kind of you to imply he has one. But I'm a realist. His job over the years must have hammered away most of the grace and kindness from his life. How can he see the goodness of God when all he ever deals with are the horrors the rest of us try and ignore? His wife was not the ... easiest of people."

Archie hoped that God was big enough even for Tom, but he wasn't sure how to say that.

"So, what are you thinking of doing tomorrow?"

"Well, I was going to walk round to the café, but I'm not so sure now. Perhaps I'll just sit in church and see what happens."

"I love doing that," said Archie. "You wander in, wondering what God might want to talk about, and something catches your eye, or you find yourself thinking of something that happened earlier in the week. Then you just see where you go."

He sighed because he hadn't found time to do that recently. There had been one time, but he'd just found himself getting stressed about the Reader course. How could he have thought he'd be able to manage it? He was bound to end up letting them both down. Anna and Pearly.

At the Reader exploratory meeting Archie had quickly realised he was the oldest by a country mile, and that normally people his age were gently turned away. He assumed Anna had pleaded and Pearly had pulled strings. The induction afternoon had been difficult. Most of the others really seemed to know what they were talking about, already took services, seemed to be dotting i's and crossing t's. When he was asked why he wanted to become a Reader, simply saying he was eager to learn as much about God as possible seemed the sort of thing a teenager might say in the first flush of conversion. He wished he'd had more time to think about the question. In the end he'd said that his vicar thought he would find it useful. The course coordinator had quickly moved on to the next person, who had a long and complicated story about her calling. Archie had almost walked out. Wanted to, except it would've made the leader feel bad, because they'd missed how difficult he was finding it all.

"Church it is then," Catherine said. "It sounds as though it might be just what I need."

***

Anna knocked and waited.

They'd given Laurence the single room at the back. A tiny space, one wall almost entirely filled by a tall sash window that rattled and sang in the wind. She hoped it wasn't too noisy.

"Come in."

There was nothing lying around that gave a clue as to who Laurence was. Anna guessed all his stuff must be in the wardrobe. The red blanket was draped across the chair. Anna would take it back to the hospital when she next went to Helston. That was a nice thought. The next time she went there this would all be over. The guests would've headed home, and she'd have her vicarage back, with nothing more pressing to think about than her talk for Sunday.

Laurence had been lying propped up on his pillows, but sat himself upright when she entered. He was wearing pyjamas and his jumper. He looked cold. She must find him another blanket or perhaps an old dressing gown. Archie was waiting behind her with the tray. She continued into the room and perched on the window ledge.

"We've bought you some dinner. You must be starving."

He nodded. His eyes were red-rimmed, and his hands were gripping the top of the duvet as if he thought they might rip it away. But then he'd just been through a very traumatic experience, was perhaps still in shock.

Archie carefully placed the tray on his knees.

"Is there anything else you'd like?" he asked.

"I wouldn't mind some water; would that be alright?"

He did sound croaky, as if he'd only just woken up. Archie was gone before Anna could even move. Laurence stared down at the plate.

"Do carry on," she said, but felt the awkwardness. Who wanted to sit and eat with someone watching them?

"Actually, could we have that talk first?"

"God, yes. Of course," she said, apologising to God for her slip of the tongue. She sounded too loud, too keen. She wished she could be more like Irene, a woman of few words and long meaningful silences that Anna always tried to fill. Mostly with all the stuff she'd got wrong or didn't understand. Irene was the best and the worst thing in her life.

"Look, your food will get cold, and here comes Archie with your water."

Laurence nodded. She really couldn't speak to him with Archie present. Archie knocked.

"Come in, Archie," Anna said, and checked her watch. She'd now only got a few minutes before Evening Prayer down at the church. Archie stood at the door, waiting. Of course, he didn't realise he was no longer required. Anna tried to catch his eye.

"Archie, thanks awfully, but we'll leave Laurence to eat." When Laurence looked surprised, she added, "I'll pop back to collect the tray." She hoped he'd understand that that was when they would talk, when she had more time.

At the bottom of the stairs Archie turned to her,

"He really looks as though he could do with getting something off his chest. He seems so weighed down."

"Yes. He's asked if we could talk, but I thought he ought to eat his food first. I'll go back later."

"But what about Evening Prayer? You haven't got long."

"I'll pop up afterwards. Won't it be wonderful when you can take some of those services instead of me?"

Archie turned away. He took ages scrabbling amongst the coats and then didn't seem able to find his hat. Today had taken a toll on all of them. At last, he looked up, ready to face the night.

"Bye," he said, and his voice came out a little gruffly, as if she'd missed something. He pulled the door shut with a bang. The wind must have caught it because Archie wouldn't dream of slamming anything, ever.

She charged back up the stairs, knocked and entered without really waiting. His fork was halfway to his mouth.

"Laurence, I've got to take the others to Evening Prayer. I don't have time to talk right now, but as soon as I'm back, I'll come straight up. I won't be longer than twenty minutes. Ten to ten at the very latest."

He nodded. What else could he do? She ran back down the stairs, was quite out of breath at the bottom, and went into the dining room. There was no-one there. Someone had stacked the plates neatly and left a plate of pudding for her. She slipped across to the lounge. Catherine, Dani and Georgie were sitting as far away from each other as possible. There was no fire in the grate, and the room was chilly. Anna looked at each of them. Georgie looked away. Anna still hadn't managed to speak to her. There was simply too much to do. Where was Harriet when she needed her? Anna felt it was all going rather badly, and she wondered who would be the first to demand their money back, who would be the first to leave.

"Is everyone alright?"

Catherine had been reading. She was the only one who smiled in response.

"Do you need a hand with anything?" she asked.

"No, no, everything is absolutely fine. Harriet is going to come down early in the morning to sort breakfast. I've only got to load the dishwasher tonight."

"How's Laurence?" asked Georgie, suddenly looking intently at Anna.

Anna had no idea how he was, not really.

"He's fine. I'll check on him after Evening Prayer."

"We are going to do that then?" Dani asked and sniffed. It'd definitely be Dani who complained, but she couldn't leave unless Georgie drove her, which was a relief.

"We'll walk down together. I don't expect Simeon will still be there at this time of night. It's pitch-black outside."

Simeon was supposed to lock up at dusk, but he might have waited for them. She felt for her own key in her pocket. She didn't want any more slip-ups today. "Oh, and wrap up warm, it can be draughty."

"Can't we say it in here like we did last night?" Dani asked, shivering.

"Oh no," Catherine jumped in. "Let's go down to the church. It's all part of the experience. Archie assures me it's a place where God turns up." Just for a second Anna detected the slightest wobble in Catherine's voice. *Not so up-together after all*, Anna thought. But deep down inside she was disappointed. Just a little. It would've been nice for Tom's mum to have been happy, at peace. Managing.

"Five minutes, out in the hall."

She walked back to her rooms, picked up her prayer book, the torch and then sat down in her favourite chair. She closed her eyes and breathed. This was tough, really tough. In future they must organise a rota so that there was someone with her at all times. When Catherine had asked her if she needed a hand, she'd been right. Anna couldn't really manage on her own and should have asked Archie to stay on a little longer.

Catherine and Georgie were waiting in the hall. Both had their coats on, hats and gloves.

"Is Dani not coming?"

"She didn't say," Georgie said quietly, turning away.

"We'd better wait another minute."

Dani appeared at the top of the stairs.

"Going without me!" she said, before descending slowly. No-one responded. They stood about while she found her things. She could only find one glove, so Anna gave her one of hers and offered her a spare scarf. Dani refused. She'd get cold, and Anna was glad, hoped she'd get really uncomfortable. Only that was mean, so she stuffed the scarf in her pocket for later.

There was an icy wind funnelling up from the sea, but the rain had stopped, and the nearly full moon made the leaves glisten as they dripped. It was a gorgeous night, and Anna wondered what it'd be like down at the cove. It was one of her favourite places. She loved to sit on the bench at the top of the steep ramp, allowing her eyes to adjust to the dark, loved catching sight of the waves heaving and rolling and flattening into the gloom. Perhaps she should take them down there and say Evening Prayer by the light of her torch. Or, even better, out at Beacon Point. Despite its history, this place, where she'd finally confronted Terry, was a 'thin' place for her, a place where she felt it easy to step into God's presence.

The lights were on in the church. Simeon was sitting in his pew. Anna nodded but didn't say anything, even though she was really glad to see him. Now she wasn't on her own. She led the three women to the front couple of pews. The lights had been on for a while, so it was reasonably bright, and once the door was closed, it was silent.

She handed out the sheets. They'd used the books to begin with, but the print had been too small in the dimness.

"There are cushions and blankets piled at the back. Feel free to go and get one at any point. We want you to be comfortable."

She waited for Dani to finish muttering about staying in the warm, then she began to speak the words. When there was space to pray for loved ones, she realised that Georgie was crying again. She reached into the pulpit and got the tissues she always kept there for when she had a runny nose. She took them down to the young woman and pressed the box into her hand, which made her jump. Catherine reached forward and patted Georgie's shoulder. Georgie bowed her head again, blew her nose and wiped her eyes.

Anna stood a moment longer and then sat down beside them and finished reading from there.

"Make your way back up to the vicarage when you're ready. I've got a torch if you have forgotten yours. The front door is on the latch. I'll be up to sort out the hot chocolate. Tonight I think we could all do with a mug."

Simeon had gone sometime during the liturgy, and Anna felt his absence. She slumped for a moment and simply breathed, allowing her eyes to rove across the familiar flagstones. She knew she couldn't stay long.

Have them, Lord. I've got nothing and please, please don't let there be anything sinister with the body and help me be there for Georgie and Laurence. And it would be good if he was still awake when I finally get back to the house. And Catherine has a chip in her soul too, Lord. At this point, Anna would have liked to have wailed, but she knew she had to hold it together. Besides, she knew he was here. Because he was always here.

There had been a moment when Anna had nearly fallen,

when Terry had tried to drag her over the cliff. She'd ended up lying on her back staring at the sky, right on the edge of the long, dark drop. There, in that terrifying place, she'd felt his presence. She'd felt held, physically, warm and safe. One sublime moment on which she was rebuilding her life, one skin-thin layer at a time.

She ran her fingers over the cold wood of the pew and breathed in the musty air of her church, his church. Knew she mustn't be long, but just as she switched off the light, before the darkness pooled into the corners, she said quietly, "I like Tom, and I know you do too, but if it's up to us, we'll never get anywhere. And I don't want to get anywhere if it's not right." She pulled her one glove from her pocket. "I'm glad we've got that straight," she said, grasping the door handle. As she tugged it hard over the squealy bit, she could almost hear God chuckling. Most of her encounters with him seemed to make him laugh, just a little. So, nothing unusual there then.

**

Laurence lay back on the pillows. He'd not slept properly for weeks, and now the worst had happened. What more could anyone do to him? He suddenly felt calm.

As the water had closed over his head, he'd thought he might never take another breath in his life. He'd hoped that the feeling of panicked airlessness wouldn't last, and it hadn't, though the cold had poured down into him. A wave had lifted him towards the dangling arms, and he'd looked up for fear that he would get tangled in them. He didn't think of the arms anymore, once he'd seen the face, hanging above. One eye was shut, the other partly opened, a line of eyeball glinting, crusted. There was a red wheal on one side of the face and purple bruising along the jaw. Laurence had only glanced up and had instantly looked away again, but the image had seared itself onto the back of his eyes.

In the ambulance, when his teeth had stopped chattering, and his legs had stopped trembling, they'd said he ought to go to hospital, but that would've taken him up the main road into Helston. He'd known he couldn't do that. Down here he felt safe, down here he was able to catch his breath, as long as he stayed on dry land. Down here, at the end of the peninsula, it felt as though he might be able to work something out.

He pulled the duvet up around his nose. It smelt of washing powder. He leant over and switched off the lamp. Then he switched it back on. He preferred the light, but now it was too bright. He turned and faced the wall. That wasn't so bad, as long as he didn't stare at the shadows.

Bob had been in terrible trouble, had needed him. You had to help a mate, didn't you? Laurence knew what vulnerability felt like. When the longing for someone, anyone, to have your back gnawed away at you until good sense fled to the margins; when the social worker was too busy, the foster carer wanted your money or, worse, your love, when you began to trust those whom common sense said you should walk away from. Like all kids at the home, he'd built a wall, but it hadn't been high enough. Now, to complicate matters, there were Georgie and her friend Dani, who she'd been with at the pub all those years ago, sleeping just along the landing. He couldn't quite believe it even now, and he'd never get used to the orange hair. What had she been thinking? Instead of being pleased to see him, she'd shouted and wheedled. He'd pushed her away. He'd turned his back on the one person who truly understood him, whom he might have talked to. Because of course that's how he dealt with things. How he'd always dealt with things. He ran away. He always ran away.

Chapter 11

Harriet arrived at the vicarage early, and this time she didn't bother going around the back. She spent a few moments trying to open the front door, only to find that Anna had left her key in the lock. It was unbelievably annoying, as she really wanted to get on. She hoped Anna would have her mobile close to hand.

"Sorry," a bleary-eyed Anna muttered as she let her in. "I'll make a note and pin it to the door. Do Not Leave Key In Lock." She stood there blinking, her pyjamas rumpled from sleep.

Oh Anna, Harriet thought as she slid round her.

"I'll get the coffee on. You go and shower."

"Are you sure?"

"Of course I'm sure. The kitchen isn't big enough for the two of us."

"And it ain't me who's goin' to leave," Anna hummed as she turned away.

Anna had obviously not done well after Tom had left. There were a couple of chocolate wrappers on the side. Harriet was pleased that she hadn't tried to hide them. It'd been a while since she'd turned to food. Through the Terry months it had been her default position. Harriet remembered one occasion, just before she'd moved out, when Anna had eaten a whole chocolate cake in one sitting. At the time she'd thought Anna ought to get some help, but then, after Terry, things settled down, and she'd even lost some weight.

It didn't take long to unload the dishwasher and get breakfast started. Harriet was happily sorting the trays when Anna came through, looking a little more up-together. Harriet handed her a coffee.

"Thanks, and Harriet, I don't tell you enough how I couldn't manage without you."

"Actually, you do, all the time. I don't feel one bit neglected." Anna looked up in surprise and then frowned as

Harriet continued, "At least by you."

"Still competing with Fiona's ghost?"

"A little. It's not that he doesn't seem to love me, it's just ... sometimes it irritates me how much." Harriet turned down the porridge as it began to gloop. "Well done, by the way."

"What for?"

"For allowing me to find my own words."

Harriet's head was a knotty mass of thoughts, so a gentle dig at Anna was just one of the numerous threads she'd not bother to untangle just now. Fiona, was one of the problems, moving was another, and Derek ... Harriet dragged herself back to the porridge. Anna was clearly struggling. The line between her eyes wouldn't disappear, no matter how much she rubbed it.

"You look so happy," Anna tried, miserably.

"I am, I think. I just want to leave the bungalow."

But Harriet wasn't sure that was going to be enough. She wondered if she'd committed to Derek too soon. She had this thing about vulnerability, about needing someone to care for. It was why she was so good at all this. She looked around the kitchen, trays ready, mixing bowl out to make more cake. It didn't take a psychologist to pinpoint her need to smother and love with whatever she could lay her hands on because inside—

"Anna, I think I need to go and sit in church."

"Do you remember when it was part of my homework to spend an hour a day in there, no agenda, no praying, no reading my Bible? Good old Irene, she is such a wise woman."

"It wasn't that long ago, Anna, and she was right. It did change everything."

"Perhaps I ought to start doing it again."

"If you do, let me know, and I'll come and join you."

Anna laughed. She probably thought Harriet was joking, but Harriet was filled with a sudden longing.

"So, how was Laurence, last night?" Harriet asked,

changing the subject.

"Exhausted. He was asleep when I got back from Evening Prayer. I'm going to try and make an appointment with him this morning."

"Does he want to talk?"

"Yes. At least he did last night." Anna got up to pour more coffee. "I hope he hasn't changed his mind."

"What about Tom?"

"Oh, I don't think he wants to talk, at least not to me."

"Well, I think you're wrong there." Harriet began to pile clean crockery onto the tray.

"He might be coming over today to re-interview Laurence. He thinks there's more to his story."

Harriet stopped for a second, her hands in mid-air.

"I would hate to be a police officer. It must take all the joy out of life," she said.

Anna stood. She rubbed her eyes.

"I'd best get going, see if anyone will be joining me for Morning Prayer."

Harriet remained standing thoughtfully at the sink. Anna had left her cup on the table. Harriet knew she didn't take her for granted; it was just that her head would have moved on, was elsewhere, was probably down at the church worrying about her charges and what they needed.

That morning Harriet had left the house before Derek had got back from his walk with Dolly. She'd felt the need to get on with things down at the vicarage. Anyway, he'd come and sat up at the bar most of the previous evening, so it was hardly as if they hadn't seen each other. Time together wasn't the issue. Harriet couldn't put her finger on what it was, but felt that they were missing something. Perhaps it was not the being, but the seeing. Seeing each other, seeing past the usual, the normal. When you looked into someone's eyes and allowed them to tell you what was there without interrupting. It had been Simeon who'd said that, which was odd coming from a man who judged you by your shoes because he didn't dare look into your eyes. But she knew he was right. Perhaps he'd read it somewhere in a book. Harriet turned on the tap and began to rinse the casserole pot from the night before. She watched the water spill over, taking with it the left-over blobs of food. It was just that when Derek looked at her like that, she was always the first to look away.

***

Simeon wondered why Derek cut short their walk that morning. They'd hardly been out twenty minutes. Belle wasn't bothered, but Simeon felt as though he ought to complete the route they usually did. He decided against it because that would mean giving in to the inner niggles, and Archie said that it was good to leave them wanting more. Instead, he left Belle curled up in her basket and went to open up the church. He thought he might even join the others for Morning Prayer.

It was only after he'd fetched the key from behind the gargoyle that he noticed the young man from the day before sitting in the porch. It was a little too late to back away, particularly as he stood up as if he'd been waiting for him.

"Hello. I'll unlock, and then you can go inside if you want to. Anna will be down soon to say Morning Prayer." Simeon didn't want to say exactly when she would arrive because she was never exact in her timekeeping. In fact, it could be ten minutes before or after an agreed time. It annoyed Simeon because it wasn't as if she had to drive miles or even walk that far. Being late suggested to him that she thought his time was less important than her own. He'd said that to her once, and she'd been horrified, though it hadn't made her any more punctual.

The young man was wearing jeans and black slip-on shoes that looked as if they had been worn many times. They were scuffed around the heels and tapered to the toes. Simeon always thought that sort of shoe must be uncomfortable. He leaned hard on the door as it stuck on the flagstones. Not as badly as last year, because Derek had come down and shaved a little off the bottom. He hadn't been able to do a really good job because he couldn't take the door off its hinges – great, black iron clasps that looked as though they hadn't been touched since the church had been built. Simeon liked them, thought they looked strong, fit for purpose.

He usually walked around once before sitting down in his pew, on the left-hand side at the back, just in front of the bell. He began to make his way down the right-hand aisle and across the front. To his annoyance the young man came down the other side and stood in front of him.

"You were the one at the point yesterday, weren't you?"

Simeon nodded and backed up a pace.

"I'm Laurence," and the young man stuck out his hand.

Simeon put his hands behind his back and said, "I'm not comfortable shaking hands. Please don't think I'm being rude." It's what Archie and Anna had told him to say when this happened.

"No problem. I'm not keen myself on sharing sticky paws with a stranger."

Simeon began to feel quite pleased with himself. He wasn't panicking, and he hadn't resorted to counting. Not yet anyway.

"Are you feeling better?" Simeon asked. Laurence may have nodded, but Simeon didn't dare look up to check. Laurence slid into one of the middle pews, so Simeon was able to walk past to his usual place.

"So, what's the vicar lady like?" Laurence asked. Simeon risked a quick glance. Laurence was two rows ahead, so it was safe unless he looked around. Simeon swallowed.

"I didn't feel comfortable with her to start with, but she never gave up on me. I told her what I was trying to do, and though she didn't agree with me, she never stopped trying to say things to help me."

"What were you trying to do?" Laurence asked. Simeon thought he might have swivelled round to face him. The tenor of his voice had changed just perceptibly, and his coat rustled.

"I was trying to jump off the cliff."

Laurence gasped.

"So sorry, mate. I didn't mean to pry. God, you must have been sad."

Simeon thought about that.

"I wasn't sad. I just didn't see the point of life."

"And you do now?"

"Yes. But it involves God and community, so if you are uncomfortable talking about religion or about family, I won't explain any further."

"Oh, don't you worry. I know all about family." Laurence began to cry, messy sobs that made Simeon squash back against the wood of the pew. He began to count, began with the cry of the rooks nesting along the lane, and then started to smooth the pew in front. A rhythmic, slow stroke of his fingertips along the bevelled edge, one side to the other. Once, when Simeon had been waiting out in the churchyard for the building to empty, he'd heard Anna howling like an animal. It had taken him quite a few months to face her after that, as he'd been afraid she might do it again. At least then he'd been out in the churchyard with the open sky above him and any number of escape routes. Out of the corner of his eye he saw the box of tissues sitting on the back table by the kettle. It took five goes before he was able to lift his hand away from the wood, and then, with a quick look at Laurence, who seemed to have stopped juddering, Simeon jumped up and made his way over. The main door, partly closed, looked inviting, or the tower room, literally three steps away. All he had to do was slip inside, shut the door quietly and wait. Instead, he picked up the tissues and walked down to Laurence, dropped the box on the end of the pew and kept going to the front, then back up the other side.

"Thanks, mate," Laurence snuffled. Simeon had to hum while Laurence blew his nose and wiped his eyes. Anna wasn't late yet, but he hoped she'd arrive soon.

"Shall I leave you alone or shall I remain here?" Simeon asked.

He had plenty of time to drop his eyes to his hands before Laurence turned to look at him.

"Don't mind. Promise not to blub again." Laurence turned back to stare at the altar, so Simeon felt safe to peer at him. Laurence rubbed his eyes. "I am so tired." After a while he said, "This place is alright though, but I wish I hadn't gone to the point yesterday. I wish I hadn't had to find him. If I hadn't found him, I'd be able to think straight." His voice cracked, but he kept his word and didn't sob.

"I'll pray for you," Simeon said, "I'll ask God what you need."

"Well, when he lets you know, mate, be sure to tell me."

Simeon turned when he heard Anna's footsteps. She came in through the door, dragging dead leaves and the late autumn sun. She was wearing her dog collar and a large, woolly jumper. She said it made things more informal for the retreats, which she thought was important. She stopped when she saw Simeon.

"Simeon, how nice to see you. Are you alright after yesterday?"

Simeon nodded and said, "Laurence is here. He needs a place to think."

Her eyes widened, then flitted about until she found him. She looked round at Simeon and mouthed, "It must have been difficult for you." Simeon nodded.

Then she bustled forward and said, "Hello Laurence. I'm so sorry we didn't get a chance to chat yesterday. Would you like to meet today?"

He shrugged. Anna stood, as if waiting for something else to happen. There was a silence that Simeon thought might be described as awkward, though to him it was just silence, space between words and breath.

"Well, we'll give everyone else another five minutes, then we'll start."

Only Tom's mother came. She sat near the door. Morning Prayer didn't take long, but Anna had prepared some questions to help them with the retreat. She began to read them out.

"Why did you come here today? What is sitting on the surface of your soul? What might be sitting just below? Is there anything bubbling away deep down that you'd like to bring to God?"

Simeon thought that he'd come because Derek had only wanted to do a short walk. His pulse was running too high because Laurence had tried to shake his hand and then had cried. That had reminded him of when Anna had howled. Which had made him think he couldn't trust her.

Thinking of trust, he wondered where Archie was. He rarely missed Morning Prayer, and suddenly Simeon very much wanted to hear his voice. He wanted to be sure that he was alright, so he slipped out to the lane, to a spot where he knew he'd get a couple of bars, and rang him.

"Morning Simeon, everything alright?"

"Are you alright?"

"Yes, but one of my gutters got blocked, and it kept me awake last night, so I thought, while it was nice and calm this morning, I'd get a ladder and sort it out."

"I would've come and helped you."

"No need. It was one of the low ones."

"Good."

"Would you like to meet for coffee? I know it's not our usual day, but I've read a couple more chapters of that book because I couldn't sleep last night, and I'd love to talk to you about them."

"Thank you, Archie. I'll go and have some breakfast and

collect Belle. Then I'll walk round."

His pulse began to slow. Archie had sounded excited about the book, which was better than when he was frightened of them.

Chapter 12

Georgie stood in the hall, undecided what to do next. When Dani had gone through to the bathroom, she'd taken the opportunity to get up and get dressed. She'd thought about apologising, but Dani was a sulker and her petulant silence was already deeply irritating. Georgie really felt it was all too much bother and definitely small fry compared to what was going on now. Dani had no idea how wearing she was or what Georgie had been through. What she was going through. No wonder the team was taking it in turns to deal with Dani. That was wise. Spread the load a bit.

She wandered into the dining room. She was a little early for breakfast and far too late for Morning Prayer. She wondered where Laurence was, whether she could go and knock on his door. She wanted to talk to him about what had happened. Falling in the water must have been terrifying, and she wasn't even sure he could swim. But it was typical; the idiot was always trying to save people, even when they were way past redemption.

Georgie had been fourteen when they'd both lived at the home. Since then, she'd changed quite a bit, but he hadn't. The pink-cheeked, skinny boy was still there, skirting around at the back of everything. Still looking as though he didn't know what was going on, still looking worn to the bone and now haunted. He'd always pulled at her heartstrings, even back when she was a kid, and what he was doing on a retreat was anyone's guess.

Harriet came through from the kitchen as Georgie debated where to go.

"Hello Georgie, how did you sleep?"

"Alright."

"They're not back from church yet, but I could rustle up some coffee for you."

"I don't suppose I could have tea?"

"Of course. Go and wait in the lounge, and I'll bring you a mug. Any particular variety?"

Georgie thought it odd there weren't kettles in their rooms like in a proper hotel. She might suggest it, if only to keep Harriet from rushing back to the kitchen. Harriet wasn't long, and she had a plate of biscuits, which was kind of her. Georgie found she was really hungry.

"We're not allowed to put kettles in the rooms. The Diocese were worried about health and safety," Harriet replied, when Georgie mentioned it. "You work for a church, so you'll understand. It's silly, really, but I'll put a table in the dining room, where you can help yourselves. I'll do it after breakfast."

"That would be great," Georgie said. "I should really have got up for Morning Prayer. My vicar would say that I'm not making the most of my opportunities."

"I think," and Harriet smiled, which made her face relax into gentle beauty, "he's not here, but God is. That's enough. Let God do his thing. He will, you know." Harriet pressed her lips together and narrowed her eyes, looking a little surprised, as if it weren't the sort of thing she normally said. Georgie nodded. Yesterday hadn't been a great start to the retreat, not a great start to the rest of her life. She'd hoped that she might feel relief, that one aspect of her past had been laid to rest, but there was still work and all its problems and Laurence too, weighing her down, making it hard to breathe and causing a sharp pain across her shoulders.

"Thanks. I'll try and let him," she said. Harriet disappeared into the hall. Georgie drank her tea and ate another biscuit.

***

Anna left the others milling between the dining room and the lounge. She went to find Harriet, who was making a reassuring clatter in the kitchen.

"Laurence came to Morning Prayer. He was already down in church with Simeon."

102

"Oh, poor Simeon. He wouldn't have liked that."

"No ..." Anna hesitated because when she'd got there, the atmosphere had felt ... sorted, despite Simeon standing at the back, gripping the pew tightly. She shook her head. "I think Simeon is managing quite well. This retreat business has him growing, almost flourishing."

"What a lovely word," Harriet said, laughing. "And to flourish, we all need a bit of God's manure around our roots."

"Now that sounds like a good metaphor for my sermon."

"Not sure, Anna, that deliberately getting—"

"Poo all over your shoes! But it would certainly make some of the old ladies in the back row sit up."

"Right," Harriet said, handing her a tray, "you take through the porridge, and I'll bring the coffee and tea."

Anna wondered if she should check her phone. She'd deliberately left it in her bedroom. She knew why too. Bloody Tom and his policeman heart, spoiling the retreat with all his suspicions. Perhaps she ought to warn Laurence that he might be back. Give him some time to get his story straight. No, that wasn't what she meant. She tried to shake that thought loose.

At breakfast Laurence still looked scared and twitchy. When Dani knocked over a glass, he almost jumped to his feet. After they'd finished mopping up the juice, Anna noticed Catherine checking her phone, a quick look, surreptitiously. Suddenly Anna wished she'd got hers too, wished she hadn't left it lying on the bedside table. She was such a child sometimes. She straightened up and turned to Laurence.

"So, you met Simeon this morning?" she said.

"Yes, I did. He is nice. Kind."

That wasn't what she'd been expecting him to say. She hadn't heard anyone describe Simeon as nice.

"How are you? It was quite a day yesterday. No ill effects?"

He stiffened in his seat, and his eyes filled with tears, but he blinked them away. For a minute he reminded her of

Archie and that stiff upper lip. Of course the rest of the table had also paused to listen.

"It was a shock, finding him. Simeon said I did it all wrong." Now that sounded more like the Simeon she knew. "But I wasn't thinking straight. I just thought he needed rescuing."

"Poor you," Georgie said.

"Well, I think you were very brave," Dani added, but she was looking at Georgie when she said it, and Anna felt she was making some sort of point.

Catherine picked up the teapot, "More tea anyone?"

"I'll go and make it," Anna said, jumping to her feet, just as Harriet came through with the second pot. She sat back down.

"So, I'm around all day today if anyone wants to talk," Anna said, trying to sound useful and wise. "The weather looks as if it might get a bit nasty. I know it looks lovely now, but we think at about ten thirty the wind will get up and there'll be rain. But the church is open. The pub too," and she laughed. "It's a nice pub." Only then she thought perhaps she ought not to be recommending it to her guests. She cleared her throat and tried again. "Lunch here will be at one thirty, as usual." She got up to clear the plates. She noticed Georgie was looking over at Laurence, but he was staring resolutely at his lap.

Dani slid her chair back and said, "I highly recommend the pub. I went there for coffee yesterday. I might walk up again today."

"Well, take a raincoat," Anna said. She plainly heard Dani mutter, "Duh!"

Anna poured one more coffee and decided to set herself up in the lounge. She'd do some reading around the sermon for the following Sunday, at least until she was needed.

The room was chilly. She looked longingly at the fire. Harriet could get it going nicely. Anna never seemed to be able to. Harriet said it was because she was in too much of a hurry. She tried to cut corners to save time, which was always a mistake. She settled into one of the single chairs. Not as comfortable as the one in her tiny back room, but it would do. She didn't like the set readings for the following Sunday so decided to go freelance. She wanted to think about the manure idea that she and Harriet had been laughing about earlier. It might have legs, or maybe roots ... The front door slammed, and she wondered who'd left the building. She stared at the empty page of her notepad and continued to stare blankly until she decided that she'd been childish long enough, that it was time to check her mobile. Sure enough, there were two messages from Tom. He was heading over and asked if she could make sure that Laurence didn't go out.

"Oh, bugger," she muttered. What if it had been him slamming the front door? She knew she needed to check, so she hurried up the stairs and was relieved to hear voices murmuring from inside his room. There was a sudden flash of jealousy. Who had he found to talk to instead of her? She knocked, and the voices stopped.

"Come in."

Georgie was standing just inside the room, but the bed cover was ruffled from where she must have been sitting.

"I was just getting back the toothpaste he borrowed," she said quickly, as if Anna had caught them doing something they ought not to be doing. Before Anna could even smile at such a thought, Georgie slipped past, pulling the door firmly shut behind her.

Laurence didn't look any better. He obviously still wasn't sleeping, unless he was a naturally pale and worn young man, who, without too much of a stretch of the imagination, could have played a good Cratchit in Dickens.

"She's a nice girl. Have you met before?" As she said it, Anna realised it was an odd question. Laurence simply turned to look out the window. Anna carried on to fill the silence. "Tom just phoned to say that he'll be popping in for another chat, so if you could stay about the place, that'd be great."

This time he nodded slowly. Anna also had to try and get Georgie to hang around. Apparently Tom thought she might have seen something. Anna didn't feel so much like a vicar as a jailor. What right did she have to keep everyone in the vicarage? How could God do his thing if people felt trapped or under suspicion?

"It's a pretty dreadful thing to have happened, particularly when you're on retreat. I'm really sorry."

"It's not your fault."

The doorbell chimed. That was probably Tom, but she wasn't going to upset Laurence before she had to.

"I'd best go and answer that."

Harriet got there first. Dani was also there, standing below Anna on the stairs. Anna supposed she was on her way out. Harriet was making a bit of a fuss about greeting Tom, offering to take his coat, asking if he'd like a drink or even some breakfast. She was obviously making a point as usual and was perfectly aware that Anna was watching them. Dani swung round. When she saw Anna behind her, she jumped and quickly moved up past her, back to their room. She must have forgotten something.

"I'll go and make the coffee," Harriet said.

"Thanks Harriet. Is the boss about?"

Harriet pointed up to Anna standing at the top of the stairs. Anna wasn't sure what to make of being called the boss. They were a team, and most of the time no-one was in charge. At least that was what she liked to think. Anna wasn't big on taking responsibility. She felt better when it was shared around.

"Do you want to drink your coffee first, or shall I go and get Laurence?" Anna asked, not bothering to come all the way down. Anyway, she quite liked him having to look up at her.

"Do you mind if we do coffee first? I'm a bit wiped."

"You've had some sleep?" Anna came all the way to the

bottom of the stairs.

"A couple of hours."

"Why so little? It just can't be anything sinister. I can't do this again." But she could tell by his face it wasn't just a random body. "Oh Tom!"

"On my way back last night I popped in to see Phil, and he gave me the man's name. I got it checked out last night. He's definitely from Exeter."

"I expect there are a lot of people from Exeter staying round here."

"Yes, all of your guests, except my mum of course." He looked over his shoulder. "Look, could we go somewhere a little more private?"

She took him into her own sitting room, a tiny place that used to be a storeroom. There was space for a small bookcase, a gateleg table and a couple of comfy chairs. She'd always loved it because it warmed up quickly. The only other person she allowed over this particular threshold was Harriet. By one of the chairs was a pile of books she didn't like people seeing as they were not really good vicar reading. Tom, of course, went straight to them. She could feel her cheeks beginning to burn.

"Anything I might like?" he asked.

"No, unless you want to read detective fiction."

"Not really. That's a bit coals to Newcastle." He straightened up, looking around him.

"Sit down, Tom."

Harriet appeared with a mug and a plate of biscuits. She closed the door quietly behind her. Tom grabbed a couple. So he'd probably had no breakfast either.

"Oh Tom, you simply can't live like this. You ought to have some rest and eat a proper meal."

He frowned. She knew such things simply didn't figure when there was a murder to sort out.

"The guy who signed into the pub was Robert Enderby. He

worked at a children's home up on the moors a few years back, and it does look as it sounds: grim and very isolated. It was shut down a couple of years ago."

"Ok," Anna said slowly. "What's your point?"

"I couldn't find any current prosecutions with respect to the home, but I did come across one of the children. There was a picture and everything." He folded his arms across his chest and looked smug. She sipped her coffee, trying not to frown.

"Who are we talking about?" Though she'd already guessed. "So, you think Laurence knew the victim?"

"It would make sense as to why he was so upset yesterday."

"Anyone would've been upset if they'd tried to fish a body out of the sea," Anna said in exasperation. "Perhaps he didn't actually recognise the man. Perhaps he was just reminded of his carer, and it brought up some old memories."

Tom smiled.

"You and your psychobabble."

Anna knew it was pointless to argue. The only way Tom would let it go was to work out the truth.

"I think he did recognise him, but didn't want us to know that he had," Tom continued.

"Why?"

Tom shrugged. She thought he loved this bit, when there were lots of possibilities, while he was still waiting to see which thread to pull, which one would unravel what had actually happened.

"So, what do you want to do?" she asked.

"I want to talk to him informally, ask if he's got anything else to add to his statement."

"You won't tell him what you know?"

"No, I don't think so, not yet. I'd like to find out a bit more about the body. I'm waiting on the boys at Exeter to come back to me on that. A simple CV check won't be enough."

"Oh dear, don't they work nights then?" She smiled

sweetly.

Tom yawned and said, "I will get some rest tonight. I promise. It's just that he's only here until Friday, so I don't want to waste any time."

"What about your mum?"

"What do you mean?"

"Well, she was expecting to spend some time with you, but if you're up to your eyeballs in death and mayhem, she'll come a very poor second."

She could see he hadn't thought of that.

"Could she perhaps stay on an extra night or two, and then I could spend the weekend with her?" His eyes were wide, his head slightly tipped to one side. Anna was a little taken aback. "Of course if it's not convenient ..."

"It's not that, Tom. I can just about manage to be on my best behaviour for four days. Stretching it to five or six would be tough."

He laughed as if she'd made a joke.

"Please Anna, just be yourself. Mum is bound to like you."

But she wasn't sure she wanted any of them to see the real Anna Maybury. Particularly not Tom's mother.

Chapter 13

Tom tried adjusting the cushion, then he tried the sofa opposite. It was no good; both seats were indescribably lumpy. He supposed Anna wouldn't realise how bad they were because she didn't spend that much time in there. From now on he'd only imagine her in that small, cosy, cluttered space at the back, where she looked so at home.

He'd been surprised to see that she'd found a 'Do not disturb' notice to hang on the doorknob of the lounge. He wondered where it had come from. He couldn't imagine her using it. Perhaps all vicars were given one when they graduated, or whatever it was that vicars did when they finished vicar school.

There was no sun around this side of the house. A small ray of light might have crept through the front windows first thing, if the sky hadn't been heavy with low clouds. It was gloomy, but it suited the job; how he felt. Through the half open door, he could hear Anna reassuring Laurence. Then he heard his mother's voice joining in. He hoped she wouldn't want to speak to him. Perhaps he ought to have gone and found her rather than having coffee with Anna. He'd wondered about that, a little resentful that he always seemed to have to choose between them. But it hadn't been his idea for her to come on retreat. He heard her laughing and then another door closing.

Anna led the boy in. He looked a bit more with it, but still had a bruised quality about his eyes. Anna was right about him looking like he was carrying the weight of the world.

"This is an informal chat. Would you like the Revd Maybury to stay with you?"

Laurence shook his head and then nodded. *Sensible boy,* Tom thought. If you were going to have anyone on your side, Anna was a good bet.

"So, Laurence, did you have a comfortable night?"

He nodded again.

"And having reflected on the events of yesterday, is there anything you'd like to add to your statement?" Like the fact that you knew Robert Enderby, Tom added in his head. He handed over the neatly typed sheet for Laurence to check through. He'd left Sandra internet-searching the children's home and its personnel. He hoped, if Exeter didn't find anything, she would. She was tenacious when it came to searching out background information. Something else to put in her reference.

Laurence glanced up, then looked across at Anna, who was watching him intently.

"Is there something you want me to say? Something I've missed?"

Either the boy had done this before, or Tom was barking up the wrong tree.

"You haven't asked me who he is." Tom knew he was getting a bit heavy. Laurence responded defensively.

"I thought it was probably someone who had fallen off a passing ship." A vain attempt to distance himself from the body. Tom wasn't fooled for an instant, but Anna caught his eye, her eyebrows up. Annoyingly, she was right. To draw Laurence out, Tom needed to treat him as a victim, not a hostile witness.

"We think the man was staying at the pub, at least for the last three nights, and a preliminary report suggests that he wasn't in the water for more than two hours, possibly less."

Laurence went a little pale, and his hands began to drum a rhythm on the chair arm. He reminded Tom of Simeon.

"So he went in earlier that morning. Did he leave a note or anything?" Laurence asked.

"Why do you think a note?"

"Because if he didn't fall in by accident, it might have been deliberate. Simeon said he'd tried to jump off a cliff round here. I thought it might be a suicide hot spot."

"You've spoken to Simeon about jumping?" Anna asked, her voice turning up at the end. She was really surprised; that much was obvious. Laurence simply nodded. "He told you what he tried to do?"

"Yes," Laurence replied, this time a little irritably, Tom thought. He could see that Anna was bursting with questions.

"We are not ruling out anything at this stage." Tom continued, hurriedly, before Anna's thoughts got the better of her and spilled into the room like a rising tide.

"So did he leave a name at the pub?" Laurence asked, his eyes still fixed on his knees, giving nothing away. Except his fingers still drummed their erratic beat.

"Yes," said Tom and waited. Anna was sitting a little to one side of Laurence, so he shouldn't be able to see her face. Her eyebrows were raised to the ceiling and she shook her head, a sharp movement that made Tom frown. He hoped that Laurence's peripheral vision wasn't particularly good.

"What name did he use?" Laurence asked, raising his head.

"Robert Enderby."

There was a long pause, and the colour in Anna's cheeks was almost glowing neon with the effort of staying quiet. Tom kept his eyes fixed on Laurence; he didn't look away for a second. There were blotchy patches down the boy's neck as if all the colour from his face had drained there. Tom waited. Always the best policy. After much examination of the floor, Laurence seemed to make up his mind. He took a deep breath.

"I knew a Bob Enderby from a long time ago." He clenched his fists on his knees. "He was a carer at the place I used to live. I suppose it could have been him, but he lives up in Exeter."

So Laurence must have seen him since the home, or how would he have known where he lived?

***

Simeon was home when he got Anna's texts. He'd been to the shop to get milk and bread.

'Come for lunch. You have met nearly all the guests now, and obviously you can leave whenever you want.'

The second text said, 'And bring Belle. She's a real ice breaker.'

He put his shopping away and looked down at Belle, snuffling at her empty bowl, ever optimistic. She was probably not a pure Labrador, but she had big, melty, brown eyes and looked soft, safe. People often stopped him and asked if they could pet her. Once or twice, he'd said they could, but that they mustn't give her anything to eat. He'd then found something to count so that he wouldn't get too nervous, until they'd stopped stroking her.

"Shall we go and see Anna?"

Belle wagged her tail. Simeon knew she didn't really understand what he was saying, but it did seem as if sometimes she sensed what he needed. Telling her what they were about to do was a new thing for him. It made him feel more in control, and as Anna obviously wanted him to do something, he needed to feel that, if only a little. He'd have to ask Anna what she was thinking because he didn't like guessing.

When he knocked on the vicarage door, the hall was full of people, and he had to step back into the drive. Anna held up a hand like a police officer.

"Let's get everyone clear, and then you'll have space to breathe."

Once the rest had filed through to the dining room and sat down, he stepped in and removed his coat. There was a bit of chatter, but it silenced as she tapped a chair for Simeon, just by the door.

"Most of you know Simeon. He's here for lunch with Belle."

"Oh, she's gorgeous. Come to mummy." Dani cried. She was out of her seat before anyone could stop her. Simeon looked at Anna in alarm. Harriet got up and took the lead from his fingers. She led Belle to the other end of the table,

114

Dani following.

"Belle is an old dog," Harriet explained. "She doesn't mind a bit of fussing, but we need to get on with lunch. There is only one rule for her, which is that she mustn't be fed titbits."

Simeon wanted to say that there were lots of other rules, but Anna quietly whispered, "Lots of rules, we know."

She was sitting to his left; on his right was Laurence. Simeon wished he'd had a chance to ask what Anna needed of him. She stood up and thanked God for Harriet's food, then she sat down again and began to hand round the dishes. Once everyone had finished serving themselves, people began to talk. Simeon always found talking and eating tricky, so he had a couple of good mouthfuls before he put his fork down.

"How are you, Laurence?" he asked as quietly as he could, staring at Laurence's fingers. They were clenching and unclenching around his cutlery.

"Not brilliant, mate, not brilliant at all."

Anna hadn't eaten much, but she got up to go and talk to Harriet.

"I have prayed for you, and sometimes talking to Anna helps."

"Yes, she seems nice. It's just that she really likes that policeman." Laurence was also whispering. Simeon could barely hear him. He was also now confused. How did Anna liking Tom stop her being a good person to talk to? He took another mouthful of food.

"Do you fancy a walk this afternoon?" Laurence asked. "You could take Belle."

"She is an old dog and has had all the exercise she needs for the day."

"Oh, just a thought."

Anna was sliding back into her seat.

"Couldn't help hearing. Why don't you leave Belle with me? She's absolutely no trouble, and Harriet will be around to make sure I don't break any of the rules."

Derek and Harriet always looked after Belle if Simeon had to go into Helston or anywhere else further afield. Anna had never offered before, so perhaps this was what she'd wanted all along, that he'd go for a walk with Laurence. Simeon felt pleased that he'd worked it out for himself and said, "Alright. Do you like walking?"

"I walk a lot around Exeter. I often don't have much else to do."

"Have your shoes dried from yesterday?"

"I don't know."

"If they have, let's go over to Kynance. I don't do it very often because Belle can't quite manage it. It is very nice."

"Cool. After lunch then?"

Simeon didn't have to talk too much after that, so he had seconds, which made Harriet's face crinkle.

***

Dani was cold. Wrapping herself in the duvet seemed the only option. She'd complained to Anna, who'd promised to put the heating up, but at the time she'd been so vague that Dani didn't think she'd really been listening. Dani took out her phone. There was no signal. She'd have to go back up into the village to check it, and she could get some chocolate from the shop. Lunch had been nice, but not very filling.

It was all so boring. She was bored and cold. She'd prayed, but it hadn't felt any easier here than it had done at home. Dani still wasn't sure she was doing it right. She pulled the duvet tighter around herself and curled into a ball. She could hear someone coming up the stairs. They creaked something chronic. Creeping about simply wasn't an option. The door opened, very slowly. Georgie put her head round.

"Sorry, am I disturbing you?"

"No."

Georgie had had to stay in that morning to talk to the policeman, though she'd told Dani she hadn't seen a thing. Dani had almost laughed out loud. Of course she'd seen something. Still, Georgie was a practised liar. Dani had watched her presenting her own personal view of events many times. Sharing a house with Georgie had been a bit of an eye-opener. Actually, sharing was not the word Dani would've used. She'd been offered the box room, which was more like a cupboard. It was right next to the water tank, so if anyone used the loo in the night, they woke her. She'd mentioned it a few times, had even left notes dotted around the landing, but every so often someone pulled the chain, doing the 'Oh, sorry, I forgot!' Yeah right!

"What are you going to do this afternoon?" Georgie asked.

"I don't know," Dani replied.

"The guys are walking across to some cove on the other side, but I don't fancy risking the rain."

Dani didn't fancy it either.

"What is there to do?" For a second Dani felt a lump forming in her throat. God, this place was depressing.

"Well, we could go and talk to Anna, or we could go down to the church and talk to God."

Next she was going to suggest they sat and read their Bibles together. At places like this, you often saw people sitting in odd corners, pretending to hide away, but actually really saying, 'Look at me!' Dani didn't want to read the Bible. It was too difficult and definitely boring. When she'd first got God, back when she was thirteen, she'd carried a Bible around in her bag for weeks because it was what the others did. It had just made her shoulders ache. She'd tried looking through it, she really had, but all that stuff on sacrifice and who was fighting whom didn't seem to have any relevance to her. She'd tried the New Testament too, but hadn't managed to get into that either. Jesus said such crazy things, odd things that made her feel as though she'd joined a sect. She'd been too afraid to ask anyone about it all because they seemed to know what was going on and she didn't want them to think she was stupid.

Anyway, it had all changed when she got pregnant. Then it was as if they had drawn a big, fat line round her. An imaginary ring that was too wide for anyone to get past.

"So, do you want to come down to church?"

She didn't, really, but literally what else was there to do? At least Georgie was talking to her again, though she still owed Dani a massive apology. Dani clambered off the bed.

Down in the hall she pulled her coat hood up. She liked the sensation of being enclosed, only being able to peer out through the matted fluff. Georgie pulled hers up too.

"You ready?" she asked.

"Yes, I guess so."

The air was filled with a drippy, drizzly mist you could almost touch. Dani stuffed her hands in her pockets.

Before she could stop herself, she asked, "Georgie, how do you pray?" Instantly regretting it, she knew she'd get the look – the 'Don't you know?', 'Everyone knows that!', 'You've been a Christian for ages' look. At least because of the hood she couldn't see it.

"To be honest, it depends." Georgie sounded a little hesitant.

Depends on what? Dani hoped she wouldn't leave it at that.

"If it's just praying for people, you know, for the things they need, then I just say it. But recently I've heard that that's not enough. We need to hang out with God, and to be honest I've no idea what that means."

Dani blew a long breath out between her teeth. That wasn't particularly helpful. As they turned into the lane, the wind hit them.

"Oh, this is horrible," Dani said, holding her hood tightly.

"Come on, let's run for it." Georgie set off. Without thinking Dani went after her. She'd been quite good at running at school. She skidded past Georgie at the gate and easily got to the porch first, with plenty of time to turn and

118

watch Georgie jog the last bit.

"You're fast, or perhaps I'm really slow."

"So how do you know Laurence?" Dani asked.

Georgie's eyes widened in surprise. Dani was really envious of her lashes, long and dark.

"I don't," she muttered.

"Bitch," Dani retorted under her breath. Because Dani had been there when they'd bumped into him, back when they were at school. And even if she hadn't remembered that, Dani would've guessed, just from seeing them together. It was so obvious she wouldn't be surprised if even drippy Anna had realised there was some sort of history. Dani was wondering if they'd arranged to meet here, but that for some reason it had to be a secret. Her mum's voice was soon echoing round her head, 'If you have to keep something a secret, then something somewhere isn't good or right.' Her mum was always saying that. So whichever way you looked at it, Georgie was a hypocrite.

When Georgie and Dani were in the lower sixth, Georgie doing A-levels and Dani doing retakes, they'd gone with some of the other girls from church to some dreadful nightclub. Dark corners and a sticky carpet, music so loud you couldn't think straight. Trying to prove that Christians were cool. They weren't. They'd all sat self-consciously in a corner until Laurence had come across to say hello. He'd stayed for quite a while to chat, or rather to shout through the din. There'd been a bit of a fumble at the end of the evening, but nothing of note. Of course Dani had filled out a lot since then and grown her hair, so she wasn't surprised he didn't remember her. But Georgie and he definitely went way back.

Georgie was pretending she hadn't heard Dani's retort. She was standing just inside the door as if she didn't know what to do. Dani was still in the porch, only when Dani tried to go past her into the church Georgie reached out and grabbed her arm, her features all crumpled and angry. Dani took a step

119

back, shaking loose her grip.

"Look, Dani, cut me some slack, will you. I'm not being deliberately horrible." Georgie swallowed and looked away. "I'm just super tired and fed up with Alf and—"

"Our vicar Alf? Alf Tripp?"

"Yes. What people don't realise is that he's a right pain in the arse. I haven't had a proper day off for nearly eighteen months. I think he's had an important meeting every Thursday since I arrived. I even asked if I could change my day off so I could get some rest, and he thought I was joking."

Dani raised her eyebrows. She made her way to the front, Georgie followed her.

Georgie continued, "I don't work normal hours, a lot of my stuff goes on in the evening, so I often do a twelve-hour day. The job has expanded and expanded. Sometimes I simply don't know where to start."

Dani thought she was being a bit melodramatic. Georgie ran a couple of groups, helped out at the Sunday services. How hard could it be? They both swivelled round as someone stepped down from a small room behind them. Anna was standing at the bottom of the steps, wringing her hands. Actually wringing her hands! It was like one of those dreadful books her mum read, all heaving bosoms and elfin beauty or warped ugliness. Never anything in-between. Dani knew which category Anna would fit into.

"How much did you hear?" Georgie stuttered, as Anna made her way over to them.

"Enough to know that you can't keep on like that," Anna spoke almost angrily.

"Please don't tell Alf I said anything. It's a good job, really, it is. Some of my friends from college have to work in supermarkets." Georgie slumped onto the front pew.

"I won't tell on you, of course I won't," Anna said, coming forward and sitting down next to her, "But you need a proper day off, everyone does. No wonder you're so … emotional."

Georgie looked up quickly and then looked away again. Dani thought Anna was right, though emotional was really just another word for weak and definitely unreasonable. It's what her mum had said when Dani had screamed that she couldn't cope, that her mum didn't understand. "I bet you get some down time, don't you, Dani?" Anna added, but without taking her eyes off Georgie.

"I don't work," Dani replied, hoping that Anna would feel bad for asking such a question. She'd tried to get a job any number of times, but looking after Selena when her mum was at work wasn't always as straightforward as it sounded. She simply couldn't guarantee her availability.

"I know I wasn't meant to hear," Anna continued, speaking to Georgie as if Dani wasn't there at all, "but I did, so do you want to come and talk a little more? Perhaps about yesterday too?"

Georgie did have the gumption to look guiltily at Dani. After all, what was she going to do if Georgie and Anna swanned off back to the vicarage? Anna must have realised.

"Look, stay here, the pair of you and then come on up about four o'clock and we can have a chat with our cake. How about that?"

Anna left smiling, bobbing down the path as if she'd done something amazing. Dani watched her through the door before turning to Georgie.

"So how do you know Laurence?"

Georgie shook her head but wrinkled her nose as if she might just smile. Dani wasn't going to give up. She'd been known at school for her dogged persistence. It had always been thrown back at her, as if it were a bad thing, but as it was the only thing anyone ever remembered about her, she thought she might as well go with it. Anyway, she was really curious about Georgie and Laurence. Deep down a thought niggled, that, perhaps if she knew just a little more about what was really going on, she wouldn't feel so left out.

"From a long time ago, when we were teenagers. We lived in a children's home, outside of Exeter. Quite a way out of Exeter, up on the moor. I guess built at a time when kids like us were best out of sight, out of mind."

"So why is it such a big deal?"

Georgie looked thoughtful.

"Not something I can easily explain."

"Have you managed to speak to him?"

Georgie nodded, but continued looking at her hands.

"Last night, when I lent him some toothpaste."

"He's a bit of a wet blanket."

Georgie laughed.

"Very good, Dani, particularly after he fell in the sea. At the home, he was nice. One of the ones that looked out for us youngsters. As you can imagine, it wasn't all plain sailing in that respect."

If she so much as hinted that at least Dani had a mum, even if she didn't get on with her, Dani would thump her.

"My mum died when I was thirteen, and they couldn't find any relatives, let alone any that wanted me."

Right this minute Dani wouldn't mind not having a mum, except of course then she'd have to look after Selena all by herself. Perhaps she should've got a paternity test done, and then Oscar or Jay could have shared the responsibility a little. But her mum would've had something to say about that. She would've totally freaked out at the notion that Dani didn't know who the father was. She definitely wouldn't want her daughter getting a reputation for … well, whatever the word, her mum wouldn't want to use it. She just didn't understand what it was like being a young woman in this day and age.

Georgie looked across at her.

She said, "It's why God is so important to me. I literally don't have anyone else."

"Alf would definitely say that that's more than enough."

Georgie shrugged. Dani had hoped that Georgie might help

her, but instead she felt all the questions she might've asked piling up behind her eyes, making her head ache as if she were getting a migraine.

Chapter 14

Simeon didn't know how fast to walk. Laurence was shorter than he was, and while he was skinny, that didn't make him fit. Simeon moved ahead of him because then, as long as Laurence didn't talk, Simeon could forget that he was there. Which meant that now and again, he had to check how far behind he was.

"Thanks for this, Simeon. I needed to get away. They all look at me as if I'm about to fall apart. I tried talking to Anna, but the moment wasn't right."

Simeon looked back at Laurence's feet and nodded. He lengthened his stride a little. Laurence didn't seem to be having any problems keeping up. They'd been walking for about forty-five minutes when they reached the car park, which was empty that afternoon, probably due to the weather. The sea below them was dull green and heaving, the sky a matt grey and the drizzle light but annoying. Simeon had his hood up, which made it hard to hear what Laurence was saying. He stopped to allow him to come closer.

"There was only one man I ever trusted enough to speak to. That's why yesterday was so dreadful."

Simeon supposed the dead man had reminded Laurence of this trusted friend.

"And to make matters worse, I know Georgie from way back. Only can you keep that to yourself please." Simeon hesitated. He didn't like being asked to keep secrets, though he wondered if keeping something to yourself was technically the same thing. Laurence nodded, then thrust his hands in his pocket and stared out over the view. "It's just that when people find out where you grew up, they get all sad. They stop treating you like a normal person. Pity is a shit thing to have to deal with. Georgie knows that, so she won't tell anyone either. We never do if we can help it."

Simeon wanted to ask a number of questions. He had to

125

press his lips together to stop the words from spurting out. It hurt keeping such things inside. He wished Anna were here. He'd then have said it anyway and she could have sorted it out. For when Anna thought he'd said something inappropriate, she usually wrinkled her nose and laughed a tinny laugh that she thought would smooth things over. To begin with it had annoyed Simeon because his questions were logical, following on from what the other person had said.

"I'd like to ask you a question about what you just said, but sometimes I don't understand what lies behind someone's words." They began to walk slowly towards the path twisting and turning down onto Kynance beach. The tide was on its way out, so there was plenty of space to walk across to the café. It was closed. A girl called Jemma had worked there across the summer and had now headed back to Cardiff to see her family. Archie had told him that. She'd lived with Jean at the shop. Simeon shivered. The thought of someone else sharing his cottage, even on a temporary basis, made his stomach clench. He bent down to pat Belle, only to remember that of course she was back at the vicarage.

Laurence looked down into the cove.

"This place is wild. I bet it's crazy when there's a storm."

"I'd never come down here when there was a storm."

The water surged around the rock, a stubborn island of granite splitting the beach in two. The tug of the waves sucked at the sparkly green and red pebbles, rolling and grinding, like rain on a tin roof.

"No, I don't suppose anyone with any sense would," Laurence said. Simeon felt as though he'd missed something. After another pause, Laurence said, "Ask your question if you want."

"Where did you and Georgie grow up?"

"Children's home outside Exeter."

Simeon picked his way down the path. As they began to make their way across the shingle, Laurence caught up with him.

"Good on you, mate."

Simeon wondered what Laurence meant. The rain began to harden. Laurence's hair darkened.

"This probably won't stop until it gets dark."

"Oh, shit. It's not going to be very nice walking back, is it?"

Simeon shook his head.

"The wind will be mostly behind us. But I could text Archie or Anna to come and meet us with a car."

"No, real men wouldn't call for help."

Simeon felt he ought to say something in reply, but couldn't think of anything pertinent. He took them across the front of the café and up the lane that made its way back onto the heathland; boggy ground stretching away to the main road, flattened grass with the odd gorse bush. Dark, peaty water seeped onto the track making long, black puddles. It was a bit of a slog, but better than the coastal path in the current conditions. He had to check on Laurence frequently, which meant turning into the rain. Simeon braced himself each time and kept his eyes scrunched half-shut. Laurence's shoulders were hunched and he was sniffing a lot, but the cold and wet did make your nose run. In the end Simeon gave him his pack of tissues.

In the distance the village lights flickered in the rain. Suddenly Simeon wanted to get back to Belle and dry clothes and solitude. He'd managed really well, but it was time to go home. He hoped Laurence would understand and be able to keep up.

***

Anna picked up a tea towel. She'd come up from the church, sneaking round the back to come in through the kitchen. Harriet switched on the kettle.

"I just saw Georgie and Dani down at the church. This isn't the sort of retreat I'd have sent them on," she said.

127

"Did someone send them?" Harriet asked, handing her a couple of mugs to dry.

"I'm getting the impression their vicar is a bit of a control freak."

Harriet turned away to chop onions. She couldn't help smiling. There'd been an almost wistful timbre to Anna's voice. Anna mostly ran behind things, clearing up the messes as she went. Harriet could see that the idea of having some sort of control might be appealing.

"So how are you, Harriet? Even with all this hoo-ha, I've still got the feeling there's stuff you'd like to say."

Harriet turned from the onions and stared at Anna.

"You and I don't normally talk like that."

Anna frowned.

"How do we talk?"

"Not usually head-on." Harriet considered for a moment, "From the side, from behind."

"Is it this?" Anna waved her arms around. Of course that would be her main worry. It had never occurred to Harriet that perhaps Anna didn't know that this was the part of her life she clung to. That here she felt in control, able to manage, to do what she was good at. She felt the same when she worked at the pub.

"No, I love this," she said, as reassuringly as she could.

Anna began to blink. Harriet hadn't managed to reassure her. She turned back to her task, her own eyes beginning to sting.

Anna got up and began to make coffee.

"Or would you prefer tea?"

And Harriet began to cry. The real tears sweeping away the onion tears. She felt Anna's arms wrap around her. She carefully put down the knife and turned, to make it easier for them both, though already she didn't need to cry anymore. Already she'd dried up.

Anna stepped back and gave her a mug. They sat down at

the tiny Formica table, a chair either side. The place where people came when they needed to work out what to do next.

"It's Derek. I don't know what I'm doing."

"You seem so happy, so settled."

"I think that's it," Harriet said, looking through the steam at Anna. "He offered security and love. I'd been lonely for such a long time."

"Do you want to move back in here?"

For a moment Harriet thought about that as an actual possibility, but only for a fleeting second. She couldn't do that to him. He'd be uncomprehending and so hurt, and she realised she was haunted by that, even here in this sanctuary.

"No. He wouldn't understand."

"I'm not sure that's the point."

"The Lizard is too small a place to go back on such a decision."

"We'd get over it."

Harriet didn't really believe that.

"Would Derek?" she asked.

"But if it's not right for you ..."

Harriet leaned across and patted Anna's hand. That statement would've cost Anna. She was there for all of them, which meant that sometimes she got caught in the middle.

"I feel heaps better now because, you know ... Let's leave it at that. These things tend to work themselves out."

Anna nodded, but she looked miserable.

"And just because I'm in a bit of a pickle doesn't mean you should stop talking to me."

"Ok."

"So what was going on with Simeon at lunch?" Harriet asked.

Anna began to sparkle as she smiled, her eyes becoming half-moons.

"Well, it was something Laurence said. I just wondered if he'd kind of made a connection with Simeon. Shared moment of trauma and all that."

"Yes, but we're talking about Simeon here. He's not exactly emotionally astute."

"I know. But he's come on heaps in the last twelve months or so. He's a different boy."

"Young man, Anna. He's nearly thirty."

"True. But I think we forget what he was like back when it all kicked off, you know, with Fiona and Terry."

"We were all different back then. More individual, I guess."

"I agree. I think, despite our differences, we've become a bit of a community." Anna shivered.

"Why is that so important?" Harriet asked.

"It just is. It feels profound."

Harriet thought this might be the perfect opportunity to ask Anna her question about church, but instead she found herself saying, "So when's Tom coming back?"

She immediately knew she should've kept quiet, that it had been silly to have mentioned him at this moment. Anna's face crumpled.

"He likes you, Anna. A lot, I think."

"But why has he got to make everything so complicated? It was just a body in the sea. But he thinks Laurence has got something to do with it, I know he does. He's got Sandra checking out his past. Bloody internet."

"Well, you have to admit Laurence did seem to be more than usually burdened when he arrived on Monday night." Harriet knew that was a ridiculous statement. What on earth was a usual burden? She ploughed on because she was too embarrassed to stop. "And since yesterday, he seems to be even more unhinged."

"Understandably! He tried to haul a man to safety, only to find that he was dead, then he fell in and had to cling onto the ramp for ages. He was frozen, in danger of drowning and dangling over him was a corpse. I can't imagine how horrible it must have been. And he did know him."

130

Harriet wondered if Anna ought to have said that.

"How did he know him?" she asked.

"From when he was a child. Years before."

"So why did he pretend he didn't?" But Harriet could tell that Anna was having none of it.

"Laurence is being treated as a suspect when he's a victim, in fact, a bit of a hero really. He tried to drag the man to safety!"

This was Anna trying to think the best of everyone. Harriet wasn't so certain. Laurence had been upset, but about what?

"I need to get on." Harriet went back to the onions. Anna muttered something about sermon preparation and disappeared into her sitting room.

**

Tom had been hassling the medical examiner all morning. He needed to know the cause of death, at least a preliminary result, as he knew not to expect too much detail at such an early stage. There was the obvious stuff: the squashed hand and the welt across the man's face, and Tom wanted to know if these could've been caused by the rocks. He was irritated, though he couldn't quite put his finger on it. It was the same feeling he'd had all the way through the year after Fiona had been found, when Anna had managed to piece together the whole picture because she'd been the recipient of all the little bits of gossip over the weeks and months. He shook his head in annoyance. Perhaps he was still irritated because she'd beaten him to it without ever setting out to do so.

Only this time the dead man was an outsider, so she wouldn't be able to help. It was up to Tom to make it right, to keep them safe. He pulled into a layby. He'd phone his mum; perhaps he could take her out for dinner. That ought to pacify at least some of the niggles.

"Mum, it's me. Do you fancy going somewhere tonight?"

"There's a nice pub over in Cadgwith. Is that far enough away?"

"Yes, yes, it is." Just by the way she breathed out he knew what was coming next.

"Shall I invite Anna?" she asked quietly.

"It's not like that," he said, knowing that he sounded the same as when she'd caught him snogging a girl in his bedroom. He'd been fifteen. It'd been horribly embarrassing for all of them. Tom couldn't remember the girl's name and he definitely hadn't gone out with her again. With Anna it was different. He really did like her. It was just that finding time for her was complicated.

"Let's talk tonight," his mum said. He knew she'd be feeling guilty about the comment. "I'll let Harriet know I won't be in for dinner."

Tom hung up and listened to the silence. Why was Anna so difficult? Why was telling his mum so hard? He supposed he'd spent an awfully long time watching his first marriage derail. Years really. Perhaps that was why he was so reluctant to waste time on something that might be doomed from the start. He dropped the phone into his lap and rubbed his eyes. He needed to concentrate. The body had been wrong. The fingers had been wrong. They'd looked broken, not scraped. He rang Sandra. She picked up on the second ring.

"Yes boss?"

"Anything more on our man in the sea?"

"Just a couple of things. I've got a complete list of kids contemporary with our boy Laurence. I'm running them through the computer."

"Are there a lot?"

"No, it wasn't a big home. Thirty when full, and it looks like it was winding down when Enderby worked there. In his last year there were only eighteen of them."

"What are you looking for, Sandra?"

"I won't know until I find it. Can I go ahead and have another trawl through?"

"Yes. Just one question. How long was Enderby there?"

"Nearly ten years. Laurence was there for three of them. Before that, Enderby worked for a home up in Bristol."

"Find out why he moved. See if there was any trouble in Bristol."

"Will do."

"And what he did after the home in Exeter."

"Where are you?"

He was still sitting in the layby thinking, but she didn't need to know that.

"I'm on my way back. I've got Georgie's statement, though she says she didn't see a thing. It's been a bit of a waste of time really."

"What's Georgie's full name?" Sandra asked. There was something in her voice. He bet she had something. He was almost tempted to put his light on and speed through the queues in Falmouth, now that there might be another link to rush back for. He hated proving Anna wrong, but it was his job. Anna would have to get used to it.

Chapter 15

Anna heard the front door open and close. It had just gone half past three. She peeked down the hallway. It was the girls, talking intently. She tried to hear what they were saying and then tried not to. They were animated at least. She looked down at her notebook still clutched in her hand. She'd written, 'We all need a good dose of manure to grow well. Yeah, we do, if we're a rose or a marrow! So should we welcome the hardships? Of course we should.' Then she'd thought of Derek and the first few months after Fiona's death. That had been terrible. No-one should have to go through that.

"But you didn't promise us a bed of roses; you just promised us life," she said quietly. Bugger, she was back to the roses again and no matter what anyone said, manure didn't smell sweet. She couldn't join it all up. Especially as Derek, who had been rescued, saved by Harriet, might have to face another trial if Harriet decided she needed more time.

Anna really hoped they'd be okay. What she wished for, what she longed for, was a happy ending. That brought her neatly back to Tom. Harriet had left her a note to say that Catherine wouldn't be in for dinner because Tom was taking her to the pub down the coast. Anna had tried to swallow her jealousy, but hadn't managed very well. She hadn't been able help it and so had had a bit of a wallow, allowing her feelings to hang around a little longer, until she'd begun to feel angry and scratchy. She'd have to tell Simeon that she knew just what he meant whenever he said he felt as if he was turned inside out.

She wasn't sure where Catherine was. She'd said she'd sit down in the church, but she hadn't been there earlier. Laurence was out with Simeon. Anna hoped that that wasn't proving a disaster, but just as she managed to stop worrying the rain began to fall. The sort of rain that meant business, when you couldn't see a beginning or an end to it. It would be awful walking back from Kynance. Perhaps she ought to go and pick them up? But then she'd promised to be around for Georgie and her work issues.

"Oh, blast!" Anna said loudly to the empty room. Why was it always so complicated? She decided to go and get the tea and cake for the four o'clock trough. She wished Harriet was around, if only for the company, but she'd disappeared after lunch to have another go at getting Derek organised for the move. Apparently, he was filling bags and then unpacking half of them again. Fiona's old recipe books, fat-spattered and dog-eared, had been put in a charity bag twice now, but both times had been retrieved. The second anniversary of Fiona's death was coming up and still it was Fiona making all the decisions. Poor Harriet, and oh dear, poor Derek.

Anna's phone rang. It was muffled in her jeans pocket. She scrabbled to pull it out. She never answered her phone calmly; it was always a race to get to it before it rang off.

"Hello Anna."

"Hello Tom."

"Can you talk?"

"Actually, I can, and I'm sorry about getting so cross this morning."

"About Laurence? Well, take a deep breath because I need to come back and talk again to another one of your guests."

"No!" Anna started to pray. What was going on?

"Georgie Harbrook. She was also at the home. Now, why didn't she tell me that? I definitely told her the possible name of the dead guy. At least Laurence admitted to knowing him, but they were both resident when Enderby worked there. So what is our Georgie hiding? Perhaps they're working together?"

"On what, Tom?" Anna replied, wearily.

Georgie and Laurence were too young, too fresh-faced for all this cloak-and-dagger stuff. Anna was beginning to long for Saturday morning, when they'd leave – jump into their battered cars and head for Helston. She had to squash the other thought that kept niggling away at her common sense – the thought that one of them by then might also have been arrested for murder. She straightened up. It was simply preposterous.

"Look, I took on board what you said about Mum, so I'm making time to take her out this evening."

Anna's jealousy flared and faded, as she felt the unkindness of it roar through her head.

"She'll love that."

He sighed.

"Except, Anna, she makes me feel as if I'm fifteen again and that she's still disappointed in me."

"I know," Anna said, thinking of her own mum. "It's like all we've done counts for nothing because we're just their kids and we still haven't managed to impress them at all."

"It was the divorce for me. I don't think she ever got past that."

"But I thought she didn't like ... your first wife." Anna hesitated using her name. She didn't want her to stand between them. The dog was easier. He'd been called Milo. Tom was still a bit cross that his wife had taken Milo when she'd packed up all her stuff.

"That doesn't mean a thing. A good son would've made a go of it."

"That's not fair. It takes two to tango and perhaps a different job ..."

He laughed.

"Are you saying I chose the wrong woman and the wrong career?"

Anna didn't know what she was saying. The door opened and Georgie stuck her head round. Anna waved her in.

"Got to go." She hung up.

"Come on in, Georgie. We'll take the trays through to the

dining room and then we'll go through to my sitting room where we won't be disturbed." It was time to use her inner sanctum. There was far too much danger of being overheard in the main lounge.

***

Georgie sipped her tea. The room was tiny; one small window looking onto a square of grass, edged with tall overgrown shrubs. It felt dark, even before the late afternoon dimness settled around them. Anna had left Catherine listening to Dani by the kettle, which Georgie hadn't felt was entirely fair on Catherine. There really ought to be two of them on duty at all times. Perhaps she'd add it to the feedback forms down on the hall table.

"I hope Laurence and Simeon get back soon. They'll be drenched by now," Anna said, looking over Georgie's shoulder.

"We got damp just running down to the church."

Anna smiled.

"Did you actually run? I haven't run anywhere for years. Too many wobbly bits."

"Actually, Dani surprised me. She was fast. Me, I don't think I can be bothered. God I'm tired." Georgie dropped her head onto her hands, squeezing her eyes shut.

"How long have you been like this?"

"The honest truth, forever. Even before saint Alf and all his boundless faith. The trouble is he has a good idea just about every day and one of us has to put it into action. He sends us long emails, says it's what God wants."

"Golly, Georgie, I don't think anyone can be that sure about what God wants. I think it's much more about muddling through."

"But that can't be right, can it? It's not what Alf says. He says that if we spend enough time praying, then we'll know and we'll get what we need. Only there isn't time to pray."

Anna's face wrinkled into a frown. She began to pick at the arm of the chair. *Crap*, thought Georgie, *she doesn't know what*

138

to say either.

"I don't think God is a slot machine, and I don't think we can earn answers to prayer by praying extra-long and with extra concentration." Anna paused and then looked straight at Georgie, as if to challenge her; only at the last minute her eyes slid sideways. "I think sometimes we ask the wrong questions or ask for the wrong things because it's all we can see. That having an answer to those questions or obtaining those things won't change anything. And God knows that."

"So, I simply hang out with him?!" Georgie was surprised at the anger blue-flaming her statement or question, whichever it was.

"I'm sorry Georgie, but yes. Unload and hang," Anna said. "Sorry if that sounds a bit rude or disrespectful. But we often drive prayer with our own needs. I'm not saying you shouldn't tell him what you want, what's going wrong, what you've been doing, but after that I think it's imperative to see where he wants to go with it all, where he wants to take you."

"But how? It sounds like you hear him really, really clearly. I can't hear him at all. I'm too tired, and I'm too ..."

Georgie started crying. She didn't want to, because the tears seemed to dredge up lots of other things she didn't want to think about, and running into Laurence had turned everything on its head. She felt bile churning in her stomach and swallowed it down. Yesterday had to stay buried if she wanted to survive this.

Anna handed her tissues and, after a little while, said quietly, "I don't hear God well at all. But I'm sure he loves me. Otherwise, what's the point?"

"But you're a vicar. Alf says he hears God all the time. Sometimes I pretend I do too."

"Sometimes I pretend that everything is alright as well, but most of the time, I'm simply running behind, clearing up after everyone."

"But surely that's not how we're supposed to live? We're

supposed to be victorious and at peace and light in the darkness." Georgie felt the words spinning across the top of her tongue. She found herself saying, "I don't ever want to go back. I want to stay here."

Anna shrugged, as if she didn't mind.

"Actually, the only person who was ever victorious was Jesus and if we get it right, it's only because God's cleared the way for us. Like I say, I muddle through, and I trust he'll do his thing because he loves me and because, patently, most of the time I won't have done my bit adequately."

Georgie wanted to wail. This wasn't what she'd been promised. It wasn't fair and there was such evil, such damaged, broken people in the world. Anna obviously didn't have a clue. Why would she, living here in her nice, comfy bubble?

"Look, Georgie, I know it's wet and cold, but wrap yourself up, take the tin of biscuits from the dining room and go and sit in the church. Let God do his thing and I'll waylay Dani so you get some time on your own. Dinner isn't until seven. You've got ages. Start from the fact that you're his beloved daughter. Nothing else matters."

It was pointless, but Anna looked so earnest. At least she hadn't told her not to worry, that everything was going to be alright because, from the age of thirteen, Georgie had known that simply wasn't the case.

**

From his kitchen window, Archie watched the rain – a dark, flat veil creeping over the point. Usually right about now he'd make a cup of tea and go and get on with something. Today he just waited. When the first wall of raindrops hit the window, he didn't flinch, even as the view was obscured and the droplets started to run together.

It was only when his back began to ping and twinge that he stretched. He wondered how to tackle the thoughts filling his head. Tuesday morning had been dreadful. It had made him feel all over the place, helpless. Watching Simeon withdraw under his hood had stretched him almost to breaking. Now Anna had told him that Simeon had gone for a walk with Laurence. She'd sounded pleased, as if it were some great breakthrough. But steps too far sent Simeon scurrying back to his blanket. After Tuesday Archie had half expected to have to go and dig him out from under it. This stretching of Simeon's character, this visiting of a country that Simeon didn't usually have a passport to was leaving Archie disconcerted.

He leaned on the sink to take the kink out of his back. He ought to go for a walk, but the rain sounded almost like hailstones, big drops of water driven by the wind, splatting against the glass. He went into the sitting room. Anna had the pink cushions now. He'd got some brown and grey ones that Harriet had said would suit the place better, would suit him better. He was sure they looked tasteful and you did need them on his chairs to counteract the slippery leather, but it felt as if they weren't his. Harriet had picked them out for him on one of her many trips to Truro or Falmouth when kitting out the vicarage. He should've gone and chosen something himself. The thought surprised him; it was ungrateful. Harriet had been doing him a kindness and he was being ridiculous. Here he was, worried about Simeon overreacting, and yet he was getting annoyed about cushions. What would Pearly say to such nonsense?

Pearly was preparing to go out to Africa to do important work for the diocese. Archie picked up the offending cushions and looked around. It did look better now. Spartan, the way he liked it, though of course he wouldn't sit down any time soon because the chairs would be too uncomfortable. He wandered into the dining room with its big mahogany table. He used it occasionally when everyone came round for shepherd's pie. Blast, Harriet would notice the disappearance of the cushions when they all got together. He'd have to put them back. But for now, this room would do for his reading. It felt less public and he could leave his books open when he'd had enough.

He worried about Simeon and Laurence; it was like a rough edge to his thoughts. How could the walk have gone well? Laurence wouldn't understand Simeon. It could take months to work him out. To distract himself, Archie went back into the hall to find the latest tome with his notes. Useful questions to ask Simeon when they next got together.

Usually, it was Thursday morning, but this week was gathering momentum and had left the usual way behind. Blast Laurence and the stupid body and Tom asking too many questions, just as everything was getting back to normal.

Archie found himself back in the kitchen watching the weather bowling in from the west. He switched on the kettle and waited for it to boil.

Chapter 16

Standing at the top of the stairs, Dani caught sight of Georgie slipping out the front door. Off somewhere else without telling anyone by the looks of it. That girl had more secrets than a ... Dani couldn't think of anything. She just knew this feeling of being left out, of being excluded. Everyone else knowing what was going on, except her. Georgie, for all her moaning, was on the 'inside', with Alf their vicar, with Laurence, even with Anna. They all seemed to speak the same language. Whenever Dani opened her mouth, there was a raised eyebrow, a slight drawing back, and she was sick to death of it. As if she were a joke, an aside to their lives that they were embarrassed by. The only person whose face lit up when she walked into the room was Selena's. Well, stuff them, stuff them all.

The front door crashed open. It was Laurence, dripping rather dramatically over everything. He was definitely going to catch something horrible, having been drenched two days in a row. He looked just like a drowned rat with his thin, pinched face. Dani waited for Anna to appear, waited for the outburst. She wasn't disappointed.

"Oh Laurence, get out of those wet things. You'll catch your death. You should have phoned for someone to come and get you."

There was a great deal of faffing about, which Dani watched with amusement, until a car alarm went off. It wailed, echoing between her ears. Laurence and Anna both jumped and then froze.

"It can't be mine; I don't think it works anymore," Anna said quickly. Catherine came out of the dining room and hurried upstairs, smiling at Dani as she passed.

"Just getting my keys in case it's mine," she said. "It has been known to do it at home." Then Harriet appeared from the kitchen.

"It's the white van." She spoke calmly, her arms folded across her chest. "I'm sorry to say it looks as if it's been broken into."

"That's mine," Laurence whispered.

Georgie had said that he was some sort of salesman or delivery driver and that he went all over Devon and Cornwall for an engineering company.

He plonked down heavily on the bottom stair. Dani squeezed past him and on into the dining room to get a cup of tea and a biscuit. There wasn't anything she could do and it was obvious Laurence was going to milk the situation for all it was worth. There was bound to be insurance so why was he making such a fuss?

Anna was asking Laurence where his car keys were. Harriet was phoning the police. Catherine must have come down the stairs because Anna was telling her not to worry as it wasn't her car.

"Did you see anyone?" Anna asked, Dani assumed, Harriet.

Dani didn't hear a reply and imagined Harriet either nodding or shaking her head. The dining room was dim and quiet, despite the mayhem in the hall. She listened with one ear as she pulled out a chair. Like everything else it didn't match. The table was large and rectangular, shiny dark wood with scratches and rings all over it. It was funny, but full of food, mats, and cutlery you didn't notice how battered it was. She rested her hand on the surface, which was cool under her fingertips. The light from the hall cast a shadow. Then the door widened and Catherine came in. She jumped when she saw Dani sitting alone in the dimness, Dani's thin shadow skating the length of the table.

"Dani! I thought I'd make Laurence something hot to drink. Are you alright?"

Dani looked up at her. Catherine reminded her a little bit of her mum, which made her think hard before she shook her head slowly. Catherine moved to the kettle, switched it on and then came and stood behind her. She rested a hand lightly on Dani's shoulder.

"Look, everyone is busy with Laurence. I expect the police will come and it's all going to get a bit messy again. So why don't you tell me what's up? I've got an hour before Tom picks me up. He's probably on his way already. I wonder if I ought to cancel our table?"

Dani could feel herself slipping down the priority list. One tiny notch at a time.

"I mean it. If you'd like to talk. I know we're not supposed to, but you seem troubled and I've got time."

A part of Dani wanted to crawl onto this woman's lap and tell her all about her mum and Selena, and Oscar and Jay, who were happily getting on with their lives. That, because it could have been either of them, neither had even hinted that they might help out. Dani had watched their friendship stretch and tear as each wondered which of them was in trouble. In trouble! It wasn't as if they'd committed a crime. They'd simply created a daughter. Yesterday had been horrible for her too, only no-one took any notice. Dani shivered.

Catherine's hand remained on her shoulder. It was held lightly and yet felt so heavy. Dani thought she'd probably tell her to get lost. Catherine didn't really care. No-one did, except about themselves.

"I think I'll go upstairs. No-one will miss me."

"Oh Dani. Of course we will," Catherine said. But when Dani got up, she didn't try to stop her.

The hall was empty. Dani imagined they'd all trooped out to the van, its alarm still wailing, its scratched and battered doors open to the world. It wasn't a new van; you could have broken into it with a toothpick. God, these people lived boring lives. Halfway up everything went quiet and for a minute Dani considered joining them, if only to find out what was going on.

The bedroom was cold, the radiators just about lukewarm. They'd begin to get hot as the evening progressed, but far too late for the room to warm up properly. Dani sat down on her bed, then slipped under the covers. She bet the policeman didn't know that Laurence and Georgie knew each other – knew each other well. Dani curled into a ball and shut her eyes. The pillow was lumpy, but at least the windows weren't rattling like they had been through the night.

She awoke to a gentle tapping on the door.

"Georgie, are you there?"

Dani flung back the duvet and swung her legs onto the floor.

"Come in."

"Oh, thank goodness." Laurence entered, but when he saw Dani, his face sort of collapsed. He still hadn't changed his clothes. His trousers below the knees were dark with rain and his short, flat hair sparkled in the light.

"She's off somewhere. I don't know where. But if you want someone to talk to, I'm not that busy."

He shook his head. A little too quickly for her liking.

"No, you're alright. Where do you think she's gone?"

"I really don't know." And she couldn't care less. "But she told me about growing up."

That brought him up short. He grimaced, then sort of shivered.

"It's not a secret. It's just that, if you tell people, they get all funny about us." But she could tell he was cross with Georgie for blabbing. He began to back out.

"So, what was stolen?"

"Nothing that I could see. I didn't have much in there, to be honest."

And he sort of smiled. *Liar*, she thought.

She said, "Make sure you shut the door properly. It's too frigging cold in here as it is."

***

Harriet leaned over the sink and breathed. She felt sick. She'd been washing up when the alarm split the air. It was dark outside, so she'd grabbed a torch, hadn't thought about safety, not to begin with, because she'd assumed it had been the wind gusting a little hard or a loose wire. She'd had an old mini that used to go off randomly at any time of the day or night. In the end she'd taken to leaving it unlocked to stop the neighbours complaining. The vicarage cars were parked off to the side behind a row of shrubs. She couldn't see them from the back door, had to walk to the corner of the house. There was Anna's elderly Fabia, Catherine's Polo, Georgie's Fiesta and Laurence's van. Not a big van, a small one. The back doors were open and one of the hazards was flashing half-heartedly. She didn't go any closer as by then she'd realised there were far too many places for someone to hide. She'd flashed her torch around and then hurried back inside.

Laurence had driven in late on Monday afternoon and, as far as she knew, hadn't been out since, so who would've known there was a van parked here? There was some random crime on the Lizard, a bit of vandalism when the kids had too much to drink, the odd burglary. But to get to the van, someone would've had to walk around the outside of the vicarage, looking for the row of cars. None of them looked worth breaking into; particularly the van, which was battered and anonymous, though Laurence said it actually belonged to the company.

When Harriet came through to tell the others, they were standing around in the hall staring at one another. Harriet could see that Anna was beginning to panic, so she knew she had to keep a lid on it. She phoned Tom. He didn't pick up, but she knew he checked his messages regularly so it wouldn't be long before he got back to them. Everyone else trooped out to inspect the damage. Laurence switched off the alarm and peered into the back. He leaned in and rummaged around a bit until Anna pulled him away. He shrugged and they all trooped back to the kitchen. Harriet closed the back door and began tending to the potatoes and the chilli, wondering if they'd manage dinner at the usual time. She began to shake. Just a gentle tremor and then she began to feel hot and light-headed. She ran the cold tap and put her wrists underneath. The water was too cold, so she simply leaned over the sink, her hair falling around her face. She reached for her phone.

"Derek?"

"Hey sweetie." There was the tiniest hesitation. "Are you alright?"

"No, I'm not. One of the cars has been broken into and to be honest I'm feeling a bit—"

"I'm on my way. I'll be down in half a moment. Stay where you are and lock the doors."

He should've at least waited for her to finish her sentence. She might not have wanted him to come down. She might've just wanted to tell him about it. She stared at her reflection in the kitchen window. There were no blinds, no curtains, but of course, with the kitchen light on, you couldn't see beyond the shiny darkness. Suddenly she didn't feel safe anymore, even here. She needed the others. As she passed the back door, she turned the key.

The lounge was quiet. Dani and Georgie were missing and Laurence, Catherine and Anna were sitting rather disconsolately, staring into their mugs. The bottom of Laurence's trousers were still damp from his walk with Simeon, but the rest of him seemed to be dry.

"I've left a message for Tom," Harriet said and perched on the arm of the sofa that Anna was curled up on.

"So have I," Anna said and raised her eyebrows.

"Me too," Catherine added, biting her lip. "It seems too much of a coincidence. Anna said you don't get that much crime around here."

"Not lately," Anna replied, smiling grimly. She looked as if

148

she were going to cry. "This retreat is a disaster. I wish we'd never started it ..." She looked up guiltily at Catherine.

Harriet patted her shoulder, hoping she'd hold it together. This was a speed bump, not a brick wall. They needed to keep going. They could do some real good. Harriet was surprised how much she believed that, how important it was to her.

"So how was the walk, Laurence?" she asked.

He almost jumped and then caught himself.

"Good, apart from the last bit in the rain."

"It's an amazing place."

"It is," he said.

Anna looked bewildered, as if such conversation was impossible. Harriet squeezed her shoulder gently.

"Where are the girls?" Harriet asked.

"Georgie's sitting down in church."

"Dani has gone up to her room. She's not getting on so well," Catherine said quietly. Laurence began to fidget.

"How long before the police get here?" he asked.

"At least another thirty minutes, I would've thought," Anna said.

All their phones buzzed at the same time.

"Ten minutes," said Harriet, the first one to get hers out.

"Could I go and find some dry clothes, do you think?" Laurence asked.

Anna nodded.

"I don't suppose there's any point me getting changed," Catherine said. "Will there be enough for me to have dinner here?"

"Absolutely," Harriet said brightly. This was something she was always prepared for, extra people at mealtimes. They all jumped when the front door vibrated with a couple of very loud knocks.

"That'll be Derek, I expect. Sorry, I phoned him, and he didn't give me much of a chance to say not to come."

Anna turned round and peered up at her, searching for

clues as to how to react. Harriet blinked, not quite knowing what she'd like her face to portray.

It was Derek. He engulfed her in a hug that almost lifted her off her feet.

"Are you alright?" he asked, holding her away from him as if she were a small child.

"I'm fine. It just made me jump. There was absolutely no reason for you to come down."

"Do you want me to go away?"

"No, but you'll have to eat your tea in the kitchen. There isn't enough room around the table."

"Is Tom coming?"

"He should be here soon. I don't suppose you saw anyone as you came down the lane?"

"No, but there was a car heading up onto the main road as I came out of the bungalow. I only saw its brake lights. It could've been anyone. Are you sure you're alright?"

"Yes, I am. Come on through to the kitchen and you can help me prepare dinner." They both heard the car on the gravel outside.

"Tom," Derek said firmly. Harriet breathed.

***

Tom climbed out of the car. Harriet opened the front door, Derek standing just behind her.

"Hiya, you two. Where's the van?"

"Parked up with the other cars around the side."

"I don't suppose anyone saw anything?"

Harriet recounted the events, even mentioning the fact that Derek had seen a car leaving, but hadn't seen it clearly enough to get any details. *Clever girl*, thought Tom.

"I'll go and have a quick look. Don't let anyone disappear, will you?"

"I'll stay too," Tom heard Derek say as he walked around the corner. The outside light was on, but it was beginning to rain again. He had a quick look around the cars and then checked around the back garden and then along the drive. Sadly, it was all long grass and gravel, not a decent shoe print to be seen anywhere.

He gave Sandra a call and told her to organise forensics and that, if she didn't have anything better to do, she could come and supervise while he had a chat with the residents. He swung round when he heard the crunch of feet on gravel. It was Anna, her big old coat loosely draped around her shoulders.

"Hey you," he said. "Is everyone alright?"

"Harriet was a bit shocked. It's why Derek is here. Laurence said that nothing was taken, but there was something in the way that he said it."

"You didn't believe him?"

She kept her eyes round about his knees as she shook her head. He stepped forward and wrapped his arms around her. Something he'd been meaning to do for a while. For a second, she stiffened and then rested her head on his jacket.

"This is not going at all well, is it?" he said.

"No," she mumbled into his shoulder. "It's probably the worst retreat in the whole history of the church, and now you'll have to talk to everyone again, and dinner will be late, and your mum will be disappointed and ..."

He squeezed her a little tighter.

"Now, where is God in all this?" he asked. Anna looked up at him, blinking back tears. She clearly hadn't expected him to say anything like this. "I mean, what do you think he wants you to do?" He hoped that she'd see he was trying to be helpful, that he was trying to understand how important it all was.

Harriet appeared round the corner, saw them and began to retreat. But Anna was already looking over her shoulder, pulling away.

"Don't worry," he said. "It's only Harriet."

"But you're on duty. It's not professional."

151

"Well, actually I'm here to take my mum out."

"Except you won't now, will you?"

"No, I don't suppose I will." He put his hands in his pocket to find his notebook. "And while you guys are eating, could I use the lounge to speak to Laurence and Georgie?"

"Use my sitting room. It means we're a bit more flexible. Do you want me to sit in?"

"No, you're alright. Sandra's on her way."

She nodded because she was way beyond trying to protect them all now.

"They'll still be informal chats, nothing more." he said, trying to reassure her.

"I'll go and make you some tea. Or would you like a plate of something? Don't worry, it's Harriet's cooking, not mine."

"Perhaps when it's all done. If there's enough you could save me some. Now I suppose I'd better go and face Mum."

She went ahead of him, pulling her coat around her, her small hands gripping the fabric tightly. So tightly the fingertips were blanched white. In the kitchen she looked around her as if she'd never been there before. He wanted to hold her again. He could see she was really struggling and he didn't blame her.

"Can you gather everyone in the lounge?" he asked Harriet, who'd begun to pile things onto a tray.

"Georgie and Dani too?" she asked.

Tom straightened up.

"Where are they?"

"I think your mum said that Dani was upstairs and I sent Georgie down to the church," Anna replied. "So she wasn't around when it all kicked off."

"It's literally on the other side of the hedge. You'd have thought she'd have heard the alarm," Tom said. "Is she on her own?" He began to back out of the kitchen. "Stay here," he called over his shoulder. Derek was standing by the front door as if guarding it. Tom grabbed his arm as he slipped past.

"Just in case, stay up here, will you, and the others too. You don't want any more bad memories."

Chapter 17

Tom was out of breath when he got to the gate. The lights were on in the church, but the door was closed, the churchyard in darkness. He shone his torch along the path, behind the tombs. He couldn't see anything. His heart was thumping as if it were an old grandfather clock building up to chime. Anna arrived behind him. He wondered if she'd ever do as she was told.

"Please stay here," he hissed. She of course shook her head. He sighed and turned back to the darkened porch. He tried the door. It was locked. He rattled it.

"Georgie, it's Tom Edwards, the DI. We spoke earlier. Are you alright?"

"How do we know it's you?" a muffled voice shouted.

"Who else is in there?" Tom asked.

"Simeon. Only he's not feeling very well. He got scared when the men came down looking for the vicarage. He's locked us in."

Anna took her key from her pocket.

"Not just a pretty face," Tom muttered. "Stand back from the door. We're coming in."

"Why on earth did Simeon lock them in, Tom?" He shrugged.

The door opened, but got stuck on the stones. Anna automatically leaned against it. *Surely*, Tom thought, *they should be able to get a bit shaved off the bottom.*

Georgie was standing behind the font. She looked really frightened.

"Simeon's over there. He's very upset."

"What happened?" Anna asked.

Tom shrugged. There wasn't much point telling her to be quiet at this stage.

"I was in here, trying to pray, as you said I should, when Simeon came running in. He said we needed to be safe and

155

locked the door. Then I heard the car alarm, and he said we should stay where we were."

Tom began to move towards Simeon, but Anna put a hand on his arm.

Simeon was sitting in his usual pew, just in front of the old bell, one of the blankets from the back draped over him. He was rocking slowly backwards and forwards.

"Tom, get hold of Archie, will you. We're going to need him." She walked to the end of the pew and perched on the edge. "Simeon. It's me, Anna. Anna and Tom and no-one else. You're perfectly safe now."

Tom walked out into the churchyard to try and get a signal. When he returned, Simeon was continuing to rock but perhaps a little more slowly.

Tom asked, "Simeon, what happened?"

Anna narrowed her eyes.

"It's alright, Simeon. Tom will take Georgie back to the vicarage and I'll wait here with you until Archie arrives."

Tom nodded. With Simeon, Anna often knew best. As he passed her, he whispered, "Find out what you can. I have a feeling we need to be moving swiftly on this one."

***

"So, Georgie," Tom said, leading the girl from the church and shining his torch along the path, though the light from the open door gave them more than enough to see by, "Did Simeon say anything else?"

"Just that the church was the safest place and that no-one was going to kick that door down."

"Had you met Simeon before?"

"Only at lunch, but Laurence seemed to think he was an OK bloke. So, when he said we needed to lock the door, it never occurred to me that it wasn't a good idea. I was a bit freaked out when he said he needed darkness and put the blanket over his head. He said that normally he'd go into the tower, but he'd sit where I could see him, just in case. Before you ask, I didn't ask, 'just in case of what?' Then he began to rock. I've known kids do that, when they needed a reboot and I know not to ask anything of them until they're ready."

"Back at the home?"

Georgie hesitated for a second and then said, "I wondered when you'd work that one out." She frowned. "Me and Laurence do know each other from back then, but I've only seen him a few times since I left."

"And was Bob Enderby still there when you were at the home?"

She kept walking.

"Bob? Golly, there's a blast from the past. I haven't seen him for a long time."

"I want a statement, Miss Harbrook. Particularly why you decided not to tell us about your shared history."

"That's easy. I never do unless I can help it. Too much pity, too many knowing looks."

As they rounded the end of the drive, Tom was pleased to see another couple of police cars parked in front of the vicarage and that it was Sandra who opened the door.

"Forensics are checking out the van for fingerprints. I've kept everyone in the lounge. What else do you want me to do?"

"We'll interview Miss Harbrook first, then Mr Weller. Hopefully by then Anna will have something for me from Simeon. I don't expect we'll be able to do a one-to-one with him until tomorrow."

Harriet had obviously been hovering; she appeared from the lounge.

"Tom, please can I serve dinner? The potatoes are already looking a little past their best."

"I guess." Then he added, "Keep some warm for Miss Harbrook and serve Mr Weller first because he's next."

"And Anna? Where is Anna?" She sounded worried.

"Down at the church, waiting for Archie. Simeon's got

himself into a tizz and Anna's hoping that Archie will be able to sort him out. I've left him a message."

"Archie went home to get some rest; he might not have heard the phone. I think it'd be best if we sent Derek to fetch him, if that's alright."

"Actually, Harriet, that would be great. I'd really like Anna about the place as soon as possible."

Harriet smiled, her annoying 'I know all about that' smile, and turned away. Quickly swivelling back, she said, "I'm assuming you'll be using Anna's sitting room for the interviews. I've had a bit of a tidy up, so it's all ready for you."

"You'd make a good copper, Harriet, if you ever want me to put in a good word."

She laughed.

"Not if it means running round after you." She turned to Sandra, who was looking a little bemused, and said, "I think you're an absolute saint!"

Sandra had the grace to shut down the smile that had begun to stretch her mouth and simply nodded. Tom thought Sandra was a woman who would go far.

"A quiet word, boss," she said, once Harriet was safely out of earshot. She quickly ran through the names she'd checked out from the children's home. Of the forty or so kids that had come through there in the ten years that Bob Enderby had been helping out, fifteen of them had been done for dealing in some way or another. Two of them had died of overdoses. Two had simply disappeared.

"Oh damn," Tom breathed. If it was drugs, then it could get messy and very, very nasty.

***

Once Tom and Georgie had left the church, it felt unaccountably empty, even though Anna was there. She was standing at the end of the pew. Then she sat down across the way from him.

"I'm here," she said. "I'll stay until Archie comes."

He remembered another time she'd sat in the church, when she'd thought no-one was listening and, in a fit of despair, had howled in anguish. Not one of his favourite memories. It made him shudder. He heard her stand up and walk to the back.

"I've got a blanket too now. It's a little chilly to sit in here without one. Would you like a drink? That would keep us both warm."

"There isn't any milk." His voice was muffled.

"I must remember to bring some down tomorrow. No point for Evening Prayer as we'll all be going back for hot chocolate." There was a little more silence.

"I hope Archie isn't too long," Simeon said, still from beneath his blanket. "Belle is alone in the house. She'll wonder where I am."

"What scared you, Simeon?" Anna asked quietly.

"I don't want to talk about it."

"You need only tell me and obviously Tom will need to know what happened."

He nodded and sat a little straighter.

"Are you feeling better?"

"Why have I got to tell you? Why can't I just tell Tom?"

"You know you don't have to tell me anything. But I thought it might help you remember everything."

"I won't forget. You know I have a good memory for detail."

"Yes, you do. But you may not realise that something is important and this gives us two goes to hear what you've got to say."

"It's like you're the police too."

"Oh no," Anna exclaimed, making him jump. "Sorry, Simeon, but my heart is far too soft to be a policewoman."

He nodded and then wondered if she could see him moving as he was still under the blanket.

"So, what happened?"

159

"I was coming over to the church when a dark SUV drew up. I'll let Tom have the make and model. There were two men inside. The one nearest me asked if I knew where the retreat was being held. I said I did know, but that I didn't think I should tell them."

"Why didn't you want to tell them?"

"They were strangers and the man's fingers were drumming on the inside of the car."

"How did you know there were two of them?"

"The driver said, 'Oh, for God's sake', and the one on the far side said, 'Calm down'. I couldn't see what they looked like; they stayed flat against their seats and only opened the window about twenty centimetres."

"That sounds a bit sinister. What happened then? Why did you come down to the church?"

Simeon came out from under the blanket.

"Your hair's all sticking out. You look as if you've only just woken up."

Sometimes Anna could get side-tracked, so Simeon spoke firmly.

"Because as I was backing away, the man on the far side said, 'Well, we can find out where he lives.' And they reversed back up the lane very fast."

"And you came down to the church because the door is thick and, when locked, would be almost impossible to batter down, whereas at home ..."

Simeon nodded.

"So Georgie was simply collateral."

"Except that if these men were looking for Laurence, then they might also know about Georgie."

"Why would they be looking for Laurence? What has he told you?" But these questions were far too big for Simeon to answer just now. Laurence had told Simeon lots of things, but some of them Laurence had asked him to keep to himself. He glanced quickly at Anna and shook his head.

"Did he tell you anything about the man who drowned?" she persisted.

"That there was only one man he'd ever really trusted, which was why yesterday was so difficult. I only asked him about Georgie. I should've asked him more about the dead man, but it felt like I'd used up all my questions."

Anna said, "I'm sure you've done brilliantly. You've stopped trembling. That's good, isn't it?"

He nodded. He did feel calmer.

"I don't suppose you managed to get the number plate."

"No, the headlights were blinding and they reversed really quickly."

Anna shivered. Simeon pulled the blanket from off his shoulders and looked at her. He wondered if she was cold or scared.

"Shall we go up to the vicarage?" he asked.

"What about Archie?"

"We can ring him."

"Let's do that. Poor man. Today must have been exhausting for him."

"For everyone," Simeon said. "Tom has driven here and back and back again."

"Yes. I never thought of that." She bit her lip, which, Simeon had noticed, was often a sign that she was worried. "I don't think that car will come back again tonight as there are police in the drive now."

He took a deep breath and stood up. His knees felt a little weak, but seemed to strengthen the more he thought about getting to the vicarage. But then he remembered that Belle was at home on her own. Would those men go there while he was with the others and harm her? Like Terry had tried to do with Dolly? He'd not thought of that.

"Anna, I've left Belle at home. I need to go and get her, but I don't think I can go on my own."

She nodded. She understood.

"What we need is a useful policewoman to come with us, someone like Sandra. She's up at the house supervising the van. Let's go and see if she can help."

Simeon wondered why she hadn't suggested asking Tom. He liked dogs; he'd understand too.

Chapter 18

Laurence sat staring at his plate. Georgie had followed the police officer into the back room where the vicar lived. She'd looked pale, her lips squashed together. He'd forgotten how stubborn she could be. She'd only tell them the minimum, perhaps not even that. He remembered a long time ago listening to the house mother interviewing her about a fight. Georgie had been the new girl back then. Two of the home bullies had had a showdown over a doughnut, and she'd witnessed the whole thing. She'd been grilled for ages, but even when she'd been threatened with the loss of TV privileges, she'd kept quiet. Afterwards, the boys had treated her as if she were on their team. Laurence wondered how tricky it would've been, walking a line between two fawning hard men in the making!

Of course he'd not really seen her since she'd got religion. Something she'd tried to explain when they'd had coffee. He hadn't understood, but it did seem to have turned her life around. Who would've thought she'd go off to get a degree? He was pleased for her if not a little jealous.

And what could he tell the police officer? That he'd spoken to Georgie on Tuesday morning? That she'd got really angry about Bob and his problems? Had even accused Bob of using the kids from the home? But Laurence hadn't wanted to admit that she was right. He'd always thought of Bob as one of the good guys. She'd left him feeling deeply disconcerted.

So, what with Georgie yelling at him and now – making matters worse – someone breaking into his van, it all left a rather nasty question hanging in the air. He'd really, really love to know what Georgie was telling the copper.

"Hey Laurence, do you want some more potatoes?" Dani, who was sitting next to him, spoke quietly so the rest of them wouldn't hear her over the clatter of cutlery and the noise of Catherine and the home team all trying their best to make it sound as if everything was alright. He looked down at his plate. He'd been pushing the food around for quite a while now and he certainly didn't need any more.

"No thanks, Dani. I'm just not hungry."

"Oh, so you do remember me then?"

He looked up at her sharply.

"Sorry, Dani, I'm not sure ..."

She scowled and looked along the table. To start with, Simeon had been sat on Laurence's other side, but he hadn't been able to cope, so he'd gone to eat his food in the kitchen with Belle.

Dani took another mouthful and then said, very quietly again, "I was out with Georgie and we bumped into you."

He remembered the evening. The time when Georgie had been with a whole gaggle of friends. Six-formers having a girls' night out. He'd enjoyed an hour when he'd been the centre of attention. Georgie had had long, straight hair and too much eye shadow back then. She'd flirted with him, but then so had all her friends and, while flattered, he'd felt more like a big brother on that occasion. Though one of them had said goodbye a little enthusiastically. He'd quickly stepped away. It would've been cradle snatching. Not something he'd been tempted by.

"You were part of the posse I met in the Dragon Cellar?"

She nodded and smiled.

"I knew you wouldn't have forgotten."

He tried another mouthful. This time he was able to swallow. It made him realise how hungry he was after all. He took another large bite just as the policewoman came through to get him. Georgie hadn't come back in. He hoped she was alright.

Anna got up and followed them into the hall. She was like a mother hen, which ought to make him feel comforted, but in fact irritated him. He needed someone who'd fight for him with claws and teeth, not a person who'd fluff up her feathers

164

and cluck.

"Where's Georgie, Sandra?" Anna seemed to be on first name terms with all the coppers.

"She's gone upstairs. Said she needed a lie down."

"What about her dinner?" The young PC looked nonplussed.

"Perhaps make her up a plate and keep it warm?"

Anna must have realised that it wasn't the policewoman's problem. She muttered 'sorry' under her breath and walked back into the dining room. The PC then nodded at Laurence and led him down the hall into the small room at the back, where the real boss was waiting for them.

"Hello Laurence. How's your day been? Feeling a little better?"

Laurence managed to nod. The DI indicated one of the easy chairs. The PC sat at the small gateleg table and took out a notebook.

"This is only an informal interview," the DI said. "We're just checking timelines and facts. Alright? Would you like anyone to sit with you? Anna or Mr Wainwright? Archie Wainwright?"

Laurence was tempted to ask if he could have Simeon, but he probably wouldn't be up to it. He'd been seriously frightened down in the church.

"Ok, so – Robert Enderby. How do you know him?"

"From the children's home. And we went for a pint a couple of times. But not recently."

"How do you think he died?"

Laurence had thought about how to answer this.

"I think he probably slipped."

The DI nodded, but his face remained impassive, his eyes cold.

"Did he do much walking, much birdwatching?"

"I wouldn't know."

"So he never went off with a pair of binoculars around his

neck, never spoke to you about the local flora and fauna?"

"Not that I can remember."

"Back at the home, did you like him?"

Before he could stop himself, before he could consider the implications, he nodded vigorously.

"Would it surprise you that Georgie didn't?"

"Georgie didn't know him that well."

"Ok, so you knew him better than she did?" He'd walked into that one.

"We probably talked more. I was older, remember."

"Old enough to go for a drink with him?"

Laurence nodded.

"Do you think he had any enemies?"

"No," Laurence said, just a second too quickly. He hoped the DI wouldn't notice. "Not that I know of," he added.

"So, do you go birdwatching?"

"Me? No!"

"Do you own a pair of Nikon binoculars?"

"No."

"Robert Enderby had a case for a pair stuffed in his pocket."

"I don't know anything about that. I never saw him with anything like binoculars."

"Any reason why they might have ended up under your van?"

Laurence stopped breathing. His mind went blank. He'd read of people freezing like that, but had not thought it actually possible. At that moment, if someone'd asked him what day of the week it was, he would've said he didn't know. What the hell were Bob's binoculars doing under his van?

"Hang on, I thought you said they were stuffed in his pocket?"

"No, the case was stuffed in his pocket."

Laurence began to feel hot and a little sweaty. Neither the DI nor the PC looked quite so sympathetic anymore.

166

"So, let's go back through your movements Tuesday morning. At what point did you realise Miss Harbrook was walking behind you?"

"Not until we were nearly at the Lizard." He felt a little guilty at that. Georgie had said that she'd called out quite a few times, but he genuinely hadn't heard her.

"Why did you pretend you didn't know each other?"

"It's what kids from the homes do."

"I've not heard that before."

Laurence dropped his face into his hands.

"It's what some of us do. We aren't ignoring each other; we simply look for an opportunity to talk without anyone else listening. It's what Georgie and I've always done. Privacy was the most precious thing in the home, and it was rare. Really rare." He looked up for a minute, his eyes moist. He wouldn't cry in front of this man. He'd gone way too far to do anything so weak. "Georgie had it tough on the moor. We both did. We spent a lot of time together in the basement near the bins. It was warm but smelly, so no-one else fancied it. It's where we could chat and read and dream a little." He shrugged.

No-one really got what being in a home was like unless they'd been a kid in care themselves. Laurence wanted to scream the next sentence, but he just about managed to speak without everything cracking open.

"I trusted Bob. He looked out for both of us."

"And yet Georgie didn't like him at all. Why do you think that was?"

"She was a lot younger."

"How did he contact you after you'd left the home?"

"I bumped into him in the street."

"By accident?"

"Yes, by accident." At least that was what he'd thought up 'til the last few days.

"Forensics will go over the binoculars with a fine toothcomb, so is there anything else you'd like to add?"

Laurence thought very hard. Someone had put the binoculars under his van. Was it Bob's drug contacts, letting Laurence know that they knew where he was? Was this the moment to dob them in, to tell the whole story? You saw it on the television all the time, the police promising protection. It never ended well and they'd managed to find him, even down here, or Bob had found him. Bob was the only person Laurence had told about the retreat.

"I feel really sick," he said, leaning forward. The room felt stuffy; if he opened his eyes, he wouldn't have been one bit surprised to see it spinning. The copper pulled him up and walked him through to the kitchen, out the back door. Simeon was sitting at the table. He stiffened, but didn't look up.

"Deep breaths, lad."

The back garden was a square of lawn surrounded by tall shrubs. Through the leaves Laurence could see the white brightness of the arc lamps around his van and then they went off. The darkness was sudden and profound. Laurence dropped into a crouch.

"It's alright. They're just shutting up shop until the morning. Goodness, you really are a jumpy sod." The DI led him back into the house.

***

Simeon sat in the kitchen, waiting for Harriet to come back through with some of the crockery. It was nice in the kitchen, very quiet except for when Tom had taken Laurence into the garden for a few minutes. Derek had left because seeing Belle had reminded him that he'd left Dolly alone for quite a while. Simeon had been very hungry. Normally, when he was eating, Belle had to go and sit in her basket, but they weren't at home, so she hadn't been sure what to do. He'd tried to ignore her head on his knee. In the end he'd told her to lie down, which she did, but then he missed the weight of her.

Georgie and Laurence must have talked together by now, so even if they were totally innocent, they could have

168

collaborated on a story to cover up their past. All Simeon really knew was that, when he'd come back from Archie's on the Tuesday morning at about eleven forty-five, Laurence had been on his own down below, trying to retrieve the body. It'd actually been eleven forty-seven. Everyone kept saying Enderby had slipped from the cliff, but Simeon thought he could just as easily have been pushed. There was a stretch of path with no edge and, before that, a shorter section just under the old café where there was a concrete wall no more than a foot high. The drop there was sheer, about a hundred feet down onto the very bottom of the ramp that led to the old lifeboat station. The sea had been at its highest, so it could easily have washed the body into deeper water and then left it sprawled across the supports before the tide turned. The man couldn't have gone over much later than when Simeon had passed him because half an hour after that, the water would've been lower down the beach and the body would've lain where it landed. But it couldn't have been right after he'd passed either because then Laurence and Georgie would've seen Enderby go over and they would surely have raised the alarm.

It had been a horrid day, squally rain forecast all through the morning, so there hadn't been anyone else around. It worried Simeon that Laurence and Georgie may have seen the man slip and had done nothing about it. Perhaps that was why Laurence was so upset, that he regretted not sounding the alarm. But on their walk that afternoon, he'd said how much he'd trusted Enderby, so why wouldn't he have rung 999 straight away? Simeon was also fairly sure that Laurence had known that the body he'd tried to rescue had been the former care worker from the home. But he wasn't sure why that was important.

Simeon yawned and decided that he'd like to go to bed. The only problem was that the men had said they knew how to find him. What did he have that they needed? What had he seen that they were worried about?

He'd seen the large, dark car on the morning of the drowning. And there'd been the other figure who'd appeared at the bottom of the road just before he'd turned away. If only he'd spent another couple of moments looking back, he might have been able to see who it was and what had happened. Tom had bitten his lip when he'd told him all that he'd seen. It was the same sort of face that Anna made whenever she was disappointed in him.

The door opened and Archie and Harriet came through. Archie looked wrinkly and tired.

"I've spoken to Anna," he said, "and we've come up with some options for you. I need an early night, so I can either come and bunk down at your place or you can come to stay with me. But I want to get going as soon as possible." He blinked and his shoulders slumped. "Golly, this has been an exhausting day."

Simeon knew what he'd like to do. He'd like to go home and feel safe, but he didn't think that was an option. He did have a spare bedroom, but it was tiny. What if Archie breathed heavily or was restless or, even worse, snored? He hated wearing ear plugs because it muffled his own breathing. So there was really no choice.

"I'd like to come and stay at your house. But we need to collect a few things from my house, so that Belle will have something to eat and somewhere to sleep."

"Anna said she'd drive us. She's waiting in the hall."

Simeon was relieved it was Anna. He wouldn't have refused anyone else, but she made it easier to contemplate what he was about to do. He decided that life was a series of choices and often you simply had to pick the one that was least difficult.

**

Once Simeon had picked up Belle's bed, some food for her and an overnight bag for himself, he sat silently in the back of the car. Archie tried to chat, but he was too tired. Anna patted his arm and he dropped his head back onto the seat rest and yawned. He didn't ask her to come in. She wouldn't have, anyway. Everyone was beyond and out the other side of weary.

She backed the car out of the drive, but didn't pull away until some of the lights came on. That was Archie and Simeon safely tucked up, tick. As she passed the pub, someone came out, the door spewing soft light across the green. She braked to give the man time to cross in front of her. It looked like Steve Parsons from the estate behind Terry's house.

She didn't know how long she sat staring at the way her headlights stretched across the village. She was blocking the lane down to Archie's, but was in no danger of holding anyone up. Apart from Steve making his way home, there was no-one else around. For a moment it crossed her mind that the men might come back, but Tom had said they wouldn't hang around in a place where everyone took note of anything out of the ordinary. She slipped the car into gear and found herself turning down towards the Lizard. She simply didn't want to go back to the vicarage. It was too full of people. Even Derek had reappeared, ostensibly to help with the clearing up, but actually to walk Harriet home. Anna reckoned she had an hour before she was due to say Evening Prayer, so there was no hurry.

The lane narrowed dramatically in the last fifty metres or so, but at this time of night she wasn't worried. She passed the entrance to the car park, the point of no return, and carried on down to the Lizard. As she pulled into the turning space, the rain began to clear and stars sparkled at the edge of the sea. She climbed out and walked down past the café. It looked a bit shabby in the monochrome of night.

Below her to the right, she could just make out the shape of the old lifeboat station in the arc of cliffs and rock, dark, heaving water and the ever-present wind, which just now was no more than a gentle breath on her face. Her phone buzzed. It was Tom.

"Where are you?"

She texted back, "At the Lizard. The house is too full."

"Are you alright?"

"Yes. Actually, it's lovely. Sorry I should be there with you, making sure everyone is alright."

"I'm just about done. Can I join you?"

She nearly texted 'It's a free country', but then she simply sent, "Yes."

She got quite cold waiting and nearly went back to sit in the car, but she wanted to be standing out in the air when he came. She stared down at the boat house for quite a long time until she realised how creepy it was – how shadows moved and became figures, how rocks became people splashing and sinking. So she moved across to stare eastwards, where the sky was open and the waves came in cleanly, just a little frilly around the edge. She was tired, so tired that, when his car swung round to park next to hers, she could hardly drag her eyes away from the view. *Stupid girl*, she thought. She should have spent the time praying, asking God what she should do about Tom because after this afternoon, when he'd folded his arms around her, she'd felt she was beginning to make a decision. But she needed God to give his blessing.

Tom came and stood beside her.

"It is lovely," he said.

"And for a minute, it's just for us."

"But you can have this any time you want, can't you?"

"I suppose," she replied, "but we don't always notice or seek out the things around us. The things that do us good."

"Or the things within us. There's beauty within you, Anna. Though I don't expect you to believe that."

For a minute she was sad that he hadn't said that she was beautiful, but then she realised that he was seeing her or thought he was really seeing her – and she was simply

172

profoundly grateful that he was looking at all.

"I don't know what that means unless it's the God bit of me. Because the Anna bit is such a mess."

"Less so than you think. But perhaps it is the God bit of you, and I know how important that is to you. Not something that I could compete with. What I mean is, I would never ask you to choose one way or the other. I wouldn't be that stupid or self-centred."

He leaned forward and tucked her hair behind her ear.

"So what should we do?" she asked. He hesitated.

"I've often thought about leaving you alone, not ringing, not letting you down again, but when I got the call about the body, God forgive me, my stupid heart skipped a beat because I knew I'd see you."

Anna turned to look up at him, her eyes wide with surprise.

"How can you feel like that about me? I'm not pretty or clever. I'm plump and lazy—"

"And you read unsuitable books and you care and speak without thinking through the consequences and you grabbed a woman tightly in a moment of madness to stop her falling over a cliff when anyone else I know would've tried to push her away. Anna, you're a remarkable woman and I don't want to leave here knowing you won't welcome me back."

Anna looked away to stare out over the waves. That was quite a speech, though she was sure she wouldn't remember it properly the next morning. The moon was behind them, nearly full and shedding enough light to see across to the rim of the horizon.

"People often say they understand about God in someone else's life and then they push a little and are hurt when he comes first." She looked up at him again. "And you're a police officer through to your marrow."

"Yes," he said, raising his annoying eyebrow, just like Harriet.

"The real problem," Anna said carefully, "will be getting

any time at all together and working out how to be us when we do. I know it doesn't always look like it, but I don't want tongues to wag because you've stayed over because ... being vicar here means something."

"I know. I really do."

"You think you do," she muttered.

"You've always got to have the last word!"

And she laughed because she might think the last word, but normally she'd never have the courage to say it.

"Could we try kissing now?" he asked.

Anna felt fear welling up from her toes, like a spring, but she said, "Yes please."

Chapter 19

Harriet brought the last of the cups through.

"I know I'm not supposed to get cross, but where is Anna? What is she doing with Archie and Simeon?"

"Can't we just lock up and go? They're all grown-ups; they don't need us to be here, do they?" Derek said, folding the tea-towel into neat squares. He carefully put it on the edge of the sink.

They were all over eighteen, but she also knew they'd found a body, had a break-in and poor Simeon had felt so threatened that he'd locked himself in the church.

"I'm sorry, Derek, but I just don't think I can leave them. Anna wouldn't want me to. You head out if you like."

He shook his head.

"I'm not leaving you to walk up the lane on your own."

Harriet nodded. The trouble was, they'd been used to feeling scared and disconcerted, so slipping back into that place was easy.

"Thanks, Derek." She rested a hand on his arm. "If you could finish up here, I'll go and make sure everyone is alright."

The house was silent. She'd served up the hot chocolate early, brought through lots of biscuits because none of the young ones had eaten much. Even Dani was looking jumpy. Harriet guessed the men in the car had been a bit of an eye-opener for everyone. Whoever Robert Enderby had been, it looked as if he'd been mixed up in something horribly unsavoury. Tom had said that he'd make sure a patrol car was around through the night, but everyone knew how stretched the police were. Even Helston didn't have regular patrols. But with the recent events, they were making a bit of an effort.

Harriet took a deep breath and pushed into the lounge. Everyone was there except Laurence. Catherine was reading. She was proving to be quite useful with some of the small things – clearing up, listening to the girls when Anna wasn't able to. Dani was playing with her phone, though there couldn't be much to do on it without a signal. Anna was going to get Wi-Fi, but most other retreat centres said they didn't bother, that it was all part of the package, getting away from the internet and all the pressures it could bring.

Georgie was staring into space, her Bible on her lap. She looked fragile, as if she were only just holding it together.

"Is everyone OK?" Harriet asked.

Catherine nodded.

"I could make some more hot drinks if you'd like me to?"

"I'm alright, thank you, Harriet," Catherine said. "Do you think Anna will come back to say Evening Prayer?"

Anna had ten minutes to get down to the church. Harriet decided to phone her. This was simply too stressful to manage on her own.

"I'll check and let you know," she said, backing out into the hall. As she did so, headlights swept across the house. Harriet was out the front door and following the car round to the side before she'd even thought about it. Anna clambered out.

"Where have you been? Evening Prayer? Had you forgotten?"

"No, I just got a bit waylaid. How is everyone?"

Harriet trailed after her into the kitchen. Anna looked pink.

"Are Simeon and Archie alright? You've been ages."

"They were fine when I left them, fussing over where to put Belle. I hope Archie's allergy holds up."

"It's a big house. I'm sure he'll manage for one night." Harriet knew she'd snapped.

"What are you still doing here? Tom said he'd left everything under control."

"You've spoken to Tom?" Again, Harriet realised how cross she sounded. She was just so tired and Anna would've forgotten that, before long, she'd be back again, as she'd agreed to sort breakfast.

"Let's get going, Harriet," Derek said quietly. He'd appeared around the corner, she supposed when he'd heard their voices. "Anna can sort out anything else that needs doing. You're exhausted."

Even his gentle voice sounded pointed and Harriet watched Anna's face as her eyes widened and her mouth opened and closed, desperately trying to think what to say. She looked so guilty and confused.

"I'm sorry. I should've come straight home," she called to their backs. Derek sort of half-turned to wave, but Harriet wanted to get home, to curl up in bed, to shut her eyes. She took her coat from Derek and shrugged into it without breaking stride.

When they arrived back home, she almost stumbled into the bungalow. There were a couple of bags by the front door, presumably for the charity shops.

"Is that all you've managed to throw out? Oh Derek, it's not much."

He shook his head.

"I've nearly finished my office, really I have. You could pop your head round the door on the way to bed." He sounded like a worried servant or a child desperate for their parents' approval. It made her want to scream. It was his house, his stuff. Why didn't he fight her, yell at her, tell her to mind her own business?

"I'm going to bed," she said. "I can't think straight."

"I'll let Dolly out," he said, as if he were doing her a favour, and that only made her want to shout that Dolly was his bloody dog. That she belonged to him and Fiona and that, really, Harriet didn't fit in anywhere at all.

When he came up and clattered about, she pretended to be asleep. She was still lying with her eyes clenched shut when he began to snore.

***

177

Georgie trailed down to the church with Anna, Catherine and Dani. She'd wondered about knocking on Laurence's door, but then had decided against it as there'd been no light coming from beneath. Perhaps he was asleep, lucky boy.

Georgie was feeling frayed around the edges and wasn't sure she'd be able to keep it together. Informal chat, my foot! The police officer had asked her if she'd wanted someone to sit with her, but she thought that might have looked as if she'd something to hide. So she'd said no, but had regretted it. His questioning had been relentless.

'When did you catch up with Mr Weller? Did you recognise him? Why did you keep your relationship a secret?'

'We don't have a relationship!'

'Yes, but you do know one another from before. What did he say to you? Did you see the black car? How long did you spend with him at the bottom of the ramp? Where did you go after that? How was he when you left him? How were you when you left him? Did you see Robert Enderby anywhere?'

At the end of it, her head had been spinning. She hadn't known how much to say, how much Laurence might have already told them. This was some bloody retreat! She was even more frazzled than when she'd first arrived, particularly now that she was definitely a suspect. She walked halfway down the aisle and sat down.

Bob was an evil man, whatever Laurence thought of him. She was glad he was dead. She shut her eyes, squeezed the lids together until she could see dancing spots. Gradually she began to realise how much her hands ached from where she was gripping the edge of the pew.

Anna's voice filled the church, but Georgie couldn't make sense of what she was saying. She wanted to go and talk to Laurence, make sure they were both dancing to the same tune because, if they weren't careful, one of them might end up paying the price for Robert Enderby's mistakes.

"Oh God, where are you in all this?"

A hand gently rested itself on her shoulder. Georgie jumped and then reached up and gripped it hard. She could feel the tears coming. She wondered who it was. A part of her wished they'd leave her alone and another part was glad they didn't. It was probably Catherine; Georgie thought she might have been sitting behind her.

Only one more day, another two breakfasts and the journey home with Dani, then she could scurry back to her job, try her best to get back to normal. She'd make up something to tell Alf, how God had spoken to her, how refreshed she felt.

***

The hand was gone, the church now silent. There was the noise of wind in the trees, a whisper of leaves and the dripping of water. The place felt empty. Georgie stood and wondered whether she was expected to lock up. She felt the beginning of fear lining her tummy because she was alone and the walk back, though short, was filled with shadows. She had to take a deep breath before she could even turn round. Straightaway she saw Anna sitting in the last pew. When she saw Georgie, she unfolded, smiling.

"I didn't want to disturb you."

"You didn't. I was worried I'd have to lock up."

"That's my job. Did the interview go alright?"

Anna shouldn't have asked that. What had it to do with the retreat? Georgie shrugged and blinked away more tears.

"I don't suppose there's another room I could use? Dani is hard work and I'm shattered. She never stops talking."

"And you kind of feel responsible for her."

"Alf said I had to be."

"Alf can't always be right or understand."

"I know, but what about all the answers to prayer, all the things he wants us to do, that he says God wants us to do? Is he deluded or a liar?"

Anna widened her eyes and blinked rapidly. Georgie supposed it was her playing-for-time face, her stalling face.

179

She obviously couldn't think of anything to say.

"Georgie, I've never met him. I couldn't possibly say. Perhaps an enthusiast? Perhaps someone who can see possibilities?" She led Georgie out into the dark churchyard.

"Just wait there, Georgie, while I switch off and lock up. Don't worry, I have a torch."

Georgie turned away from the building and stared. Even with her back to the church she couldn't see much, but then Anna switched off the lights and the churchyard came to life. It sprang into three dimensions, navy blue and dark grey, black and green shapes, rustling and moving in the wind. Deep shadows from the gravestones lining the path that was edged with fuzzy grass. Georgie stopped and stared and breathed.

Anna came up behind her and said, "Are you ready?"

"In Exeter everywhere is lit up at night. Even my bedroom is orange from the streetlamps and last night the police officer had a torch."

"Don't be scared."

"I'm not scared. It's beautiful. I think I would like to live in the dark. It's so ... complete."

"Perhaps tomorrow, as long as the weather's not too wild, we'll walk over to Beacon Point and say Evening Prayer up there. Sometimes just standing on the edge, staring out at the horizon, can change who you are."

"Is that God?" Georgie asked, a little desperately.

"Of course it is. If we believe in him, then we have to believe that he's in everything. If you start looking for him, you'll start finding him, particularly in the everyday."

"Do you truly believe that?" Georgie asked.

"When I remember, because I'm horribly ordinary, as the others will tell you."

It wasn't quite the reassurance that Georgie wanted – or perhaps it wasn't the reassurance that she was used to.

She'd begun to think that God was having difficulties

making himself felt in her hard, broken heart. Yet though Anna was quite ordinary, her faith in his presence was real. For Georgie it was as good a place as any to start.

Chapter 20

Laurence lay on the top of the bed. He was cold, but he couldn't be bothered to move. It was his own fault, as he was still wearing his damp trousers. He wondered if this was how people died of hypothermia. His stomach growled. He wished he'd managed to eat more tea. But at the time, it had been like waiting for his first job interview, when he'd felt a nervous twitch crossed with the mother of all sick hangovers. The incredible thing had been that, even though he'd felt awful, they'd still offered him a job. Ok, it hadn't been the job he'd gone for. It turned out to be a fancy-named dogs-body in a warehouse, but it was better than nothing. Once he'd got to know everyone, he'd actually begun to enjoy the work. At that time simply turning up for his shift every day had done more for him than any fancy CV. Within a couple of years, he'd been virtually running the warehouse, but the money was terrible, which was why he'd applied for the new job as a van driver. He hoped that at some point, if he kept his nose clean, they'd see his potential, would perhaps give him some sort of engineering training.

Amidst that flush of renewed hope and new horizons, or at least Devon and Cornwall, Bob had reappeared. It had been a while since he'd been in contact and they'd gone for a drink. Laurence hadn't hesitated. Before this last couple of weeks, he'd always thought Bob a nice man, that Georgie was wrong, that it was a shame she'd taken against him right from the start. It had made things awkward. Back at the home he'd always tried to be her mate, had stood between her and the worst of the bullying and really wished her well when a family took her. He'd heard later that it hadn't worked out, but by that time he was off on his own, managing his bedsit and the many job applications.

How had it all become such a nightmare? And the binoculars! Who'd put them under his van, so clearly in sight?

It had to be the men from Exeter who'd moved them. They must have followed Bob, not trusting him to find Laurence and the missing consignment. Then, when they'd broken into the van, they'd used Bob's binoculars as a warning. Letting Laurence know that they knew exactly what had happened. Laurence leaned over and retched into the bin. There wasn't enough in his stomach for it to be worthwhile; it just made him feel sore and empty. It was all so crazy and terribly out of hand. Why couldn't Bob have left him alone, given him the time he'd wanted? Laurence had never asked Bob for any favours in return for digging him out of this awful hole because that's what you did for a mate. Wasn't it?

Laurence didn't want to think about any of it, but of course it was all he could think about. He'd seen for himself that, though the sea hadn't been kind to the body, there were other bruises poking out from under his friend's shirt, that he looked as though he'd been well worked over by someone with big fists. Laurence retched again.

It wasn't fair. He wouldn't admit to everything. If push came to shove, he'd rather go away for drugs than for murder. He couldn't let Georgie down, not again.

He really must try to get his story straight, particularly about what happened that morning in the lead-up to landing in the water. He had to find out what Georgie had said, what she'd seen or done after she'd stormed off. She'd been so angry with him, yet all he'd asked – no, begged for – was that she gave him some time to think things through. No-one ever gave him enough head space. He lay back. His brain felt overloaded. There was too much fear, too much that was wrong, too much that he was responsible for. He just wanted to make one decision where he wasn't running to catch up with himself.

Walking back from Kynance with Simeon, there had been a moment when he'd seen things more clearly. He wondered if such clarity was God. Did God exist? Did he really care about him? It would be nice; no-one else had ever given a toss, except Bob and Georgie. But both of them had come with strings attached – long, tangled strings. Now Bob was gone and there was this ache inside, regret deeply rooted, that he was beginning to resent because he couldn't see what he ought to have done differently. He'd been on this track from the day he'd moved to the moor.

The house creaked and groaned, the radiators popped and gurgled as they cooled and the wind rattled the window. It reminded him of the home. He felt comforted and ... really cold and very hungry.

He got up and pulled on the dressing gown that Anna had found him over his clothes. He really must get into his pyjamas at some point. That felt better. He slipped out onto the landing. Anna did keep saying to treat the place as their own and he was starving. A glass of milk would do it, though what he really fancied was a cheese sandwich.

The kitchen was quite small and he tried to manage with just the light from the fridge, but it didn't reach high enough. He decided to risk the main switch. He was a grown-up now. They couldn't ground him or say how disappointed they were in him or, worse, accuse him of stealing.

There was an uncut loaf, covered in seeds that he didn't like the look of, and then he found some sliced bread that they used in the mornings for breakfast. He only needed a couple of pieces. The butter was hard, so it ended up tearing holes in the soft bread. But the cheese was good. He decided to make a cup of tea, but then couldn't wait for the kettle. He was famished and most of the sandwich was gone before the water had finished boiling. He was so intent on the next mouthful that he didn't notice one of the doors swinging open. He'd thought it was another cupboard. Anna stood there, blinking sleep from her eyes.

"I'm sorry. I didn't mean to disturb you," he said, his mouth full of bread.

"You didn't. I noticed the light when I nipped to the loo and thought I'd left it on. It has been known."

"I was really hungry. I'm sorry. I won't eat so much at breakfast so there's plenty for the others."

"Laurence, let me make you another sandwich. We have tons of bread and it's really good to see you eating something at last. There's some cake in the tin too."

He frowned. This wasn't the reaction he'd expected.

"Has the kettle just boiled? Cup of tea?" she asked.

Laurence nodded.

"Cake or another sandwich or both?"

She made him another round and then cut herself a small piece of cake. "Mm! Harriet's cakes are something else," she said.

Laurence hadn't really noticed Harriet's cake over the last few days, but once he'd finished his second sandwich, he did have a piece and it was good. Finally he was beginning to feel full, and a little tired. It was as if the food was squashing down the nasty stuff. So far Anna hadn't asked him anything. Perhaps at this time of night there was an embargo on trying to help your guests. He hoped so.

"Thanks," he said, standing up. "I really needed that."

"Good," she said. "I hope you can sleep now." She looked up at him.

"I don't believe in God. I shouldn't really have come on a retreat like this. I'm a bit of a waste of your time." The words were out before he could stop them.

"You're not that," she said carefully. "Why did you come?"

"It was Georgie. When I met her for coffee all those months back, she said I should give God a chance and then I saw your advert on the notice board at work."

"We don't have an advert. We simply sent a note to the Diocesan Office. I guess someone must have printed it off."

She gave her head a little shake and then said, carefully, "I think that believing God exists is a big step, but a much

186

bigger one is to realise that he loves you, deeply and profoundly."

She sounded as though she believed that, but that she needed to reassure herself that she'd said it properly. He wanted to laugh. If God did care so much, why hadn't Laurence been born into a family who'd loved him, instead of a family that had been so addled by drink and drugs that, at six months, he'd been removed for his own safety? He'd never met his mum or dad and neither of them had ever come to find him. He'd waited, like all the other kids, hopelessly, year after year. He'd hoped they'd get clean because they loved him so much. Then, at some point, he'd given up, had let them go. Perhaps one day he'd look into what had happened to them, but right now he doubted he'd ever be that strong. At least Georgie's mum had died. She'd not had to come to terms with the mess of unrealised hope that he'd had to deal with. It must have been an easier place to launch herself from. Laurence had always been a little jealous of her. She had nothing weighing her down or holding her back, except perhaps lately Dani, who always seemed to be hanging around. Apparently she'd even moved into the house where Georgie lived. He had seen over the last few days that that was driving Georgie nuts.

"I am ready to sleep now. Thanks again for the sandwich. I'll set the alarm and try to get down for Morning Prayer." He felt he owed Anna that much at least, though her answering frown said it all.

***

Dani lay in bed staring at the ceiling. For all that Georgie was supposedly upset, she'd had no trouble dropping off and was now snoring. It was mega-annoying. Dani wished she'd brought ear plugs; the sort of thing her mother would've thought to pack, if she'd ever gone on holiday. She ought to try and get away sometime – it might stop her whingeing about how tired she was.

Dani decided to give Georgie another five minutes, then she was going to prod her over onto her side and hope that it'd be enough to stop the pig impressions. The real problem was that Dani's own heart was hammering away in her chest and when she pressed her head down into her pillow, she could hear the blood roaring around her ears. It had been like that for most of the day; at least since she'd realised that, if the police had searched the place properly, she would've been in trouble.

She kept replaying the fifteen minutes she'd spent down on the point, where she'd walked along the veranda of a building all boarded up for the winter. It had looked like an old café, with yellowing menus in the window and a rusty ice cream sign. Dani didn't particularly care; it was out of the wind.

She didn't have gloves or a hat and it was bloody freezing. She'd stood and stared out, not getting what all the fuss was about. There'd simply been a lot of sea, and it'd been all so grey, grey and dull green. She'd seen the café down below her, but it had looked small and shabby, probably unable to do a decent cappuccino.

She'd decided to walk back up to the pub and had been about to turn away when she'd seen the man coming along the path. Even at a distance, she'd recognised Enderby. At first she thought that it couldn't be, not down here, all this way from Exeter. Still, she'd shuddered, remembering the man who'd very nearly screwed up her life more than it was screwed up already. It had surprised her how much just the possibility of him had made the blood roar in her ears.

Back in the bedroom there was a long silence until Georgie suddenly juddered and growled from the back of her throat. Bloody Georgie and her pathetic orphan thing. She'd no idea how difficult life could really be. One day Dani would fill her in on a few salient facts, if only to shut her up.

Georgie sighed and rolled over and for a blessed couple of

minutes the room was silent. Dani rolled over too, only then of course she needed a pee. She never usually had to get up in the night, except when she'd been pregnant – then, it had been all the time. This was Georgie's fault for keeping her awake. Dani lay a bit longer, but knew she'd never drop off now, so she got up, not bothering to be too quiet. What was the point? The bed creaked, the door creaked, the stairs creaked. The stairs were creaking now; someone was coming up though it was nearly two o'clock. Dani peered through the crack of the partly opened door. It was Laurence. He'd stopped at the top of the stairs and was looking along the landing, staring at her. Dani quickly stepped away from the gap, even though she knew he couldn't possibly see her. But his look had frightened her. He'd glared at their door with something akin to hate. He didn't know her that well, so it must have been Georgie at whom the look was directed. What was going on between those two? And what had he been doing downstairs?

Dani waited until she saw the light come on under his door and then slipped to the bathroom at the other end of the landing. She didn't care if the cistern woke Catherine; the lucky cow had her own room so there had to be some disadvantages.

When she climbed back into bed, Georgie thankfully was silent, a small mound of duvet. She didn't seem to take up any space at all. Dani rolled onto her tummy and tried to fluff up the pillows. It didn't help the lumpiness. Fortunately, there was only a day to go, just two more nights in this frigging awful place.

Chapter 21

Anna swung her legs out over the side of the bed and onto the rug. Her eyes felt scratchy and tired. She yawned, a long deep satisfying yawn that, just for a moment, muffled the screaming voice in her head.

"I made a decision yesterday, God," she said and groaned. "I'd thought I'd wake up all happy and floaty, but instead it feels as if you haven't had a proper say because I wanted what I wanted." She hunted about on the floor for her slippers. "I'm still not sure I'm ready. How can we make such a relationship work?" She stood up and stretched. "It's impossible."

Her phone jangled on the bedside table. She sat back down and reached for it. Tom! She answered, her heart beating a little faster.

"Anna, we've just been contacted by my colleagues up at Exeter. I'm afraid there's a link to a drug ring up there. All of your guests at some point or another have either been under suspicion or had to make a witness statement." She was disappointed that he'd not started a little more gently, the memory of the night before still warm and fuzzy inside her. She also wanted to say, 'Surely not your mother!', but she managed to bite her tongue. "They're sending someone down to help us out, someone with a bit more background knowledge," he finished.

"Drugs!"

"You've only just woken up. Sorry."

"And I didn't sleep well," she said, stifling another yawn.

"Me, I had the best night I've had in years." He sounded smug.

"So you believe you're making progress with the investigation?" she asked.

"No, you numpty." His voice dropped to a whisper. "Because yesterday you said we could give it a try." He was probably in a room full of colleagues with ears like elephants, but Anna didn't care. Tom was happy, not regretting what had happened the night before. Still speaking very quietly, he said, "Anna, if there's a drugs link, please be careful. These guys aren't nice. Enderby's hand was crushed and someone certainly thumped him."

Anna didn't understand the significance. Tom sighed. "Probably a car door. It's not uncommon".

Anna shuddered. "But surely they won't come back?" she said, desperately trying not to picture a door slamming shut on someone's fingers.

"We don't know if they found what they were looking for. There's a possibility that Laurence has hidden something."

"Are you saying Laurence is involved with drugs?" She knew she was stating the obvious.

"Look, I can't say any more for now. I'll be over again as soon as I'm done here."

"Do I need to keep anyone in, waiting for you? Should I warn them?" She knew she sounded sarcastic.

"No, I don't want them knowing that we know what we know."

Anna needed a coffee. She pulled on her dressing gown and went through to the kitchen. It was still a bit early for Harriet. While the coffee brewed, she went for a quick shower. She found herself thinking carefully about what she'd wear and was annoyed for worrying about that, when she'd never bothered before. Only she realised that wasn't true either because most of her clothes were dark and baggy, as anything fitted would've shown too many lumps and bumps. She went back for the coffee. Harriet appeared at the back door. She looked tired too. They all looked tired.

"Do you think we can manage?" Anna asked her, once Harriet had taken off her coat.

"Manage what?" Harriet replied, unpacking her bag onto the counter.

"All this," Anna said, turning slowly around. "I thought

Archie looked exhausted yesterday. And you. Could we give him a lie-in?"

Harriet nodded.

"But phone him straightaway. He's normally up with the lark."

"Tom rang this morning," Anna said, sending a text instead.

"What did he want?"

"There's a drug connection."

"Oh, that's not good. With the man who died? Enderby?" Anna nodded. "What's the connection?"

And Anna realised she wasn't sure.

"He's coming back over sometime today. More questions. Do you think we should offer them their money back?"

"No, it's not our fault. It's what an insurance company would call an act of God."

"Only it isn't, is it?" Anna said sadly. "It's nasty men who shut people's hands in doors and prey on the vulnerable just to make money. Oh God, it's so depressing."

"Did you say they shut his hand in a door?"

"Something like that."

Harriet's cheeks pinched white around her nose. "I guess we do live in a bit of a bubble down here. Nasty life doesn't often impinge."

"Apart from the odd murder." They giggled because it was all getting a bit much. Anna poured more coffee.

"How are you getting on?" she asked. "Derek was here a lot yesterday. I wondered if it helped or ..."

"On one level, it was good to have him around. He did help me get things sorted, particularly when we had to wait around for you." Anna felt a surge of guilt. Her snatched moment. A significant moment, she reminded herself, now lost in Harriet's gentle dig.

"I'm sorry. It's just that, suddenly, I couldn't face coming back here and I did take you for granted."

"I forgive you."

Anna looked down at her hands, picked at a nail.

"And ...?" Harriet said.

"Tom came to meet me down at the point. It was only for a few minutes."

"And ...?" Harriet said, her arms crossed, her foot beginning to tap.

"We're going to give it a try. He said some nice things about me. But I should have kept a closer eye on the time."

"No, no, you shouldn't have. You should have braved my wrath and stayed away until the sun rose." Harriet spun around slowly, stretching out her arms, but not too far, so as not to knock the kettle or the toaster off the side. "At last, at flippin' last!"

"It's only a try-out."

"But he kissed you, didn't he?" she said, almost dancing from foot to foot.

"I can see that you're pleased for me, but, Harriet, all I'm feeling is pressure and I don't know if I can do it. Juggle life and Tom and faith and ... everything."

"I am the last person to put you under any pressure, but I'm just glad that you're at least trying. If it doesn't work out, I won't under any circumstances make a judgement. It would make me the biggest hypocrite on the planet." She blew Anna a kiss. "Now, we need to get breakfast going and you need to do Morning Prayer." Anna swore she heard Harriet say, under her breath, "Silly old bear!"

***

Archie woke with a start. Simeon was leaning over him.

"You missed your alarm, so I've made you a cup of tea," he said, hurriedly stepping back.

Archie rubbed his eyes. *The battery must be flat*, he thought. He definitely wouldn't have slept through the annoying beep of his alarm clock.

"What time is it?" he mumbled, suppressing a yawn.

"Eight o'clock."

"Blast, I'm supposed to be down at the vicarage for breakfast."

"May I use the bathroom?"

"Of course you can," Archie replied, frowning. Surely Simeon knew he didn't have to ask?

"It's just that, if you wanted to get up and dressed quickly, you'd need to go in first."

"No, don't you worry. I'll text Anna. I'll go down later, unless she says she needs me urgently."

What he really wanted to do was to roll over and go back to sleep.

"Oh, and thanks for the tea, Simeon. It's a real treat." It was. He reached for his mobile and switched it on. Anna had already left him a text to say that he could give breakfast a miss. She'd also typed, 'Only one more day to go' and had added a smiley face. The fact was they were all feeling the strain. He picked up his Bible and read a couple of chapters. He got up to shave once he was sure that Simeon had gone downstairs. Finding Simeon leaning over him like that had given Archie a bit of a start and it had taken quite a while for his heart to settle down again.

Simeon had headed out into the squally wind to walk Belle. Archie pottered around the kitchen and put some washing on, but wasn't quite sure what to do next. He should probably get over to the vicarage, despite Anna's text. One thing they were learning was that the more of them about the place, the better. It was not a normal retreat, if you could call it that at all, and he felt they all needed to be on duty.

**

To Anna's surprise, everyone was waiting at the bottom of the stairs. She checked her watch. She wasn't late; they were all early.

"Good morning, how lovely. Good rest?" she asked generally. There were murmurs in reply. Once she'd shepherded them outside, she made sure the front door was pulled shut, so that if anyone did happen to come searching, Harriet would be safe. They walked to the church in silence. She'd forgotten her key, but picked up the one behind the gargoyle. Once inside, Anna did a quick recce around the tower room, the vestry and behind the altar. Though, to be honest, there wasn't really anywhere you could fit two large men and she had a feeling that hiding wasn't their style.

"Before we start, I want you to spend five minutes in silence. Don't worry, we won't be late for breakfast and I'll let you know when we are done." She waited for them to find a space, to go and sit hunched in the pews. They spread out, like dry leaves in an autumn breeze. Anna stood at the back with her book in her hand, where she could see a little of the path through the partially opened door. She wanted warning of any surprise visitors – though what she'd do if anyone came striding along with menace, she wasn't really sure. She wondered where Simeon was. He often appeared for Morning Prayer, but then she remembered that, of course, he was over at Archie's house.

"This is their last day, God," she breathed. "And I know you'll go on working, but this is one of the few moments when their lives will be defined by this stillness, by being here." She checked her watch. She was a terrible judge of time.

"Worship the Lord in the beauty of holiness," she began and watched the shoulders drop and sheets lift as they began to follow the words. Catherine remained with her head bowed. She'd know it by heart. Anna, too, fell into the familiarity of the liturgy, was enveloped in it, so that she began to feel cocooned and safe, buoyed up by the weight of the sentences.

At the end Catherine hung back.

"Anna, do you mind awfully if I miss breakfast? I'm simply not hungry and I'd like to try and get over to Kynance."

"Of course. Watch the weather and grab something off the coffee table for elevenses."

When Catherine had gone, Anna closed her eyes for thirty seconds, no more, and allowed God to do his thing. When she got up, feeling less responsible, she saw Simeon and Belle coming down the path. Unaccountably pleased to see them, she stepped out into the light.

"Hello you two, how are you?"

"I am well. Belle doesn't seem to have minded staying at Archie's."

"I expect that, where you're happy, she's happy."

"Has Tom spoken to you any more about the men in the car, Anna?"

"Only that we need to be careful. That they may have been looking for something."

"That means that Laurence is involved somehow. Does Tom think he killed the man he tried to pull from the sea?"

"That's a bit of a jump, Simeon."

"Yes, but Tom said the man had only been in the water a short time, which means that, from when I last saw him alive, there was a limited amount of time for someone to hurt him."

"You've thought about this a lot."

"Of course. It means that five people could have done it."

Anna's mouth dropped open.

"What do you mean, Simeon?"

"I saw the people in the car. They could have parked in the car park and come down by the steps. I saw Georgie following Laurence. It could have been her, while Laurence was in the café. It could have been Laurence at any point. Or it could have been the other person I saw, who stopped at the end of the road just before I turned away. I now wonder if that could have been Dani."

"You said it was a man."

"I said I thought it might have been."

Anna had to think about this before asking, "What about

the two walkers having their coffee or the girl in the café?"

"They are each other's alibis. Tom said he couldn't find a link."

"I bet it was those horrid men in the car. They were probably looking for stolen drugs."

"Does Tom think Laurence is involved with drugs?" Simeon's voice was almost normal, but his fingers were beginning to clench and unclench. Anna nodded. She didn't want to upset him, but felt that he needed to know what might be going on. They all did.

"Well, he didn't say exactly that; just that there might be a drug connection," Anna corrected herself.

"Oh dear," Simeon said matter-of-factly. "I think I'd like to stay with Archie for a few days more. Do you think he'd mind?"

"I wouldn't have thought so."

"Laurence must have had drugs in his van."

Anna thought that was probably the case and yet ...

"If he was trying to steal them," she said, "why didn't he go and get rid of them as soon as he could and then get as far away as possible? Why on earth did he come down here, on a retreat of all things? He doesn't know anything about God. He doesn't even believe there is one."

"Neither did I once, but everyone has to start somewhere."

Anna sighed. Of course, everyone had to start somewhere, but just because Simeon had been on that particular journey didn't mean that everyone else he met was too, and it still didn't explain the drugs.

"I'm sorry, Simeon, I've got to get back. As Archie's having a lie-in, there's only me and Harriet to hold the fort."

"I took Archie a cup of tea when I realised he hadn't got up. When his alarm went off, it beeped for a long time before stopping."

"A cup of tea ... I expect he enjoyed that." Anna wondered when had been the last time that Archie had had tea in bed?

Probably back when his wife had been alive. Of course, the alarm would've driven Simeon nuts, which made Anna smile.

Chapter 22

When Archie got to the pub, he was quite surprised to see Catherine crossing the green. He waved and she cut back to meet him.

"Out for an early morning walk?"

"Yes, I had a cup of coffee to get me through Morning Prayer and then I simply wasn't hungry."

Not hungry or couldn't face the other guests, Archie wondered. From Catherine's point of view, they were probably all a bit young and needy.

"The age range is not what we expected," he said.

She laughed.

"Are you saying I am older than you'd like or that they are younger?"

Horrified, he said quickly, "That they are younger. Your age is exactly ... if anything, it's also a little young."

"Well caught, sir," she said, laughing and gave a little bow.

"I really didn't mean to say that you were old."

"And I didn't take it like that. Relax, Archie, I'm not offended. I thought I'd walk over to Kynance and then back round the point. Everyone has been waxing lyrical about it."

"It's a wonderful walk, but I'm not sure this is the morning for it," he said, squinting up at the sky. It was blooming a ceiling of grey that felt as if it were already too heavy for itself.

"Really, I could have sworn there was a large patch of blue when I set out."

"There often is. One thing you can say about the Lizard is that we have ragged skies, which doesn't really help when trying to decide what the weather is going to do all day."

"Ragged skies ... what a lovely way to describe it. You do love it here, don't you?"

And he stopped for a second, looking behind her, across to the coast.

"Yes. It's where I am."

"Again, sir, deeply profound."

"Sorry. It's because I haven't had breakfast either."

"Archie, is that you?" Phil was emptying the bins around the side of the pub.

"Have you met Phil?" Archie asked Catherine. "He's the landlord and a good man."

"Did you just call me good, Archie?"

"I did, though I shall expect some form of recompense when next I darken your doors."

"How about right now? I could do with getting the coffee on."

Archie smiled at Catherine, "Would you like to join us? He makes a very good coffee."

Turning back from the front door, Phil said, "And excellent bacon butties for those who can't face one more healthy breakfast."

Catherine laughed.

"They are very nice breakfasts. Harriet has everything under control." Which was true in every sense, but Catherine still followed Archie into the pub. It was dark inside. Phil put the lights on over the bar. It smelt a little damp, the morning after the night before.

"Pull up a stool and let's gossip," he said.

"Something we never do," Archie said firmly.

"Something you'd never do," Catherine said quietly.

"You are right, of course, Mrs Edwards. I do all the gossiping and Archie keeps me on the straight and narrow." Of course, Phil would know exactly who she was, without an introduction being necessary.

"Call me Catherine."

"Phil."

Archie pulled himself up onto a stool and relaxed. He was used to being here. If there wasn't a church meeting or a book to be wrestled with, he often came up for a rum.

"Am I allowed to ask questions about what's happening?" Phil asked, pouring coffee. "Bacon won't be a minute."

"Phil will know more about what's going on than any of us."

"All villages are like that," Phil said, grinning as he disappeared into the kitchen.

"Does he know that I'm Tom's mum?"

"Probably. But we can tell him if you'd like. I wouldn't want him to say anything ..." Archie realised where that sentence was heading.

"About Tom or just the police in general?"

"Sorry, Catherine, it's just that Tom turns up whenever we're in trouble. He has a way of disconcerting Anna that's hard to fathom."

"No, Archie, it's not hard to fathom at all. I think he's been in love with her for quite a long time. When he told me about what had happened, what Anna did when that woman attacked her, he sort of glowed. I knew then."

"Really? In love?" Archie was a little put out; he felt that was far too dramatic.

They sat in silence, listening to Phil whistling in the kitchen.

"You really think he loves her?"

"Who's in love?" Phil asked, coming through with a plate piled high with sandwiches.

"That does look good," Catherine said. "And you're right, this coffee is wonderful."

Phil tipped his head on one side.

"Just in case you need reminding," Catherine continued, "I am Tom's mother."

Archie looked up and caught Phil's eye. As expected, Phil had known full well who she was. He pulled up his stool and made himself comfortable.

"So do you approve of our lovely vicar?"

"Phil, you can't ask Catherine that!" Archie sounded

genuinely shocked. He knew Phil could be a little forthright sometimes, but such a question would put Catherine in an intolerable position. Though he had to admit that he'd immediately made the assumption that Catherine wouldn't like Anna, that she wouldn't come up to the mark.

The thing with their Anna was that you had to get to know her, to see beneath the slightly insecure, muddly exterior. Anna was, Archie felt, a rather remarkable woman and one who cared passionately about them all. But it wasn't always obvious.

"I suppose not," Phil responded, but he still had that annoying twinkle in his eye. He was such a nosy man.

"Actually, I do like her," Catherine replied, laughing. "The problem is whether Tom will be enough for her. As much as it breaks my heart to say it, he doesn't share the most important thing in her life. It's got to be an issue for them."

Archie stared at Catherine in surprise and breathed out.

"Yes, it's what's been worrying me. God means such a lot to her, and if she and Tom do get together, won't there be a conflict of interests?"

"There could be," Catherine said quietly. "But it would be a shame."

"They're grown-ups! Can't they work it out?" Phil spoke crossly. "I think they'd be great together, whenever they can be together."

"Being married to a police officer is tough, no two ways about it," Catherine said. Archie wondered if she was thinking about Tom's first marriage.

Like being married to someone at sea, Archie thought, remembering Moira and those first hours after a long stint away, when they'd moved around each other, afraid to exchange more than a stilted greeting. Their letters had been passionate enough, barely able to contain themselves when they'd first been married, but that initial moment had been almost painful, the car journey back to the house uncomfortable and strange.

"So do you open the whole day all the way through winter?" Catherine asked Phil and Archie relaxed a little. She was closing Phil down. Quite right, too.

"Not all the time. But definitely just before lunch. You'd be surprised by the number of people who come down, if only to get a breath of fresh air."

"And somehow end up in the pub!" Catherine said and Archie couldn't decide if there was a disapproving tone to her voice. "I don't suppose the retreat helps much with your profits," she added.

Phil laughed.

"You wouldn't have thought so, but people of faith – or certainly people who are seeking faith – are my best regulars."

That made Archie smile because it was true. Derek and Harriet, Anna, he himself and sometimes Simeon all found their way into the bar, where they sat and talked and wondered. Archie realised those times were precious to him.

"And do some of the retreaters use your facilities too?"

Phil nodded, "Yes. In fact, on the morning that poor man drowned, one of the young women was in here after she'd been for a walk down to the Lizard. Dani. She didn't seem to be particularly impressed with our main attraction. Kyle, on the other hand, seemed to impress her greatly." He laughed.

"How is Kyle coming along?" Archie asked.

"He's no Harriet. I think he finds it all a bit boring, the sheet-changing in particular."

"Harriet is marvellous," Catherine said. "She's a wonderful cook and seems to arrive just when Anna needs her. Though ..." Catherine ground to a halt. Archie wondered what she'd been about to say about Harriet. That was the problem with this place: it invited you to share confidences.

"She's not been herself the last couple of weeks," Phil said, beginning to wipe the bar with a towel. "A bit sad, almost

205

worried."

Archie frowned. He hadn't noticed. He hoped that Harriet wasn't having second thoughts about Derek. It had been such a wonderful turn-around for them both and everyone had been delighted. They'd all needed a bit of a happy ending after Terry. So it would be a little awkward because any wobbles would happen under the spotlight of everyone else's expectations.

At least with Anna and Tom, there were none of those, none whatsoever.

"It's coming up two years," Phil said quietly, "since the death of Fiona."

Archie shook his head. Surely it couldn't be as long as that?

"Tom couldn't give me details, but it sounded like it was a difficult case," Catherine said. "I can't imagine what it must have been like, wondering for all those months who'd killed her."

"I think mostly we convinced ourselves it was simply an accident," Archie replied. "The grains of stone in the wound were so very few, so very inconclusive."

"Not like it is on the telly! Any more coffee?" Phil asked, leaning across with the jug.

"No thanks, I think I will try for Kynance and then come back round as planned. Will I have time before lunch?"

"You'll have to walk briskly," Archie replied. "Why don't you save Kynance for another day? Simply walk around the point – then you can enjoy it."

"I will bow to your local knowledge," Catherine said, smiling. She picked up her bag to get out her purse, but Phil shook his head and smiled.

"My treat. Now out the pub, turn left and left again. Follow the lane down onto the path. You can't get lost."

Once Catherine had closed the door behind her, Archie slipped off the stool and pulled on his coat.

"I'd better head out too. Go and see how they're all getting on down at the vicarage."

***

Laurence had managed to sleep, mostly because he was so shattered, but also because he was reassured that Anna would hear if anyone tried to get at him. He'd certainly revised his view of her. She'd defend them and Tom would get a squad car to come over really fast if he thought she might be in danger.

Lying in bed that morning, he knew he was in trouble whichever way he looked at it. Coppers talked, didn't they? Rang each other up and said, 'What do you know about ...?' And because Georgie was here, they would've made all sorts of links. He really wished they'd had time to get their stories straight. Then there were the binoculars turning up under his van. He'd thought it had been the guys from Exeter, but what if it hadn't been them sending a message? What if it had been someone else trying to point the finger? It was getting more and more difficult to work out what to do next, how much to say.

Sitting in church was weird. He listened to the words of Morning Prayer for a few seconds. Anna read very slowly. They didn't mean anything to him, but he could tell she believed them, every syllable. She was a funny woman. He'd liked to have had a mum like her or perhaps an elder sister. Someone to keep an eye out for him. Someone who'd have warned him about life's pitfalls. Someone he would've listened to when they'd said that Bob was a waste of space.

Thinking of Bob made him feel sick, so he tried to concentrate on Anna's voice. They were beginning the Lord's Prayer. Now that was something he could remember, just about, and he joined in, if only to drown out the image of Bob's face, water streaming from his hair as he loomed closer each time the waves lifted Laurence towards those outstretched arms. Was such an end truly what Bob deserved?

If what Georgie said was true, then yes, he supposed it was.

Laurence couldn't wait for breakfast. He felt as though he wouldn't be able to eat enough to fill the hole inside. Harriet initially looked gratified and then alarmed. She offered to go and make extra porridge, but he refused. Instead, she kept bringing more and more toast until his stomach finally felt tight – suddenly unpleasantly so, as if, before this moment, he'd simply been numb.

"It's nice to see you've finally got an appetite," Anna said. He could see that she was pleased. He decided she was one of those people for whom you wanted to make the world right. Like Bob. Only that made him wonder what she might ask of him. He supposed she might be satisfied with some form of admission. Perhaps he could talk to Simeon about that. Now there was a bloke who thought things through, who thought in straight lines. Laurence would definitely ask his advice. It would be sensible to get things organised in his head before the policeman came again. Because he would be back.

Laurence had to consider the possibility that he wouldn't be driving home to Exeter with the others. He wondered what would happen to his van, his job. He guessed the police would take care of most of it. He had to talk to Georgie because this morning, when he'd woken up, he'd made a decision – that whatever happened, he wanted her to get through this unscathed. She wasn't to be contaminated by his bad decisions.

Chapter 23

Dani had a plate of porridge. She usually couldn't see the point of it, but it was warm and Morning Prayer had chilled her to the bone. At home she just had cereal while watching something on TV, her mum always complaining when she left the bowl on the side. Except just now she wouldn't mind being at home. She wondered for a second if this was what homesickness felt like.

After the break-in the day before, she'd got into a bit of a panic; it had been such a close call. Thank goodness she'd had the foresight to put the binoculars back.

What a nightmare! At some point Mr Plod was bound to take the place apart and she knew how stressful it was watching someone hunt for something you'd hidden. She'd watched her mum do it at home. The first time she'd found a few grains at the back of a drawer.

The second time Dani had been too clever for her, though her mum, melodramatic as ever, had cried. She seemed to know that there ought to have been something there to find. The third time had been when the police had come round with a warrant. Their search had made her mum look like a rank amateur. They had gone through every square inch, including Selena's room. Dani even had to lift her out of the cot, so they could look under the mattress.

It had been horrible because that time her mum hadn't cried at all. She'd stood in the hall, biting her lip and staring at the floor.

They hadn't found anything because by then she'd been clean for a couple of months, mostly because she'd been steering clear of Enderby. He'd tried a couple of times to offload some of his excess onto her, but she knew how to deal with men like him and had threatened to dob him in if he didn't leave her alone. The really annoying thing had been that – even though the police came up empty-handed – she and her mum had rowed spectacularly that night because she wouldn't believe anything Dani said, her reassurances clanging and tinny even to her own ears. She'd thought it would serve her mum right to stew for a bit, so that's when she'd moved in with Georgie.

Dani reached across for the coffee. Catherine was late coming to breakfast, which was a pain because Dani preferred talking to her. The rest of them were a bit lame. Georgie and Laurence were sitting opposite. Anna and Harriet were over by the door, but Harriet was up and down the whole time, bringing through more toast. Laurence spoke out of the side of his mouth to Georgie.

"Fancy a walk after breakfast?"

Pathetic, really, trying to speak so she couldn't hear them. She turned and stared out the window. She was surprised when her bottom lip began to quiver and her throat filled with unshed tears.

"Stuff it," she said loudly and pushed her chair back.

She made it through to the lounge before she actually began to cry. Now who was being pathetic? They would think it was because she felt left out, but it wasn't that. No, what she felt was scared. Everything was in such a mess. Georgie and Laurence needed to be really careful. If Georgie kept her head, she could still go home, back to her sweet life. Laurence, not a hope. Dani herself needed to be really tough or someone would join the dots and figure out what she knew. She wanted to get back to Selena and her mum, though she wished her mum wouldn't think what she was bound to think. Just for once, it would be nice if she'd fight for her daughter. Dani drew in a gulp of air. She hadn't meant for it to be such a mess. She really hadn't. Anna came into the lounge.

"Dani, I've brought you a fresh cup of tea." Anna came and stood next to her. She carefully put the cup down on the windowsill in front of them and fished a pack of tissues from her pocket. Three packets fell onto the floor and Dani wondered if she normally carried so many around with her. Crying was gross, so Dani tried not to do it too often.

"Come and sit down. The last couple of days have been really difficult. The police being here all the time can't have helped."

Dani wondered how much Anna was assuming about her and then thought that perhaps she ought to give her the benefit of the doubt. Anna wasn't that clever; she wouldn't get what was really going on.

"I'd hoped to get away from it all, but everything has just followed me down here."

Anna nodded.

"I'm really, really sorry about that. This is our second murder in as many years."

Dani hadn't been talking about the death.

"It might not be murder. Couldn't he have fallen off the cliff by accident? How can they be sure?" she said.

"Tom says the medical examiner has been going over the body with a fine toothcomb and there are telling signs, apparently."

Dani shook her head. She just couldn't see how that worked.

"And there are the binoculars, which definitely belonged to him. Phil from the pub recognised them and Enderby had a case in his pocket that matched."

Dani's brain began to fire.

"But he can't be the only one with a pair like that. A tourist might have dropped them."

"I suppose," Anna said, looking puzzled. She tucked a strand of hair behind her ear.

"Would you like to talk? You seem so upset. Are you sleeping alright?"

"I wish I'd got my own space."

"I'm sorry you don't seem to be getting on with Georgie."

The room suddenly sounded abnormally quiet. As if all the

211

normal noises had been sucked away. Anna annoyingly remained silent too. She'd put on her listening face, which Dani thought made her look like a frog. And yet ...

"People just don't seem to like me. Yesterday I thought Georgie and I were getting on alright. We ran down to the church, but then, when you turned up, it was like I didn't exist anymore. I was invisible. I'm always invisible. The only people who see me are Mum and Selena and neither of them have a lot of choice."

"Why do you think people don't like you?"

"Because as soon as they get a better offer, they're off like a shot. They think it's alright to do that because I'll be too thick to notice."

Anna winced.

"Only you're not, are you? You notice a lot of things."

"Sometimes." Dani decided this was the perfect moment. "Georgie's upset about work. No question she's angry with saint Alf, our vicar, but she knows a lot more about the man who died." Dani felt a little mean saying that, but this wasn't about Georgie; this was about her. This was about someone listening to Dani for a change and not thinking she was a complete waste of space.

Anna nodded. "But we're all a bit jumpy, aren't we? I'm not sure it's good for us or the retreat to keep going over who was where or what might have happened."

Anna was clearly missing the point, so Dani persisted.

"But if it's drugs, Anna, while Laurence is here, we're all in danger."

Now Anna looked shocked. She sat there wide-eyed, just like a frog.

"Dani, do you know something?"

Dani squashed her lips together. Anna had this way of asking a question that you found yourself answering. She mustn't forget that Anna and Tom were obviously an item, even if they were trying to keep it a secret. She probably told him everything, even though she'd assured everyone that whatever they said was confidential.

"I need to get out of here."

"Tomorrow will come soon enough," Anna replied.

"No, I mean I need to get out now. Go for a walk or something."

"Of course. But wrap up warm. The weather front that has just passed through is dragging some nasty cold air behind it. They're even forecasting snow flurries."

Dani almost laughed. Anna was now a weather forecaster.

"I like snow. I like the way it makes everything sound softer."

"Yes, all muffled and crunchy," Anna added.

"If it snowed, we could build a snowman and have a snowball fight."

"Has Selena ever seen snow before?"

"No, I don't think so."

"Well, her first snowman will be really special then."

Dani thought back to when she'd last built one. It had started snowing while they'd been at school and by the time they'd got to the youth club, there'd been a good four inches on the ground. She'd walked because she'd thought it would be nice, but her feet had ended up like blocks of ice, her fingers tingling with pain.

Oscar had lent her his coat, but it had been Jay who'd kissed her in a dark corner. Building the snowman had been fun, but without gloves or a hat she'd been frozen and when he'd begun to fumble under her clothes all she'd been able to feel had been icy bruises.

She'd thought that she and Jay were now an item. But when it'd been time to go home, he'd climbed into his mother's car, turning back at the last minute to wave, but half the group had waved back, so it hadn't been especially for her.

In that same week, Oscar had been waiting for her after

213

school and had fallen into step beside her. The snow, now in patches, had been black-edged and mucky from the cars. It had made her sad; she'd loved the thick-white covering, which had even made her house look welcoming and pretty. She and Oscar had walked across the park and behind the folly he'd kissed her ... She'd thought of Jay for a moment, but he'd been invisible since the Sunday, not even a chance meeting in the corridors at school. Anyway, nobody owned her; she could do what she liked.

It had only been later, when she'd seen the two boys laughing together, that she'd started to think something might be wrong. The youth worker had been horrified when she'd finally begun to show. She guessed he'd had some hard questions to answer. Certainly everyone had started covering their backs. She hadn't wanted to think about it, who or when, so she'd left school. She'd carried on at the youth club for a bit longer, but all of a sudden everyone had seemed really childish. Jay and Oscar had begun to show up less and less and when they had come, there'd been a ring around her a mile wide. She should've said something. She should've named names, but she'd known what clever boys would say about a girl like her. And God – where had he been in all that?

Dani had soon realised she'd no longer been getting the termly diary from the youth club or letters about trips or even Bible studies. So, when Selena had been born – not a couple of days Dani was ever likely to forget – she'd taken the card signed by her church friends and dropped it in the bin.

She had no idea why a couple of years later, she'd started going back, except they had a crèche and her mum got a lie-in on a Sunday morning.

It was depressing. Her whole story was just so pathetic and she still didn't know how to pray or read her sodding Bible.

"Well, when it snows, let me know."

Anna looked startled. Dani let herself out the front door and began to walk up the road. She walked fast because it was cold. The pub's lights were on and she wondered if Kyle might be about. He'd been fun to talk to, even if it'd meant the landlord throwing them dirty looks and finding him stupid jobs to do. She didn't care. She'd simply had to get away from the awful vicarage.

***

Georgie felt bad about Dani, but she had far too much on her own mind to worry about. When Dani had jumped up from the table, Anna had gone after her, so at least it meant that Georgie could talk to Laurence without being overheard. He looked as if he might burst into tears himself.

"Poor kid," he whispered. "We ought to make more of an effort."

"Why? She's been horrible to me," Georgie hissed at him.

"I expect she's just a little jealous. You do seem to have pulled yourself up by your bootstraps. Dani's still down in the crap."

"Not true, Laurence. You were always a sucker for a sob story." Georgie knew she was being harsh, that Laurence had been extraordinarily kind to her, his pretend kid sister. He'd helped her with homework, had found things that had gone missing, had even stood up for her with the carers. He'd made a lot of the moments bearable.

He, as usual, took her comment on the chin because that was what Laurence did. She sometimes wished he'd fight back, call her a cow, tell her to stop being so mean, tell her to be the Christian she professed to be.

"I'll see you down at the bottom of the churchyard," he said, biting into another piece of toast. He did look half-starved.

"Will the policeman come back?" she asked.

"Of course he will. Someone's died. It'd be nice and neat if they believed he was killed by one of the men from Exeter, but I have a feeling that they'll keep digging."

Georgie stared at her plate.

"Why couldn't it have been them?" she said. "He was not the man you thought he was ..." She stopped because Laurence turned to look at her, but he only looked through her, as if she were not there. Georgie didn't want to lose him again. She needed someone who understood. She'd missed Laurence over the years, really missed him.

"Not here, Georgie, not now."

For a second, she felt the panic rising up from her stomach. She pushed back her chair, said brightly, "I'm off to get sorted" and was gone before Laurence could say a word.

She ran up the stairs and into her room. She leaned her forehead against the window and breathed, but a headache began to bubble around her eyes. She knew it would gather in intensity and hover about all day, and there wasn't anything she could do about it, nothing she could take that would touch it. She slipped along to the bathroom, wondering where Dani was now, whether she was still grizzling to Anna. Georgie hoped she'd keep her mouth shut, but was rather afraid Dani was actually beginning to piece things together.

It was a bit too early to go and wait in the lane. She'd freeze and there'd be too much time for someone to see her hanging about, but then she really didn't want to be trapped by a petulant Dani. In the end she decided to risk the lane.

It was cold and though she'd put on an extra jumper, she still wondered if she'd ever feel warm again. Turning out of the drive, she checked up and down. It was empty, but the fear still prickled down her spine like icy water. What if the men came back? Where could she run to? The lane had such steep sides. In the end, she tucked herself into the dead end of a path at the bottom of the churchyard. As she did so, Simeon and his dog came past. He hesitated; he obviously knew she was there, but he didn't look at her. Laurence said he was alright, that he was honest, straightforward, that he knew all about God and how to find him, which had been a strange thing for Laurence to have mentioned. Georgie had been

216

fairly sure that Laurence wasn't interested in faith, which made her feel desperately sad and very lonely.

"Simeon!"

He stopped, but didn't turn around. It looked as though someone had simply switched him off. His hood was over his head, so she couldn't see his expression. The dog looked back though and wagged its tail. As if that was the test, Simeon turned towards her, but still kept his eyes fixed on the ground.

"I'm sorry to stop you. It's just that Laurence said you were ... good ... to ..."

Georgie didn't know how to proceed beyond that.

"I'm sorry if I freaked you out in the church. What would you like to talk about?" Simeon said to her knees.

"Could I stroke your dog?"

"Yes," and he allowed the lead to run so that Belle could come to her, which meant of course that Georgie herself didn't need to go any closer. She dropped down onto her haunches. Belle allowed Georgie to pat her and even to put her arms around her neck. She was at least a barrier against the wind funnelling up from the sea.

"You pray, don't you?" Georgie said quietly into Belle's fur.

"All the time."

"How do you do it?"

"Sometimes I speak. Sometimes not. He's everywhere, so he's always with us, even when we're doing things that make us forget that. You have to decide what you believe about God and then live accordingly."

"But do you ever feel anything?"

"Yes." He waited for her to say something else, but Georgie wanted more, so she swallowed her impulse to add in her own story. Eventually he said, "Sometimes I feel something. Not often."

"What's it like?"

"A hand that is not there, resting on my head or my shoulder. A fizzing in my stomach that is not anxiety. A prickle across my scalp. Stuff like that," said Simeon.

"Do you ever think you've done something that is beyond redemption? I mean, beyond his forgiveness?"

"Redemption is a big word," Simeon said quietly. She felt that he perhaps thought she wouldn't understand the true measure of it. Only then he said, "But his forgiveness feels bigger."

She looked up into his face and caught him staring down at her. He immediately looked away.

"What could you've done that made you need such big words?" she asked.

"We all need them. Every single one of us. It's the whole point of Jesus." He spoke evenly, as if she were a small child who would have difficulty understanding any of this, but she'd heard it a million times.

"Jesus died for our sins so that we can come into the presence of God," she sang.

"You sound like Anna used to, when her voice said things that her head didn't seem to believe."

"I'm sorry to be rude," Georgie said, standing up suddenly, pulling her gloves back on. "But please, what have you done that made you need his forgiveness?"

"I didn't want or appreciate the life he'd given me and did not notice the people he put around me to help me."

He stood there staring at the ground. Belle had gone back to his side; she was almost leaning into him now. *And the two became one,* Georgie thought, hopelessly jealous.

"Do you have any other questions?" he asked.

"No, but thank you," she replied, hoping he wouldn't notice the catch in her voice. He looked sideways, left and right, his eyes scooting across her face as if it were too marred or ugly to look at properly. Yet despite the fact that he didn't seem able to look at her, she suddenly felt as if he'd managed to do just that. He turned away and walked up the road. As he got to the church gate, Laurence came around the corner.

They stopped and talked together. Laurence looked at his watch and nodded. Simeon seemed to be in demand.

Georgie waited for Laurence to come down to her. He hadn't filled out from when he was a boy, long, skinny limbs that his brain didn't seem to know how to work properly, shoulders stooped and short spiky hair. He wasn't handsome. She fell into step beside him and they walked on down to the sea. At the bottom he led her to the left, up behind the holiday cottages. As the land rose ahead of them, a path splintered off towards the sea. They followed it until they were standing on the narrow spit of land that was the northern side of the cove. The edges were sheer, dropping steeply into the water. Though they were not hugely high, for a moment Georgie felt almost dizzy. Not far along there was a bench, its feet buried deep in the turf. Sitting on it, they could see down into the cove and the path leading up the other side to the lifeboat station. There were people staying in the round house; a light sparkled behind the door and a single car was parked across the way. Georgie wondered what it was like inside.

"I saw this place yesterday. It's in plain sight, but no-one will be able to creep up on us to listen," Laurence said, rubbing his eyes as if he'd just woken up.

"It's not exactly sheltered though. I'm so cold."

"Actually, it is, more than you think. When we're done, walk along to the end and see what it's like without the land protecting you. Down there you'll have to be careful you don't get blown into the sea."

"Like Bob," she said, bursting into tears. Laurence wrapped his arms around her.

"Oh Georgie, what have we done?"

219

Chapter 24

Derek was up early and brought Harriet a bucket-sized cup of coffee before heading out with the dog. He left the house whistling, which enabled Harriet to get up and get on without anything else filling her head. She decided that, as it was the last night of the retreat, she'd do a roast chicken. There was a new recipe for lemon stuffing she wanted to try. She cheerfully planned timings and a shopping list of extras she'd need.

It was only when she opened the front door of the bungalow and her eyes were drawn across to Terry's front garden that she flipped back into harsh reality. The garden was beginning to look a little overgrown and unkempt. Terry had been sectioned, though, as Simeon rightly said, it wouldn't be forever. She was far too clever not to be released at some point.

Fear shimmered at the edge of Harriet's thoughts, but she couldn't allow it a foothold, not with everything else that was going on. She was glad that she and Derek were moving further down the lane, so even if Terry did come back, there'd be less chance of bumping into her. Of being reminded.

She closed the door firmly behind her and marched purposefully down to the vicarage.

***

Once breakfast was over and the dining room had emptied, Harriet collected the two big trays from the kitchen and returned to make a start on clearing up. Anna had also come back to help, but was sitting slumped at the table, her chair pulled away so she could stretch her legs out.

"I was worried we'd miss Catherine for breakfast, but Laurence ate us out of house and home. I'll have to get more bread," Harriet said. Anna looked up puzzled. Harriet didn't think she'd heard a word. "Pass me the clean cutlery, would you?" Anna stood up and began to gather knives and spoons, clean and dirty together.

"We're missing something here," Anna said, holding a knife in each hand. "These three know each other and two of them knew the man who died."

"Robert Enderby."

Anna nodded, her lips pressed together tightly. She started picking up napkins.

"You're always so good at remembering names."

Harriet didn't think she was particularly, but definitely better than Anna.

"Come on, Anna, let's go through to the kitchen where we won't be disturbed every five minutes."

Harriet passed her one of the trays. It would save her another trip.

"Goodness, Harriet, didn't Laurence eat like we hadn't fed him for the last couple of days!"

Anna was only listening to what was going on inside her own head. It was a good job Harriet wasn't feeling quite so fragile as earlier; only the thought of Terry still made her shudder.

"What's the matter?" Anna asked. "You look as if you've seen a ghost. Did you hear something?"

"No. I was thinking about Terry. I'll be glad to move, get away from having to look at her house every day."

"You'll still have to pass it to get up to the pub or to the shop."

"Thank you for reminding me."

Anna bit her lip and the sudden colour of her mouth made her cheeks look pallid.

"I suppose I could always go round by the coastal path," Harriet added.

She leaned across to pat Anna's arm. Sometimes upsetting Anna was too easy.

"Not a very efficient use of your time, though you'd get very fit."

That'd be nice, Harriet thought. She didn't manage to get out as much as she used to. Derek walked the dogs now, Dolly with Bowzer from the pub. Lately she'd hardly had time to do more than power walk up to the shop and back.

"I've just drunk enough tea to sink a battleship, so why do I really fancy a coffee?" Harriet asked, filling the kettle.

"That's not like you, but it's just like me. I use tea and coffee to punctuate my day, to demarcate the sections. That was breakfast with the guests and this is chat-with-Harriet time."

"Oh, how long have I got?"

"As long as you want. Or at least until Archie or Tom turn up. I hope Archie's alright. He's been looking a little ..."

"Old ... Is that too mean, Anna?" But he'd been looking wrinkly, a bit patched up, not his usual dapper self at all. Dapper was a word that Harriet only ever used for Archie. It normally suited him very well.

"I'm worried that he's worried about the Reader course. I thought I was doing him a favour, getting Pearly to waive the rules, but ever since he went to that introductory meeting, he's been very quiet."

"I suppose he's a little old for it. Doesn't the course take three years?" Anna nodded. "Have you talked to him about it?"

"Yes. He said it was fine."

"Oh dear. Not good then."

"The trouble is, Archie thinks he'll be letting me down if he doesn't go ahead with it."

"And of course, neither of us ever thinks like that about anything, do we?" Harriet said sweetly.

"Oh, ha ha!" Anna said, laughing. Then in a high-pitched, wheedling tone she continued, "Oh, I couldn't possibly leave Derek, even if it's the right thing to do. The village would never forgive me."

Harriet sat down and buried her face in her hands.

223

"They wouldn't though, would they?" she said, her voice muffled by her hands.

"Oh Harriet, I'm so sorry. I meant it as a joke. Only it's not one bit funny."

Harriet looked up at her friend, leaning forward, wanting to help, always wanting to help.

"On one level though, you're right. I do need to say it out loud. I need to voice my concerns, face them and you're the only one with whom I can do that. But please, please, Anna, can we keep it between ourselves?"

She could see that Anna was hurt as she pulled her hand away and got up to make the coffee. It was true, though. Anna was always blurting things out without thinking and Harriet's worries about the future mustn't get back to Derek. It would devastate him. Damage limitation would never be enough. Harriet knew that.

"Of course. Whatever you say to me is confidential," Anna said quietly.

"Anna, it's just that, if it got back to him ..."

"I'm sorry I'm so unreliable."

That was the problem with Anna. She could take any moment and wrap it around herself. Now she'd believe that that was what everyone thought of her and Harriet would have to spend much precious time working her back from that particular notion.

"You're not unreliable. It's just that sometimes you forget who told you what, and people do tell you things because you are kind and very reliable."

"But not if I then blurt those things out at inappropriate moments."

"Anna, please don't make this about you."

Harriet froze. She'd just made it a thousand times worse. There was a tap on the back door. She stood up and squeezed past Anna to let Archie in. He looked pink from his walk across the village.

224

"Coffee?"

"Yes please."

"How are you?" Anna asked, biting her lip. She stepped back so he could slide a chair out.

"I'm alright, just tired. It's been a bit of a week and now Simeon is staying. I don't mind of course," he added quickly.

"You can mind if you want to and it has been a bit of a week," Harriet said with feeling.

"Is it too much for us, do you think?" Anna asked, plonking down. Harriet slid mugs across the table to each of them.

"No, I don't think so," Archie replied, but he was frowning. "After all, we won't have a murder every week, will we?"

"But even without that, it can get really hectic. Dani and Georgie hate sharing, poor Catherine has been positively neglected and Laurence ... well, he has ..."

None of them wanted to fill the space left by that sentence, though Harriet thought it might be better to do just that, to actually say what they were all thinking, to say that there was a possibility that Laurence might be a murderer. Perhaps they'd all feel better if they got some of the unsaid things out into the open. She'd felt better talking about Derek, except that, despite their previous conversation, she was now nervous that Anna might try and help by saying something to him.

"I don't think he did it," Anna said. "He simply doesn't look as if he's got it in him."

"In which case, who else?" Harriet prompted.

"The men from Exeter," Archie said quickly. "They're obvious candidates."

Anna shook her head.

"Tom said they left the village after they'd spoken to Laurence. Jean from the shop saw them go." Harriet could see Anna was wondering if she ought to be telling them things that Tom had said. But the hesitation was short-lived and with hardly a breath she continued. "It was a big car and surely someone would've noticed if they'd come back."

"They could have parked further out, even down by Kynance and walked to the point along the coast," Archie said. He didn't often speak with such forthrightness. "Pushed the man over and then jogged back to their car."

"But surely they would've been spotted by someone," Anna persevered. "You can see that bit of the path for miles and there were men working on the car park at Kynance. Tom said they were pretty sure they hadn't seen anyone."

"Ok then, who does that leave us with?" Harriet asked.

"Either he fell or it was Laurence and Georgie. They were the only people down there at the time," Anna said.

"I thought Simeon said he'd seen someone else come down the road," Harriet looked thoughtful, her voice hesitant.

"Oh yes, but he couldn't tell if it was a man or a woman," Anna replied and shrugged. "He wondered if it might've been Dani."

"I expect it was Dani." Archie said, shifting back in his chair when both women swung round to stare at him.

"How do you know that?" Anna asked.

"Because she told Phil that she'd been down there, before she went back to the pub."

"As far as I know," Anna said, "she didn't tell anyone else that. Certainly not Tom. He's never interviewed her, never thought she had anything particular to add once she said she'd only been to the pub."

"Ok, well, leaving aside the murder and the mystery person being Dani, someone from here must have been down there because otherwise how did the binoculars get under the van?" Harriet asked, remembering Tom's worried frown when forensics had pointed them out to him.

Archie spoke, reluctantly, "Either Laurence, Georgie or Dani must have picked them up and brought them back, perhaps without realising what they were." He raised his mug to his lips and took a sip.

"But then why keep quiet about them and why put them under Laurence's van?" Harriet said. The binoculars and their appearance back at the vicarage had always bugged her.

Anna looked confused. Then she said slowly, "Unless whoever it was was trying to point the finger. They'd seen something happen down at the Lizard, but didn't want to say and brought the glasses up here in the hope that the police would find them?"

"But they wouldn't have found them, if Laurence's van hadn't been broken into," Harriet pointed out.

Archie shook his head.

"I think the obvious answer to all of this is that the men from Exeter killed the man from the pub and then left his binos under the van as a warning to Laurence." Harriet could see Archie didn't want to let the drug dealers off the hook. Admittedly, the alternative was too horrible for words. "A warning to toe the line, to keep his mouth shut or else he'd end up like the man in the sea."

"Oh, that's quite a good theory, Archie," Anna said. He nodded, but Harriet wasn't satisfied.

"That means that Laurence either hid something that the Exeter men were looking for or he saw them killing Enderby."

Harriet was a little shocked when Anna giggled.

"Of course, we're missing a very obvious suspect."

"Simeon!"

"No, not him," Anna said, her lips squashed white as she tried not to laugh. She pushed her chair back for dramatic effect. "Catherine. Perhaps she got fed up with waiting for Tom to come and see her and decided to murder someone so that she'd get his full attention."

Harriet began to laugh too; she couldn't help herself. Archie didn't. He wasn't finding it funny at all. There was a tap on the back door and Anna flushed pink.

"We were only kidding, Archie," Harriet said, patting his shoulder as she turned round to open the it. "Oh hello Tom.

We've solved your murder for you. Haven't we?" she said, turning back to the table. Anna was blinking now and shaking her head. Archie looked really upset. He tried to stand, but there wasn't enough room. They needed a coordinated effort to get up from the tiny kitchen table. Harriet hoped that Tom knew them well enough not to worry that they all looked so embarrassed at his arrival, as if they had something to hide.

***

Anna finally managed to get up and slid to the door. All they needed now was for Simeon to turn up and they'd have the whole set. No, Derek was missing, but for now it was probably best to have either Harriet or Derek, not both. Anna was worried about Archie. She'd never seen him look so angry before. She wondered how she could have disregarded the Reader course so much; it was obviously weighing him down. She needed to be his friend for a change.

Tom looked shiny. He'd combed his hair, tried to flatten it at the back. She'd fancy him again in two weeks when it had grown a little. He'd also put on a clean shirt.

Was that what being together meant? That you noticed when someone changed their clothes? She looked down at her jumper. There were a couple of bits of porridge sticking to her left boob. She hurriedly picked them off and smoothed her own hair behind her ears.

Archie was squashed against the door into the hall. She wondered what he'd do now. What should she do? What did Tom need? Harriet was pouring him coffee.

"Archie, can I have a quick word?" she asked. Archie looked up and nodded. "I'll be back in a minute, Tom," she said.

Anna took Archie through into her sitting room. She didn't think he'd be particularly comfortable sitting there – it was too small, too cosy, but she didn't want to use the big lounge as there they would definitely get interrupted.

"Have a seat, Archie." The two easy chairs were knee-touchingly close. He sat, but was at attention. This was how he used to be with her, on guard. She tried to slump a little more so that she wasn't sitting quite so formally herself.

"What's going on, Archie? I can see that something's really bothering you."

She watched him trying to work out how to answer her. It was like sitting opposite Simeon on a bad day.

"Take a deep breath and spill the beans. Surely you know I'm here for you."

"It's just that it's personal."

"Oh Archie, I'm sorry." How could the Reader course be personal? "You don't have to do it, you know. If it feels too much, no-one will think any the less of you."

He frowned.

"What will be too much for me?"

"The Reader course."

He smiled and his shoulders sagged.

"That I had already decided. I was going to speak to Pearly next week and of course yourself." He looked down at his hands, now clasped on his lap. "I was waiting for a quiet moment to tell you. I'm really sorry, but I'm simply too old. There's a new twelve-week course they're going to try out, which might be better. Lay Worship Leading. More helpful to you and more appropriate for me."

Anna's head was reeling a little. So what was bugging Archie, if it wasn't the course?

"But something is upsetting you."

"Yes, but like I said, it's a bit personal and I'm not sure it's something I can discuss with you."

"What about with Pearly, I mean, the bishop?"

"Absolutely not."

Anna breathed a deep breath from between tight lips.

"Well, if there's nothing I can do to help, I'm a bit stuck."

"I'm praying about it a lot. Hopefully it'll sort itself out. I'd talk to you if it was appropriate. You know I would. The problem is, Anna, we can't see into other people's hearts and neither should we, but we're responsible for each other. I certainly care about what happens to you, deeply."

Anna frowned. He'd just said a lot of things, but she wasn't sure she understood which was relevant to this precise moment.

"I know you care deeply, for all of us. We often only go ahead because we know you have our backs. It's the whole community thing."

"And we're important to you, aren't we, Anna?" To Anna's ears, there was a note of desperation in his voice, a little catch at the end, a slight emphasis on the 'we'.

"Of course. You guys are my life. My family."

And he nodded.

"Well, I'm just going to pop down to the church. Anything you'd like me to pray for?" he asked brightly, as if everything was resolved.

"No thanks, I'm alright for now." They both stood up, awkwardly. She hated this; she didn't want it to be like it used to be. "Archie, whatever you need, we're all here for you. You know that, don't you?"

He smiled, but it was more of a tight grimace and did not reassure her at all.

***

Anna would've liked to sit back down to think through what had just happened, but she thought she ought to get back to Tom. It hadn't looked great that she'd walked out as he'd walked in. But she was a vicar; this was her job and she didn't know if Tom was here as a police officer, a son or as a ... boyfriend. Boyfriend! What a childish word. It didn't suit what they were trying to be. Not one bit.

The kitchen was empty, but she could hear voices in the lounge. Tom was sitting on the sofa, both hands closed around a mug of coffee. Harriet was standing in front of the fire, a few logs burning in the grate.

"I could do with a word with Archie," Tom said. "And, of

course, Dani. I thought she must have been down there. That madam will need to be told what's what."

Anna said quickly, "Archie's just gone down to the church and Dani is ... She probably didn't realise that what she had or hadn't seen was important. Please don't be too cross with her. She's only just stopped being a child herself."

Tom looked sad, disappointed.

"I won't," he said. "I have done this before, you know."

Anna looked down at the floor.

"I'm sorry. I didn't mean to imply you aren't professional or anything," she said quietly.

Harriet cleared her throat.

"Do you know what I think you two need?"

They both turned to her. Anna's stomach lurched, a panicky sinking that made her put her hands on her tummy and press. What was Harriet going to say? Would Tom be cross that Anna had spoken to Harriet about what had happened the night before, like two silly schoolgirls?

"Some boundaries," Harriet said, shrugging.

Anna thought that feeling like a giggling schoolgirl was quite apt. Tom pressed his lips together, his mouth becoming that tight, hard line he used when he was formulating how to retort to any slight on his professionalism.

"Now Tom, before you get all prickly," Harriet said, beginning to look a little uncomfortable, "it's just that you're a police officer and Anna, you're a vicar twenty-four-seven. It must be difficult for either of you to know what you're meant to be like when you're together. For goodness' sake Tom, you're investigating a murder!"

"It's true that sometimes I'm not sure whether to treat you as a police officer or a friend."

"It's not always straightforward, I grant you," he said.

"So what can we do?" Anna asked. Last night she'd imagined Tom walking in that morning, coming over and kissing her. She hadn't really got past that bit. When he'd

231

knocked on the door earlier, she hadn't known what to do and Archie had stood between them like a giant sore thumb.

"Put in place some rules," Harriet continued. "You can work them out between you."

"What sort of things?" Tom asked suspiciously.

Anna began to nod her head.

"If it's about police work or I'm patently being my vicary-self, then we behave as colleagues. But when we meet for, say, coffee or dinner or a film together, then we can be normal, like other couples."

Anna was quite pleased with herself, except suddenly she felt scared, remembering other times when she was paralysed with fear of saying or doing the wrong thing. "What about around your mum?" she said.

"Perhaps Tom can find some time when the three of you can be together and he's not being a police officer and you're not being a vicar. What do you think?"

"Ok, this all sounds good and sensible, but Anna, I think sometimes we'll have to switch it up a bit to make it work," Tom said carefully.

"How do you mean?"

"If you intend to say goodbye this evening as a professional colleague, I shall get very upset." He raised an eyebrow.

Anna bit her lip and Harriet laughed. A good laugh.

"I think you'll both get the hang of this quite quickly," she said.

"Speaking of which, I haven't seen Mum this morning."

"She's gone out to Kynance. Will be back for lunch," Harriet said.

"Well, I'll go and find Archie then. If you could keep Dani here, I'll come back and interview her later."

Harriet turned, picked up an empty tray and left the room. Anna stood up as Tom stepped across to her.

"Just for a second, can we switch off the vicar and the

policeman?"

So they did. Anna's only problem was switching everything back on again afterwards.

Chapter 25

"Shit! Shit! Shit!" Laurence shouted out across the sea. It was a good day to yell. The wind was at his back, propping him up, taking his words and spraying them out over the edge. Standing here he reckoned he could scream at the top of his lungs and no-one would hear him, no-one would ever know. He'd been wondering if it was worth slipping back to the vicarage to pick up his stuff and then making a run for it. There must be somewhere he could go, somewhere he could start again. He didn't have much to leave behind, nothing that should make him hesitate. But how did you start again in a new job, when filling in paperwork would always be a risk? He simply couldn't imagine himself living well while looking over his shoulder all the time. The last few months he'd felt hunted – shapes out of the corner of his eye, sounds in the night he couldn't place. It had been horrible, but if he ran, the police would simply assume that he was guilty. There ought to be due process. He'd heard that on a TV programme and it had stuck. But kids like him didn't seem to have the same rights as others. He'd sworn he'd never fall back on that tired maxim either. The 'poor me, I was brought up in an orphanage' routine. The 'Take pity on me, I was used by a man I trusted'. Would a lawyer insist they play that card? In which case to hell with due process.

He saw Belle making her way towards him. She snuffled around his ankles and he bent down to rub her ears. They were the softest thing he'd ever felt. She looked back to check that Simeon was still coming. Laurence had hoped they'd have time to meet before the DI arrested him.

Laurence held out his hand to greet Simeon until he remembered that Simeon didn't do touching. He dropped his arm. That was fine by him because from now on, neither did he. Earlier, he'd held Georgie while she'd sobbed until she'd stopped. There'd been a few little gulps and then she'd wiped a tissue across her eyes, blown her nose and sat back.

'He deserved it and we deserve better. We deserve a chance,' she'd said. He'd asked her if she wanted to talk some more. She'd said no and walked away. Laurence had been sad and then hurt because there was plenty he'd wanted to say to her, but he couldn't follow because he'd already agreed to meet Simeon and that was important too. He'd been intending to ask him a bit more about God, but now he'd something else he wanted to do.

"Shall we go back and sit on the bench?" Laurence was staring down into the cove. The tide was high, the water surging up the ramp. As it sank back, it hit the next wave coming in so that there were lines of white foam criss-crossing the swell. A stream filled with brown water was pouring down the cliff and splattered into the waves, a spray of droplets forming a permanent rainbow, pale and diaphanous. The noise of water falling, waves turning and tumbling up the inlet, surging round the spine of rocks, filled the air. Even talking to Simeon, standing just a metre or two away, meant raised voices. All three of the houses below them looked empty, blinds down, doors shut. The car had gone. A couple of small boats and a kayak had been hauled up out of the way, but apart from those signs of life – splashes of red, white and orange – everything else was the dull green and grey of early winter.

The bench was damp Simeon took a cloth from his coat pocket and wiped it. Laurence was impressed.

"Do you always have a bit of old towel in your pocket?"

"Yes. It's for Belle. In case we go and visit someone and she is muddy." He then pulled a carrier bag from his pocket and dropped the towel into it. He peered at his fingers and pulled his gloves back on.

"This place tears at your—. Actually, I'm not quite sure what I want to say."

"I think it tears at your soul," Simeon said matter-of-factly.

"The bit inside you that is God. This place, this cove in particular, resounds to the rhythm of the waves, the wind. It emphasises the presence of God all around us without being overwhelming."

"You have an incredible way of putting things."

Because Laurence had felt something pulling gently at him. Niggling away underneath.

Simeon said, "I've had lots of time to think about things and when I think something is important, I write it down. Then I wait and watch."

"And you truly believe that it's God who speaks to you?"

Belle was sitting up, leaning against Simeon. Now and again, Simeon moved his hand to rest on her head.

"Yes, I believe that it's God who speaks to me." He pulled a book from his pocket. He held it in front of him and flicked the pages. It was a notebook, about a centimetre thick, full of small, tidy writing.

"I don't want to let you look at it because it's full of things about me. Also, I don't like people touching my possessions."

"That's alright, mate. I just don't know why I have to believe in God. What has he ever done for me?"

"He's given you life. He's brought you here to talk to me."

"That could sound a little arrogant, Simeon. Like you're the answer to all my problems."

"Not arrogant, but I might have some of the answers to your questions, simply because we're sitting here talking about God."

"But that was because I asked you."

"Why did you ask me?"

"Because you're a straightforward and honest guy and there aren't that many of them in my life right now."

"So I'm exactly the right person for you at this minute. I don't think God likes to waste any opportunity."

Laurence raised his hands. Talking to Simeon had made sense, like walking a well-trodden path, where all you had to

237

do was take another step, but suddenly he felt that the path had dropped away and he was expected to fly.

"Do you mind if we stop talking about God just for a minute?" Simeon nodded. "The thing is, Simeon, I think the DI will arrest me today." Simeon didn't move a muscle, continued to stare out over the water. Laurence liked that about him. If there was any judgement, he guessed Simeon would simply speak it out. "I'm guilty of quite a few things. In fact, I'm surprised I'm not in custody now."

Of course that might simply be because, just after breakfast, just after Anna had said a prayer of blessing over each of them, he'd slipped out of the front door. How did they know that he wouldn't go far because no-one had come running after him?

This was a good place; he could see all around, though it also meant that he could be trapped on this little spit of land and he didn't like the thought of that.

"Can I tell you my story, Simeon? I want someone to know what happened. It'll get twisted and pulled about by the coppers, but I want someone to hear what I have to say."

"But if you tell me you've done something illegal, I'll have to tell Tom."

"I know. But he's not here now and that'll have to do."

Simeon turned and stared out at the horizon. His hand was on the dog's head. She was looking up at him as if she knew there was something important going on.

"This is not something I've ever done before," Simeon said. For a moment, he turned quickly to look at Laurence. They were sitting at opposite ends of the bench, a gap between them, but close enough that, if Laurence stretched out his hand, he could touch this man, Simeon, who said quietly, "Please tell me your story. If I don't understand, may I ask questions?"

"Yes, if you like," Laurence replied, already feeling lighter. "I'd like to start back when I was sixteen and Georgie arrived at the home. She was just fourteen and so small. She'd had a terrible time."

***

Dani was sitting on an uncomfortable chair. It seemed to be padded in all the wrong places, the fabric rough and pulled. She wanted to tuck her legs under her, but, although the police officer had said it was an informal interview, she had a feeling he hadn't meant that informal. He was sitting opposite; the policewoman was behind Dani at a small table. They both had notebooks. He'd asked if she wanted anyone to sit with her, but the only person she could think of was Catherine. But Catherine was his mum, so she hadn't bothered.

"Could you please tell us again your movements on Tuesday morning?" There was the slightest stress on the word 'again'. Dani heard it and decided to ignore it.

"Where would you like me to start?" Honestly, what a bore.

"What time did you leave the vicarage?"

"I'm not sure. Just before ten." It hadn't been long after Laurence and Georgie, probably about ten to. She wondered what the police officer wanted. Perhaps someone had seen her after all, though she'd checked and checked again. Even the big car park had been empty. Anyway, she'd run really fast, kept her ears open and had been back up at the pub in no time at all.

"How long were you down on the point?"

"I can't remember. A few minutes. Five-ish. I don't know."

She knew she'd got back to the pub at ten-thirty, but she wouldn't tell him that.

"Did you see anything?"

"A lot of sea and a couple of grotty buildings."

The policeman glared at her. He sat slightly forward. Dani began to feel really intimidated.

"I'd like to stop now," she said, her voice thin and scratchy.

"I have more than enough to caution you with wasting

police time, so I'll say when we stop."

This was getting difficult. Bloody Georgie and Laurence and that horrible, horrible man. She'd have to keep her wits about her if she was going to tell this story straight.

"So, what exactly did you do? Start from when you came past the car park."

She bit her lip, making a fuss about remembering. As it was, she'd never forget what happened. How could she?

"I did see the big 4x4 coming up the lane. It shot by me, going far too fast."

"And yet you didn't stick to the footpath through the car park, but instead went down by the road? It's very narrow and can be dangerous for a walker."

"I've never been there before. I didn't know I had a choice."

"There are signs. If another car had gone up or down, you could easily have been knocked over."

She shrugged. She'd been about halfway along when she'd realised it was a bit dodgy because the big black car had been going quite fast. Luckily there'd been another small drive further down where she could have nipped in, out of the way, if she'd had to. Over the last thirty yards the sides of the lane had been particularly steep, sheer and close-cropped, topped with dense thorns. She'd jogged that bit, down to where everything opened out, where she'd felt that, if she didn't cling onto something, she'd slip down into the sea. She'd taken the first path on her right, which had brought her into the garden of a bungalow that turned out to be an old café. It'd been dusty and shuttered, with dog-eared signs dotting the windows about opening again in the spring. It hadn't looked as though it ever would. She'd scooted along the front veranda until she'd gotten to the far side. When she'd felt secure, she'd checked out the view, out across the point, over the coastal path and onto the roofs of the café below. She'd just been able to see where the track leading to the sea disappeared around the end of the buildings. Far down below there'd been another roof. Of course now she knew that it was the old lifeboat station. It'd looked a wreck of jagged, rusting metal. Romantic it certainly wasn't.

"So once you got there, what did you do?" The woman at the table was frantically taking notes. Dani could hear her pen scraping the paper.

"It was really cold, so I turned round and walked back up to the pub. I couldn't see what everyone was making such a fuss about. You can see a lot of sea. Big deal!"

The policeman shook his head. Dani would've liked to see the expression on the face of the woman behind her.

"You didn't see Georgie or Laurence at any point?"

Dani shook her head.

"And you are absolutely positive you didn't see anyone else on either of the paths, going west or east?"

Again, Dani shook her head.

"What time did you get back up to the pub?"

"I'm not sure, but I bet the landlord could tell you. We chatted until a friend of his came in. The man who helps out at the vicarage, Archie something or other. He seemed to be upset, so they went off to talk at the other end of the bar."

She twisted round to see if she could see what the policewoman was scribbling in her notebook.

"Are you sure you didn't walk a little way along the path to the west?"

"Which way is that?"

"Did you see a pair of binoculars? Anywhere?"

The woman behind her made her jump by asking, "Thought perhaps someone might have dropped them and that you could hand them in somewhere?"

It was all just a little too late. Because she'd seen them, hanging from the shoulder of that bloody man as he walked towards her, when she'd pressed herself back around the corner of the café. She was still almost certain no-one had

241

seen her because if they had, these two would've been asking a whole set of different questions.

The policeman said, "Don't go far, please. We may need to speak to you again to clarify some of the details."

Actually, she could go where she wanted. She knew her rights. It was a shame she didn't have her own car because then she could just drive home. What could they do to stop her?

She grabbed a coffee from the front room and climbed the stairs. Georgie was lying on her bed, staring at the ceiling. As Dani walked in, she rolled onto an elbow. She looked a bit red-eyed.

"So, what did they want?"

Dani wanted to ignore her, but that didn't seem to be the sensible option. Not anymore.

"Oh, the usual. 'Where was I when it was all kicking off?'"

"Right, and you of course didn't see anything because you were safely sitting in the pub with Kyle."

Dani was half into another sweatshirt. She must have hesitated for a microsecond, certainly no longer. She swore under her breath.

"You were there, weren't you?" Georgie said sharply.

"Actually, I did pop down to the point for a minute, but I really didn't see anything."

Georgie was staring at her.

"Did you see Bob? Did you see what happened?"

She'd swung her legs onto the floor and was leaning forward. Her cheeks were flushed and her fingers were screwing the duvet into tight whorls.

"God, Georgie, back off, will you! I wish I'd never come to this bloody place. I bet you wish you hadn't either. Seeing Laurence has just been one big laugh."

"Laurence is alright. It's not his fault he's such a softy. Bob was always able to wind him round his little finger, from the first time he ever met him. I told him, and told him he needed

242

to be careful, not to trust anyone. But Laurence was just so desperate to trust someone."

Dani looked up in surprise because she'd just made a guess about something and she bet a thousand pounds she was right.

"You were just too young for it to be you, and he won't see you as anything other than the little girl he helped when you were kids," said Dani.

Georgie looked startled.

"It's not like that. Really, it's not." But she sounded sad.

"Like what, Georgie? You'd do anything to help him out, wouldn't you? But would he cover your back like you're covering his?" Dani immediately regretted saying that because Georgie clambered off the bed and came towards her. Dani was suddenly quite frightened.

"You have no idea what you're talking about. You really don't. So, if I were you, I'd just keep my big mouth shut. Because I'm not stupid and I saw your dirty knickers all over the floor." For a moment Dani thought Georgie was going to hit her. She leaned back, biting her lip. But Georgie just grabbed her coat and walked out, leaving the door open. Through the gap Dani saw her at the top of the stairs, her face pinched and furious.

Dani sat down on the bed. Well, she'd certainly hit the mark, but she hadn't liked the dig at her dirty knickers. She'd pulled them out of her case in a bit of a panic while hunting for the binoculars she'd hidden inside there. She'd thought they'd be safe, at least until she knew the police were on their way back.

How much easier would it all have been if she'd not had to share the room with the mad cow. And what if Georgie had put two and two together? She certainly wasn't stupid.

Chapter 26

Georgie looked around the hall. There was nowhere to go except out, and earlier, when she'd met Laurence, she'd got really cold.

She didn't think Dani would be down for a bit, which was a relief, only now she felt the guilt roar up through her. She sat down on the bottom stair and put her head in her hands. It wasn't Dani's fault that Georgie was in such a mess, but she'd definitely taken it out on her.

It had felt so good, rather like kicking an annoying puppy. No-one would understand how close to the edge Georgie was and all around her people were keeping secrets and telling lies.

She wandered into the dining room. Harriet had been as good as her word and on the table there was a flask of fresh coffee, a kettle and a pile of biscuits. Yesterday they'd been home-made; today they weren't, but were big double choc-chip cookies. A real treat. The staff at church were lucky if they got a pack of custard creams. Georgie bit into one while she poured a coffee. She topped it up with milk and then added a spoonful of sugar, as Harriet's coffee was always a bit strong.

She took another couple of biscuits and went over to sit at the table. The two big windows were filled with sky, but it was dark and heavy, so the room felt dull. She almost went over to put on the main light, but that would've meant advertising her presence and, just for now, she wanted to be alone, needed to calm down, to get a grip.

The front door opened. She heard the rustle of a coat being pulled off. There was a second or two of silence, as if whoever it was couldn't decide what to do next. Then the door into the dining room opened and Catherine walked in. For a second, she didn't see Georgie and Georgie had to decide whether to move or not.

"Hello Catherine."

"Oh, hello Georgie. I was just going to make myself a cup of tea. Do you want anything?"

"I've got one," she said, lifting her mug in the air.

"Sorry, I'm disturbing you."

"No, it's alright."

Catherine switched on the kettle and reached for a mug, but then she suddenly hesitated. Without turning around she said, "Do you want someone to talk to or would you rather I went next door?"

Georgie sighed, which sounded rather more pathetic than she'd meant it to. The sort of pathetic that would invite questions.

"The trouble is we go back tomorrow. I just don't feel I've had enough time." She hoped that wasn't too specific.

"Three whole days at the start of the week sounded like forever, but you're right, before you know it, you're sitting down to another meal and another slot has passed."

"I don't want to go back. But I don't think I can stay here."

"And you have to take Dani home," Catherine said, turning round at last and smiling, as if it were a good thing.

"She could catch a train. Except she probably couldn't afford it. I don't have any money to give her."

Georgie knew she sounded as if she were asking for help, but all her energy had drained away and she couldn't be bothered to second-guess anyone. She knew she'd have to go back, continue her job, work out her penance. The alternative of being found out was too terrible to contemplate and Alf would be waiting, expecting her to be all bright-eyed and bushy-tailed; only she was too exhausted to pretend anymore and there was still that pile of admin to do, neatly stacked at the end of her bed. She'd promised herself that she'd sit down and work through it on the Friday evening she got back. It had sounded so plausible then, but not now. There was no way she'd be able to tackle it after a journey with Dani. She'd simply slide it onto the floor and cover it with her own dirty laundry.

"Sorry. That sounded as though I was asking you for money."

"Georgie, you've got so much going for you. What is it that's weighing you down so?"

"I suppose seeing Laurence again has brought a lot of things to the surface." Bob and all those memories. "The thing is, Catherine, we don't have any family at our backs to catch us or anywhere for us to run to. Even Dani has a mum, who, despite being a bit full-on, is always there for her, who's killing herself to allow Dani a bit of life, even though Dani would rather die than admit that. So when Laurence and I see that ingratitude, it hangs a bit heavy because he and I stand alone. Sometimes it makes us a bit desperate, a bit unbalanced in how we view things."

"I've never thought of it like that," Catherine said.

She'd probably never thought about it at all. Georgie felt the anger beginning to simmer again.

"It's not your problem."

"It shouldn't be yours either. What sort of society treats its children like this?"

Georgie looked across at her. Catherine seemed to be a genuinely nice lady, kind, caring, but what could she do? What could anyone do?

"Perhaps I'll meet a nice, ordinary bloke some time, one who has parents and a home."

Catherine stayed silent. Georgie wished she'd make a joke, say something facetious. But Catherine's eyes were shiny and Georgie prayed with all her heart that she wasn't about to cry. That was exactly why she didn't tell people about her past. Because the pity welled up and overwhelmed them.

Suddenly the light came on and they both jumped. Harriet was backing into the room carrying a tray laden with cutlery and plates.

247

"Oh, I'm sorry, ladies. I didn't realise you were in here."

Catherine stood up.

"Let me give you a hand."

"There's no need, but if you really want to, I wouldn't say no. We're running a bit behind today. Tom is here. He wondered where you'd got to."

Georgie watched Catherine's face light up at the mention of her son's name and her own heart folded in on itself. It hurt, it actually physically hurt, to see Catherine's love.

"What's he doing right now?"

"I think he's gone down to the church to speak to Archie."

For a few minutes Georgie watched the two women laying up the table. It was a comforting moment. Then Harriet cleared away the dirty mugs and checked to see how much coffee was left.

"Lunch will be in about an hour. Can I get you two anything in the meantime? There's cake and more biscuits."

"Actually, is Anna about the place?" Georgie asked. "I wouldn't mind having a bit of a chat." As long as Tom was safely out of the way, then Anna might be alright. She wasn't perfect like the rest of the people who'd tried to help Georgie and perhaps she could help her work out what to do. How to go forward. Georgie certainly didn't have a clue herself.

***

Tom stood in the churchyard by the tomb where Fiona had died, where she'd lain for some time, her eyes filling with rain. It was horrible that that was the last thing Derek would ever remember about her, lying twisted, staring through half-closed eyes, her cheeks pallid, almost green in the torchlight. Tom rested his hand lightly on the stone. Simeon said a lot of people did that without realising they'd stopped at the spot. It had become a strange place of pilgrimage; definitely not the sort that Anna would approve of. Tom shook his head and continued on down the path. The church door was ajar and he hesitated for a moment before pushing it open. Speaking to

Dani that morning hadn't really helped at all. It had confirmed to him that he didn't particularly like the girl and he certainly didn't trust her. She was adept at saying what she thought she could get away with. Telling the truth, the actual truth, didn't seem to matter, as if such things as the law and decency didn't apply to her. To others certainly. She'd be the first in line if there was a grievance, if she was a victim. He smiled a little grimly. Such judgements he'd keep to himself. He could imagine what Anna would think of his intuition. But he'd been interviewing people for a long time and, unlike Anna, he didn't always think the best of them.

He now knew that Dani had been down at the point when Robert Enderby had been killed. He was also sure she wasn't telling them everything. Not by a long chalk.

The trouble was that all of the guests were carrying burdens and what Tom had to work out was which ones were fresh and new and relevant and which ones were old wounds not yet healed. Those he was only interested in as part of their back story. What he'd really like to do was lock them all in the vicarage with Anna for another couple of weeks. She'd get them sorted and then he could arrest his murderer. Of course, there was still the possibility that it'd been the men from Exeter, who had known not to stop at Tesco or Sainsbury's to fuel up, so no registration had been caught on camera. There was nowhere else in Helston with CCTV, which was a pain.

Archie was sitting in the front pew, his head bowed, his eyes tightly shut. His lips were moving and Tom felt that he was intruding on something desperately personal, that the man was scraped down to the bone. If he hadn't been a police officer, he would've turned and walked away.

"Hello Archie. I'm really sorry to disturb you, but I need to clarify a couple of things."

"Tom!" Archie jumped to his feet.

"It's just that you spoke to Harriet and Anna this morning

about something Dani said."

"You really need to speak to Phil. He was the one who told me. From my lips it will be second-hand at best."

"I will speak to Phil, but you …"

Archie frowned and tipped his head to one side. Tom knew that Archie didn't particularly like him, though he'd never admit to such a thing. He was surprised by a sudden yearning for this man's approval. There was an air of authority about Archie, a quiet certainty. Tom would've liked to cultivate something like that in himself. He felt that, most of the time, the men and women under him were simply waiting for him to trip up. Good people like Sandra would take their exams and disappear off, promoted to the dizzy heights that Tom had always despised. Probably because he was too scared, too frightened to think he could make it. He'd perfected his disdain, turned away with practised ease from any hints or possibilities of promotion dropped onto his desk by his superiors.

Tom stood up a little straighter and said, "So, what did Phil say to you?"

Archie went over what he could remember, but he told Tom again that he hadn't seen Dani arrive at the pub and he hadn't seen her leave. Phil would be much more useful.

"So, what do you think of her?"

"Miss Erskine? I don't think I should talk about her at all. It feels wrong as she's currently under our care."

"But Archie, she's a possible murder suspect."

"Oh no. I'm sure it wasn't one of our guests. I think it must've been the men from Exeter."

"I'm pretty certain it wasn't. Simeon saw Mr Enderby after they'd driven back up the road and the pathologist reckoned he'd gone into the water round about the same time or pretty soon after, otherwise the tide wouldn't have carried him out. So it has to be either Mr Weller, Miss Harbrook or Miss Erskine."

"Couldn't it have been an accident? He simply slipped and fell?"

"There's a heel print on the hand that was gripping the vegetation, probably for sheer life, which kind of makes that difficult to swallow. Surely, if it'd been just a slip, why didn't whoever was there raise the alarm, try to do something? And then there are the binoculars we found back at the house."

Archie looked thoughtful and very sad.

"But someone did try to do something."

"Only he'd been in the water an hour by then. We can be pretty sure of that, as long as we believe his watch. It stopped working at ten twenty-two. It's a bit Agatha Christie-ish." Tom laughed. Archie smiled weakly in response.

"Didn't Simeon say that he'd seen Georgie and Laurence at the bottom of the ramp round about then?"

Everyone knows everything or at least they believe they do, Tom thought crossly.

"No, he saw Laurence at the bottom and he saw Georgie beginning to head down the ramp and, at ten-fifteen, possibly Dani arriving. Any of them would've had plenty of time to go up and knock Enderby into the water – Laurence then going back to the café, Dani heading back to the pub and Georgie going on round the path that I think comes up by your house. I don't suppose you saw her?"

"No. I let Simeon and Belle in at about ten-fifteen, but the path is down behind the hedge. You could have a whole battalion go past there and I wouldn't notice them."

"And no-one else in the village saw her come through," Tom said. He really didn't have a thing to go on.

"Have you tried Jean from the shop? She normally keeps a good eye open."

"Thought of that already, Archie. Sadly, she'd just had a delivery and spent most of the morning unpacking coffee and biscuits."

Tom sighed. He really was getting nowhere fast. His Exeter

colleagues wanted Laurence in custody as a possible carrier, but Tom was sure there was more going on. Why had Robert Enderby been down here? Why had the heavy mob from Exeter made an appearance? They had been blatant, out in the open. Surely, if they'd just knocked someone off, they'd have been less blasé. Scaring Simeon like that was about sending a message, but this was not their territory. Or perhaps they didn't think the law stretched this far, that they were just dealing with inexperienced country plods. That stung. But if they'd come down to recover drugs from the back of the van, had it been because they hadn't trusted Enderby to sort it out or Laurence to deliver them to the right place? Tom rubbed his face with his hands. Then there were the bloody binoculars. He was ninety percent sure that they'd belonged to Enderby because of the case stuffed in his pocket, but any fingerprints on the binoculars themselves were smudged. Not one of them was good enough for a proper ID. And how had they ended up under Laurence's van? Unless Enderby had been there himself. Perhaps looking for the drugs that Laurence had for some reason not delivered?

Archie was still standing next to him. He looked worried.

"You're not really getting anywhere, are you?"

"No. I need someone to tell me something I don't know already."

"Have you tried Simeon? He's very observant."

"Remember he was a bit freaked out. Bad memories from before, so he saw things, but didn't catch details."

"But since then, he's been spending quite a bit of time with Laurence. Anna's been throwing them together as much as she can." Archie sounded a little disapproving, as if Tom had asked her to do it.

"I didn't know that. What do you think was on Anna's mind?"

Archie looked surprised.

"You're asking me?"

Tom shrugged. Fair enough. Archie was right. He ought to know what was on Anna's mind, better than Archie at least.

"The thing is, Archie, I think the world of her, you must know that, but she's a vicar first and I'm a police officer. I don't know if either of us can ever truly step away from our calling."

"Whatever else you think, no-one can step away from God," Archie said and looked slightly over Tom's shoulder. It reminded Tom of something that Simeon would do and say.

"Neither would I ever ask her to."

Archie straightened up.

"But you can't share what's of most importance to her."

"She can't share my job either." Tom knew he sounded peevish.

"You can't possibly think that being a police officer and having faith can be compared?"

The problem was, he probably did, therefore, Archie was never, ever going to approve of his feelings for Anna. His love for her. Perhaps it was all insurmountable. Tom turned to go. He didn't have a clue what to do next.

Chapter 27

After Tom had left, Archie couldn't settle. He couldn't get away from the fact that Tom had been asking something of him and, as per usual, Archie hadn't been sure what. He needed to clear his head. No, he needed to fill his head with thoughts. Work out what was going on inside.

He texted Simeon. Almost immediately, Simeon replied that he was on his way back up from Church Cove. Archie walked out into a patchy sunshine, pulled on his gloves and marched to the end of the path, where Simeon appeared with Belle and Laurence.

"Hello you two. Have you had a good walk?"

"We didn't go for a walk," Simeon said, but Archie was watching Laurence.

"We had a good talk," Laurence said, "sitting down at Church Cove."

"It's a lovely spot. Are you going back up to the vicarage?"

Simeon nodded.

"We are cold and could do with a warm drink and Laurence needs to do something."

Once again Archie watched the boy's face carefully. Laurence shrugged and, for a moment, Archie could see a small boy struggling to get out past a very old man, twisted and bent into shape by the path he'd had to travel.

Archie finally turned to Simeon and said, "I wouldn't mind a chat sometime, Simeon."

"In demand, mate! See what I mean. What you have is precious."

Simeon very quickly looked up at Archie and nodded. Even though Archie often told Simeon how good he was at listening, Simeon had never really believed him. Archie wasn't one bit surprised that it'd taken a stranger's voice to find its way through.

"Archie, I'm cold. Could we have a drink at the vicarage and then perhaps we could talk on our way back to your house?"

"I'm staying for lunch. Anna needs the support. Perhaps you could stay too?"

"It'd be great to know you were around, Simeon," Laurence said.

"I'll need to ask Harriet, in case there's not enough food."

The three of them trailed up the lane. No-one spoke.

Anna was in the hall, sitting on the bottom stair. Tom was standing in front of her. She looked pink and, for a minute, Archie was angry that Tom was able to mess her about like that, to override the important things just by his very presence.

"Archie, it's good to see you," she said, standing up. "And Simeon. Do you want to stay for lunch?"

"If there's enough."

"There always is. You know how wonderfully Harriet over-caters."

"Detective Inspector," Laurence said quietly, "I need to speak to you." For a second everyone held their breath.

Archie didn't know what he was going to do until he actually found himself stepping forward.

"Look, I know I'm not a lawyer or anything, but let me sit in with you. Would that be alright, Tom? I know not to say anything and I know that I don't have the right to ask as Laurence is over eighteen. It just feels important."

Tom glared briefly. Archie could imagine what he was thinking. Something about old busy-bodies poking their noses into places they weren't welcome. But Archie could also see Anna's face and she was nodding and smiling with relief, and that outweighed Tom's disapproval by a country mile.

"Mr Weller, as long as it's alright with you?"

Laurence looked surprised, then nodded.

"Thanks, Tom," Archie said. Out the corner of his eye Archie saw Simeon nod too. Poor Tom was surrounded by them, the do-gooders. He didn't stand a chance.

"Come on through to Anna's sitting room. It means we can talk undisturbed," Tom said and no-one missed the threat, gentle though it was.

Archie and Sandra sat at the small gateleg table, and Tom and Laurence in the easy chairs.

Laurence leaned back and then forward. He began to talk abruptly. Sandra had hardly got her pen ready.

"After I'd left the home Bob and I met for a drink now and again and I took him to work a couple of times, when he'd lost his bus pass. I was grateful that he'd looked me up. He was someone familiar who didn't need me to explain my whole back story. Before long, I realised Bob was involved with some very horrible people." Laurence looked across at Archie. Archie didn't know how to respond, didn't know what Laurence needed from him and before he could even smile, Laurence looked away again. "To begin with, I had the impression that Bob was simply in debt to them. I even offered him some of my own savings. I didn't have much, but, anyway, Bob didn't want them. He explained that, to pay off what he owed, he had to take a package down to Plymouth. Except he had a couple of shifts at the hospital. He was a porter there and I knew how much he loved the job; how much he wouldn't have wanted to let them down." He glanced at Tom. "I know how dumb I must sound, but I offered to do it, without a thought. It was only when I was telling Simeon I finally saw how right Georgie had been from the very beginning.

"I didn't even have to go out of my way. Bob must've known about the route – not difficult, as when I drove him, my list of deliveries was on the front seat of the van." He took a large breath. "So, I took a small, brown parcel and delivered it to a betting shop in one of the back streets of Plymouth. I think I can give you an address, though I'll have to check on Google maps first."

Archie was surprised to find tears coursing down his own

257

cheeks. He surreptitiously wiped them away. Sandra rested one of her hands on his arm for a second. This time, when Laurence looked across, Archie managed to pull himself together and quickly smiled back in what he hoped was an encouraging fashion. Laurence nodded and then continued.

"It wasn't long before Bob asked me to do another trip. He implied that, after that, he'd be off the hook." Laurence shifted in his seat. "I tried not to think about what I was delivering and, when I did, I pretended that it was something innocent. I know how completely stupid that sounds. Anyway, after that it did go quiet for a couple of months and then Bob phoned to ask if we could go for another drink. I knew I was in trouble when he turned up with a black eye. After that, I delivered packages every two or three weeks. Mostly I didn't have to go far off my route, but once or twice I did have to put extra fuel in the van. Bob offered to give me something towards it, but I always refused. That way I could still believe I was simply helping out a mate." Laurence shook his head, but remained staring down at the floor.

"Over the last couple of months, I'd start to feel sick each time he got in touch. I began to wonder how much the local drugs squad knew about me, driving down through Devon and Cornwall with such regularity. I stopped sleeping and even considered going to the police before they came to me."

Laurence looked up at Tom, who remained still, his face a professional mask. Archie desperately wanted him to show some form of humanity towards the boy. Laurence lowered his head and carried on.

"I should have gone to the police; except, I didn't know a lot. I could say where I took the packets, what they looked like and that it was Bob who handed them over with the addresses. But I didn't know anything about the organisation itself, who was in charge or who else might be involved.

"The turning point came just last week, when Bob gave me two packages. They were bigger than usual. One was to a regular drop-off. I did it, but when I was not far from the new address I suddenly pulled into a lay-by. I simply couldn't do it. A new place meant the network was expanding and I was helping it grow. Delivering drugs is killing people, no matter which way you look at it. That's what I couldn't get out of my head sitting there beside the A30, even with the traffic roaring past, rocking the van with the speed of it. When I finally decided to pull away, I couldn't feel my feet they were so cold. I'd been sitting for hours. I'd already booked onto the retreat, though I hadn't ever been on one before, but from the advert it looked as if I might get some thinking time. I'd been down to Helston to deliver parts with my proper job, so I knew it was at the back of beyond."

Archie looked at Laurence's face. His cheeks were flushed with the telling. Tom was still sitting motionless. Sandra was scribbling furiously. Laurence had just confessed to supplying drugs. The boy would go to prison; there was no doubt about it. Tom sat back and crossed his legs. He looked as if he were having a normal conversation and Archie wanted to yell at him to at least have the good grace to sit up as this young man spilled out his life.

"So, Laurence, what happened when you arrived on Monday?"

"Well, I'd been absent by then for three or four days. I was supposed to deliver the second package on the Wednesday morning. From Thursday onwards, I got tons of missed calls and texts from Bob. He was patently freaked out.

"I stupidly told him that I was still going on the retreat. He knew I'd been thinking of it ever since I'd seen Georgie and then the advert at work. He must've remembered enough to come down to find me. After all, there can't be that many places running such things at this time of year.

"Apparently, while I was sleeping in my van trying to stay out of harm's way, he was at the pub keeping an eye out for me. I arrived early on the Monday morning to see what was

259

what. I still wasn't sure what I was going to do, but I was fed up with sleeping in the van; it was bloody freezing. When I got to the village, I parked out of sight down behind the pub and had a bit of a walk round. Bob must have come out after breakfast and seen the van. All he had to do was wait for me to come back to it."

"So you did see him on Monday!"

"Yes, but only for about five minutes. I told him that I hadn't decided what I was going to do. Told him to leave me alone. But I could see they'd had a real go at him this time. He showed me his hand. They'd slammed his fingers in a door." Archie shuddered and Laurence looked across at him and sort of nodded. Archie felt ashamed. He was supposed to be here for Laurence and the boy was clearly trying to reassure him.

"They meant business. He said it wasn't too late to make the delivery, but I kept thinking about the number of kids I was destroying. He never once offered to take it himself." Laurence's fingers were clenching and unclenching. "Now I can see him for what he was, but even then I still thought I could detect some honour, some fatherly feeling ..." Laurence began to cry.

Archie was horrified. Laurence had been trying to do the right thing, but the man had been relentless. There was no doubt in Archie's mind that Laurence had been pushed too far, with fatal consequences.

"I said I wanted four more days. I suppose time to get my head straight. I said he owed me that much. I got really angry with him," Laurence's voice faded, so that Archie had to lean forward to hear what was said next.

"How angry were you?" Tom asked, finally uncrossing his legs and sitting upright.

"I threatened to shut his other hand in the door, if he didn't leave me alone."

Archie could feel the boy's shame. He looked over at Tom, willed him to look across at him. But he could see that Tom was only focussed on Laurence; the wolf, as it were, had the deer in sight.

"Tom," Archie said, "shouldn't Laurence have a lawyer present?"

Tom grimaced and Archie knew he'd be angry at an interruption at such a critical moment.

"Mr Weller, do you want a lawyer present?"

"No," Laurence said clearly. Archie felt his heart judder; he felt quite breathless.

"So, tell me again what happened on Tuesday morning."

"Georgie followed me after breakfast, though I didn't notice until we were nearly at the point. She wanted to find out what I was doing here. I think she'd hoped I'd had a conversion or something. She's always had a bit of a thing for me."

"And you? For her?"

"No. She's done well for herself. I wouldn't want to hold her back. If truth be told, despite both of us being in Exeter, we'd only bumped into each other a few times." He spoke, sadly. "Nearly a year ago, we had coffee and a bit of a catch-up. Before that, when she was still at school, I bumped into her and her girlfriends at a club." Laurence looked down at his hands; they were twisting and turning in his lap. They looked grubby and the nails were clearly chewed down to the quick. He looked back up, not at Tom, but at Archie. "The thing is, I'm a bit ashamed of that first meeting. I was pleased to see her. She was obviously still holding a bit of a torch for me, so I played along with it. We all had too much to drink and, in the end, one of her mates followed me out to the loo. I think it was Dani, but I can't be absolutely sure. I hadn't realised what was going on until we were out the back and she was—"

"How old was she?" Suddenly Tom and Sandra were both alert, leaning in.

"I knew she was only sixteen. As soon as I realised she'd got the wrong message, I backed off."

"You're telling me a young woman was throwing herself at you and, though you'd had a lot to drink, you walked away?"

"God, yes. She was Georgie's friend. I realised I'd messed up badly, couldn't face Georgie, so I told the girl, Dani I now realise, to go back in and tell her I'd catch up with her another time. Who knows what Dani told her because I didn't see or hear from Georgie again until our coffee in the shopping centre."

"And that was that?" Tom asked. Laurence nodded.

Archie wanted to believe Laurence, but he thought he was holding something back. Laurence should have gone to the police straight away about the drugs, but the death of Robert Enderby would have complicated that. Still, the link with Dani wasn't good news, because even though Laurence said he hadn't taken advantage of her, someone else clearly had for her to end up as a mother at such an early age. Poor girl.

"Tom, we need to take a break."

"No, Archie. Laurence needs to tell us what happened on Tuesday."

Laurence nodded at Archie, once again reassuring him. It was all the wrong way round. Even though he'd come up through the Navy and had spent some time working the lifeboat, Archie felt that he'd not lived a single day on the edge like this boy had.

"When Georgie caught me up, I wasn't exactly pleased to see her, but she seemed so glad to see me that I agreed to meet her down by the old lifeboat ramp. Anna had been going on about it at breakfast and I'd decided to take a look. While Georgie was up at the loo, the big car came down. They asked if I knew of anywhere nice to stay. I said no and they turned around and drove back up towards the village. The thing is, even if they were the bad guys, I wouldn't have known them. I only ever dealt with Bob, so perhaps they didn't realise it was me either. Anyway, I walked on down to the sea. It's an amazing place. Georgie joined me not long after, but I was struggling with the whole Bob thing. I asked her to leave me alone, promised we'd talk later in the week. I told her I'd got tangled up in something and that I needed to think it through. She seemed to know more about it than I'd told her, so I guessed Bob had tried it on with her too. She was so angry, but I couldn't deal with it; my head was too full. She stormed off. I spent another few minutes watching the water, but it was so cold and I hadn't had much breakfast, so I went back up to the café. I don't know how long I was there; you'll have to ask the girl. She was wiping tables by the window when I walked in and then we spent a couple of minutes at the counter choosing cake. There were other people in there too. They would have seen me. Afterwards I walked back down to the boat house."

"Why?"

"Because it was an amazing place and I still wanted to get my head straight. But when I got down there, I could see the body and it looked just like Bob and I thought it was my fault. I thought I'd made him jump because I wouldn't deliver those drugs."

"You think he jumped?"

"I did at that moment and that I'd made him do it."

"We've only got your word for it that you didn't meet him again that morning."

"Ask Georgie. She carried on round and says she didn't see him either. If she didn't, then I couldn't have."

Unless the two of them were in it together, Archie thought. He shook his head crossly. Someone was lying and he could feel Tom's frustration. Tom wasn't bothered about the drugs – he'd hand that all over to Exeter – but the death of Enderby was his baby and he wanted it sorted. While Laurence had just been incredibly courageous, it didn't really help Tom at all; Archie could see that.

"Okay, we'll stop there," Tom said. Sandra closed her notebook.

"But aren't you going to arrest me?" Laurence cried out, his face smooth with shock.

"What would you like me to arrest you for?"

"Delivering the drugs!"

"My Exeter colleagues will do that once you've signed your statement. There's a chap coming down tonight to take you back, and you will indeed help them with their enquiries. They'll want descriptions of the men in the SUV for a start; times and dates of deliveries and whatever else you can remember."

Laurence slumped.

"Inside or outside prison, I'll never be free or safe, even though they've got the package back."

"So something was taken from the back of the van? I suppose we could hold you on wasting police time."

Archie felt sorry for Laurence. He looked so miserable. Completely defeated and, whatever happened now, he surely was in danger. Tom must be able to see that? Archie simply couldn't understand how someone like Tom could have captured Anna's kind heart.

Chapter 28

After interviewing Lawrence, Tom pulled Archie to one side.

"You don't let him out of your sight," he said, fiercely. Archie simply nodded. Anna, standing in the doorway, flinched, but Tom didn't see her. He looked about ready to scream, tension crackling off him like static. Laurence looked shocked, pale faced as he backed away down the hallway.

Anna heard Tom say to Sandra through gritted teeth, "That lad may have said he didn't do it, but he might just be clever enough to cop to the drugs to mask the murder."

Then Tom sent Sandra outside to stand watch. His mum came out from the dining room with a sandwich for him. Anna wished she'd thought of that. Catherine gave a little shrug as if she understood, as if this was all quite normal. Anna followed her back into the dining room to say grace and to get lunch on the go, but she couldn't settle. She excused herself and returned to the kitchen.

Tom had just taken a bite when she opened the door. He stood up, though she wasn't sure why.

"It's alright. Finish your food."

"It's just that I'm starving. I didn't manage breakfast this morning."

"What about Sandra?"

"She said she was alright."

"I'll take her a cup of coffee." Anna filled the kettle and switched it on. Staring out the window at the long grass and tall straggly shrubs she became aware of her fingers gripping the edge of the sink. She let go. Turning back to him, she said, "What are we supposed to do, Tom? Are you going to take Laurence away?"

"Not yet. Exeter want him and we've agreed to it – county cooperation and all that. And I do have concerns that this could be a safeguarding issue, which I will pass on." He rested his elbows on the table, as if he were about to rest his head in his hands. "But not until I'm sure he didn't push Enderby over the cliff."

"How are you going to be able to work that one out? No-one saw anything."

"No-one said they saw anything, but they all had time and they were all nearby."

"But why?" Anna almost wailed. They were her charges and he was trying to pin a murder onto one of them. She could feel the tiny hope she'd had at the beginning of the week, that she might help them, if only just a little, crumbling away.

"Because Laurence was being exploited by Enderby. Georgie knew that and she was angry that Laurence was still being taken in by him. Dani knew Laurence. I'm not sure why or how she would've known Enderby, but she's definitely not telling the complete truth. Her home was searched for drugs a couple of years back and they don't do that unless there's firm evidence. I'll find out more tonight."

Tom ran his hand through his hair, so that it stuck up all around the crown.

"You shouldn't have it cut so short. It doesn't suit you," Anna said, before she could stop herself.

"Sorry, love, it's just one of the things I have done. If the barber cuts it close, I don't have to go back so often."

She hooked her hair over an ear; it was just long enough now for it to stay there for a moment. Tom rubbed his eyes.

"Perhaps I've been too soft. Perhaps I should just pull them all in and grill them until someone tells me the truth."

Anna sat down.

"I think they're all telling the truth. I think they're just missing out bits. None of them finds it easy to trust us. No-one seems to have been on their side, no-one has ever fought for them. Even Dani's mum seems a little hard. Surely, if your daughter got pregnant, you'd want to know who the father was? To take some of the responsibility off her shoulders, no matter how shameful you thought it was?"

"So why didn't Dani just rat on him?"

"Because her mum didn't want her to. She was worried about what people would think."

"In this day and age?"

"She was a member of a church youth group. Some of them can be very straightlaced. I think Dani was more ashamed that she'd been used. It may not have been about her mum at all."

Tom caught up Anna's hand. He laced his fingers through hers.

"Where do you stand on such things?" he asked.

Anna suddenly wasn't sure. What did she believe? What did she want?

"I couldn't do anything that would upset my parishioners."

"So it's marriage or nothing?"

She supposed it was but felt a terrible urge to swallow it down, to be a woman of the world. To say that that particular part of her belief was outdated. Only it wasn't just about sleeping with him; it meant other things too. That love was more than a fumbled moment. That it was about her and who she was, not what she could give in return. But that felt as though she'd set the bar ridiculously high. No man could love like that.

"I'm not saying that." *At least not for now*, she thought.

"But Archie would, wouldn't he? He'd say I was interfering with your duties. Coming between you and your faith and that I was not good enough."

Anna suddenly wanted to run to Archie, to fling her arms around his neck and say thank you.

"Tom, this is not the moment. Not in the middle of ... all this." She began to step away.

"No, of course not. Sorry. We've got enough on our plates."

But he didn't let go of her hand.

"Look, Tom, I know you don't want any of them to leave,

267

but is there any possibility we could take them out on the cliffs tonight? It's just that it's a full moon and the weather forecast is good. It could be beautiful and I want them to be touched by this place, by God, particularly as tomorrow they're all heading back to such difficult lives."

"Where exactly?"

"Beacon Point. If we use the lane down to the new lifeboat station, there's only the small climb at the end."

"What about going down to the lookout by car and walking back from there? It's much closer."

"But the lane is rutted with mud. The farmer is always having to pull cars out and he gets really cross about it."

"I got my car down there."

"And if I remember rightly, you had to pretty much reverse it all the way back up and it was in a dreadful state." Tom nodded and grimaced. The car had dripped cow pats for weeks.

"So please can I take them? Do Evening Prayer by moonlight? Allow them fifteen minutes to breathe the air and listen to the sea?"

"To breathe free air. Anna, I'm pretty sure one of them is responsible for the death of Robert Enderby and one of them – could be the same one – delivered drugs for a hobby."

"But we can't penalise the others. It feels important. Of course, they might not want to do it. I can imagine Dani wondering why."

"Don't be too harsh on her, Anna. I don't like her much and I'm sure she knows more than she's telling, but having a kid at her age can't have been fun."

Anna felt admonished. She should've said that, not Tom. But Dani always left her feeling as if a rash of irritation were about to break through her skin; losing her temper was the least of it. A clever, young woman who used the child in her to get her own way.

"We'll have to get a couple of constables to watch the

paths. I'll have to come with you, and Sandra too," Tom said firmly.

For a second, Anna's brain flashed an automatic spark of jealousy. The wonderful, ought-to-go-for-promotion, I-can-definitely-see-she-has-potential Sandra. But the feeling was short-lived and didn't stop her in her tracks like it used to. Even she could see that, if Sandra did move on, Tom would miss her. She had his back and Anna was glad that someone did.

"I need to get back to the others," she said.

"I'll speak to Dani and Georgie again, see if we can find something that links them to Enderby."

"And the drugs!"

"And Anna, we need to find out who brought the binoculars up to the vicarage and why they hid them under Laurence's van."

When Anna walked back into the dining room, Harriet looked up, smiling, but only half-heartedly. Anna shouldn't have spent so long with Tom. It had felt like an indulgence. She sat down between Dani and Georgie. Both girls turned to her. Anna didn't know who to acknowledge first, but found her head turning towards Dani. Georgie sort of slumped. Anna guessed she was used to Dani being first in line.

"How are you managing, Dani?" Anna asked. Dani shrugged. "Would you like a chat? Sometime this afternoon?"

Georgie rose.

"Hang on, Georgie, there's plenty of time. Why don't we meet too?"

Harriet nodded imperceptibly. Thank goodness she'd noticed Anna was at least trying to be a good vicar. Anna cleared her throat and addressed everyone.

"Tonight there'll be a full moon and for once the weather looks as if it might be dry and calm. So I propose we go up to Beacon Point to say Evening Prayer." Laurence turned to face the window with a look of such yearning. He was probably thinking he wouldn't be allowed to go, that surely by then he'd be on his way back to Exeter. Anna didn't quite know how to reassure him. She could hardly tell him in front of the others that it was alright, that Tom said he'd arrest him afterwards. Oh, and, by the way, he was hoping that Laurence would confess to murder while he was at it.

"You'll need to wrap up warm and wear walking boots. There are one or two sticky patches on the way up."

"Can I have a word, Anna?" Catherine asked.

Anna tried to behave like a grown-up. Kept calm, did a bit of deep breathing. What helped was that Harriet was trying not to laugh. It was an absolute pain having someone sitting opposite who knew you too well.

"Come along to the kitchen."

Before she'd even closed the door to the dining room, Anna swung round.

"Look, this has been a terrible week. It was supposed to be all calm and spiritual. As it is, it's been … and you've been horribly neglected."

Catherine tipped her head to one side in the way that unaccountably reminded Anna of Tom.

"I've had lots of time to walk and pray. It's not been restful, but it has stirred up lots of things I thought had been settled a long time ago."

"Would you like to talk?"

"I'm not sure that would be right for either of us. Tom stands rather large between, don't you think?"

"Yes. Yes, he does." Anna felt a load slide from her shoulders.

"You're such a lovely woman. I can see why he's drawn to you, but the faith thing will always be an issue."

"Has he ever believed?"

"Yes, there was a time, when he was a teenager. He read his Bible a lot, seemed to be praying. Even asked about baptism, but then he met this girl and it all became a passing phase. He said my faith was simply my crutch, what I used to cope with his dad."

"Can I ask what happened?"

Catherine straightened a little and for an awful moment Anna thought she'd say no.

"He left me and then he died. A heart attack. I had to arrange everything because there wasn't anyone else, knowing all the while that he hadn't wanted me anymore. It was the toughest few months of my life." She turned away and Anna wished she hadn't asked. She put on the kettle, just to have something to do.

"Was your husband a Christian?"

Catherine folded her arms across her chest.

"That's the problem, Anna. He wasn't. I thought it didn't matter, but as my faith grew and took up more of me, it meant there was less and less for him. He said he left because he'd become an add-on to my life, one I wasn't particularly bothered about."

Anna sat down with a bump and stared at her hands.

"No wonder you're not happy about Tom and me. Have you spoken to him about it?"

"I don't think I ever specifically told him about what happened between me and his dad, not from my point of view. I always expected him to ask, particularly when his dad moved out, but Tom never did. I suppose they might've spoken about it when he went to stay, but I just don't know."

"But that's not fair," Anna said. "He needs to hear your side."

"Even if it means he walks away from you?"

Anna didn't want the lump in her throat to get any bigger, tried to swallow it down.

"Wouldn't it be worse if he stayed?" she said. "Because then, despite everything, he wouldn't believe that faith was worth the bother."

Catherine stood up slowly.

"I'm not going to hug you because if I do, I'll start to cry. And if I start, I'm afraid I'll never stop. I don't want to do that."

"Was that what you wanted to talk to me about?" Anna asked.

"No. Tom wondered if I could stay on an extra couple of nights. But after everything, it seems a terrible imposition."

Only now Anna didn't think it was at all.

"Please stay. Though the catering won't be so great once Harriet is not involved. I eat a lot of toast."

"I like toast and I could always take you out to the pub to say thank you."

"Friday night is fish and chips from the chippy. It isn't open more than a couple of days a week. It's one of my favourite things."

"Where do you go and eat them?"

"It depends on the weather and the wind direction, but down at Church Cove is wonderful."

Catherine rested her hand on the doorknob, hesitating, then turned round.

"I know I'm not supposed to, but while you're talking to Dani, I'll try and keep an eye on Georgie. Something's really eating away at her."

Anna nodded. She wasn't sure what else she could do. Once Catherine had gone, she slumped in her chair, covering her face with her hands. She hoped Harriet would come through soon. She needed to tell her about Tom's dad. It was a game changer and she was feeling terribly lost.

"Won't you do some kind of heart miracle?" she asked God. "I don't really want to spend the rest of my life alone and, now that you've dangled Tom in front of me, that doesn't feel fair."

When she took her hands away from her face, Harriet was sitting opposite her.

"So, what gives, Anna?"

And Anna told her what Catherine had said. Harriet's eyes filled with tears.

"Marry me?" Harriet said. "I'll be faithful and I can cook and above all else I'm not a police officer."

Anna knew she should laugh, but instead she laid her head back down on her arms and blinked a lot.

Chapter 29

Simeon decided to go home. He was feeling less and less anxious about the men in the SUV coming back. If they'd found what they were looking for in Laurence's van, then why would they hang around, particularly as the death of Bob Enderby was now the main focus of attention? They'd definitely want to get as far away as possible from that. He was pulling the front door of the vicarage behind him when it swung back and Georgie followed him out.

"Hi Simeon."

Simeon kept his eyes fixed on her boots. They were old-fashioned leather, mucky with mud. He couldn't see what colour her socks were because she'd pulled her jeans down over the top. Not sensible because now they'd get dirty too.

She said, "Laurence has to stay in the house. He promised Tom." Simeon wasn't sure why she'd told him that.

He told her, "Tom has two constables in the village. One at the top of the lane, the other down on the main road." Just in case she was still worried about the men in the SUV.

"The thing is, Simeon, if Laurence makes a promise, he keeps it."

"That's good."

Simeon wasn't sure what she was getting at or what to do next. He didn't want to hang about in the cold. He wanted to make sure that his house was still locked up, safe and sound. After all, he'd left in a bit of a hurry and hadn't gone through his usual checklist.

"Georgie, I'm sorry, but I need to go and see that my house is alright."

"Can I tag along? I promise I won't be any trouble. I have to be back here soon anyway to see Anna."

"Alright."

He began to walk up the drive. He couldn't see her, but he knew she was just behind him. At the top of the lane there was a police officer.

"Hello Mr Tyler."

Simeon simply lifted a hand.

"Do you know everyone around here?" Georgie asked.

"I know everyone in the village and can tell you where they live. I know that police officer because when Fiona was killed, he was here with Tom."

"What's Tom like? Really like?"

Simeon turned off the track and up the side of his cottage. A one-storey bungalow really. He led her round the back and across the garden. The gravel path was weed-free, just as he liked it.

"What a lovely garden," Georgie said. "If you cut down the bushes, you'd have a great view over the fields."

"I like the bushes," Simeon said, pulling out the key. He only kept the path weed-free and raked; the rest of the shrubs he allowed to grow as tall and straggly as they liked. They formed a good barrier against the wind.

The house was cold; he'd at least remembered to turn the heating off. "You should keep your coat on. It'll take one hour and ten minutes to warm up."

"Thanks Simeon. I'll do that. You must live alone."

"Yes. Do you?"

"Yes and no. I share a house with a couple of others, but they tend to get home late and I'm busy on the weekend." She sighed. "I hardly see them at all."

"I thought Dani was living with you?" Simeon didn't look up, but he could see Georgie's fists clench.

"That's only temporary. While she has a break from her mum."

"And her little girl?"

"Exactly. To be honest, Simeon, I think she's a bit of a spoilt brat. She certainly gets her own way all the time."

"Some people are like that."

"Clever and manipulative. Others are innocent or idiots.

Laurence is an idiot. He needs to stand up for himself more. That Bob Enderby was a user. I'm sure he'd earmarked Laurence from the very first time he met him. You know he tried his tricks on me a few times? Told me a sob story about getting mixed up with bad people by mistake."

"Does Laurence know that?"

"Yes. I finally told him down by the old lifeboat."

Simeon looked around. He needed to think, but she was also a guest in his home.

"Would you like a cup of tea?"

"If you're going to make one."

He always hated this reply to what he considered a straightforward question. If you wanted a cup, you should just say so and he hadn't been going to make one. He wasn't sure there'd be enough milk. He put on the kettle and checked the fridge. There was an unopened pint and, with a careful sniff, he decided it'd be alright.

"Do you think Dani knew Mr Enderby?"

Georgie seemed to think about that for a moment.

"I'm not sure. But she's exactly the sort of girl he'd single out. I've known her forever from school, so he might even have got to her through me."

"You should ask her."

"Why?" Georgie asked.

"Because then she'd be a suspect too. At the moment, it's just you and Laurence."

Georgie reached out to hold onto the edge of the unit. Simeon hoped she wasn't going to faint or anything. He wondered if he dared look at her face, whether it would help or not.

"I do think she knows something about the binoculars," Georgie said quietly.

Simeon turned his back to make the tea. He heard her sit down on one of the kitchen chairs. She hadn't asked if it was alright, though at least now he knew where she was. Belle was standing between them. She knew he wasn't happy.

Georgie continued, "I think Dani saw the binoculars, thought she'd take them, perhaps that they were worth something, and then panicked when Tom said he was coming back to talk to everyone again. She wouldn't have wanted them found among her things."

"Why are you so sure she took them?" he asked.

"Because ..." Georgie hesitated. "Because I saw them earlier, under one of the cars. Anna's, I think. Not under the van. So I was very surprised when Tom said that's where he'd found them. I thought for a minute he was just another bent copper and he'd moved them to incriminate Laurence." Simeon shook his head. Tom could be fierce sometimes, but he wouldn't break the rules.

"Yes, but the really important question is, who brought them up from the Lizard?" Simeon said firmly. "And if it was Dani, why did she move them?"

Georgie didn't reply for a minute.

"When I went up to our room on Wednesday morning, Dani's case was all over the place, as if she'd been looking for something in a hurry. I think she had to get the binoculars from where she'd hidden them, knowing that Tom was on his way. But putting them back under Laurence's van seems a really deliberate way of pointing the finger. It was really cruel. He's got enough on his plate without some spoiled brat getting her revenge on him."

"Revenge for what?"

"Apparently, he made a play for her when we were all at some dreadful club. Only then he dropped her, as if suddenly he couldn't be bothered. It sounded a bit callous, not like him at all. I bet he hadn't realised what was going on, but I know Dani wouldn't take that kind of rejection well."

Simeon didn't know what to say to that. It seemed like a long time to hold a grudge. He thought it might be something more recent. He sipped his tea, which he didn't really want, so he put the mug on the draining board.

Georgie continued, "What Dani described didn't sound like the boy I knew. He's not mean. He's kind and a bit soft. It's much more likely that Dani tried it on and, when he wasn't interested, she felt a bit stupid. We were all a bit silly back then."

"Do you think Laurence killed Mr Enderby?"

Georgie went very still and Simeon's heart rate began to make the blood roar in his ears. He was getting terribly hot. Why had he asked such a leading question? It was a stupid thing to do. What if Georgie had killed him? That would mean that he'd invited the killer into his kitchen. He closed his eyes; he could feel everything coming apart. Georgie was now angry. Her voice scratched at his eyelids, demanding a way in. He tried not to listen, but he couldn't help himself.

"... and he doesn't deserve the use of 'Mr'. Not by any stretch of the imagination. Bob Enderby was an awful man. He followed us around, looking for kids he could use, exploit. He didn't deserve to live. I'm glad he's dead. Really glad."

Through the anger, he could hear her tears. He grabbed the kitchen roll and pushed it towards her.

"Please go. I don't feel very well."

Georgie went quiet. He couldn't even hear her breathe and he didn't know what she was doing because his eyes were tightly shut.

"Sorry, Simeon. I didn't mean to get so angry," she whispered. "And I didn't want to talk about this stuff at all. I wanted to talk to you about God ..."

The room emptied, all the what-ifs sliding through the door. Simeon almost felt himself being sucked out after her, until he heard the lock click. Then everything settled. He counted to three hundred before he moved or opened his eyes. He very carefully checked every room. Then he took Belle into the bedroom and closed the curtains. He crawled under the blanket, pulling it over his head. Belle lay down next to him.

After focusing on his breathing for a long time, he fell asleep. When he woke, before he could stop himself – he found he was reliving the walk to Archie's house. He remembered turning back to check that no-one was coming after him and catching sight of the figure at the bottom of the road. Had it been Dani? He'd then passed the man, Enderby, just down from Archie's, the binoculars hanging from his shoulder. Simeon had had to press himself into the hedge, feeling trapped and held by the brambles.

It could have been Dani at the bottom of the road. The timings worked. But why would she have pushed Enderby over? Georgie had thought it was possible that she knew him, had been targeted by him. But Georgie was only guessing.

She said that Enderby preyed on the vulnerable, that he'd have watched out for people just like Dani. Simeon shivered. His phone began to beep. It was Archie, worrying about where he was. Simeon texted back to say that he was safe, back at home with Belle. Eventually, after running through what he'd seen a few more times, he got up and made himself a fresh cup of tea.

***

"So, Dani, how are you getting on?" Anna's voice sounded stupidly cheerful, not how she was feeling, and even though Dani hadn't said a word yet, Anna felt as if she wanted to shake her, to tell her that she ought to count her blessings, that –despite the difficulties of her life – there were lots of people looking out for her.

Dani just shook her head and opened her eyes wide, her head tipping just a little to one side. She held people at bay with a shield of put-downs and sarcasm, and now a look that Anna felt was just rude.

"I wish you wouldn't do that," Anna said and then wished she hadn't spoken out loud.

"What have I done now? I've not said a word." Dani's

sullen retort was to be expected.

"Sorry, Dani, that was unkind. It's just that people try to help you and you usually fend them off with sarky comments and hurtful remarks. In this case a look."

Dani scowled and, for a second, was speechless.

"I don't," she said eventually. But Anna almost danced around the room. She'd hit the mark.

"So, tell me what's been happening for you through this week."

"What do you mean?"

"Where's God in all this? For you?"

Dani visibly deflated. Her shoulders slumped and she released a long stream of air. It seemed to drag her forward, hunch her over.

"I haven't a clue. I've never really understood any of it."

"Ask me a question and I'll try to answer it as honestly as I can."

Dani looked as if she was genuinely thinking about what to say. Anna was pleased there hadn't just been a quick retort.

"The prayer thing. I ask for stuff, but I never seem to get what I want or need. So am I asking for the wrong things or am I simply not hearing the reply because I'm too thick or too sinful?"

Anna almost shuddered and wished that Simeon was here. He'd answer clearly, whereas inside Anna's head, there were about thirty different replies. Couldn't Dani have started with something easier, like, 'Is there a God?'

She thought for a moment and then said, "Prayer is a funny thing. It doesn't always feel easy, though fundamentally, it should be. David and the Psalms teach us to be real, to not pretend, to lay it out and then listen." She looked out of the window. There was so much she could say and, for a second, Dani's face had been disarmingly young, open, waiting. "Jesus took himself off all the time to pray. So it's important to set aside time. I know that lots of people, if

281

they're carers or something, can't do that, but most of us can and most of us should."

"Do you?"

"Not as much as I ought to." Anna shrugged. "I try to find time every day, but acknowledging my need of God in a place of complete honesty doesn't happen as much as it should."

"And you're a vicar!"

"A very flawed one."

"So what are you going to do about the DI?"

Anna looked up sharply, side-swiped. She was about to say something like, 'We're not here to talk about me', but instead she replied quietly, "I don't know, Dani. I really like him, but he doesn't share our faith and somehow that feels like a deal breaker."

Dani nodded and said, "And how do you know you've heard from God? Vicar Alf is always saying things like, 'I was praying, and I felt God say …'"

"Now that's all a matter of trust and practice. God speaks to us in so many different ways." Anna smiled. "Actually, the best place to start is assuming that it is God who's speaking, using whatever is to hand to get our attention, even our imagination. When your mind wanders, invite God into the wandering and see where it takes you."

Dani didn't look terribly impressed. Anna pushed on.

"Sometimes we demand things to go away that are part of our journey. I think if God gave us everything we asked for, we'd be spoiled brats with a capital B and we wouldn't ever get to the bottom of who we really are." Anna sat back. "We'd skate across the top of life without ever really experiencing it."

Dani shrugged.

"Ok, Dani. Hard question, which you do not have to answer. Would you rather have Selena in your life or not?"

Dani looked up through narrowed eyes. Anna could see she thought it might be a trick question.

"Just think about it."

"I love her and so does Mum. But Mum's never forgiven me for not saying who the father is and I couldn't because I wasn't sure." She shrugged again. Her narrow, bony shoulders didn't seem strong enough to hold up the weight of her head. "Mum would've been so ashamed that I'd been with two blokes who didn't care. Who treated me as everyone else does, a throwaway. Single use only."

"Oh, Dani, that's awful. One thing for certain is that God doesn't think you are disposable."

"But everyone treats me like that. Everyone."

Anna was suddenly struck by a terrible thought.

"Did you ever meet Bob Enderby?"

"Yes, but I only delivered for him once or twice and when he came back to give me more, I threatened to go to the police. I told him I was going to say he'd tried to rape me or something like that. He backed off. He was a bully, but he did it on the sly. Buying you a drink because ... well, why do men buy any girl a drink?"

Anna's mind slowed to a halt and when it started up again, she knew she was going down the wrong track, but she didn't know how to stop herself.

"You need to tell Tom – DI Edwards – that you knew Mr Enderby."

"But then I'd be a suspect like the others and you won't tell him because what I said was in confidence."

And the old Dani was back, her hard shell shining brightly all about her and it was Anna's fault. She knew she'd missed an important turning.

"What about the binoculars? Did you see them down on the point and bring them back up to the vicarage?"

"Are you doing his work for him now? You know I'm not going to say one way or the other because that would incriminate me."

But if she hadn't touched them, then surely she would've

simply denied it? Dani shrugged those sharp narrow shoulders of hers and stood up.

"Are we all done?" And she walked out.

Anna didn't know what to do with the shame and remorse that roared up from the bits inside that counted. In her mind, in a row were the faces of Harriet, Archie, Catherine, Simeon and – slightly less clear, but looming very large – God. And they all looked disappointed.

Chapter 30

Harriet finished laying out the food for later. It filled the kitchen table. There was still an hour before she had to put anything in the oven, so she wandered through to the dining room. It was empty, the kettle warm from when someone had just made a cup of tea. She could hear voices murmuring from Anna's sitting room. She walked into the lounge. The fire was smouldering. She added another log and gave it a prod. She turned round and jumped when she saw Tom and his mum sitting in the corner. She'd been so engrossed in herself she hadn't seen them.

"Sorry. I didn't mean to disturb you." They were both pink-cheeked and Harriet wondered if they'd let the fire die down because it had been a bit too fierce.

"Actually Harriet, you might be able to help me with some advice." Tom smiled his crooked smile. "You're good at that."

For a second, she wondered if he was being sarcastic. She hoped not. Catherine had turned her face to the window as if she wanted no part of it.

"You and Derek live together. You have a strong faith from what I can see, but does he? Does it matter?"

This felt too personal, and she and Derek were nothing like Anna and Tom.

"Sorry, Tom, I can't help you. My situation with Derek is complicated. I think even though we started off in very different places, we're building a sort of understanding together. And neither of us are vicars, which I'm afraid I do think has a bearing on it."

Tom seemed to slowly deflate. Harriet knew she ought to stop, but she couldn't. "Otherwise, why is Anna agonising over you? Why is Archie curled up tight with worry over it and why have you and your mum been arguing?" Both of them looked at her with wide eyes and she knew she was right, at least in some respects. She just wished she could be as good

285

at looking into her own life.

"So you're saying, for Anna and me to work, I have to believe in God?" As Tom said this, Catherine drew in a sharp breath that broke Harriet's heart.

"You don't believe in him at all?" Catherine asked, her voice catching with every syllable. "Not even after all these years? My faith means nothing to you?"

Tom looked confused and a little angry. He stood up, backing towards the door. Harriet wished she was anywhere else but in this room, having stirred the pot so efficiently.

"I'm in the middle of a murder investigation. I cannot switch that off. I need to concentrate. When it's over, I'll answer those questions." He didn't slam the door, though it might have been better if he had. Catherine began to cry; silent tears that ran down her face.

"The trouble is," she said, wiping them away, "there's always an investigation. Always something that's more important because he can't switch off what he does. It's his own version of God."

Harriet handed her the box of tissues, wondering what to say. Catherine uncurled and walked to the fire, leaning over to give it another prod. A log at the back disintegrated in a shower of sparks. Still with the poker in hand, Catherine turned back to Harriet. "To him, it's better to be a policeman than a man of God because people who love God don't have enough love left over for those they ought to care for. This is all about his dad. This is my fault. I've let them both down."

"Oh no, I'm sure you haven't," Harriet said, but she faltered because she knew that people did get things wrong. Perhaps back then, when Tom was a teenager, even Catherine.

"Well, I think I have!" Catherine stood rigidly, her arms crossed over her chest, as if holding herself together. "God is unconditional love and I could only manage to love so poorly, so sparsely, that the man I promised to have and to hold, to cherish, left me. He just left me. There was no-one else; he just didn't feel I cared enough. What sort of person does that make me?"

Harriet moved across to Catherine and wrapped her arms around the sobbing woman. Anna came in.

"What's happened? Has someone been hurt? Tom! Is Tom alright?"

Harriet shook her head.

"Can you get Catherine some water?"

"Of course."

She was gone a few moments, returning with a teacup so full that it dripped across the carpet. For a second Harriet felt a flash of anger. Couldn't Anna have found a proper glass? Been more careful?

"I'm so sorry, Anna," Catherine gulped. "I've managed to ruin your life as well as my own."

"But your life isn't ruined. You're so ..." Harriet wondered what words Anna wanted to say.

"My own son despises the one thing I have to offer him."

"I think despise is too strong a word," Harriet said. It was. She didn't think Tom despised the faith he saw all around him. He just didn't think it mattered. Only it did and, unless he had a bit of an epiphany, he was going to lose at least one of the two women he cared for most in the world.

"I've got to try and meet Georgie. I promised. But please, please can we talk, soon?" Anna begged. Harriet almost smiled. Anna, in one sentence, had just broken every single rule they'd ever made about the retreat. Catherine, though she couldn't possibly think it was a good idea, simply nodded.

Poor Anna. Tom would have to take a back seat while his mum crept into the picture.

***

Anna went to sit on the stairs. Not on the bottom step, but about halfway up. It felt less in the way and it was a good place for people to come and find her. A second later Archie came down the hall from the kitchen. She could see a patch where his lovely thick hair was thinning, right on the top at the crown. He was clutching his beany in his hands as if it were an offering. He caught sight of her and nodded.

Good old Archie! He never seemed surprised where he came across her. She knew she took him for granted. After her encounter with Terry at Beacon Point, he'd helped her in from Tom's car, caked in mud and shivering with shock. Tom had explained what Terry had done.

Archie hadn't asked any questions, but had simply poured her a whisky and run a bath. Then, when that was all over, he'd sat at her elbow through the administrative chaos that had come from their plans to run the retreats and the overhaul of the vicarage after the fire.

Sadly, it seemed that, recently, whenever he looked at her, there was a small frown line that wouldn't disappear. She moved down a couple of steps, so that they were more eye to eye. That felt better.

"Hope I've not been needed. I went for a quick walk."

"No, you're alright, Archie. I'm waiting for Georgie. Don't go into the lounge though. Catherine's a bit upset."

Archie's face became very still. He must have, like the rest of them, been sure that Catherine was fine. That she'd simply come to spend some time with God.

"Tom is sitting outside in his car. It looks as if he is working," Archie said, without quite looking her in the eye.

"There is no space in here. Every room seems to be full of sad people." Archie looked so concerned that Anna took pity on him. "If you like, you could go down to church or across to Simeon's. If we need you, we'll ring."

"Alright, Anna. I'll go and find Simeon. Make sure he's alright. If I move on to the church, I'll text and let you know."

With his hand on the latch, he slowly turned back to face her.

"Will the police be with us until everyone goes home?"

"I don't know, Archie. I ought to know, but I don't."

And Anna put her head in her hands.

*　*　*

It took Archie a couple of minutes to get to Simeon's house. Poor Anna! Tom was such a nuisance. He disconcerted her and, if truth be told, she didn't always act logically or rightly when emotionally stretched.

He knocked and then called, "Simeon, it's me. Archie." He heard Belle snuffling behind the door. He knew to be patient. Simeon often had to work out whether he wanted to see people or not. The door opened just a little.

"Hello Archie. Do you want to talk to me about faith or about the murder?"

"Neither, actually."

The door swung open.

"Good, because I don't want to be anyone else's listening ear. I hadn't realised how hard it is. If it's like this every time we hold a retreat, I'll have to reconsider my involvement."

Archie was a little taken aback. Simeon rarely made jokes, so what he'd said had to be serious. Archie was also used to Simeon voicing complete thoughts, but this felt as if he'd missed far too many of the steps leading up to it. He followed Simeon into the lounge.

"What's going on?" Archie asked, sitting down in his chair.

Simeon had bought four easy chairs, purely for when people came to visit. Archie had had to take receipt of them. It had been Archie who'd disposed of the packaging, Archie who'd signed all the paperwork. Such a thing was way beyond Simeon back then.

Archie found the chairs rather uncomfortable, but Simeon had bought them online and it hadn't occurred to him that he ought to have tried them out first. Harriet had provided cushions. *She seems to spend a lot of time sorting out cushions for her muddled neighbours*, Archie thought guiltily, remembering the ones he'd piled in the cupboard under the

289

stairs.

Belle came and wagged her tail, her nose resting gently on Archie's knee. He gave her ears a tug. Her duty done, she dropped down at Simeon's feet.

Simeon was sitting side-on to the window. He didn't like to face the light, as he found it too bright. His hands rested either side of his knees and Archie wondered if he was as uptight as he sounded.

"Laurence and I went for a walk. That was fine. He talked a lot, but I stayed ahead of him, and it was raining, so I was able to have my hood up." Archie smiled. Simeon always had his hood up, regardless of the weather. "But he told Georgie that I was a good listener and that I understand God, which made her want to talk to me. Only, Archie, no-one really understands God. They both ask me questions all the time, then they tell me things that I think perhaps Tom should know. But when we did that listening day with Anna's spiritual director, she said that we should treat everything as a confidence."

"She's absolutely right."

"But did she think we'd be dealing with suspects in a murder investigation?"

Archie laughed.

"No, I don't expect she did." Then he said quietly, "But what we must remember is that only one of them may have pushed Enderby off the cliff. The other two are simply our guests."

"Two of them could have been in it together," Simeon said, pedantically. He glanced up at Archie. "But you're saying that we should give them all the benefit of the doubt until we know for sure who did it."

"Yes, I think so. And trust that God and Tom know what they're doing."

Archie wasn't sure he did trust Tom enough. He readjusted the cushion as his back was starting to twinge.

"Are you going to Evening Prayer up on Beacon Point tonight?" Simeon asked. Belle sat up to rest her head on his knee.

"Yes. What about you?"

"I'm not sure." Simeon turned to look out the window. "The weather will be good."

"It will be beautiful and perhaps Tom will see that Anna's faith is important." Archie realised that he hoped that with every fibre of his being.

"I think he knows that already. But I think he's in denial. He is simply hoping that it'll go away. People often do that."

Archie nodded. He could see how Simeon might have come to that conclusion, though none of them had ever seen Tom and Anna together as a couple.

"Yes, people do bury their heads in the sand," he said, "but Tom and Anna will need to make a decision soon."

"And you're very worried that it'll be the wrong decision."

Archie slumped.

"I'm not sure that there's a right or wrong choice."

"Short term or long term?" Simeon replied carefully. Archie wasn't sure of the relevance of the question and so shrugged. Simeon continued, "If Anna decides to give up Tom, she'll be lonely and sad, but she'll come through that. We know she's very strong. And God is enough for anyone; otherwise there would be no point to him." He flashed Archie a look. "But Anna will have to work that out practically."

"So, in the short term, letting Tom go will be hard, but in the long term it'll be better for both of them?"

Simeon hesitated.

"Except God's ways are not our ways and his thoughts are not our thoughts. Sometimes, when things are difficult, we do work out what's important. So what if, in trying to make a go of it, Tom comes to realise that not only does God exist, but that God loves him?"

Archie looked across at Simeon. His hair was long again,

down past his ears. There was stubble on his cheek and lines under his eyes that never quite went away. Only some of those lines were from where Simeon smiled or laughed. Anna often made him laugh. She was good at that.

Simeon looked at Archie. It was an unusual stare, straight into his eyes, so Archie knew that what Simeon was about to say was important.

"We love Anna and we have to care for her, whatever she chooses to do. We can only tell her our opinions. After that, we just have to help her through all the messy bits. Like you all did with me."

Archie was about to protest that helping Simeon hadn't been messy, but he stopped himself. It had often been messy, and exhausting.

Simeon carried on. "I spoke with Anna many times. I told her that I wanted to die. Each time I said it, she got into a state or a muddle. Once or twice, she got cross, but most of the time, even at seven in the morning when she was hardly awake, she still made me coffee and was prepared to listen. She was a very important part of my journey."

And so was I, Archie wanted to say.

"You then taught me all about friendship and how to handle certain situations. I still use most of the phrases you and Anna came up with to get me through the things I find difficult. Earlier I told Georgie I didn't feel well, so she left, even though she hadn't finished her tea."

"Georgie was here?"

"Yes. So I learn things from all my friends every day."

"That's good, Simeon." Archie was still reeling from the fact that Georgie had been to the cottage and Simeon had made her tea. At last Archie felt able to gather his thoughts sufficiently to say, "As per usual, you've set me straight."

Simeon dropped his head, as if to acknowledge what Archie had said, though he was probably just checking that Belle was alright.

Archie excused himself and wandered back to the vicarage. Simeon had said a lot of things that he needed to think about, but, right now, he thought that Harriet might need a hand.

Chapter 31

The hum of the oven's fan filled the vicarage kitchen. Harriet normally found it a soothing noise. It had taken her a little while to get the hang of the thing and she didn't overcook everything quite so often now.

She looked around at the preparations for dinner. Derek was going to pop in later with the stuffing and veg, which she hadn't been able to manage that morning.

She frowned as she tried to concentrate on timings and what she would do if the evening went pear-shaped, but the gentle background of the oven wasn't enough to blot out everything that seemed to hang in the air. She felt a sudden frisson of panic and had to lean on the sink. She wished Tom would get on with it and simply arrest someone, so the rest of them could relax. So it could be over and tomorrow morning she could serve breakfast, hug them, wave them off and shout to their tail-lights that they were welcome to come back anytime. That was how it was supposed to be – not this horrendous tangle of feelings that made simple thought almost impossible.

She gave the half-full tray of peeled potatoes a critical glance. They weren't particularly good potatoes, but with plenty of oil she could make do. Whenever she organised a roast dinner, even Simeon seemed to look forward to it. Harriet smiled. Simeon had been remarkable over the last few days. Going out for walks, helping with questions of faith and how to pray. She wondered if Anna had ever thought it possible that he'd turn out to be such an important part of the team. The only problem was he'd got a bit overwhelmed with everyone's need of him. Archie had been quite concerned. They'd have to watch that next time. No-one should feel they carried more than their fair share of the load.

Harriet realised that she'd just made the assumption that

there would be another retreat. That things would go on.

The back door juddered in the wind and a shadow passed across the window. For a second, she froze until there was a knock. An intruder meaning harm wouldn't knock. She sighed, allowing her shoulders to relax. She was getting unnecessarily fearful. She'd definitely have to put a stop to that.

Archie was standing at the door, waiting politely. He could no more walk in uninvited than slouch, though now and again he did put his hands in his pockets.

"Hello Harriet. I came to see if you needed a hand."

"That's kind, Archie, but I can't do a thing until Derek brings down the next load of veg."

"I could fetch it if you like."

"He said he'd be here in the next half hour, which is fine. Coffee?"

"Yes please. But I'll make it. You sit down. You'll be on your feet for most of the rest of the day and then back again for breakfast."

She didn't argue. She was beginning to get tired. It had been a long week.

"I was thinking about this evening," she said, watching him measuring the coffee with precision. She suppressed a smile. He didn't have an ounce of slapdash in him. Another gust of wind hit the back of the house. "I thought Anna said it was going to be calm."

"I'm hoping that's the last few gusts and then it'll settle. Between blows it doesn't feel so bad."

"Do you think it's wise going up to Beacon Point?" she asked, wondering if there were any biscuits left.

"No, I don't. I'm a little worried that the Beacon is a little too exposed, too high. We should try and persuade Anna to change her mind."

"She can get a little fixed on things, but she's as jumpy as the rest of us. The cove would be lovely. We could always go

296

up to the bench on the westward side."

"And the drop wouldn't be quite so ... terminal," he said, turning to glance at her. Harriet finally allowed her face the freedom to smile properly.

"Golly, Archie, why's everything so life-and-death?"

"It never used to be," he said, thoughtfully.

"Have you got any ideas about who could have done it?" she asked, as he brought the mugs to the table. He stopped mid-step and his eyes wandered round the room. "You have, haven't you?"

"If it's not those awful drug people from Exeter, then there aren't a lot of other options."

"Laurence?" Harriet whispered.

"Laurence, I guess." Archie sounded so sad. He'd taken a real shine to the boy.

"Oh poor Archie. You just don't want it to be him."

"No. No, I don't. I wondered if I might write to him when he leaves. Do you think I'd be allowed?"

"Of course. It's a nice idea."

"I just don't want him to feel so alone. At least maybe, if he knows there is someone somewhere thinking of him who now and again sits down and writes a letter, it won't be as bad. Though I'm a bit worried he might think I want something from him, you know, like that Enderby chap."

"Archie, no-one could doubt your motives and – let's face it – with trust the proof of the pudding is in the eating. You'll write if you say you will and gradually he'll believe you, as we all do."

"Thanks, Harriet." He hesitated for a moment. "There's something else I wanted to talk over with you."

She took a sip of coffee.

"Anna and Tom?"

"Yes," he said, his eyes widening when he realised she'd known exactly what he was going to say. "I know it's none of my business, but I'm quite worried about it, and Catherine getting into a state caught me off guard. I wondered what you thought?" He looked at her, blinking earnestly. "Please only speak if you're entirely comfortable. This is more about me than Anna and Tom I think."

Harriet leaned across and patted his hand.

"Archie, I've been worried too. Am worried. Tom seems to genuinely care for her and it's not like he hasn't a clue or anything, but not sharing faith might leave a huge elephant in the room, and no relationship can withstand that."

"I pray for him every day."

"Do you? Anna would be comforted to hear that."

"Simeon says we've got to let them get on with it and simply support them whatever happens."

"I think he's right, Archie. There are too many variables floating about and it doesn't feel the most important thing just now."

Archie pushed himself back in his chair and sat up.

"That's true. I'll keep praying, but I guess they've got to work it out for themselves, just them and God. Despite what Tom thinks."

The door clattered open and Derek came in loaded with carrier bags.

"Hello Archie. How are you?" he called out, filling the room with his smile. Harriet almost laughed at how much space he managed to take up. Archie had to squash back against the wall.

"Thanks, love, perfect timing," she said.

"Can I do anything?" he asked, shrugging out of his coat and bashing his elbow on the still open door.

"If you could finish the potatoes, that would be great," she replied. So that Archie wouldn't feel useless, she added, "And Archie, could you go through and check to see if we need to top up the tea or coffee?"

Once Archie had gone, she slipped across and kissed Derek on the cheek. When he half-closed his eyes and leant his head towards her, she wrapped her arms around him and for a second or two, they just stood there, his hands in the sink, the potatoes bobbing about in the muddy water.

***

The car felt like a haven, out of the wind and rain, away from their desperate faces. As a precaution Tom had sent Sandra back into the dining room, in clear view of the front door. He could just about see the back door himself.

Laurence might make a run for it; except where would he go? Georgie or Dani might run too. At least then he would have his answer.

The obvious person was Laurence. He'd trusted Enderby and that gradual realisation that he was using him, fuelled by Georgie's fierce anger, might have pushed him over the edge.

Tom smiled grimly. Laurence tipping over might have caused him to tip Enderby over. It didn't make him laugh. Laurence had been distraught and shocked when he'd been pulled from the water, but it could have been the realisation that he'd actually killed a man.

Tom rubbed his eyes. But after pushing Enderby over, would he have gone and sat in the café? That felt very cold. Tom decided to talk to the waitress again. Finding out how Laurence had been when he'd first come in was critical. But then there was the possibility that Laurence had simply thought he'd caused Enderby to commit suicide or that Georgie had done it.

Georgie could easily have met Enderby on the path. She'd walked back that way, but she'd said that she hadn't seen him. It was just possible that she was telling the truth, that, if she'd run really fast, she could have got up past Archie's house before Enderby had started down. She'd always believed he was a bad guy, hated him, hated what he was doing to Laurence, of whom she seemed particularly protective. Bumping into the actual man on the path may have simply made her see red. Then, in panic, she could have made her way back to the village along the next available path. No-one had seen her until lunch and Anna had said she'd seemed really upset. Anna had thought it'd been due to a fall-out with Dani, but it could have been that, in a fit of rage, she'd shoved the drug-pusher to his death.

Tom's head felt about ready to explode as he inevitably came to Dani. She'd definitely had the opportunity to do it. She might have had some prior contact with Enderby. The only link would've been through Georgie or Laurence. But again, if she was involved, would she have calmly walked into the pub? She would've had to run most of the way back for the timings to work and no-one had suggested that she'd been out of breath.

Sitting in the car, getting colder and colder, he decided that, of the three of them, it was most likely to be Georgie. But he couldn't say definitively; she'd simply had more of an obvious opportunity. He jumped as Anna tapped on the window.

"Stop being an idiot and come inside," she said, as he wound it down.

"I'm not being an idiot, I'm trying to work out who killed Bob Enderby," he replied.

"Well, come and sit in my room where at least you'll be warm and able to have something hot to drink."

He began to clamber out. His feet were actually numb with cold.

"I'm thinking Georgie."

She turned back to him, slowly, and he could see she was biting her lip. There was a retort there, but she turned away and carried on to the kitchen.

"What are you thinking?" he pushed. She often saw things intuitively, was annoyingly right when she wasn't hopelessly wrong.

"I wish he'd fallen over by accident. Caught sight of Laurence through his binoculars and slipped. The binoculars

300

left on the edge, where Georgie or Dani pick them up."

"What about the heel print on his hand?"

"Done when he was beaten up by the men."

"Can't have been. It would've shown as old bruising."

"Then whoever was there tried to rescue him, slipped and put their foot on his hand by mistake and that caused him to drop."

He shrugged. Anything was possible. They needed a confession.

"Look, there's a constable at the end of the drive. I want to go and talk to the girl at the café again. Then I'm going to come back and we're going to put some pressure on Dani."

"Have something warm first," Anna said.

He reached out to catch her wrist just as they got to the back door, but she didn't notice and he let his hand drop. Perhaps she was right. This was one of those moments when he needed to be a police officer.

As he passed her in the hall on his way to the coffee station, she said quietly, "Georgie. I think she could've done it. She's so very stretched and so very angry. But Dani is also —"

She stopped, her brow furrowed. He wondered what she knew that she didn't think she could tell him.

"What about getting their shoes checked for skin or something?" she asked.

"I spoke to forensics. Everyone walked home in the wet, so the chances of there being anything useful are vanishingly small."

"Not even in a groove?"

"No, because the skin was marked, not broken."

Anna hung her head and sighed.

"I'm going on down to the church to pray. If anyone needs me, that's where I'll be."

Tom watched her slip out through the front door, caught sight of her walking across the drive from the dining room windows. She'd obviously decided that she needed to be a vicar just then too.

**

Laurence hovered at the top of the stairs. He really just wanted something to drink. A cup of tea would do and one of Harriet's biscuits, but he wasn't going to go into the dining room while the police officer was there. He slid back into his room, wondering again about making a run for it, but there were coppers everywhere.

He was in two minds about running. He realised that, even before he'd come here, he'd been preparing to face up to the consequences of the drugs. He wanted to hold his hands up and say, 'Punish me'. Delivering drugs was murder. It was simply doing it one step removed and very slowly. But now, having been face to lifeless face with Enderby, he was changing his mind. This was a different matter altogether. This was up-close and personal and would affect everything. He couldn't go back to his old life now, even if he wanted to. He leaned his head against the cold glass of the window. The square of wild grass was blurred with rain. Anna had promised them a dry evening, but just now it was pouring. If he twisted his head until his cheek was flat against the glass, he could just see the cars. At least the corner of the policeman's Audi. Laurence squeezed his eyes shut. He'd had a chance at life and he'd screwed up. He'd made bad choices all along. Georgie hadn't. At least not until now perhaps. If he could, he'd help her; she was worth saving.

Perhaps he'd do them all a favour and jump. It's what Simeon had been trying to do, before he found God. He wondered if he'd be able to do it. Step out into space and fall. No. Even the thought of it made him shaky. He really needed that cup of tea.

"Ok, God, if you're there, find me a way out of this, one where I can live with myself. Bob wasn't a good man, but I don't think anyone deserves to die. So I don't know what to

302

do with that on my conscience."

He stood and waited for something to happen. He wrapped his arms around himself, but he still felt empty and hollow. Surely by now the DI would've gone somewhere else.

He crept downstairs, pushed open the dining room door. He jumped when he saw Catherine and she jumped when she turned and saw him. Everyone was creeping around. She flushed pink to match her eyes and he realised with a pang that she, too, had been crying. *This place, this awful place*, he thought. It scraped you bare.

"Hello Laurence. Something hot?"

"Yes. A cup of tea would be lovely."

She switched on the kettle and moved to the front window, so that, when she turned back to speak, she was framed with sky.

"It's been an interesting week," she said, holding her cup up to her chin with both hands. He leaned back against the kettle table.

"That's a bit of an understatement."

"I'm sorry about your friend."

"As I've learnt to my cost, he was no friend of mine or of any of us kids at the home."

Catherine took another sip.

"How did you manage when you left?"

"I managed. We all do. After all, the one thing we don't have to cope with is homesickness."

Catherine dropped her head. When she looked across at him, she was frowning.

"Georgie said you hate it whenever anyone shows pity. Which is why you don't tend to tell people where you come from. But I don't know what the difference is between being horribly sad for what you went through and the pity that you seem to dread so much."

He turned back to the kettle and dropped a tea bag into a cup. The milk jug was full and there were biscuits. Good old

Harriet. While his tea was brewing, he took the tin across to Catherine. For a second, he thought she was going to refuse, but then she smiled and her shoulders dropped.

"Thanks. These are really good," she said.

"They are delicious. I wonder if she'd send some to me when I'm ..."

And for a minute he was in a tiny cell, which didn't feel much different from where he was now.

"We can't bear the pity because it's like watching someone else suffering when you've got the wound." He pressed the teabag against the side of the mug. "And nothing changes."

She turned away to stare out of the window. He knew she was trying not to cry, which he thought was kind.

"So, what about you and Tom?"

"Me and Tom ... what do you mean?" she said, swinging back to face him. Laurence shrugged.

"He's your only son, but you live a long way away and he doesn't seem to get you."

"I don't think sons are supposed to get their mothers. That's not how it works."

Laurence was disappointed because, if he had a mum, he would've made darn sure he'd be around for her. Of course, if he had a mum, he probably wouldn't realise how precious she was and he'd be moaning and whingeing about how she interfered in his life, just like Dani.

"I thought Tom would find his own way back. I let him go because it has to be his choice. Only now I wish I'd made more of a fuss. Screamed and yelled and held onto him a bit, so at least he'd know I care and that it was really important."

Laurence laughed.

"He knows you care. He definitely knows that. He's just running scared because he does understand how important it is to you." He took a sip of tea. "Simeon speaks of God so matter-of-factly. It made me desperately want what you all have."

"How come you get it?" she asked, turning to look at him. He knew it wasn't because he'd just professed a longing, but because she was desperate for her son to get it. Tom was bloody lucky. Laurence reached for another biscuit. He offered them to Catherine. This time she shook her head. There were no happy endings for people like him, just a hard slog and lots of difficult choices.

"I guess I understand because I'm standing back from it all," he said with a mouthful of crumbs. He took another biscuit. They were so good.

"Have you tried praying?" she asked.

"What, like, 'If you're there, make this all go away'?"

"No, something like, 'If you're there, help me dig deep and get through it.'"

He supposed he'd tried that earlier, only it hadn't made any noticeable difference.

"But that's normal life for me."

She turned away again, her eyes on the floor, as if she'd dropped something. He hoped with all his heart that she'd manage to keep the tears at bay. When she turned back, her eyes were still dry. She moved past him to the door and, as she did so, rested her hand on his arm.

"I believe in a God of power. So I'm praying for a miracle."

"Like Bob Enderby having never been born," Laurence muttered to her back. "Then he wouldn't be dead and then I wouldn't have to take my punishment like a man."

He sat down heavily and took another biscuit.

Chapter 32

Dani stood at the top of the stairs, listening to the murmuring in the dining room. She'd left Georgie lying on the bed, staring at the ceiling. When Dani had tried to speak to her, she'd simply rolled over to face the window, away from the proffered hand. At that moment they might well have been in separate rooms. Dani knew she'd guessed about the binoculars and that, when Dani had put them back, she'd put them under the wrong car. She'd dropped them with relief under the nearest wheel. It had been a stupid mistake.

If only she'd put them back under Anna's old Skoda, none of it would've mattered. The police might not have even found them, and then they would've had to put Bob Enderby's fall down to the men in the SUV because of the drugs. Okay, Laurence would still be facing a charge for dealing, but the rest would've quietly washed away. Dani began to tremble. This was serious and getting out of control. She wouldn't grass on Georgie unless she absolutely had to, but she had to hold her nerve. That bloody man had deserved to die, no question. She wondered if not telling the police about Georgie was a risk. She didn't want anything to come back on her. She wasn't going to miss Selena growing up or give Oscar and Jay an excuse to think she was a write-off. She wanted to show them that she could make something of herself, be a good mum. It didn't matter that she hadn't named and shamed them. They'd always wonder if Selena was their daughter or if, one day, Dani might come asking for money.

She began to cry. It had been bubbling up for hours. Quiet, little sobs that she tried to hold in.

How was she going to manage the next part of her life? She couldn't be a screw-up anymore. The first priority was to get away from this place.

A tissue was pushed under her nose. She looked up from where she was standing. Catherine was a few stairs down. She didn't ask Dani if she was alright, for which Dani gave her brownie points. Unaccountably, at that moment, Dani decided to go and sit in the church. She'd take all her questions to God. Why not? No-one else had anything useful to say.

"I'm going to the church. I couldn't borrow a pair of gloves, could I?" She'd wrap up warm because she didn't want to be distracted. She sniffed. Catherine handed her another tissue. She looked tired, old.

"Absolutely. Now that is something I can find for you." Catherine swivelled around and headed down. Dani followed her. On the side table were the pile of gloves and scarves that everyone had brought with them and peeping out from underneath was Dani's notebook. She knew it was hers because she'd scribbled her name on the front as if she were back at school. Catherine handed her gloves and a scarf and then fished about in her coat pocket and came up with a pen.

"Just in case," she said.

There was a constable at the top of the road, but before he could say anything, Dani called out that she was just going down to the church. He nodded.

It was relentlessly cold and overhead the clouds were scudding by at a tremendous rush. Too fast to drop rain, for which she was glad. The church door was ajar, and the building suddenly became bright with sunlight when, just for a second, the sun came out from behind a cloud. Dani shook her head and laughed.

"It's a bit obvious," she said to the ceiling. She walked to the front and sat down. On the simple altar under the east window was a wooden cross, nothing else.

"So what do I do?" she asked. She got out her notebook. She looked at the blank page and began to scribble. She started at the edges as if she were drawing a border and then began to work her way into the centre. She scraped and scratched at the paper, wanting to cover it in black ink; she didn't want a single patch of white to show. Finally, the page tore and, with a scream, she flung the book from her.

"I don't know what to do. Tell me what to do!" she cried.

Someone slipped in beside her. She jumped and then subsided back into a heap. It was only Anna.

"About what?" Anna asked.

"About Selena. About my life. I don't want what those boys really thought of me to define me. I want to show them."

"What's stopping you?"

"Being on the outside, not understanding how it all works and, before you say anything, I just don't."

"Oh Dani. None of that matters."

Dani swung round angrily.

"How I feel doesn't matter?"

"No, what others think and feel about you doesn't matter at all. Where you have to start is ..."

"With what God thinks of me!" It came out wearily.

"Yes!" Anna said loudly. She stood up and then sat down again, a little sheepishly. "It was only when I concentrated on him and me that I began to realise that it was him and me, then him and us. My little band of parishioners. But I honestly couldn't see them until I began to understand where I started and ended. I'm loved, and not just by a bunch of normal human beings. I'm loved by God. I'm not really sure of anything else, but when I screw up, that's where I start from. That's where I go back to."

"But how do you know?"

Anna laughed.

"Because I'm surrounded and cared for by the most gloriously flawed, damaged and well-meaning people in the world."

"But I'm not surrounded by anyone like that!"

"I wonder." Anna faced forward. "The people in my life! Let's start with Simeon. One of the most important. He's on the spectrum, you know, won't look you in the eye, tells the truth as he sees it without thought or feeling as to how it

309

might affect you. Then there's Archie, who's still grieving for his wife and he's angry with her and therefore a little overprotective of all of us, particularly me, I think. Harriet is kind and loving and terrified of happiness. Whenever we have a moment, she always says something to push me away. And Derek and Phil and ..."

"And Tom," Dani said.

"Yes, and Tom." Anna sounded sad. She looked sidelong at Dani and said, "Who do you have?"

"Mum and Selena," Dani said instantly, though she was cross with herself for not hesitating a little.

"That's a good place to start."

"But my mum's such a cow."

"Harriet can say some awful things too, but she's my best friend. I expect your mum is all sorts of things as well as being a cow."

"She's disappointed mostly."

"And working hard to allow you to be as free as you can, which will make her tired. You're living with Georgie. I know it's only temporary, but Selena will be hard work without you to take up the slack."

Dani wrinkled her nose, clasped her hands together and then placed them either side of her knees.

"Mum did say she'd hoped to go back to college, but I put a stop to all that. She can't afford it now."

"Why don't you do her a deal – why don't you go to college first and then, when you've got a job, tell her you'll support her while she goes?"

"That's a bit long term. Anyway, I'm not sure what I could do."

Only she knew exactly what course she'd like to try. The only GCSE she'd enjoyed or been any good at was PE and, at the local college, there was a life coaching course that was all about fitness and health. It was part-time over two years. She began to wonder what exams she might need and whether she'd have to repeat a couple, which would be a bore, but ultimately worth it.

Dani took a quick peek at Anna, who was looking at the altar. She smiled to herself. She'd got a few months to look into it and perhaps her mum wouldn't give her such a hard time if she was doing something apart from collecting benefits.

Anna stood up.

"I'm back off to the house. I still want to try and speak to Georgie. And Catherine, for that matter. Can I make you a drink before I go?" Dani shook her head. There was no loo and any more tea or coffee would not be a good idea. Anna carefully picked up the notebook from the floor, ripped out the first couple of pages and put it beside Dani on the pew.

"Don't forget, he speaks through the simple stuff. It's just a matter of trusting that it's him speaking."

***

Georgie woke up, rubbed her eyes and yawned. She was incredibly surprised that she'd fallen asleep. She'd thought that Dani would have a go at her, then had listened to her leave. Now, through sticky eyes, the room was dull, but she didn't want to switch on the bedside light because that would make the dimness gather in the corners. She really wanted to hold on to the daylight, no matter that it was fading. The panic inside began to gather momentum. She hugged her knees to her. She hoped against hope that Enderby hadn't targeted Dani through Georgie herself. She wished and regretted, a maelstrom between her ears. Why hadn't Laurence simply delivered the package and had his crisis of conscience later, when he was safely back up in Exeter? Bloody Laurence and his forgiving heart, trying to explain it all to her. Bloody Enderby and his manipulative evil. And he must've been evil to target young people who had such little hope to begin with.

Georgie got up and stared at the blank window. In one

sense, it terrified her – she was so open to the world – but nothing on earth would make her pull the curtains and shut it all out. There was a knock on the door and Georgie sat back down.

"Come in," she whispered. Of course it was Anna, moving carefully, as if the air was thick, as if she had to push through all the feelings of despair emanating from Georgie.

"You look as though you've had a sleep." She made it sound as if it were a good thing. Georgie smiled because Anna clearly hoped so much that everything was going to be alright.

"Oh Georgie. I wish you'd let go of whatever it is that's squashing the life out of you."

Anna had an unusual way with words, but it was exactly how Georgie felt. Back in some ancient time, there'd been a particular punishment for a person who refused to plead one way or another in a court case. They were laid on a sharp rock and weights were piled on top of them. Over the weeks, they were loaded down more and more, until they either pleaded or died, often of a broken back. It was called pressing. It must have been beyond agony and so drawn out. Georgie had written a short essay on it for her A-level history; she'd been horrified at the barbarity of it. Now she felt as though it were her being pressed down, flattened by the weight of what was happening to her and Laurence. She couldn't get enough breath down into her lungs. Yet what did she expect, when she was still refusing to come clean to God?

Anyway, it was all too late. She was heading back tomorrow and she was well-practised at pretending. She'd look for another job and somehow keep going in the meantime. She supposed it might be possible, as long as she could leave all this behind. The room began to spin.

"Head between the knees."

Instead, Georgie stood up.

"I need air."

"Then let's go down to the cove. As long as I go with you, no-one will mind. We've got about an hour before it gets really dark."

In answer, Georgie simply picked up her shoes from under the bed.

***

The cove was quiet, the tide dropping, so that the spine of rocks and the concrete pipe were beginning to show. All three houses were dark and there were no cars. Anna led Georgie down the ramp and across to a rickety bench just above the line of boats hauled beyond the reach of high tide. Georgie knew that above them was the bench where she'd sat and talked to Laurence, invisible from where they were now. A couple of gulls were screeching and there were jackdaws picking at the grass growing near the top of the rocks. Some small birds were darting about, but she had no idea what they were. The seat was damp, but at least out here she could breathe and she didn't feel quite so sick.

"Better?" Anna asked.

Georgie nodded. Would Anna expect her to start talking now? To spill her heart and ease the packing around her soul? Georgie felt stuffed to the eyeballs with stuff, filled to the brim with all the things she'd put in place to make her life work.

"I couldn't have done it," she said quietly. Anna nodded. "You believe me, don't you?" Anna nodded again. But Georgie thought that Anna could've watched her do it and she'd still have nodded just then. She was such a gentle soul, understanding that life was grey and fuzzy around the edges, that the moments of clarity were far-spaced and, instead of leaving you feeling comforted, they often left you feeling bereft and hollow.

"Whenever this all gets sorted, however it turns out, Georgie, if you ever need somewhere to run to, come here – make a fresh start here. We don't have the answers, but we

313

won't ask anything of you."

Georgie turned to stare at this woman with her fine hair and pink, round cheeks. There were rings under her eyes and the beginnings of a double chin. Did she realise what she'd just offered?

"Do you mean that?" Georgie asked, a whisper of hope. For a long moment Anna didn't reply.

"Yes, I do. I think you need somewhere to jump from. We all do, and until you can work out how to do life without your burden, then we're as good a place as any."

"I do believe in God."

"I know you do, Georgie. But I expect he feels a long way off." Georgie nodded. "And you can't hear him or see where he's working." Georgie nodded again. "Just let me have one thing to pray for, so that there's one less thing for you to carry."

Georgie shook her head, her eyes spilling tears; she couldn't speak. Anna pushed a pack of tissues into her hand.

"Give me the first thing that popped into your head just then. If you can't say it now, write it down when you get back to the vicarage, but please give it to me before you go."

"Do you think the police officer will let us leave?"

"He'll hopefully work it out before tomorrow."

"Like you?"

Anna closed her eyes.

"I'm trying to understand."

"So why offer me what I don't deserve then?" Georgie said, standing up.

"Because that's the whole point of God – it's precisely what he does offer. Love, though we don't deserve it; worth, though we don't believe it, and a job to do."

"But I can't do it; not now."

"Yes, you can. But let me have that one thing to pray for. It's important."

Georgie nodded.

"I'll tell you before I go. I promise." She stood up and began to make her way back to the vicarage. Anna didn't follow her immediately. It was only when Georgie looked back from higher up the lane that she saw Anna following. She'd probably promised the copper to keep any eye on her.

Chapter 33

Simeon had tried to go to church. He'd thought it would be empty, but the girl, Dani, had been wandering about and talking. He'd hoped that, with no distractions, he'd be able to pray. He needed to order his thoughts and God usually highlighted what was important. He might as well go home and pray there. Anyway, his feet and fingers had begun to tingle and the light was fading. Simeon scooted along the path to the gate. He was about to turn right, when the merest whisper of a breath made him turn left. He began to walk down to the cove.

The weather was settling, the clouds running less frantically across the sky. Anna might get her quiet, gentle Evening Prayer tonight, though, with all the unresolved issues, Simeon wouldn't have suggested Beacon Point. He was very surprised that that was where she was thinking of going. It was where Terry had tried to push her over and, after all, they did have a murderer in their midst. Most of the cliffs round there were high and in the dark.

He gave a start when, just a short way further on, Georgie appeared out of the gloom.

"Hello Simeon," she said. But she didn't stop and question him, which was a relief. He carried on to the steep bit, where the road became concrete, ridged to stop you slipping. The tide was low and Anna was at the bottom, just beginning to walk up too.

"Simeon. Are you alright?"

"The church is full and I'd like to pray."

"The little bench is free and, as you can see, none of the houses seem occupied."

"Are you alright?" he asked, peering past her to the cove.

"Yes, I think so." She put her hands in her pockets. She was smiling when he glanced at her face. "Actually, while having a conversation with Dani and now Georgie, I think I've made an important decision."

"About Tom?" he asked.

"Yes. How on earth did you know that?"

"Do you really want me to go through all my reasoning?"

She smiled again.

"No, I don't suppose I do. But do you want to know what I've decided?"

"Perhaps Tom should be the first to know."

She shook her head and made a small noise in her chest, as if she were about to laugh out loud.

"Yes, I suppose he should. It won't be news to you anyway, will it, Simeon?"

"You look happy, that's all."

"I am. This minute I really am. Though I'm still really worried about the young people, particularly Georgie. She's so uptight I think she's going to spring apart if she doesn't talk to someone soon."

"Have you told her she can speak to God about everything?"

"Sort of. Not as clearly as that perhaps. Maybe you should try and have a word with her?"

Simeon shivered and took a step back.

"I promise to try if an opportunity presents itself."

"Oh Simeon," Anna said, her voice breaking, cracking with tears, "You're an incredible person, you know that?" For a second, she stared intently at him. Then she slowly turned away and headed up the road.

Simeon continued on to the bench to have a long talk with God. He allowed his mind to unpack itself into the stillness, calming him as he systematically mentioned everyone, what he thought they needed and then asking God what he thought they needed. He asked for the courage to speak to Georgie if the situation arose, which meant that he should definitely go to Evening Prayer that night. Then he remembered that he'd been going to tell Anna that he thought Beacon Point was a bad idea. He sent her a text and got an almost immediate reply, suggesting he come up to the vicarage for dinner. He took a long, deep breath. Anna was probably already arranging a moment with Georgie or possibly Laurence.

"I don't want to speak to them and I need to be calm," he prayed as he strode back up the lane, but when he walked into the dining room, he was surprised to see Tom standing at the window. He frowned.

"Hello Simeon. You alright?"

"Yes, but I don't think we should go to Beacon Point. After all, someone in this house is a drug dealer and someone might be a murderer and it would be hard for you to keep your eye on all of us at once."

"Already thought of that. Archie is also worried."

The frown got deeper.

"Don't worry, I'll have a word with her." Tom looked across at Simeon, who hadn't been expecting it and so didn't quite drop his eyes in time. "Simeon, have you figured anything out yet?"

Simeon bit his lip.

"You've got an idea, haven't you?" Tom persisted.

Simeon didn't dare move. He stared down at Tom's very scuffed shoes. Brown boots that looked as if they hadn't seen a shoe brush since the day they'd been bought.

"Simeon, is there anything you think you can tell me? Anything I ought to know?"

"I think you should speak to Anna."

"I'll go and find her and get her to agree to the cove."

But that hadn't been what Simeon had meant.

**

Anna felt overwhelmed. She'd thought she knew where everyone was, but was suddenly really scared that one of them might've made a run for it. Yet what could she do? She wished Tom would make up his mind. What she needed was five minutes on her own, with a cup of tea. To curl up on her

319

favourite chair and stare at the wall. When she opened the door into her tiny sitting room, there he was. He was making himself at home. He stood up, like some old-fashioned, well-mannered gentleman, though he spoilt the image by sitting straight back down again when he realised it was her. He looked grey and pale.

"How are you doing?" she asked.

"I'm stuck. Pondering. Muddled. I just can't work it out." He did look stuck, a little lost. "I don't have any evidence for anything and the girl at the café was no help."

"Oh Tom, I'm so sorry." For a minute she wanted them to confess, to make a clean breast of things, to make it simple and straightforward for him.

"No tips or hints from the man upstairs?" he asked a little desperately.

"If you mean God, then say so," she said and then bit her tongue. She hadn't meant it to come out quite so sharply; truly, she hadn't.

"Anna, don't get cross with me. Not right now."

It wasn't fair. She wasn't being cross; she just wished he wouldn't relegate her faith to a euphemism.

"The trouble is, Tom, you say something like that and it makes me think you still don't understand how important all this is for me. That it doesn't matter." He shook his head in annoyance, which didn't help. "And while you think it doesn't matter, I know you don't get it." He looked at her, his eyes narrowing just a little with the weight of the frown creasing his forehead, his hands balling into fists on the arm of the chair.

"I promise never to resent or get between you and your duties," he said through gritted teeth.

"We aren't talking about my duties; we are talking about my God and I want you to share him," she said emphatically. Where did all this sureness come from? He looked away, as if to clear his head.

"No couple shares everything."

"But Tom, they do share the really important bits."

"So you're saying that we can only be together if I find God."

That's not what she'd meant to say. It wasn't the conclusion she'd come to when she'd been with Dani. Then, she'd decided to trust God for Tom, to step out for a change. How had she just managed to argue herself into the opposite corner?

"Anna, I really care for you. Isn't that enough?"

It ought to be enough. Why couldn't her life be simple, like other people's? Why wasn't she able to just fling herself into his arms and get on with the next bit?

"I did think it was enough. Earlier today. I wanted to give us a go."

He stood up, disappointment deepening the lines around his mouth.

"This is just what my mum did," he growled. He struggled to get the words out and they fell between them, piling up messily. He sat back down heavily; his legs unable to support the weight of what she was doing to them both. Anna felt the tears spill over and run down her cheeks.

"No, it's not," she replied. She picked up a tissue and blew her nose, but the tears kept coming. This was so bloody hard. She wanted to say, 'Find God, and then come find me. If you still want to.' But it sounded like blackmail. She began to cry, really cry. He came over and wrapped his arms around her.

"Don't cry. Please don't cry."

"But it's all so impossible," she gulped and grabbed more tissues. "It's horrible because we can't pretend. It has to be real. And I'm forcing you into a terrible place. God is all about love and I'm making it all about choice. I really care for you, but I'm terrified I can't choose you."

She scraped the tissues across her eyes.

"Do I get any say in the matter or is it just you and God?"

"I think, by the very nature of him, he's going to get the deciding vote."

Tom pulled out his warrant card and stared down at it.

"Please don't say no just now. I need to focus on the murder and I need to be allowed to hope just a little longer." She tried to look up at him, but her eyes wouldn't focus.

She wasn't sure when he left. She just noticed the absence of him. There was a pain; it made breathing hard. She didn't think she'd ever feel quite right again. Now it was time for dinner and she had to wash her face and walk back into the other room, full of those who had an equally important call on her time.

***

Harriet loaded up the tray. Everything was ready, but she'd heard Anna and Tom arguing and then he'd exited stage-left, tight-lipped, and hadn't even seen her hovering in the kitchen. Luckily, he hadn't slammed the back door because the glass would've probably fallen out. She heard Anna crying. *What an absolute bloody shame*, Harriet thought. She'd really hoped they might have tried. She'd thought that was what Anna had decided. But there was so much going on, and now that Catherine had jumped into the mix, Tom and Anna didn't stand a chance. Poor loves.

She tapped on the door. Anna didn't reply, so she pushed on in. She shouldn't have really, but Anna sounded distraught. She was standing in the door to her tiny bathroom, rubbing a towel over her face. It hadn't helped – she looked red-rimmed and soggy.

"Another misunderstanding?"

"The trouble is I really want to talk about it, but this is patently not the right time, so it keeps getting heated and then we say things we don't mean."

"And then really annoying people come along and tell you it's time for dinner."

Anna smiled a little weakly.

"You're not really annoying."

"Only a bit," Harriet said. "Do you have any cream? I think your face could do with a bit of TLC."

"But it's time for dinner."

"Go and put some on while I rally the troops. See you in a minute." Anna turned obediently and disappeared back into the bathroom. Harriet headed down the hall. It was dark, the ceiling light barely lifting the gloom. Catherine was just coming out of the lounge.

"Simeon's here," she said brightly. Harriet wondered if she'd heard the row too.

"Shall I go and get the girls?"

"Yes please," Harriet replied, trying to match Catherine's smile.

The front door opened and there was Archie with Dani. Harriet turned to look up the stairs and saw Laurence, rubbing his eyes as if he'd just woken up. He looked haunted and jumped as he nearly bumped into Georgie.

"Dinner, Laurence, Georgie." She wanted to tell him to go and wash his hands because he looked about six, with his hair sticking up and his clothes all rumpled. Georgie didn't look much older and Harriet noticed how hard they tried to avoid each other as Laurence stepped back to let her past.

Anna appeared at the kitchen door and suddenly Harriet felt like a light attracting the moths. That they'd all come and dance round her and her wonderful cooking, their fragility outlined by her own solidity, her own rootedness going deep because that's what they needed. She began to back into the dining room, as if to draw them all in.

Everyone was here and yet the room felt empty. Harriet caught Archie's eye and he followed her out to fetch the trays.

"It's all a bit awkward, isn't it?" he said, looking back over his shoulder.

"Just a little. Though you'd thought we would've gotten used to entertaining murderers." That made Archie wince.

"Sorry. Perhaps just people who have hurt other people."

"We've all hurt others. I think the thing that's bothering us is the viciousness of the deed." Harriet thought there was something in that.

"Is Simeon alright? Will he come with us tonight?" she asked.

"Yes, I think so. He's leaving it to the last minute to decide. He's finding it a bit of a strain, being sought out by everyone."

Harriet pointed to the trays.

"We should get a trolley," Archie said. "Then you wouldn't have to make so many trips backwards and forwards."

That was quite a good idea. She suddenly longed to sit down with her laptop and order one. A normal, ordinary thing, off Amazon or eBay.

When they returned, Catherine and Anna were talking at the far end of the table. The others were sitting with a space between them. They were silent.

"Not exactly a celebration," Anna said quietly. "I'll say grace." She stood up, pushing her chair back. She prayed for God's presence and wisdom, for him to continue to meet with them. She didn't mention the food and, for a second, Harriet felt a sliver of irritation. She watched Anna's face carefully and, sure enough, she realised just as she reached for a plate of chicken. She looked over to Harriet and shrugged. A worried, 'I'm-really-sorry' shrug. Harriet smiled back and blew her a kiss. Dani was watching them intently. When she realised that Harriet had noticed her staring, she dropped her head. The bravado, the hard shell was still there, but it was battling with something else. Harriet wondered what was going on inside.

Catherine was going to stay on an extra couple of nights, so that Tom could spend some time with her. Harriet wondered how that was going to work after the altercation with Anna. She might check with Phil to see if he had any space available. If Anna and Tom had split up for good, it'd be awkward for everyone to have Catherine at the vicarage. That made Harriet wonder how Derek was getting on with the packing. She should've asked him earlier. The storage container was coming on Monday – a moment she realised she was looking forward to. She loved living out of a suitcase, loved the simplicity of managing with only just enough. The house they were going to rent was already furnished, so they were literally hanging on to their clothes and the can't-do-without kitchen and bedroom items. Derek wasn't managing and kept packing lots of things, just in case, but if they were desperate for something, they'd borrow it. It was such a simple way to live. She hoped he'd learn to love it like she did.

Anna cleared her throat.

"I'd just like to say a big thankyou to Harriet for all her hard work. She's a wonderful cook and it means that you never have to battle with hunger while you're here."

There was a smattering of applause. Laurence only nodded. To be fair he'd mostly eaten toast. Georgie clapped loudly, almost fiercely, so that Dani looked across at her and raised her eyebrows.

After the main course, when Harriet started to clear the table, Catherine and Anna got up to help. Archie started to rise too, but Anna shook her head. It didn't need all of them.

"So, are we ready for this evening?" Harriet asked Anna, as they took the dirty plates through to the kitchen. Pudding was warming in the oven. A rhubarb and orange crumble with a jug of custard. Easy. Anna nodded. Catherine came in behind them, carrying some of the cutlery.

"I'm going to do Evening Prayer, but with big gaps for us to hear from God. We'll go and sit on the point to the left of Church Cove, just down from the seat, and I'll take some bin bags and cushions, so people can make themselves comfortable."

Catherine said, "Looking down on the sea with the moon above will be beautiful."

"What should I do when it comes to confession?" Anna chewed her lip. It was beginning to look quite sore. "I'm worried it might be a bit pointed if we all sit there in silence?"

"Perhaps that's where we do our own thing, don't you think? As long as you explain," Catherine said quietly.

"Then it's between us and God. Good idea. I'm not responsible." Harriet could hear the relief in Anna's voice.

"Will Tom be with us?" Catherine asked, again so quietly that Harriet could hardly hear her.

"Yes. At least near enough to hear what's said and to prevent anyone from making a run for it," Anna replied. She sounded almost normal apart from a slight catch of breath at the end.

"The culprit will think they've got away with it," Harrient said, "so it would be pointless trying to run." At least she hoped this was the case.

They began to troop back into the dining room.

"I suppose it just depends on the level of guilt and what they truly believe about confession," Catherine said.

"But surely you'd be quite entitled to simply ask for God's forgiveness and no-one would be any the wiser," said Harriet.

Anna looked thoughtful.

"They could," she said. "But God would know. We still have to do our bit, even though his love is all pretty much one way. We don't just simply receive; we also have a part to play. The fact that we can do so with a clear conscience is one of the perks of our faith."

Anna opened the door. The four around the table looked up. Harriet peered at each of the young people and wondered what they'd walk away with tonight, what God would lay out for them to pick up and take home from this crazy week.

Chapter 34

Georgie hadn't bothered to have much pudding and had made a quick exit at the end of the meal. When Dani followed her up, Georgie was standing in front of the window. Dani tried to creep in. She didn't want any more grief, but a floorboard creaked and Georgie swung round as if she'd been waiting.

"Sorry," Dani muttered. Georgie looked terrible. Pale, almost green under the eyes. "Are you alright? You look as if you have a hangover."

"I wish," Georgie replied, slumping onto the bed. "I'm just not sure I can keep this up."

Dani narrowed her eyes.

"Look, if it's about the binoculars, I'd just stay quiet."

Georgie stared, her large, dark eyes boring into Dani. Then she said matter-of-factly, "I knew you'd taken them from under Anna's car." Dani wondered how much there was to worry about. Despite Georgie's tough upbringing, she seemed to be collapsing under the strain.

"But it was you that brought them up from the point," Dani said. "Laurence might've done it, but he wouldn't have left them outside like that. I expect he'd have simply tucked them away in his van. Why didn't you put them in your car, by the way?"

"I didn't have my keys with me." Georgie sighed. "I was, as you can imagine, in a bit of a panic."

"Oh, I'd not thought of that," Dani replied. She'd wondered about the appearance of the binoculars. It had seemed such an odd thing to do, to bring such incriminating evidence up to the house. She guessed none of them had been thinking particularly clearly that morning.

"But, Dani, you saw them under Anna's car and you took them!"

"I thought they might be worth something and I didn't think it was a good idea for them to be found at the vicarage."

"So why did you put them back?" Georgie almost wailed.

"Because I didn't want them to be found in my bag. I was doing a bit of damage limitation and giving them a wipe. Only of course then those stupid idiots came to get their drugs and Anna called her boyfriend in."

"Why under Laurence's van? You could've chucked them in a hedge, into the sea, anywhere."

"So could you. But like you, I wasn't exactly thinking logically. I didn't deliberately put them there. I just shoved them back where I thought I'd found them."

Georgie sighed, which annoyed Dani as, really, she hadn't done anything wrong. She'd only spotted the binoculars because she'd been outside trying to find a signal on her phone. Anyway, the police probably would've seen them under Anna's car just the same.

Georgie began to tremble.

Dani said, "You know that I know what happened."

"You saw?"

Dani nodded. She'd seen it all.

"So, what are you going to do?" Georgie whispered. "Will you tell the police?" Dani watched the tremor for a moment; Georgie was like an old woman.

"Why would I? What would I have to gain? They've got nothing on either of you, apart from Laurence's confession to the drugs and, if he'd kept his mouth shut, I reckon he'd have got away with that too."

Dani realised that, for whatever reason, she had total control over what was going to happen next. She held all the power. So why didn't she feel better? Why did she feel so bloody? She took a deep breath and turned away to pick up her bag. She had to hold her nerve just a little longer. Keep all this forgiveness crap at bay until she got home, got some distance, saw Selena again.

"I'm going to speak to Laurence," Georgie said, standing up very slowly, as if she were afraid she was going to faint.

"Why? You don't have to help him anymore. He's not worth it; he was never worth it."

"You don't know what he's like, what he's worth," Georgie retorted. "You don't know how kind he was when I was a kid. I had no-one and he looked out for me."

"But he didn't protect us from Enderby, did he? He wouldn't believe what a shit he was. How many of us did Enderby screw over? And stupid Laurence went on trusting him way beyond any reasonable doubt. Don't you see what a fool he's been?"

"How did you meet Enderby?" Georgie asked.

Dani shouldn't have replied, but it felt really good to tell someone the truth at last.

"Just after you went back into care again, when you moved to Yeovil. He started helping out at the youth group. Not for long. But enough to know who I was, what school I went to and the fact that I was a bloody loser."

"I'm so sorry."

"Why? It wasn't your fault." Dani felt like slapping her.

"It wasn't Laurence's fault either," Georgie replied, tears beginning to flow. "He was a fool, that's all. I'm sorry, Dani. You know what I did, but I can't let Laurence take the blame for me." She moved across to the door.

"He's not going to though, is he? He's held his hands up to the drugs, but he's never tried to help you beyond that. Laurence was stupid over Enderby; don't be stupid over him." Dani was almost shouting. She was worried that someone might hear them. Georgie's hand was on the knob. It dropped down to her side as she turned away. Dani really did want to hit her stupid, doe-eyed face, but instead she took her arm, led her to the bed and sat her down.

"Look, I'll get you a glass of water or something. You'll be alright."

Dani looked at her watch. They still had another half hour before they were to meet down in the hall. She had until then to get Georgie back up on her feet and breathing again.

***

Laurence was also sitting on his bed, trying to finish a cup of coffee, but it had gone cold. How long had he been staring at the wall? He wondered what Georgie was doing. Poor kid. If he'd not been so blind about Enderby, perhaps he and Georgie might have been able to ... Why hadn't he believed her when she'd tried to tell him that Enderby wasn't to be trusted? From the last few months in the home together to pretty much every time they'd met since, she'd had a go. They'd never been able to get past it. Georgie was the only person who'd ever tried to care for him and he'd believed the drug pusher rather than her. He'd been so incredibly stupid and, finally, when he'd seen what an absolute idiot he'd been, there'd been no relief because it'd been too late. He'd liked to have gone and asked her forgiveness, but Simeon said that such things often took a while to work through and Laurence knew he'd run out of time.

If only Enderby had let him alone one day longer. He'd been working it out. He'd been going to try and face up to what he'd done. But there was Bob, standing in front of him, his cheek swollen, an eye half-closed, holding his hand like a claw. Nag, nag, nag. Pushing him away, screaming at him had felt so good. Like a release, but afterwards all that had rushed in was an overwhelming tightness at what he'd done. The wrongness of everything, each stupid choice he'd made along the way, closing down his life. Seeing Georgie had been like putting a thumb in an open wound and the pain had overwhelmed him.

There was a gentle knock on the door. Laurence jumped and the dregs of his coffee soaked into his pillow. He quickly turned it over and shuffled to the edge of the bed.

"Come in."

It was Archie, so upright, so shiny.

"I wanted to say that I'd like to stay in touch when you go

back to Exeter." Laurence felt his heart shrivel. What did the old man want? "Just to have someone on your side, as it were. But only if you'd like to, of course."

Laurence shrugged.

"Why?"

Archie frowned and shook his head.

"Because you don't have anyone else and the penal system can be tough."

Penal system! It was like Archie was living in another century. Still, he did have a point. While Laurence was waiting for his hearing, he could be sent anywhere in the country, particularly as bail was out of the question. In prison no-one could guarantee his safety against the guarantee of his silence. He'd be another overdose before anyone could do anything about it. So it'd be good to have someone thinking about him. Only Exeter was a long way away. It'd probably be out of sight, out of mind.

"What do you know about it?" Laurence said.

"My life hasn't always been as straightforward as it is now."

"Look, Archie, thanks and all that, but you don't need to do this. You really don't."

Archie nodded and his eyes narrowed just a little.

"The thing is, Laurence, I'd like to. I'd really like to be there for you."

"I don't believe, you know. I have no faith in your God."

"That doesn't matter. I have faith and I pray that, one day, you'll get it too."

"What if I don't?"

"You're a young man. You've got years stretching ahead of you in which God can do his thing."

"He wouldn't want someone like me." Laurence turned away, but the wall was too close and he had to step back.

"That's the whole point, Laurence. You're exactly the sort of person he loves most. Though, of course, he loves us all the same," Archie said hurriedly and stepped back too, just a little. "Are you coming tonight?"

"I don't think I have a choice."

"Well, I'll see you there then." He handed Laurence a piece of paper. "My details. Then it's up to you."

Archie smiled, nodded and pulled the door closed behind him. Laurence looked at it. There was a mobile, a landline, an email address and a proper address. Archie hadn't left out a single thing. It was pointless keeping it, but he tucked it into his wallet just the same.

He turned the pillow over and tried to soak up some of the coffee stain with his towel, but it had well and truly sunk in. Pointless trying, really. He'd have to tell Harriet what he'd done. Tell her he was sorry for that, at least.

***

The front door was open and Tom could see them all milling about inside. A murmur of noise and shadows. Over and over again, he went through all that had happened on the Tuesday morning. It had only been the day before yesterday. Still he couldn't get anything to slot into place. Tom clenched his jaw and jammed his hands in his pockets. By rights, Laurence should've been on his way back to Exeter. Why was he allowing this charade to take place? Sandra hadn't been able to disguise her surprise when he told her what was going to happen. That he was granting Anna her wish in the hope that this final act would make one of them let something slip, anything he could use to get to the bottom of what had actually happened down at the Lizard.

He'd just got off the phone with forensics. There was no doubt now. Someone had placed the heel of their boot on that man's hand, up near the wrist, as he'd clung on for dear life. The fingers, already mangled from the car door, meant he hadn't stood a chance. They'd looked down at him and pressed so hard they'd broken small bones, leaving a deep indentation in the skin. The drop, then the rocks and the sea had done more damage, but it had been that heel that had made Enderby fall.

Tom turned away. Anna believed in them all, but didn't believe in him. At least not enough to trust him. She came out and walked over to where he was waiting. She'd brushed her hair, but nothing could mask the paleness of her cheeks.

"Are you ready?" she asked. He nodded. "Thanks for this, Tom. I know it's a lot of trouble for you."

"Don't worry," he said, "there are constables on each of the paths, at the top of the road and Sandra and I will be in sight at all times."

"That's not what I meant," she said. He'd known that, but didn't want to stray into no-man's land. They had to keep the boundaries in place tonight.

"Truce for now, Anna. I'll be a police officer and you obey your calling. I won't get in your way, but neither must you get in mine."

She looked up at him, straight into his eyes, and then her gaze slid over his shoulder, as if what she'd seen was a disappointment. His mother stepped down onto the gravel, pulling on her gloves. She nodded, but didn't approach. She must be absolutely miserable too. The others filed out and then the outside light flickered on. As security systems went, it was hopeless.

"You'd best lead the way," he said to Anna. She nodded and tried to smile, but it was as if her face was stiff with cold and would crack if she tried too hard. She began to walk up the drive. Archie and Catherine hung back, allowing Laurence and the girls to follow behind her. At the top of the lane Simeon was waiting with Belle. She wagged her tail and then sat down while everyone walked past. There was no chatter and it reminded Tom of a funeral cortege. Anna walked slowly, a blue woollen hat with a furry bobble pulled down over her hair. It looked faintly ridiculous and didn't lend the scene the dignity it deserved.

Sandra fell into step beside him.

"How do you want us to play it, Boss?"

"To be honest, I'm not sure what I'm expecting. Anna reckons that they're all close to breaking. I reckon they all know more than they're telling us; at least one of them deliberately 'helped' Enderby to fall. So stand as close as you can without cramping anyone's style and let's see what Anna's God can do." That wasn't what he'd meant to say. He added, "Once we get back to the vicarage, we'll arrest Laurence and take him to the guy from Exeter. He should've arrived by then." That felt better, more professional.

"You're not worried we're allowing a murderer to escape?"

"Of course I'm worried. But I don't know what else to do. Without a confession, we've got nothing to keep any of them here."

Anna turned back to look at them, then quickly looked away again. She'd always been a little jealous of Sandra. He'd quite enjoyed that; the possibility that she thought that someone as attractive and clever as his constable might be interested in someone like him. If Anna knew him at all, she'd know he'd never even think about it. The job was hard enough as it was without crossing that particular line.

It didn't take long to reach the steeply ridged concrete at the last part of the lane and as they began to descend, the moon slipped out from behind the clouds. Tom heard footsteps behind them and the clatter of claws. Derek and Harriet appeared with Dolly. Harriet also wore a woolly hat with an over-large pom-pom, but on her it looked perfect. She was an attractive woman and the way Derek held her hand, hugged close to his chest, showed he was patently aware of it. Derek saluted him as they went past, Tom nodded in reply. As long as Harriet wasn't in danger, Derek would be a useful bloke to have around.

Using the moonlight, they walked through the gate onto the north path. He knew that one of his constables would be up around the corner, muttering about bosses who didn't care who froze to death in the line of duty.

Just a few metres beyond the gate, the track turned east out along the spit of land that protected the cove. The first part was sheltered, as the path was halfway down the slope, worn into the land by the countless footsteps of visitors lured out by the possibilities of the sea and a view along the cliffs. Just below the crown was the bench; beyond that, the path wound its way down onto a narrow wedge of grass. They were about thirty feet above the water. The nearly-full moon sparkled across the sea and into the cove. It reflected off the windows of the houses down below them. The sea was well out, exposing the rocks and sand and the seaweed-covered outfall. Just as Anna pulled her book from her pocket, a cloud snuffed out the moonlight, as if someone had switched it off. Anna laughed.

"It's going to do that a lot, I think. But don't worry, I have a torch to read by and I will explain any responses. Mostly, I'd like you to get comfortable. Archie and Derek have cushions in bags for you to sit on and there's the bench. Just stay close enough that you can still hear me, so you know what's going on."

There was a lot of rustling from the plastic bags. Harriet and Derek came and perched on the bench. Tom's mum took a cushion and walked right out to the end, as far away from him as she could get. Simeon and Archie flanked Laurence, who sat on a row of rocks looking out towards the lifeboat station. There were a couple of lights at the bottom of the steep steps, but it didn't look as if anyone was actually there. The two girls didn't seem to know what to do until Anna dropped a couple of cushions near their feet.

Tom could see the lights of three ships out on the horizon. They weren't moving; probably just waiting for a cargo. Mooring out at sea was free. Now that sounded like a nice, simple life. Would they take on an ex-copper? He wondered how long he'd have to be away before anyone noticed he'd gone.

The moon slipped out from behind the clouds. It was a bright, brittle light and Tom suddenly felt as if it were scraping away the top layer of his skin. Bloody Anna and her God. And his mum. He could almost feel their prayers piling up around him, snagging his feet, muffling his thoughts.

There was hardly any wind, yet his eyes began to blur. He had to be able to see everyone that he needed to see. It shouldn't be this difficult; the promontory was small – it's why he'd allowed Anna to bring them down there. Blinking rapidly, he reminded himself that he needed to be a police officer, with hard edges and sound reasoning.

Anna took a breath and suddenly he was afraid for her. She was always taking care of people, looking after those broken and damaged souls who'd lost their way. Tonight, he was here, his constables all over the place and, at the first crackle of a radio, they'd come running, but there'd be other nights when she wasn't protected, other times when crackpots and lost souls might want a chat, might take out the unfairness of it all on her. He shuddered, instinctively stepping forward, just a yard or two, so that if anyone did have a go, he'd have a fighting chance of getting there first. Of course, if any of them lunged at his mother, she'd be lost, sitting all the way over there. Twenty feet, no more, but way beyond him. He'd have to rely on Archie or Simeon to realise what was happening and to react really quickly.

Tom shook his head. They were out here for Evening Prayer. Nothing more. He was crazy if he thought anything more dramatic was going to happen. It's just that there'd been a time when it had and that had been the moment when he'd realised what a remarkable person Anna really was and how much he'd do to keep her safe.

Chapter 35

Anna's eyes flitted over each of the scattered group in turn and finally came to rest on the end of the promontory. Her hands shook. She was nervous. Tom had never heard her take a service before. She was also at the end of, had presided over, the worst retreat in history. She'd even booked an emergency session with her spiritual director, Irene, knowing she'd need to make some sense of what had happened, was still to happen. She breathed, took her time. Unusually, there was very little wind – only a gentle breath across their cheeks. The beauty was settling about them, the moon huge and glittery, the sea rippling but flat to the horizon and the cliffs a dark greeny-blue. For a second, Anna shut her eyes, visualising each of them and how they were sitting, so that the image was burned onto the back of her eyelids.

She wondered if Archie would ever like Tom, whether he'd forgive her for even contemplating a relationship with someone who didn't understand God. Whether Catherine would ever forgive herself for pushing away the man she'd promised to love. Would Simeon, for that matter, continue to creep out from under the label that everyone was happy to give him? And Harriet, would she allow herself to love and be loved without the expectations of the village crushing her?

They were a screwed-up bunch, even without taking into consideration Dani, Laurence and Georgie. Anna almost spoke that thought out loud, but managed to catch herself just in time.

She spoke the opening sentences and then paused. They'd all done this enough times now to know that she wouldn't hurry.

"As this moment marks the end of a day, it also marks the end of a week dedicated to God. Regardless of where you are on the journey, he loves you. It's the only thing I am absolutely certain of.

"Is there anything you'd like to say to him? Anything you've been meaning to talk to him about? Now is the moment. Nothing is off limits."

There was a wonderful silence and Anna poured her heart into it, making a God-shaped space for each of them. Laurence cleared his throat as if he were about to say something. That wasn't what she'd meant; it was supposed to be between them and God, inside their heads. She caught Catherine's eye, who smiled reassuringly. But Anna should've made it clearer.

Laurence began to speak.

"I'm still not sure you're real, but I'm getting glimpses of something I don't understand. So, if you are there, I'm really sorry for delivering those drugs. Making it so easy for others to do evil."

Anna was stunned. Her eyes blurred with tears. She hadn't expected that. Georgie then gave such a sob, almost a wail, that made everyone jump. Anna felt, rather than saw, Tom tense. Harriet went and wrapped her arms around the girl. Dani inched away, turning her back to look southwards.

"I'm sorry too, so sorry," Georgie whimpered, the words breathless and sharp. "I lie all the time; I just go along with everything around me and I get so tired I can't think straight." She looked over to Laurence and said to him, "I thought I'd only shoved him out of the way." Then she whispered, "I didn't realise he'd gone over. I really didn't know what I'd done until it was too late. I didn't even notice I had the binoculars until I was coming past the pub."

Tom stepped forward, but stopped when Anna turned and looked at him through narrowed eyes. She shook her head sharply, willing him to back off. He'd promised her this half hour and Georgie was going to get as much time as she could give her. Laurence moved, though. He came and knelt at Georgie's feet next to Harriet. It was getting quite crowded around her.

"Georgie, it was my fault. You always understood what sort of man Bob was and you always tried to tell me, to show me. But I allowed him to carry on exploiting everyone. No wonder you were so angry. It was my fault. Not yours."

Catherine walked over to them, handed out tissues and then returned to where she'd been sitting. Anna wished that Tom would go to her, but then there'd only be Sandra guarding the way back.

"I don't think I can keep this up much longer either," Laurence said.

"Don't try to," Anna said quietly. "The more we pretend, the worse it gets. Honesty with God is the only way forward."

Laurence nodded violently in agreement and turned to Simeon.

"I wish I'd met you sooner, Simeon," he said.

Simeon raised a hand in acknowledgement, but kept his eyes on the ground.

This was going a lot better than Anna had expected. She was about to do one of the readings when Catherine took a deep breath.

She said very quietly, almost to herself, "I've been really lonely of late. Pretending everything was alright. A close friend died recently and I miss them. They were a huge part of my life at home."

Anna desperately wanted to turn and look at Tom, but didn't dare move. She understood that it was nothing to do with her. This was between them.

"Come and live here," Archie said firmly. "You'd be nearer Tom and we'd love to have you."

Catherine mouthed a silent 'thank you' at him and turned away to look out over the sea.

Anna wanted to say, 'Are we done?', but instead started counting. She decided on sixty slow seconds before she began the next bit. Dani was the only one who'd remained silent and though, usually, she hated to be left out, tonight was not

339

usual on any level. She still had her back to them and only Simeon or Catherine would have any hope of seeing what was going on in her head. At fifty-two seconds, the pieces fell into place, as Anna realised what she should've seen all along. That what had been on the edge of her mind when Simeon had spoken earlier suddenly took centre stage. This was all about a window of opportunity, and a narrow one at that.

"Dani," said Anna, "this would be a good moment to tell Georgie what happened."

Tom stiffened.

"You'll feel better if you tell the truth."

Dani swung round. She glared at Anna. She looked furious and the words she then directed at Georgie seemed to force themselves from between her lips, as if they were made of something more than air.

"It was your fault that Enderby got to me. He came to our youth group because you led him there. I know you said you were sorry, but you don't know what it's like for people like me."

Georgie couldn't hold Dani's gaze. She buried her head in her arms. Laurence closed his eyes as Dani turned on him.

"Oh, don't worry, Laurence, I never believed anything he said. He was a first-class user. He asked me to run errands for him. But unlike you, after a while I said no. I knew what kind of man he was. There, are you satisfied now?" she said, swinging round once more to face Anna. Though Simeon was looking down at the ground, he suddenly began to nod. Anna wasn't one bit surprised that he'd now worked it out too.

Dani froze, her eyes wide as she watched Anna and Simeon exchange a glance of understanding.

Tom was frowning. Anna could see he wasn't sure what to do. She wanted him to stay back. Dani was too close to Simeon and the edge. At that moment Simeon moved.

"I need to go now," he said and turned his back to the sea. Dani reacted like a steel trap, grabbing his arm and pulling

Simeon towards her. The moon disappeared behind a cloud as Anna shouted, "No!", though it came out as an inarticulate sound from deep within. The sea had become dull and she suddenly couldn't see anything clearly enough. In slow motion, she saw Dani pulling Simeon's hood from his head. His eyes were squeezed shut, but he must have felt her breath on his cheek.

"You don't know anything. Tell them, Anna!" Dani shouted, her voice harsh, insistent. Simeon wouldn't be able to think, let alone breathe. Dani had twisted his arm behind his back. Belle was standing just in front of them, and she looked back at Archie as if to ask him what she should do. Archie's face was a mask of pain, anger and impotence. The drop behind them wasn't huge, but it was onto rocks and the concrete-covered pipe. The moon slipped out from behind a cloud and the sea sparkled.

"Dani, this isn't helping your case. Let Simeon go. You can't understand how much this will distress him," Anna squeaked.

"There isn't a case. Why are you saying that I did it? Georgie pushed him. Georgie made him let go. I saw her. She said she pushed him. You all heard her."

But Georgie didn't stamp on his hand, Anna thought. *You did.*

"Calm down. Everyone stay exactly where you are." Tom's voice was firm, his hands raised in front of him.

Simeon dropped his head and moaned. He tried to twist away, but Dani just pushed his arm higher up. He was grey with pain. Archie was visibly trembling and Anna could hear him taking ragged breaths, his face pale and waxy. Anna turned to him and said, "Archie, are you alright?" But there was nothing she could do when he dropped to his knees and groaned.

Tom was finally beginning to move towards Dani as Simeon screamed and wrenched away from her. Anna thought

341

she heard a popping noise and he gasped, but he was already kneeling down by his friend.

"Archie, breathe slowly. Concentrate on your breaths, not the pain," Simeon shouted, leaning over him.

"It's not my fault," Dani was crying. Tom had her by her arm, handcuffs dangling.

Catherine moved quickly over to Archie and spoke quietly but firmly. "Get him sitting with his back to the rocks. Simeon, try and calm down; it'll only upset him more if you're upset."

"An ambulance is on its way," Sandra said, taking hold of Dani's arm. She pushed her up the path ahead of her, Dani still sobbing as she stumbled along. The others were clustered around the point, staring at Archie, now sitting propped up where Derek had hauled him. Anna was stuck, incapable of moving. All she could think was, 'Not Archie, not Archie ...'

* * *

The ambulance stopped up by the lane to the lifeboat station, where it could turn. They brought a stretcher down and carried the now unconscious Archie away. Simeon stumbling behind, wrapped in a red blanket, his arm dangling at his side. Tom began to walk after them. Anna was still having difficulty thinking straight. She hesitated until Harriet stepped forward and patted her arm.

"You go to the hospital and be with them. Derek and I will go back to the vicarage and make sure everyone there has what they need. Come on, Georgie, Laurence, Catherine," she said, gathering them up.

Anna walked as quickly as she could, almost jogged until she couldn't breathe anymore herself. She decided another heart attack wasn't useful at this point, so she slowed down. Tom was waiting at the top of the drive.

"I know you want to go with them. One of my people will take you. Simeon needs someone to be there who understands. And Archie ... you need to be there for Archie and you shouldn't drive in this state."

She was still out of breath, so she simply nodded, grateful as he spoke into his radio.

"What a mess," he muttered. "What a bloody mess."

She bit her lip because she didn't know what to say. She managed to touch his sleeve with her hand. He looked at it for a minute, but when he raised his face to her, all she could see was the police officer. She didn't have time for him; she needed to get to the hospital.

Chapter 36

Simeon was lying on a trolley in a side room. He was woozy, but not in any pain. They'd got his shoulder back into its socket and given him an injection. Anna had explained to the doctor that Simeon wouldn't speak and would keep his eyes shut until it was over.

He'd only opened them a little when he was sure they were alone. The lights would be too bright and the sounds too clattery for him to be comfortable.

"I expect Tom will come soon to ask us to explain what we know," Anna said.

Simeon nodded.

"Does it hurt?" she asked.

"No. Not yet."

"I'll stay with you."

Simeon nodded again and squeezed his eyes shut once more.

"Archie's in the best place now, hooked up to all sorts of monitors. He's not well, but, Simeon, he's not dead." She bit her lip hard to squash the tears down. Simeon would hate her to cry. It'd be too much for him in this difficult place.

"If you need to cry, Anna, you can. I'll count."

"It's alright, Simeon. I don't need to now." And she didn't; his permission had somehow taken the edge off.

She'd never thought about Archie dying. She supposed he was nearly seventy, but that didn't feel that old and he looked after himself, looked after them all. It was much too soon to be contemplating such a loss.

"Please don't let him die," she whispered.

At that moment, Tom appeared. He grasped her hand, holding it down at his side. She squeezed it and felt calmer.

"Hello Simeon. Does it hurt?" Tom asked.

To Anna's surprise Simeon glanced up at Tom and then back down again.

"It doesn't hurt, though the doctor said it'd be quite sore tomorrow and, for the first few days, to take the full dose of painkillers."

"Very sensible. Why suffer needlessly! Are you both alright to talk? I want to interview Dani and I need to be sure that what I think happened did actually happen."

They both nodded.

"Can you help me sit up?" Simeon asked. "Then I can look at the floor and I'll be able to concentrate better."

Tom pulled him upright very gently and Simeon swung his legs round so they were dangling over the edge of the trolley.

"So, what happened?" Tom asked, pulling over a chair and sitting down.

Anna took a deep breath.

"It fell into place for me when Simeon said that he'd promise to try and say something to Georgie if an opportunity presented itself. I kept thinking of 'windows of opportunities' and of course Dani had admitted that Enderby had made her do a couple of jobs for him. I couldn't say anything, Tom," she said. "Dani tied me in knots with confidentiality. She is quite clever ..."

Tom nodded.

"Enderby's death was the logical outcome of four people being down on the Lizard at a particular moment," Simeon said firmly. "Georgie and Laurence started the process. When they argued down at the bottom of the ramp, he yelled at her to leave him alone. He was trying to work out what to do about the drugs and he felt that everyone was crowding around him, that he didn't have space to think." Anna was impressed that Laurence had told Simeon that part. She wanted to say so, but didn't want to disrupt his flow. "Georgie was terribly upset and ran back up the path. Laurence followed her, but not straight away. He said he felt really bad about getting angry with her. He knew it wasn't her fault and she was only trying to get him to see the truth." Simeon took a sip of water. "The ramp there is quite steep, so when he finally got to the top, he couldn't see her anywhere and was quite out of breath. He gave up any thought of going after her because she could've gone anywhere, so he decided to go into the café. He'd not managed much breakfast and, by then, he was quite hungry."

Tom looked up from his notes. Anna knew he missed quite a few meals himself, so he'd know what that felt like. Simeon, on the other hand, never missed food, unless it was absolutely necessary. Feelings of emptiness or hunger were very disconcerting for him.

"Georgie must've been literally a few yards further along, just round the corner on the west path," Anna said. "I suppose she was hoping Laurence would follow her." Anna's heart went out to the girl, still carrying a torch for the boy, even after all those years.

"If he had, then perhaps Enderby wouldn't have died," Simeon said. "Except Enderby was putting Laurence under a lot of pressure, so perhaps something else bad would've happened eventually."

Anna had to agree. "Georgie and Laurence care for each other deeply. It's obvious. I expect to begin with it was like brother and sister, but now their relationship seems more complicated," she explained.

"Anyway," Simeon continued, "by the time I passed Enderby, just before he got down onto the coastal path, everyone was in place. Dani was standing on the veranda of the old café, out of sight. Enderby and Georgie were on a collision course. Laurence was in the café."

"Georgie must've been beyond angry at what Enderby had done to Laurence. How he'd come between them, how he was still coming between them," Anna said. "No wonder she reacted when she saw him, coming towards her along the path like that."

"It was incredibly lucky for her that he didn't fall

immediately," Simeon said, flashing a look at Tom. "And he couldn't have, not straightaway."

"No-one wants to fall to their death. The cliff edge was badly scuffed where he tried to hang on," said Tom.

Anna shuddered. "But I think Georgie was simply trying to get past him. She shoved him hard and then began to run. She didn't look back. She would've tried to help if she'd realised that Enderby had gone over."

Tom nodded. "So, when she did find out, she assumed that she'd killed him – that she'd pushed him over. No wonder she was in such a state," he said.

"Yes," Anna replied. "From that lunchtime onwards she looked awful. I couldn't understand it at the time, but of course it makes sense now. Worse still for her was that perhaps Laurence thought she was guilty too."

"So, what do you think happened next?" Tom asked, glancing at them both in turn. Of course Simeon's eyes were still firmly fixed on the floor.

"Well, obviously, Dani went over and stamped on his hand," Anna said.

"Yes," said Simeon, "but the timings are critical." Anna had wondered about that, but this was the first time she'd tried to put it together. Simeon flashed her a look. She smiled and he carried on.

"I think Dani waited until Georgie rounded the corner. What she couldn't know was that the waitress in the café was wiping tables right by the window up until the moment that Laurence came in. If that girl had looked up, she would've seen Enderby hanging on and Dani standing over him."

And it must have been a terrible moment for Enderby. Perhaps, for a second, he may even have thought he was saved, but then she stamped down and all hope was gone."

Tom narrowed his eyes, "But Simeon, it could've been Georgie. Why are you so sure that it was Dani?"

"Because of the tide and because the girl in the café was

wiping the tables when Laurence came in. Also because Laurence sat facing to the right and didn't have a book with him."

Simeon adjusted his arm lying limply across his lap. Anna hoped it wasn't beginning to hurt quite so soon.

Simeon continued, "Remember, Laurence wasn't that far behind Georgie. If Enderby had gone over when Georgie had pushed past him, the girl wiping the tables would've had a clear view and, even if she hadn't looked up from her task, she would've noticed the movement out of the corner of her eye. But she didn't notice anything. When Laurence had placed his order and went and sat at the window, he also saw nothing and he didn't have a book or anything to read."

"He would've definitely seen someone fall or at least seen Dani or Georgie standing up there," completed Anna. "Which means, if we believe Georgie and Laurence, then Enderby went over when Laurence was at the counter and Georgie had already disappeared down into the dip where it leads up to Archie's house."

"And it had to be then because Enderby's body was picked up by the last of the high tide and lifted onto the stanchion under the old ramp. It couldn't have been any later because he would've fallen to the foot of the cliff and remained there or just ended up in the water. It was a dull, wet day and the swell wasn't that big and you know that Laurence didn't spend that long talking to the waitress, so the window of opportunity was tight." At this point Simeon looked up at Anna and smiled. "Enderby must've fallen just before Laurence sat down, otherwise he would've seen him drop. Do you see?" Tom nodded; it was complicated, but he did see.

They were done. Simeon carefully slipped off the trolley, cradling the sling in his good arm. He took a couple of steps and halted.

"I'd like to go and see Archie now."

"So would I," said Anna.

Tom remained in his seat making notes. Anna wondered if he'd noticed them leaving at all.

***

So it all hinged on a woman wiping tables, Laurence not having anything to read and the hope that Georgie and Laurence weren't working together. The duty solicitor looked about twelve years old, with shiny cheeks and her hair pulled back tightly into a ponytail. Tom hadn't worked with her before and she was clearly nervous; probably hadn't expected a murder case.

Dani looked around her as if for the first time. She'd stopped crying in the car. Had started demanding things not long after.

"I'll make a statement about what I saw. But that's all," she said loudly, her voice bouncing off the walls of the interview room. "I saw Georgie push him and then scarper and then I walked back to the pub because I was so upset."

"But not so upset that you told anyone what you'd seen or even sounded the alarm," Tom said.

"He was not a nice man. You heard what he tried to do to us. If he suffered, then all well and good. If anyone deserved to fall, it was him."

The solicitor placed a hand on her arm and shook her head.

"My client is clearly upset," she said. Anna would've agreed, would've told Tom to back off. Her capacity for compassion always astounded him. But Dani knew what she was doing and, if she stuck to her story, it'd be the timings that were important and they could easily get complicated in a trial.

He needed to sit down with all the witnesses and check again what they remembered in light of Simeon and Anna's timeline. That was the only hope now of getting a conviction.

"You must've hated what that man did to Laurence; how upset he and Georgie were. They were your friends."

"Not Laurence. Georgie, yes. But they were both so weak. 'Don't tell anyone we were once in a children's home, they might pity us'," Dani said, using a child's voice. Tom suppressed a shudder. "Keep it all secret! They were so stupid because you only had to see them together for ten seconds to know all about it. God, they were pathetic."

"Pathetic?"

"Well, what would you call it?"

"A little sad. A way of coping."

Dani pursed her lips and narrowed her eyes.

Tom stayed quiet for a moment and then said, "You always felt you had to look out for everyone, didn't you? Selena, your mum, even Georgie who was supposed to be looking after you. And there was Enderby clinging on for dear life."

"Georgie literally screamed at him to leave them alone." Dani grinned. "The idiot tried to reason with her, but she was hysterical. He reached out to her, those stupid binoculars hanging from his arm, and she grabbed them and pushed past. He sort of teetered, but she was running by then." Dani stopped and, looking straight at Tom, she said quietly, "I was right to use the word pathetic. Laurence thought it was his fault because he'd believed in Enderby in the first place and that Georgie had done it because she was so angry with him. Georgie thought she'd simply pushed him over. Those two couldn't organise a booze-up in a brewery."

"So you sorted it for them."

Dani stared at the table.

"I'm cold and I want a hot chocolate."

Tom was suddenly relieved. There was no magic to it at all. He'd just needed to know which buttons to press. He felt a real pang of sadness for the baby and knew that Anna would be terribly upset. At least it hadn't been premeditated, so Dani wouldn't be in prison forever. Enderby had been an abuser by all but the lowest standards. Tom switched off the machine and went to get Dani a drink.

351

Catherine and Anna had both ended up in church. Both had throws around their knees and cups of tea to hand. Anna had spoken Morning Prayer and then they'd prayed for everyone they could think of. Archie was still in hospital and Phil had promised to take Simeon back to visit later. Derek and Harriet were also on standby. The doctors would probably fit a stent in the next couple of days. Archie was fragile and on a new regime of pills and potions that made him feel vulnerable, but Simeon said that he'd look after him.

That morning Tom had rung to say that he'd be over for dinner. Catherine had said she'd sort out the food, which was good because that meant that Anna could concentrate on worrying about everyone. Georgie hadn't been in a fit state to drive home. She was in fact sleeping in, having been at the police station half the night. They'd delivered her back just after 3 am, looking white-faced and terribly young. Giving her statement had not been straightforward.

Anna had made her a hot drink and sent her straight to bed. At least she wouldn't have to share a room anymore. Laurence had also finally been arrested and was now on his way back to Exeter in the custody of the visiting police officer. His van had been collected by a recovery truck very early that morning. Anna wondered how much sleep Tom had managed. Then she wondered if she ought to ring Alf, Georgie's vicar, and fill him in on what had happened, perhaps take the opportunity to tell him to ease up on his employees.

She might then invite Georgie to stay a bit longer for a proper rest. Tom had been reassuring about her, saying that – though she'd pushed a man and told some lies to protect her and Laurence – he was fairly sure that was all she'd done. Anna believed it too, had always believed in Georgie. She'd forever feel guilty about not always believing in Laurence and there wasn't much she could do for him, though Tom said they were going to contact his old social worker to make sure he had plenty of support.

"Are you and Tom going to give it a go?" Catherine asked, blowing on her mug of tea. Anna jumped.

"Sorry, I was miles away."

"I shouldn't have asked. Forgive me."

Anna thought about it for a few moments and then said, "I'd like to, but I want to talk to him first. Talk to him without thinking there's a murderer waiting in the wings." Then she added quietly, "I was so muddled before; now it seems clearer. Particularly seeing Archie go down like that. It never occurred to me I might actually lose him. It was awful." She took a sip of tea. "You see, I love them and I realised that Tom doesn't necessarily have to get God, but he does need to get how much I care about these people. My charges, my friends."

Catherine nodded.

"That's quite profound," she said. "And I'll think hard about moving closer. I'd like to spend more time with him."

"I think you'd fit in really well," said Anna, though she wondered how hard it would be to argue with Tom or get annoyed with him knowing that his mother was going to be staring up at her the following Sunday. "I tell you what, though, I'm hoping there won't be any more murders around here for a while."

"Was it murder, though? I think Dani was just tidying up. Took advantage of a moment."

"It's still a little chilling," Anna said and shivered. "I don't know if I can run any more retreats. I had this picture of people coming and telling us all their problems, God turning up and them leaving happy and refreshed. But Dani, Georgie and Laurence had long-term, deep-seated issues. It was really scary and we were just not qualified to help them."

Catherine laughed. Anna turned to look at her.

"I think you're wrong." she said. "You're not here as a psychologist or even a counsellor. You simply did what you were supposed to do, which was listen and worry and care.

We've all changed. Even Dani dropped her guard once or twice. Georgie now knows that what's expected of her is too much, that Alf is an exception rather than the rule. Laurence has found Archie and Simeon and perhaps something else far more important. Don't you think Archie will make the most wonderful mentor? He might not make it up to Exeter, but he'll write and he'll text and phone and pray." She laughed again. "And then there's the healing properties of Harriet's cooking and of course you, loving everyone to distraction."

"Thank you, Catherine. Stay as long as you like."

They sipped their tea and Anna pulled the blanket more tightly around her. There was a patch of dappled sunlight spilling across the floor, but it didn't make the place any warmer.

"Do you mind if I do something a little odd?"

Catherine frowned and tipped her head.

"Of course not."

"You see, we never finished Evening Prayer and I'd like to. It feels important."

Catherine simply took the book that Anna held out to her.

Anna began to read the closing sentences, determined to finish what they had started. She didn't hurry, but neither did she pause too long. The important thing was to end well. She felt the words as she spoke them, felt them spill over each of the people she was there to love, as if she were once again saying a blessing over them.

Over all of them.

Acknowledgements

Authoring is a very solitary occupation, but book production is a team effort and I'm very grateful for the many who have helped me along the way.

In particular, I would like to thank Jutta Mackwell–one of the most important people on my journey–an editor who encourages like a friend and edits like the professional she is. I really would have given up years ago if it wasn't for her gentle persuasion and her enthusiasm for all that I have written.

My thanks also to Bridget Scrannage, whom I trust implicitly to make my stories work. She is the best structural editor and I learn so much from her comments.

Thank you to Kate Yates, who read this book right back at the beginning in its rawest state. It takes time to read a manuscript, and even more time to make notes and spot errors. I am so grateful for her kindness.

A huge thanks to those who have listened when I've felt overwhelmed, particularly Karen Fleet. Thank you Sam Mackwell for tech support. He is constantly patient, and creative. When I've been almost weeping in frustration he's always come back with a solution. He's a good man. Likewise, Joe House, who is so easy to work with. While I am of the generation that is afraid I will click something and lose it all he, thank goodness, is not! My website and I are grateful.

Thank you to my readers for your kind words and suggestions. I hope this books satisfies the itch.

And lastly, because they are first, thank you to my family, who still ask me how I'm getting on, even when I am not.

Not just a team, but an entire community – thank you.

CPSIA information can be obtained
at www.ICGtesting.com
Printed in the USA
LVHW050405161021
700579LV00005B/32

9 781999 7102